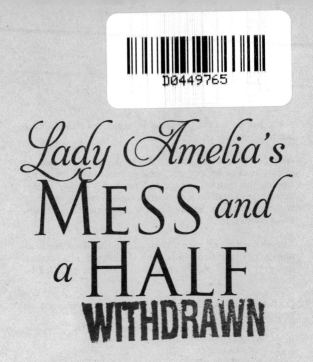

Lady Amelia's MESS and a HALF

WITHDRAWN

SAMANTHA GRACE

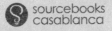

sourcebooks
casablanca

Copyright © 2012 by Samantha Grace
Cover and internal design © 2012 by Sourcebooks, Inc.
Cover illustration by Aleta Rafton

Sourcebooks and the colophon are registered trademarks of
Sourcebooks, Inc.

All rights reserved. No part of this book may be reproduced
in any form or by any electronic or mechanical means in-
cluding information storage and retrieval systems—except
in the case of brief quotations embodied in critical articles or
reviews—without permission in writing from its publisher,
Sourcebooks, Inc.

The characters and events portrayed in this book are ficti-
tious or are used fictitiously. Any similarity to real persons,
living or dead, is purely coincidental and not intended by
the author.

Published by Sourcebooks Casablanca, an imprint of
Sourcebooks, Inc.
P.O. Box 4410, Naperville, Illinois 60567-4410
(630) 961-3900
FAX: (630) 961-2168
www.sourcebooks.com

Printed and bound in Canada
WC 10 9 8 7 6 5 4 3 2 1

New York Times and *USA Today* Bestseller

The Heir

by Grace Burrowes

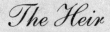

An earl who can't be bribed...

Gayle Windham, Earl of Westhaven, is the first legitimate son and heir to the Duke of Moreland. To escape his father's inexorable pressure to marry, he decides to spend the summer at his townhouse in London, where he finds himself intrigued by the secretive ways of his beautiful housekeeper...

A lady who can't be protected...

Anna Seaton is a beautiful, talented, educated woman, which is why it is so puzzling to Gayle Windham that she works as his housekeeper.

As the two draw closer and begin to lose their hearts to each other, Anna's secrets threaten to bring the earl's orderly life crashing down—and he doesn't know how he's going to protect her from the fallout...

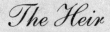

"A luminous and graceful erotic Regency...a captivating love story that will have readers eagerly awaiting the planned sequels."—Publishers Weekly (starred review)

For more Grace Burrowes, visit:

www.sourcebooks.com

New York Times and USA Today Bestseller

The Soldier

by Grace Burrowes

———— ❧ ————

Even in the quiet countryside, he can find no peace...

His idyllic estate is falling down from neglect and night-mares of war give him no rest. Then Devlin St. Just meets his new neighbor...

Until his beautiful neighbor ignites his imagination...

With her confident manner hiding a devastating secret, his lovely neighbor commands all of his attention, and protecting Emmaline becomes Devlin's most urgent mission.

———— ❧ ————

"Burrowes's straightforward, sensual love story is intelligent and tender, rising above the crowd with deft dialogue and delightful characters."
—Publishers Weekly (starred review)

For more Grace Burrowes, visit:

www.sourcebooks.com

For Jodie, the brave and generous of heart. You have been with me from the beginning, and I can't thank you enough for your guidance and encouragement. But you are more than a mentor. You are my Bibi, only better behaved. Thank you for your unwavering friendship. It is a gift I will always cherish.

One

JAKE HILLARY WAS A KEEPER—KEEPER OF HIS FAMILY'S secret, keeper of his wayward brother, and most tragically, keeper of a hopeless love for his best friend's wife. But at least for now, he wouldn't think on the torturous evening to come of admiring Amelia from afar. His brother was due for a thrashing, and Jake planned to deliver it.

Yanking on his watch fob, he extracted the gold timepiece from his pocket. He could barely make out the hands in the dim light.

"Blast and damn."

He slipped the watch back into his pocket. There wasn't enough time to pound Daniel before the party. Instead, Jake hammered his fist against the door of his brother's rented room, rattling it in the frame.

"Aye!" Daniel bellowed.

Apparently, his brother had discarded common courtesy *and* manners while he was at sea, although Daniel had never been one to adhere to etiquette. Based upon his ill-mannered response, it seemed unlikely he intended to cross the room to admit Jake. Irritated, he threw the door open and barged inside.

"Dan—"

"Right there, luv." Daniel threw his head back against the chair as a blonde burrowed her face into his crotch. "Oh, yes!"

"Damnation." Jake covered his eyes and spun on his heel, cracking his elbow against the door frame. "Ouch!" He muttered another curse under his breath.

"What the hell, Jake? Haven't you heard of knocking, you reprobate?"

"I did knock. Next time I shall make more noise," he drawled. Surely all that pounding could have been heard on the other side of Mayfair. "Inform me once you have set yourself to rights."

Jake shook his head as he strolled into the corridor to wait. What a sight to stumble upon, his brother getting his butter churned. And all before dinner. It was enough to spoil his appetite.

When the foul smell from the stairwell hit him again, his lip curled. Daniel might indulge in whores and spirits, but he wasn't throwing away his fortune on rented rooms. Paper peeled from the walls in great sheets, and stains of an unknown origin splattered the scarred floor.

Smells like the bloody mews in here. Fitting, given his brother was behaving like a jackass.

After a series of bumps and muffled curses, the door flew open. His brother filled the doorway, every bare inch of him.

Jake smirked. "I asked you to summon me *after* you had dressed."

"Get in here."

Pushing away from the wall, Jake reentered the apartments. "Is your guest decent now?"

A crooked leer replaced Daniel's scowl. "Why? You want a turn?"

"Show some respect. The woman deserves at least as much for tolerating your vulgarity."

A feminine giggle drifted from the back room. "Thank you, Mr. Hillary, but I find the captain's vulgarity tolerable indeed." The young woman appeared in the threshold, her nudity now concealed with a faded ruby dress. Her lackluster hair was pinned up in a haphazard coiffure.

"Oh, my!" Her brown eyes rounded as she looked Jake up and down before turning back to Daniel. "Your brother is delicious, Captain Hillary."

Delicious? Like a meat pie? Jake coughed into his fist, uncomfortable with the nature of her compliment given there were no rules to dictate his response. Yet, he considered it bad-mannered to discount her outright. "Yes, well. Thank you."

Daniel winked at her. "You fancy the rotter, do you?"

She wandered over to Jake's brother with a smile pulling at her plump lips. "I would wager he is the most handsome of the Hillary clan."

"Aside from me."

"Aye. That goes without saying." The woman accepted the purse Daniel offered and pressed a kiss to his cheek. "Same time tomorrow, sir?"

Daniel swatted her behind. "I'll send word."

Jake moved aside to allow his brother's, um… *friend* passage into the corridor.

As she moved past him, she grazed her fingers over the lapel of his jacket. "You're definitely the pinkest of the pinks. I would be happy to pay *you* a call sometime."

Jake's smile was forced. "That's a generous offer, miss."

"Not at all, sir." She tipped her head to the side and batted her lashes, looking up at him in expectation. When Jake offered no encouragement, she heaved a sigh and sauntered to the stairway.

Daniel chuckled. "What are you about, choirboy?"

Jake closed the door and walked farther into the apartments. "I cannot decide which smell is more offensive, the corridor or you. Get cleaned up. You haven't much time."

"Time for what?" Daniel flopped onto the tattered chair in a perfect display of insolence, among other things.

Jake looked up at the ceiling to avoid catching another glimpse of his brother. "I have it on good authority you received the invitation to the dinner party Mother has planned in your honor, although you did not bother responding. *Again.* Now, get dressed. The guests will be arriving in…" He checked his watch again. "Forty-five minutes."

"Is that tonight?"

"Yes, and you can either make yourself presentable, or I will drag your smelly arse across Town as is. Either way, you are attending."

Daniel smirked. "I'd like to see you attempt it. Come on. Make me attend Mother's boring dinner party."

Jake cracked his knuckles and rolled his neck. "Must we go through this *every* time? You learned nothing from the last time I thrashed you. Why do I bother?"

Daniel threw his head back and laughed. "I only vaguely recall the incident now, but you had the advantage since I was foxed."

"You're not far from that now," Jake said dryly.

"Put some clothes on. Mother has expended a lot of effort on your behalf. Try to show a little gratitude."

"Mummy, Mummy, Mummy," Daniel mocked, a spark of enjoyment brightening his eyes. "One would think you're still in leading strings."

"You must discover novel ways to abuse me. I grow weary of the same insults." Jake refused to be bothered by his older sibling. He had too many serious concerns on his mind at the moment, such as not making a cake of himself in front of Amelia this evening.

"Would you hurry?" he snapped when Daniel made no move to ready himself.

"Oh, very well." His brother dragged his carcass from the chair and lumbered toward the back room. "Who will be in attendance? Anyone interesting?"

Jake folded his arms and rocked heel-to-toe, toe-to-heel, impatient with Daniel's tardiness. "No one important. Unless you count your *family*."

Daniel stuck his head through the doorway, a jaunty grin in place. "I said anyone interesting. Do you ever listen?"

"If you would only pay a visit to our parents when you return to London, Mother wouldn't orchestrate these affairs."

"Mother would be as happy to forget me as she is her past. She has ulterior motives for this evening's event."

Jake didn't bother arguing this time. It was true their mother was too sensitive to her bourgeois origins, but she desired the best for her children. Sometimes Jake wondered if Daniel's decision to captain his own ship had been designed simply to upset her. If so, his efforts were jolly successful.

Daniel walked from the back room dressed in his best and looking like a proper gentleman. Of course, he still smelled like a barrel of rum, but Jake couldn't do anything to correct that unfortunate problem. The acrid scent emanated from Daniel's skin.

"Pay Mother one call when you arrive, and you needn't trouble yourself with her motives," Jake said.

"I would like to see how quickly you would run home to Mum after being at sea. The first thing I need is the touch of a woman, and *not* the one who gave birth to me. Unlike you, I'm not content to dote on Mother."

"Sod off."

Jake craved a woman's touch, too, but not just any female. Daniel knew well where his allegiances lay. Unfortunately, the woman he desired didn't want him. And thanks to his maniacal rant in her foyer months earlier, she no longer spoke to him either.

Daniel donned his coat and adjusted his cravat. "How is Lady Audley these days? Enticed her to your bed yet?"

Searing heat crept up Jake's neck to the tips of his ears. "My personal matters are none of your concern." The last thing he wished to disclose was how he had ruined any chance for an attachment to Amelia while his brother had been abroad.

Daniel's eyebrows arched in question. "I will take your grumbling as a no. Pity. What has it been? A year?" He strolled to the outer door and tugged it open. "Perhaps *I* will try my hand with the lady tonight."

"The hell you will."

The thought of Daniel touching Amelia under *any* circumstances set Jake's blood on fire, but after what he'd walked in on a moment ago… "Just stay clear of the lady. She deserves better than the likes of you."

"Like you, Mummy's Boy?" Daniel chuckled as he disappeared into the darkened corridor. "I tire of waiting for you to woo the lady. I say tonight, may the better man win the lovely widow."

Jake stalked after his brother. "I am the better man."

⁂

Amelia, Lady Audley, leaned against the carriage seat, dreading the coming evening. She would rather be any place than a guest in Jake Hillary's home, but she couldn't snub the Hillarys, not after their generous donation to the children this afternoon. Besides, Mrs. Hillary had always been exceptionally kind to her. Amelia could face Jake this evening for his mother's sake, even if the task required herculean strength.

Amelia's dearest friend and silent partner in the foundling house renovation project, Bianca Kennell, leaned forward with a frown. "Amelia, you look as if we are attending a funeral instead of a dinner party. At least *try* to appear enthused for my sake. You know how I love parties."

"I am not attending this affair for my own pleasure. Mrs. Hillary has spoken with Lady Eldridge and the Duchess of Foxhaven about the renovation. She assures me both ladies are amenable to publicly lending their support, but they wish to inquire into my specific intentions."

Bibi yawned loudly, covering her mouth in a grand gesture. "Oh, pardon me. All this talk of orphans and charity is putting me into a sleeping trance."

Amelia shook her head, smiling reluctantly. She really should be more severe with Bibi, but her dramatics amused more than vexed her. "How thoughtless of me, dearest. I shall endeavor to be more stimulating in my conversation."

"Thank you." Bibi pinched both cheeks, patted her ebony curls, and then readjusted her breasts so they swelled over the neckline of her emerald gown like rising dough. "How do I look?"

"You look lovely, as always."

Bibi flashed a brilliant smile, a wicked twinkle in her eye. "Good enough to eat?"

Amelia grinned cheekily. "Mrs. Hillary serves three-course meals. You needn't worry about anyone stuffing an apple in your mouth and serving you on a platter."

Bibi huffed and lifted her nose in the air. "You have a sharp wit tonight, Lady Audley. Try not to slice anyone to ribbons with it."

"I shall wield my weapon with care," she answered with mock graveness.

"See that you do." Bibi crossed her arms and slumped in her seat, her bottom lip protruding as she practiced her pout. "You comprehended my meaning."

Amelia lifted one shoulder, the heat of a blush flooding her cheeks. Unfortunately, she did know her friend's meaning. "Must everyone be privy to your private affairs?"

"Just because you have chosen to remain celibate does not mean I must."

Amelia hadn't chosen celibacy. Her life was simply too complicated to entertain thoughts of a liaison at the moment, and she had sworn off complications the day Jake had condemned her in her own house. She certainly didn't have time for the caliber of gentlemen Bibi took to her bed. One scoundrel had proven one too many for Amelia.

Bibi tossed her head. "What other benefit is there to being widowed if I can't enjoy a tumble or two here and there?"

As the carriage rolled to a stop, Amelia recited a silent prayer of thanks. She didn't wish to continue this discussion.

"Do whatever you like, Bibi, but please practice discretion. I need the support of the ladies attending tonight."

"Prudes."

Amelia's brows lifted. "Must we hurl names at them?"

Bibi didn't answer. The footman opened the carriage door and offered her his hand. As she climbed down the steps, she tossed a look back at Amelia. "You were more fun before Jake Hillary attached that millstone of guilt around your neck."

Amelia's heart leapt into her throat as she noted other guests alighting from their carriages or wandering into the house. "Hush, silly girl."

She joined Bibi on the drive and they linked arms, both staring up at the massive Italianate home. Despite visiting Hillary House many times, Amelia never ceased to be amazed by the grandeur. Why, the Hillarys could house hundreds of children without ever crossing paths with a single one!

The foundlings would not have as grand a home as the wealthy landowner, but their living conditions would improve by no small amount once she had the support of a few more philanthropic souls. Of course, she couldn't approach the true holders of the purse strings, which meant she must convince their wives to do so on her behalf.

Amelia's stomach churned. Perhaps it had been a mistake to arrive with her friend. Lady Kennell had been deemed bad *ton* by several of the ladies who had developed a disliking for her. She hazarded a sideways glance. Bibi flashed an enthusiastic smile, causing Amelia's heart to soften. When she looked at Bibi, all she saw was the loyal friend who had been with her since childhood. *To the devil with those ladies.*

She hugged Bibi closer to her side and whispered in her ear, "Thank you for accompanying me tonight."

"Where else would I be?"

Indeed. Bibi remained Amelia's constant ally in whatever ventures she undertook.

As they approached the front doors propped open to admit the elegantly attired guests, Amelia patted her dearest friend's hand. "Are you ready to face the *ton*?"

"Face them? I am prepared to conquer, my dear."

Amelia laughed softly. "Well, go easy on them for my sake."

If she had any hope of helping the orphans, she needed the ladies to view them as benefactresses of a worthy cause, not the wanton widows of Mayfair.

❧

Jake tried to focus on the conversation between Lord Hollister and his brother, but his attention strayed to the drawing room door every few seconds. Amelia had yet to arrive.

He must stand vigilant if he wished to spare her from Daniel's boorish company, which meant enduring his brother's ill manners himself. Daniel was not one to alter his conduct for polite society. If possible, he became even more offensive in such circumstances. Jake only hoped this time he didn't send their mother to her bed for days afterwards.

Lord Hollister inclined his head, preparing to take his leave at last. "Good evening, gentlemen. I trust your stay in Town will be pleasant, Captain Hillary."

Daniel wiggled his eyebrows at Jake. "I'm certain my time in London will be exceptionally pleasant."

"Over my dead body," Jake said through a tight smile.

His brother's mouth twitched in amusement.

Lord Hollister wandered away then paused to scan the room, likely searching for another unfortunate guest to regale with tales of his hounds. The marquess moved toward a group of gentlemen clustered in a far corner. Jake chuckled as panic lit Lord Gilford's eyes when he noted the gentleman's approach.

"Egads!" Daniel rammed his fingers through his hair and released a loud, groaning sigh. "Does the man bore *everyone* to tears?"

Lord Hollister was out of earshot, but a few twitters indicated guests standing close by had overheard.

"Mostly." Jake handed his brother a drink.

Daniel took a swig then sniffed the glass. "What the hell *is* this?"

"Lower your voice," Jake scolded. "It's cordial water. Mother insists you wait until after dinner to hit the brandy."

Daniel sampled the drink again and snarled. "This

tastes like piss," he whispered. "Bring me a drink suited for a man, not some blasted chit."

"Retrieve it yourself." Trusting in his brother's negative review of the beverage, Jake placed his untouched cordial water on a passing footman's tray. Daniel followed suit.

A flash of color at the drawing room entrance caught Jake's eye, and he turned in time to see their sister and her husband arriving. His heart warmed as it always did in her presence. He nodded in their direction. "This party should gain more life now. Lana has arrived."

Daniel glanced up. "Good God, she's become fat."

Jake elbowed him in the side. "She is with child, half-wit."

Their younger sister's smile widened when her sight landed on them, and before her husband could escort her, she hurried across the room and launched herself into Daniel's arms.

"You're back," she cried, hugging him vigorously.

Despite Daniel's sullen demeanor up to that point, he chuckled and hugged Lana in return. Lifting her feet off the ground, he placed a loud smack on her cheek. "Pumpkin pie, so good to see you."

Jake shook his head, wholly entertained by his audacious siblings and happy at least he knew how to conduct himself in public. If their mother had expected either Lana or Daniel to behave with any decorum this evening, she would be disappointed.

Lana pulled back when Daniel returned her to her feet and wrinkled her nose. "You know I hate that name, *Danny Boy*."

Jake smirked at her use of their brother's hated moniker. Served him right for teasing her. "I was just sharing your good news with Daniel," he said.

Their brother snorted. "Untrue. He said you had grown stout with marriage when clearly you are with child. Little Jakie can be quite the cur."

Lana rolled her eyes but grinned all the same. "Yes, Jake is the culprit, I'm sure." She placed her hand on her husband's arm when he joined their group.

"Drew, I would like to introduce you to my brother, Captain Daniel Hillary. Daniel, this is my husband, Lord Andrew Forest."

Daniel nodded, his dark frown returning. In Forest's less-domesticated days, everyone had known him, at least by reputation. This would not be the first time their paths had crossed, but for once Daniel held his tongue.

"It is a pleasure, my lord."

"Likewise." Forest placed his hand on the small of Lana's back. "If you will excuse me, lady and gentlemen, I have a matter to discuss with your father."

"Wait. I'll come with you." Lana linked arms with her husband to halt his retreat then leaned forward to speak to Jake and Daniel as if Forest couldn't overhear. "Papa seeks his opinion on another bit of horseflesh he is considering acquiring. They appear to be in competition to see who can make the most frivolous purchases this year. I declare, our mews would be bursting at the seams if not for my vigilance."

Forest shrugged good-naturedly. "It's my only vice, Lana."

"Well, when you state it that way, I suppose I have no cause for complaint, do I?"

Forest winked. "Satisfaction *is* my aim, love."

An attractive flush infused Lana's cheeks. Since it was no longer Jake's calling to protect his little sister from scoundrels like Forest—unless, of course, she requested his assistance, in which case he would gladly step forward—he overlooked the veiled comment. The firm slant to Daniel's jaw indicated he might not be as magnanimous this evening.

"Neither of you may take your leave before you've danced with me," Lana said and blew a kiss their direction before wandering away arm-in-arm with Forest.

Once they were across the room, Daniel whirled on Jake. "How did that mutton-monger end up married to our little sister?"

"It's a long story," Jake said with a sigh. He didn't wish to rehash his failure to safeguard their dear sister from one of the biggest satyrs in Town. He still hadn't forgiven himself. But he had to admit Forest made her happy, and by all accounts, the gent had reformed. Any scandalous whispers about the former rake now included his wife and their penchant for dark corners.

Jake glanced toward the doorway. What was taking Amelia so long? Most of the guests had already arrived. Perhaps Daniel would forget about his interest in luring her to his bed if Jake could send him sniffing in another direction.

"Father keeps brandy in his study. Shall we help ourselves?"

"Brilliant suggestion." Daniel headed for the side door.

Jake made to follow but froze in place.

Amelia lingered in the threshold, a cool smile sliding across her perfect lips.

Hellfire. He might have just swallowed his tongue. Taking a deep breath to shore up his courage, he squared his shoulders. Tonight he would approach her, because surrendering her to Daniel was out of the question.

Fools rush in where angels fear to tread. Well, Jake was a fool, and Amelia's beauty rivaled any angel's. He pulled at his cravat and rolled his neck. Hopefully, that was the only similarity she shared with the heavenly creatures, but with his luck, she too had a taste for vengeance and a fondness for smiting.

Two

AMELIA AND BIBI STOOD SIDE BY SIDE, THE FACES around them a blur. Amelia's mouth felt gritty as if she had eaten sand.

The footman, attired in dark blue and goldenrod livery, a perfect bookend to the manservant standing attendance on the opposite side of the entrance, cleared his throat. "Presenting Lady Audley and Lady Kennell."

Amelia clutched her friend's arm to quell the tremor in her hands as a few curious stares wandered in their direction.

Really, her nerves were unforgiveable. One might think her a recluse newly venturing from her cave to join society. But tonight was different. She had two weeks left to garner support or the board of directors at the foundling hospital would quash her plans.

Bibi lifted herself to her full height, every inch of her diminutive frame regal, and flashed a blinding smile. She commanded the room, drawing attention away from Amelia, and in turn, Amelia would attempt to keep her friend out of trouble tonight. Not always an easy task.

The other guests' attention was fleeting, and they resumed their conversations, their voices melding into a low rumble. Amelia's eyes flitted around the room in search of Jake. When she didn't locate him, she released a pent-up breath.

Perhaps he wouldn't come. Although the possibility settled her nerves, it brought her little comfort. *How I've missed him.*

She swallowed against the tears burning at the back of her throat and forced herself to shake off her ridiculous sentiments. Though her heart often refused to cooperate with her resolve to forget Jake, she was an intelligent woman capable of overriding her traitorous emotions. Jake had no place in her life—and he never had.

As the crowd absorbed her and Bibi, Amelia spotted Jake's sister on Lord Andrew Forest's arm. Lana gifted her with a wide smile and an enthusiastic wave, boosting Amelia's morale. It was reassuring to have at least one friendly face in attendance this evening.

Lana had always been a delightful young woman. The darling girl had gone to great lengths to reach out to Amelia, which couldn't be easy for any wife.

Forest inclined his head in polite greeting, never seemingly troubled by their past intimate association. She returned the gesture and averted her gaze. To think she had fancied herself in love with the man at one time. Now, with more clarity, she could see he had been a lousy salve to soothe her injured heart when Jake had hied off to the country. All she had gained from the ill-advised affair was bruised pride and a tarnished reputation. And in the process, she had destroyed any chance for a future with Jake. He had made it clear last autumn what he thought of her.

Bibi leaned close. "I suppose you would like a drink?"

"Yes, I'm parched as usual. Thank you."

"Follow me, my dear." Bibi fluttered her full lashes at the gentleman standing closest to them before sauntering toward the punch bowl with a sensual swing to her hips.

Amelia held back, not wishing the same attention Bibi received from the men in the room. Whereas Amelia strove to change the opinion others held of her, her friend thumbed her nose at their contemporaries. Snubbed by the other ladies of the *ton*, Bibi exacted her revenge by courting the notice of their husbands.

As Amelia joined Bibi by the punch bowl, Mrs. Hillary approached with a genuine smile. "Ladies, thank you for coming this evening."

Amelia returned her warm greeting. Jake's mother had always been so kind to her, especially after Audley's death. The good lady's encouraging notes had been appreciated more than Mrs. Hillary could know.

"I am always grateful for your invitations, Mrs. Hillary."

"As am I." Bibi offered a charming smile to their hostess, proving she had listened to Amelia's pleas to be on her best behavior. "Has the guest of honor arrived?"

"Daniel is here somewhere." Worry lined Mrs. Hillary's forehead as she looked around the room. "Heaven knows where he is keeping himself." When she glanced at Amelia again, her expression brightened. "I may have two more donors for you, Lady Audley. I'm certain once they learn of your good intentions they will wish to do their part."

"Mrs. Hillary, I can't thank you enough."

"It's my pleasure. Of course, I haven't broached the subject with either of my sons, but how could they refuse? Daniel and Jake will be captivated by your ideas when you explain everything to them over dinner."

"You are seating me near your sons?" She fought to control the panicked shriek threatening to break through her words. She couldn't imagine a worse fate than being seated close to Jake, pretending his disapproval had no effect on her.

Mrs. Hillary patted her arm. "Heavens no, dear."

Amelia tried not to melt into a puddle on the floor.

"You shall dine *between* them," Mrs. Hillary said.

"Oh, my," Bibi murmured. "Who do we have here?"

Amelia's head snapped up to see what had caught her attention. Her gaze glossed over Captain Hillary and settled on Jake.

Her insides quivered. Why did he always stare at her in that way? His intense hazel eyes passed judgment with a mere glance. Amelia chided herself for allowing him to cow her. Intensity and intimidation might work to his advantage in court, but she would not be so easily handled.

Jake's mother touched Bibi's forearm. "Lady Kennell, have you met my son, Captain Hillary?"

A slow smile spread across Bibi's face. "I do not believe I've had the pleasure."

The seductive lowering of her eyelids left no doubt in Amelia's mind that Bibi would like the situation remedied at once.

Mrs. Hillary motioned for her sons to join their party. As the men approached, Amelia spun away to avoid

Jake's stare by retrieving a glass of punch, but Bibi blocked the table.

She cleared her scratchy throat. "May I have a glass of punch, Lady Kennell?"

Bibi blinked. "Punch?"

"Yes." Amelia pointed. "The punch at your elbow. I would love some. May I?"

"Oh, by all means." Without taking her gaze from Captain Hillary, Bibi fumbled for a glass, almost tipping it over, then held on to the drink instead of passing it to Amelia.

She reached to pry the glass from Bibi's fingers. "*Thank* you."

"Pardon?" Bibi barely glanced at her. "Oh, think nothing of it."

"Indeed. I shan't." Amelia drained the beverage then turned with the glass clutched close to her chest as if crystal held special powers to shield her from the man who had broken her heart.

"Daniel, I would like to make an introduction," Mrs. Hillary said as the men reached them. "May I present Lady Kennell? And you recall Lady Audley, do you not? Ladies, this is my third-born son, Captain Daniel Hillary, and I'm certain you are both acquainted with my youngest, Jake."

Captain Hillary bowed low, sweeping a magnificent leg, and offered a grin. "Why Lady Audley, you are even more beautiful than when I last saw you." His grasp was gentle as he placed a kiss on her gloved knuckles. "Mother tells me you've taken on a good-will mission. I do hope you will share all the details with me this evening."

"I would be delighted, Captain. The children are dear to my heart."

Captain Hillary turned a bright smile on Bibi. "Lady Kennell, what an enchanting vision you are. Tell me. Are you real, or a figment of my imagination?"

Bibi chuckled and held out her hand. "I assure you, Captain, I am real."

He placed a kiss on Bibi's hand and held her bold gaze. "I believe you tease me cruelly, my dear, for surely I have died and gone to heaven. No earthly beauty could ever compare to yours."

Amelia resisted the urge to roll her eyes. Captain Hillary was an excellent example of the manner of man for which Amelia had no use.

He raised his eyebrows as he released Bibi's hand. "Kennell, you say? As in Kenny's viscountess?"

"As in the *widowed* Viscountess Kennell. Surely you heard of his demise last year."

"I had heard, but I had forgotten he had a lady wife. May I offer my deepest condolences for your loss, my lady?" Captain Hillary's lascivious grin contradicted his expression of sympathy.

A flash of annoyance crossed Mrs. Hillary's countenance when she regarded her older son. "I must beg your forgiveness, ladies and gentlemen, but I must partner the guests for the promenade. Daniel, would you please escort Lady Kennell? I have placed you between the viscountess and Lady Audley. Perhaps Lady Audley could share her ideas for the foundling home over dinner."

"Splendid," Captain Hillary said and winked at Amelia before offering his elbow to Bibi. "I'm feeling generous this evening. Perhaps I could present you with a substantial gift later tonight, Lady Audley."

"That would be lovely, sir."

"I shall give it to you in private so no one is the wiser."

Jake's jaw tightened and his glower bordered on murderous. *For heaven's sake!* Did he not believe charity work to be a worthy endeavor? Perhaps he found fault with everything she did.

As Captain Hillary led Bibi away to form the queue for the promenade, Mrs. Hillary touched Jake's arm. "Jake, please see Lady Audley to her place."

He drew back as if she suggested he dine with a snake, but he recovered quickly. "Of course, Mother. It would be my pleasure."

Hurt pierced Amelia's heart. Jake's harsh attitude toward her obviously hadn't softened over the last several months. Sometimes she wished to return to those evenings when she had believed he might love her, but it was a foolish desire. She couldn't change what she had done, and Jake held no forgiveness for her.

Mrs. Hillary bustled away to partner the other guests.

"Perhaps you would prefer a different dining partner," Amelia said.

Jake's blue-green gaze met hers, his expression blank. "I consider it an honor to escort you to dinner, Lady Audley."

She sighed, wishing he would just rail at her once and for all and end this horrid false politeness.

❧

Jake held the chair for Amelia as she assumed the spot next to his brother at the table. He shot a warning look at Daniel when he turned an appreciative eye on her. His brother paid Jake no mind, gazing overly long at her neckline, although the creamy mounds peeking over the lacy edge of her bodice were hard to ignore.

Jake's teeth clashed together and added to the dull throb at his temple.

His mother knew of his affection for Amelia. She had known immediately when he had fallen in love, and she had comforted him when Amelia had given her hand in marriage to his best friend instead of him. To place her within Daniel's grasp, a man legendary in his ability to charm the drawers off most females, was cruel. Not that Jake believed his rakish brother possessed any chance of bedding Amelia. *Unless she fancies him.* Jake nearly groaned aloud from the misery that possibility brought him.

Amelia shifted on her seat when he slipped into the chair beside her. The light floral fragrance she wore wrapped around him, reminding him of a stroll through Vauxhall Gardens in early summer.

Glancing sideways, he stole a peek at her profile. A fiery heat consumed his body as the sweet taste of her flooded his memory. He wanted nothing more than to have no care for propriety. If Jake were a scoundrel like his brother, he would whisk Amelia to his chambers and toss up her skirts.

But he *was* a gentleman, the bouillabaisse was just now being served, and Amelia was no trollop.

Jake yanked at his cravat. The bloody thing was attempting to murder him this evening. He loosened the knot and drew in a deep breath.

Amelia tipped her head to the side and studied him. "Mr. Hillary, are you ill?"

"No." Jake snatched his wineglass and drained it.

Amelia nibbled her bottom lip, so pink and plump. *Dear Lord.* An image of her beautiful lips wrapped around his shaft popped into his mind. His pulse sped and beads of sweat formed on his forehead.

Damn his rakehell brother! Had Daniel never heard of a lock? Jake had entertained many fantasies involving Amelia, but never this one, and never in polite company.

"Mr. Hillary, are you certain you are well?" Her concerned voice distracted him from her movement, so when her hand brushed his leg, he jumped, banging his knee on the table and sloshing wine from her goblet onto the table linens.

"Good heavens, Mr. Hillary."

The puddle of red soaked into the white linen, changing to a lighter shade of rose as it spread. Looking up, Jake's gaze landed on his sister staring at him in alarm with her spoon paused in midair. At least Forest pretended not to notice instead of smirking in the irritating manner he possessed.

A footman rushed forward to blot the mess while another hurried to replace Amelia's wine. A flash of doubt crossed the wine steward's face as he refilled Jake's goblet. Jake held his gaze until the servant looked away.

"I beg your pardon, my lady," he said, as he returned his attention to Amelia.

She sat with her spine stiff, refusing to look up as she took dainty sips of the fish soup.

Daniel smirked at him over the top of her head then leaned to whisper something to Lady Kennell. The viscountess snickered and craned her neck to peer at Jake.

Amelia refused to acknowledge him for the remainder of dinner, instead turning her back on him while answering Daniel's questions about the foundling house renovation.

He suppressed a frustrated sigh. All of ten minutes in her presence, and he had proved himself a first-rate gaby.

At the conclusion of the torturous meal, his father pushed from the table and rose when Jake's mother stood.

She gestured toward the door. "Ladies? Shall we leave the men to discuss their politics?"

Daniel was on his feet within seconds to pull Amelia's chair out. His fingers grazed the bare skin of her shoulder.

"Thank you, Captain Hillary," Amelia said. She held herself rigid as she stood.

"My pleasure, Lady Audley. Perhaps we shall cross paths later. I should like to contribute to your worthy cause."

"Certainly, Captain." She didn't spare Jake a glance as the women glided from the dining room.

A low growl rumbled in Jake's chest. His brother met his glower and smiled. Jake clenched his fists against his sides to refrain from delivering a dowse to his chops. In addition to the scandal, Mother would disapprove of staining her Aubusson with Daniel's blood. But as luck would have it, Gentleman Jack and the patrons of his boxing saloon were not as persnickety. Tomorrow Jake would teach his brother a lesson about leaving be what didn't belong to him.

"Gentlemen, shall we retire to the blue drawing room? Cigars and brandy await."

The men followed his father from the dining room. Daniel matched pace with Jake. "Lady Kennell has a commonplace mind. I admire that in a lady."

"I'm glad you are enjoying your last night of walking."

His brother laughed and dropped to the settee, propping his arms across the seat back. He appeared as a giant on the diminutive piece.

"Aren't you surly this evening? I hesitate to request your advice, but I do have a dilemma," Daniel said. "No denying Lady Audley is attractive, but Lady Kennell is a tempting armful, too. How am I to choose between them?" He winked as he lit the cigar clenched between his teeth. "Perhaps I won't be forced to limit myself. They seem close."

Jake dropped his chin, meeting his brother's direct gaze in challenge. "Stay the hell away from Amelia or there'll be the devil to pay."

Daniel took a drag on his cigar before blowing the pungent smoke in Jake's direction. "Ah, so it's Amelia, is it?"

"Lady Audley to you."

His brother cocked a grin. "I've made a few deals with the devil. Maybe that's a price I'm willing to pay."

"Leave her be."

Daniel's eyebrows shot up. "Well, little brother, I say we settle the matter tonight. Sign her dance card before the first waltz or she's mine. I refuse to wait any longer while you dangle after her."

Jake's muscles twitched as his fists tightened at his sides. "And if she dances with me, you stay away from her forever."

"Such high stakes attached to the lady. I do believe you care for her."

"And you care nothing for her, so do her a favor and leave her alone." Jake turned on his heel and stalked across the hazy room where Forest was leaning against the sideboard, appearing bored with everything.

He lifted his snifter as Jake approached. "Couldn't help but to overhear. Your brother is as big an arse as I recall."

"He makes *you* look saintly."

Forest clunked his drink down and reached for the decanter. Glass clinked against glass as he poured a hefty portion of scotch into a tumbler and passed it to Jake. "I can't say I have attained sainthood, but I am on the path of righteousness, my good man."

"Lucky for you, Forest." Jake accepted the glass and sipped the amber heat, trying to calm his riotous breathing. "Otherwise my sister would serve your bollocks for breakfast."

Forest flinched. "Hell's teeth. *Damned* lucky for me I'd say."

Three

AMELIA SAT ALONE ON A POMONA GREEN SOFA WHILE
Bibi visited the retiring room. Ladies she had known
for years surrounded her, but no one spoke to her.
Most wouldn't meet her eye.

She was not oblivious to the consequences of her
association with Bibi. Although her friend had always
been impertinent, her troubles with a certain baron a
few months ago had made her brazen beyond the pale.
Lord Banner didn't help matters by poking the grumpy
goose, so to speak. His wife was less than pleased by his
blatant interest in Bibi and made it her charge to punish
Amelia's friend at every opportunity. If the overbearing
woman had her way, the entire *ton* would shun Bibi.
Fortunately, Lady Banner's influence was not far
reaching beyond her circle of well-dressed minions.

Amelia sat up straighter and adjusted her skirts. Bibi
would never turn her back on her, and she wouldn't
abandon her friend to win favor with the *haute ton*. Still,
the evening was a disappointment. If no one would
even look at her, how would she garner their support
for the children? Mrs. Hillary had assured her there were

members of the Mayfair Ladies Charitable Society who had praised her efforts at their last meeting, but those ladies didn't appear to be in attendance this evening.

"There you are." A kind voice broke through her thoughts. Amelia glanced up to discover Lana Forest standing by the settee. She returned the younger woman's warm smile.

"Do you mind if I join you?" Lana asked.

"Please do." Amelia scooted to make room for Jake's sister on the tufted piece.

Lana had a way of bringing cheer to a gloomy room, and Amelia could use some cheering.

"How go your efforts on behalf of the foundling hospital?" Lana asked.

"Not as I had hoped."

"Take heart. Forest will lend his support, as will several other gentlemen of his acquaintance." Lana's smile was wicked as she leaned close to whisper, "I have convinced him to call in their vowels."

"Their vowels?"

"Gambling debts owed to my husband."

"Lana." Amelia chuckled at the young woman's cleverness.

"Only what they can afford to spare, of course." She set her skirts to rights then folded her hands. "Do you mind if I speak plainly, Amelia?"

She paused for a beat, a flutter starting in her belly, before shaking her head to indicate Lana had permission to be candid. One could never be certain what the lady might say from moment to moment.

"I noticed my brother was friendly with Lady Kennell." Amelia released her breath, sinking against the cushion. "Yes, you may want to dissuade Captain Hillary. Bibi can be… difficult to please."

"Then I shan't worry for Lady Kennell. Perhaps my brother has met his match. But I feel it is only right to caution you."

Amelia drew back. "Me? Why caution me?"

"Daniel can be charming when he wishes, which is not often enough in my estimation. He plays the doting suitor well, but he tires quickly of a lady's company." Lana placed her hand over hers. "Amelia, he watched you at dinner when you weren't paying notice. He will approach you next."

Her body heated at the insinuation. Did everyone believe her to be such a willing bed partner? She did practice discernment.

"You paid me a similar kindness at Irvine Castle," Lana said. "I would like to return the favor."

Amelia smiled, but she couldn't look at the young woman. She had done her best to caution Lana against Andrew Forest, to disallow him to ruin her chances of finding a decent husband.

"My advice was off the mark," Amelia said. "Your husband is quite doting."

Lana sighed and furrowed her brow. "And I wish I were wrong about Daniel. Heed my warning; he cares for no one but himself."

Amelia nodded, unsure how to respond given she had no interest in Captain Hillary. "I will take your warning under advisement. Thank you."

"Splendid. The matter is settled then." Lana tossed her head, causing wispy tendrils of auburn hair to slip from the pins. Her lively green eyes sparkled. "Now

Jake, on the other hand, is a different breed of man. Extremely loyal and not given to whimsy. I would venture he would make a delightful husband."

Oh, good heavens. Amelia flicked open her fan and waved it to cool her hot cheeks. Lana had a reputation for successful matchmaking, but she apparently knew nothing of her brother's disdain for Amelia. "Yes, well, thank you for your kind guidance, Lana. I will make note of your concerns."

Jake's sister sank back against the cushions with a slight frown. "Indeed? You have nothing more to say?"

Amelia almost regretted thwarting the young woman.

She spotted Bibi and hailed her, eager to end any conversation that might encourage Lana to meddle further in her affairs. "Ah, Lady Kennell. You return."

Bibi grinned at Lana. "My lady, your brother is a gem, and so very handsome."

She returned Bibi's greeting with a polite smile. "So I am told, Lady Kennell."

Bibi lowered into a chair, removed her long white glove, and held her hand out to study her fingernails. "I'm eager to become better acquainted. Perhaps we'll even become close, intimate friends."

"Yes, I see," Lana said.

Bibi's slender brow lifted, and she flashed a mischievous grin. "Captain Hillary is a handsome swell, too."

Amelia bolted upright. What was Bibi implying? If she thought to pursue Jake Hillary, she would receive blistered ears for her trouble. He might not be Amelia's to defend, but she wouldn't allow her lusty friend to devour him. Why, the idea left her downright indignant.

Lana gawked at Bibi. "Uh…"

Amelia cleared her throat. "Of course, Captain Hillary is *more* to your liking, wouldn't you agree?" She hoped her friend would follow her lead and stop hinting at her desire to make Jake her next conquest. She couldn't imagine Lana would take kindly to Bibi toying with her favored brother.

Bibi's cocoa eyes darkened. "I disagree, dear Amelia. I find Jake Hillary undeniably enticing of a sudden. I'm entertaining the most enjoyable thoughts about him right now."

Amelia silently pleaded with Bibi to be quiet.

Lana flushed bright red, her chin jutting forward. She seemed as protective of Jake as he had been of her before she married, which did not bode well for Bibi.

Amelia's gaze flickered back and forth between the two ladies. She held her breath. Perhaps she should intervene, but aligning herself with either against the other wouldn't do. Lana's complexion slowly returned to its normal shade of ivory, and she replaced her scowl with a neutral expression. "Lady Audley, visiting with *you* has been a treat this evening. I hope you will excuse me."

Amelia offered her widest smile, eager to make up for Bibi's offensive behavior. "I enjoyed our visit as well, my lady. And thank you for your kind support of the foundling house renovation."

"It's my pleasure."

Once Lana left, Amelia whipped around. Her friend's cheeks pinked under her intense scrutiny. "What are you about, Bibi?"

"You may offer your gratitude later." She tried to hide behind bravado, but her rosy complexion communicated her chagrin.

"Why must you push everyone away?"

Her friend picked at her nail and scoffed. "Those ladies care nothing for us. We are outsiders, impure women set on corrupting their steadfast husbands. If that is what they think, why disappoint?"

Amelia sighed and shook her head. "I think Lana may be different."

"Doubtful." Bibi's demeanor changed in an instant. She lit up like a firework and clapped her hands. "Great heavens! I was serious about Jake Hillary. His brother leads me to believe the man is inexperienced in the bedchamber."

Amelia gasped, her gaze darting around to be certain no one overheard. "Bibi," she whispered fiercely, "that is a horrible rumor to spread about Mr. Hillary."

"Horrible? What's horrible about his state of purity?" Bibi's eyes narrowed. "You are behaving oddly, as if you don't wish for me to seduce him. Do you fancy the gent for yourself?"

"Absolutely not!" Amelia had never shared information about Jake's visits. She had told herself it was to protect against rumors. After all, she had been in mourning when he visited her at Verona House bearing gifts from his mother. But the truth was Amelia had kept their association secret out of fear if she spoke of him to anyone, he would disappear. A ridiculous superstition since he had vanished anyway.

Bibi clasped her hands to her chest and grinned like a child with a new toy. "Splendid, then I lay claim to him. I have never had the pleasure of educating a young man in the art of lovemaking."

Amelia's stomach squeezed painfully. She couldn't

hear another word of Bibi's inane chatter over the rushing sound in her ears. If her friend thought to use and dispose of Jake like a used frock, she had never been more wrong. If indeed he required *education*—and Amelia couldn't believe for one minute that he did after the way he had kissed her—Bibi would not be his tutor.

◈

Jake's fingers tightened on the punch glass, the cut crystal imbedding diamond patterns into his palm. He drew in a deep breath, trying to ignore the tempest in his belly. Across the ballroom, Amelia chatted with her dark-haired friend, Bippi or something equally bizarre, who kept glancing in his direction with a smile stretching her bloodred mouth.

What was so funny that Lady Kennell watched him with obvious amusement? With his luck, the lady knew of Daniel's challenge and had already shared it with Amelia. Perhaps Amelia whispered all the ways she might humiliate Jake as she gave him the cut direct. Even if he deserved her contempt, he wouldn't enjoy the ridicule of his fellow gents on the morrow. He could only go so many rounds in the boxing ring.

Jake sniffed, disgusted by his doubts. It was a dance. She wouldn't dare deny him one dance. The act required little on her part. He would do all the work, leading her around the floor with his hand on her back. Several respectable inches from her tiny waist, which innocently served as a transition from her splendid breasts to her curvaceous hips and rounded bottom.

Jake groaned under his breath and wheeled around.

He couldn't approach Amelia with his breeches tenting like the pyramids of Egypt. Why mere thoughts of Amelia accomplished what the accommodating widow Mrs. Lovejoy had failed to do on two occasions baffled him. He had begun to fear something was broken, and while he was relieved to learn all was in good order, perhaps he should send around an apology to the widow.

The start of a melody floated on the air. He didn't have much time. The first dance had begun, and the fourth was a waltz. An image of his brother with Amelia cooled his ardor in a hurry, although it flared his temper.

He turned and plowed into his sister. Lana teetered and flung her arms wide to regain her balance.

"Lana!" Jake lunged, catching her around the waist before she toppled backwards, but he didn't have his footing. She gasped as they twirled and slipped. Frantic and fearful of hurting her, he held on tight and managed to plant his foot before they crashed to the floor. Although not as noticeable as falling on his sister, his display drew enough unwanted attention.

"Damnation," he muttered.

Forest hurried over followed by Daniel, Lady Kennell, and Amelia.

Reaching Lana's side, her husband wrapped his arm around her waist; a fretful line creased his forehead. "Are you injured?"

Jake's sister laughed. "Jake and I are a touch out of practice, but I think we still show a good flair for dancing."

"I'm sorry, Lana. I should have been watching where I was going."

Forest drew her to his side. "I've never met a gent as luckless as you, Hillary. Nevertheless, your sister is unharmed."

"Yes, don't fret. That was the most exhilarating event of my week."

Forest frowned at her. "Indeed? The *most* exhilarating?"

Lana hugged his arm and beamed. She always smiled these days. To see his younger sister happy made Jake's heart swell with tenderness. She deserved joy after everything she had experienced.

Daniel slapped Jake's back. "That was the worst footwork I've ever seen." His boisterous voice boomed in the great room. "No lady who values her toes will consent to dance with you after that demonstration."

"Don't be so sure, Captain Hillary." The silken tones of Lady Kennell's voice demanded Jake's attention. "I would take great pleasure in a turn at Mr. Hillary."

The dark-haired beauty slanted her head, her heated gaze roving over his body. Lady Kennell was a brazen one, convincing him the rumors circulating about her at Brook's had merit.

His eyes narrowed and a pulse of resentment surged through his veins. Had she influenced Amelia's decision to take up with another gentleman while he was away? "Indeed, Lady Kennell? You wish to *dance*?"

"Yes, indeed." She batted her dark lashes, a lazy smile spreading across her lips. The lady misread him greatly. "Well, Mr. Hillary? Would you like to claim the waltz?" She flicked her dance card toward him, clearly expecting him to take it.

He caught the slight shake of Lana's head then

glanced toward Amelia. Apprehension clouded her blue eyes as she studied him with such graveness, he hesitated in his response. He wouldn't hurt her ever, and from her expression, he was treading on sensitive ground. Unfortunately, he didn't know which action would be the inciting factor: snubbing her friend's advances and setting tongues to wagging, or dancing with another woman who promised more than a dance.

He looked to his sister for an answer.

Jiminy! When had she developed that odd twitch with her neck?

Lady Kennell chuckled. "I'm waiting with bated breath, Mr. Hillary."

Just as he opened his mouth to decline her invitation, Amelia thrust her dance card at him. "Mr. Hillary, you requested a waltz earlier, did you not?"

Amelia's grim expression suggested a turn about the floor would be as pleasurable for her as a tooth extraction, so her actions made no sense. Then again, ladies rarely behaved in any predictable fashion in Jake's experience.

He latched onto her card before she could snatch it back. "I have not forgotten, Lady Audley." He scribbled his name beside the waltz and returned her card with a smile. The corners of her lips inched upward, but he wouldn't go so far as to classify it as a sign of contentment.

He handed Lady Kennell's card back, hoping she wouldn't notice he hadn't claimed a dance. Amelia had made her wishes known, and he would abide by them.

The ladies huddled as they moved away.

"*I* wanted to be first," Lady Kennell complained. Amelia shushed her to no avail. "You only needed to say you fancied him, Amelia."

"Be silent," Amelia hissed.

An elated smile kicked up the corners of his mouth. Amelia did fancy him still, didn't she?

When he swung his attention back to his sister, she huffed. "Don't you dare dance with *that* woman."

His smile faded. "What do you have against Lady Audley?"

"Not her, you ninny. The other one."

Forest gently took Lana's arm and aimed her toward the refreshment table. "He didn't claim a dance, love. Calm yourself."

"And he shouldn't. She is not a proper lady."

Forest drew her away. "Your brother can manage his affairs without your assistance. Come along."

When Lana shot her husband a silent warning, he simply chuckled, which earned him a full-out glower. Jake had seen that look many times. He didn't envy Forest his evening.

Once alone with Daniel, Jake lifted a brow—a move he had practiced in the looking glass for years in imitation of his elder brothers. "Amelia is not meant for you."

"So you claim." Daniel crossed his arms over his massive chest. "Do you plan to keep both ladies for yourself?"

He couldn't refrain from gloating. His brother wouldn't spare him if their positions were reversed. "How would I ever choose between the two?"

Daniel leered. "Indeed. Well done, Jake, my boy."

"Tomorrow morning. Gentleman Jack's at ten o'clock. You are overdue for a thrashing, old man."

"Brazen pup."

Jake walked away with a smile of satisfaction.

Four

AMELIA HUSTLED TO CATCH UP TO BIBI AS SHE STOMPED to the retiring room. "Please wait for me, Lady Kennell. I must speak with you."

Bibi didn't break stride as she passed a group of debutantes and their chaperones returning to the ballroom. The young girls stopped and stared with wide eyes.

"Did you see Lady Kennell's gown?" one of them said in awe.

"It is gorgeous," her companion replied, before turning to speak with an older lady Amelia didn't recognize. "Aunt Charlotte, may I go inquire after her modiste?"

"Absolutely not, Penelope. You shan't ever speak to that woman."

Aunt Charlotte's pinched expression and haughty tone sent a fresh wave of irritation through Amelia. She halted in front of Penelope. "I'm certain Lady Kennell will be happy to recommend you to Madame Girard, Miss…?"

"Penelope Cummings, my lady. Oh, how splendid."

The girl bubbled over with enthusiasm, her brown curls springing as she bounced on her toes. "Thank you."

"My pleasure, Miss Cummings." Amelia held Aunt Charlotte's gaze, daring her to speak ill of Bibi in her presence.

"Yes, thank you, Lady Audley," the girl's aunt said with a touch of humility. It would be foolish to decline an offer for a personal recommendation to the coveted modiste, even if Aunt Charlotte held one of Madame Girard's best patrons in contempt. It would be even more foolish to test the bounds of Amelia's overtaxed patience.

She nodded then continued on the path Bibi had taken. Her friend sat at the dressing table when she entered the otherwise empty retiring room, excluding the maid standing in the corner. "Will you excuse us a moment, please?"

The young woman curtsied and bustled from the room.

Bibi glared into the looking glass, opened her reticule, and yanked out a silver tin of lip rouge. Popping off the top, she dipped her little finger in the paint and applied the rose red to her lips.

Amelia planted herself beside the dressing table with hands on her hips. "You have no cause to be angry with me, Bianca."

Bibi rubbed her lips together before pursing them as if blowing a kiss. She replaced the tin lid and returned the rouge to its proper home. "I am your dearest friend, Amelia, and you neglected to mention you have a soft spot for Jake Hillary."

"I do not." When Bibi narrowed her eyes, Amelia repeated her claim with less conviction. "I really don't."

"Then *why* did you shove me aside to hand Mr. Hillary your dance card?"

"I didn't shove you."

Bibi's thin brows lifted.

"Shoved is a bit exaggerated, would you not agree?" Heat infused Amelia's cheeks. "I may have nudged you. A little. But it was accidental."

"You nudged me. A little." Bibi smirked. "That was no accident, Amelia Audley. You are not a clumsy ox, although I'm unsure the same can be said of Mr. Hillary after his performance this evening. I believe you have your work cut out for you in the bedroom, my dear."

"Bibi, stop." Amelia couldn't look at her friend. "Mr. Hillary and me? How ludicrous."

"Ludicrous?" Bibi issued an audible sigh. "Simply tell me if you plan to tutor him in the bedroom or not."

"Of course not. And neither will you."

She headed toward the door, intent on returning to the ball.

"You're a cruel woman, Amelia. Very cruel."

Bibi's sharp tone brought her to a skidding stop, and she spun around.

"Cruel? You think I am *cruel*?"

"Yes, I do." Bibi lifted her chin and nailed her with a look that froze her in place. "It is obvious Mr. Hillary carries a torch for you. Had I known you returned his interest, I never would have considered him. But he is untried at five and twenty. Bed him, please. Because if you don't, I will be forced to do the deed. I cannot stomach the suffering of a handsome gent."

Amelia's hands fluttered to the heart pendant around

her neck. "Captain Hillary has played you horribly. No gentleman retains his innocence at Jake's age." She reached for the door handle but turned to address Bibi once more. "And Jake Hillary has no use for me. He despises me, so rid yourself of these silly notions."

Bibi rolled her eyes. "Yes, darling Amelia, now run along and allow him to despise every inch of that beautiful body you possess, the one Mr. Hillary cannot take his eyes off. *Ever.*"

Amelia shook her head in disbelief. Her friend had gone mad, and one could not argue with someone bound for Bedlam. "I'm returning to the ball."

"Don't keep the gorgeous man waiting," Bibi called in a singsong tone.

Amelia pulled the door closed behind her. This evening had turned into a disaster. Not only was she making no progress with garnering support for the foundling hospital, she had thrown herself at Jake, proving herself no better than the wanton he believed her to be.

When she reentered the ballroom aglow with hundreds of tapers, her sight landed on him whisking one of the newly presented debutantes onto the floor, a friend of Miss Cummings. Jake was taller than most, with a slender build, so he stood out in a crowd.

Amelia's palms grew moist inside her gloves, and she swallowed against the panic rising in her throat as she watched them bow to each other. Jake's dance partner glanced at him and giggled. While he acknowledged the young woman, he offered nothing more than a polite, albeit strained, smile.

Amelia's fear released its grip on her heart, but her

relief was fleeting. He may have no interest in the young miss on his arm, but he might find someone to his liking this season. There were many beautiful, young innocents to vie for his notice. At some point, he would take a wife, but no amount of rational thought on the topic had prepared her for the inevitability.

Amelia couldn't look away as Jake joined hands with the girl and sashayed down the line of dancers. Tonight he cut a dashing figure in his gray breeches and charcoal jacket. He was handsome beyond what was fair. Instead of growing stout or developing a balding pate with age, Jake had become more pleasing to the eye.

She had been taken with him her first season. Unfortunately, he had held a *tendre* for Lady Delilah, although their match had never materialized. Amelia frowned.

Jake had much to recommend him, but she supposed a title carried more weight with some ladies. He was dashing, charming, and hailed from generations of wealthy landowners. And now he boasted a fortune of enviable proportions after the inheritance of his grandfather's shipping company. He was a prize for any young miss wishing to make a tidy match, which only served to increase her misery. He would not remain unattached forever.

Jake escorted his dance partner from the floor and bid her farewell. The disappointment on the girl's face caused a sick feeling in the pit of Amelia's stomach. Had she shown her emotions as readily at that tender age? Most importantly, could she keep her feelings hidden this evening as she waltzed with him?

He looked around the great hall until his gaze landed on her. Her heart fluttered as he moved in her direction. *Oh, please don't giggle like a ninny.*

Jake Hillary possessed elegant good looks. His sculpted visage rivaled any work of art and rendered him much too appealing to lack experience in the bedchamber. Captain Hillary was a scoundrel to spread lies about his brother, and Bibi was a fool to believe him.

Jake bowed when he reached her. "Lady Audley, I believe I have the next dance."

"Mr. Hillary." Amelia placed her hand on his arm and sensed the tensing of his muscles. She glanced up, fearful she might discover disgust on his face, but his expression remained neutral.

He escorted her to the floor and they took position for the waltz. His long fingers, graceful like a musician's, closed around hers. A blend of citrus and rosemary filled the air.

Good heavens. He smelled good enough to eat.

As the music swelled, Jake guided her around the floor. He was an agile dancer and always had been. Amelia had often pondered this about Jake and his siblings. Every Hillary was light on his or her feet.

"Mr. Hillary, how is it you and your siblings are all accomplished dancers?"

His eyebrows pulled together. "Are you mocking my earlier performance with my sister?"

"Not at all. I've simply noticed you exhibit a great aptitude for dance."

He grinned, his eyes crinkling at the corners, giving him a boyish charm. "You have noticed? How delightful to hear. What else has come to your attention?"

"Oh, never mind, Mr. Hillary." She wasn't interested in playing games of cat and mouse. Her interactions with gentlemen invariably proved an ill use of her time, and tonight was no exception. She should keep to her work with the children.

She and Jake moved in time to the music, silent for several beats.

"Father employed an instructor at Mother's urging," he said at last. "The man was relentless. You either learned to dance properly or suffered his tantrums."

Amelia's mouth formed a silent *oh*.

Jake's smile slid from his face as he stared at her lips, or at least she thought that was where his sight landed. His Adam's apple bobbed. "More than once, he stomped my toes for performing the wrong step."

"That's awful, a truly appalling technique."

"Yet effective." A spark of mischief lit his blue-green eyes. "I now have gained a great appreciation for the pain a lady would endure if my rather large feet trod upon her."

How like a gentleman to boast about the size of his feet. Amelia chuckled, the tension draining from her shoulders. Maybe they could be civil to one another if nothing else.

His thumb moved in a gentle arc on her back and sent tingles racing through her limbs. She yearned to be held by him again, to have him kiss her like he had that night almost a year ago. Being close weakened her resolve to forget him.

When he led her into a turn, she caught sight of Bibi dancing with Captain Hillary. Her friend flashed a ridiculously wide smile. Why, one might think she'd done something miraculous, like invented a cure for measles. Amelia looked away when Bibi tried to mouth something to her. Something about the garden?

The music faded, but Amelia and Jake stood there holding each other's hands. Their gazes met, something unspoken passing between them and making her tremble inside. She drew in a shuddering breath and dropped his hand before stepping from his embrace.

"I suppose you should find your next dance partner," she said.

"I suppose I should." He didn't escort her from the floor or falter in his stare, and a flash of heat washed over her. "Amelia, there's something I wish to tell you. Let's find a quiet place where we will not be disturbed."

A shrill screech gave her a start. She whipped around to discover Bibi on the ground holding her ankle and whimpering. Captain Hillary crouched down beside her.

Amelia raced over to her with Jake following closely behind. "Bibi, what happened? Are you all right?"

Pain marred her pretty features. "My ankle. I twisted it."

Captain Hillary lifted her amid shocked gasps from the crowd gathered around them.

Mrs. Hillary pushed through the crush, her face pinched. "Oh, dear. Bring her to the green drawing room at once, Daniel."

He followed his mother with Bibi cradled in his arms while Amelia and Jake trailed behind.

Bibi peered over Captain Hillary's broad shoulders. "Mr. Hillary, I'm afraid you cannot sign my dance card now."

Jake grimaced. "Perhaps another time, Lady Kennell."

Her head lolled back as they exited the ballroom, a tortured cry on her lips, which sounded oddly like a woman in the throes of ecstasy. Amelia's posture grew more rigid. Now she stood no chance of winning the favor of the ladies of the *ton*. Not after Bibi's outrageous behavior. But what vexed Amelia even more was her friend's assumption that Jake wanted to dance with *her*.

In the drawing room, Captain Hillary eased Bibi onto the settee where Amelia had sat with Lana earlier. He knelt at her side and reached for a slipper.

She slapped his hand. "Don't touch it. It hurts."

Captain Hillary scowled and stood. "You should remove your slipper before your foot swells too much to do so."

Bibi shook her skirts, covering her foot and ankle. With a sweet smile, she glanced up at the captain. "I'm certain you are correct, sir, but I cannot bare my ankle in mixed company."

Amelia bit the inside of her cheek to keep from laughing aloud. Bibi rarely exhibited such restraint, as evidenced by her scandalous performance in the ballroom.

Mrs. Hillary fluttered around Bibi, fluffing pillows to place behind her back. "Oh, my dear Lady Kennell, I am so very sorry for your injury. Is there anything I can do for you?" Her gaze traveled the room. "Perhaps a brandy? To ease your pain, of course."

Bibi placed a gentle hand over Mrs. Hillary's trembling one. "Please, don't fret. It was my own clumsiness. All I require is rest."

Captain Hillary smirked. "Might I offer you an escort home?"

Amelia's eyes narrowed on Bibi. Was this a ploy to leave the party with the gentleman?

Her friend shook her head. "Thank you for the kind offer, sir, but I imagine Lady Audley would allow me the use of her carriage. Perhaps the footman could call for it now?" She held her ankle and winced.

Oh, dear. Bibi must have truly suffered an injury to compel her to rebuff Captain Hillary's offer. Amelia's annoyance evaporated.

Mrs. Hillary looked to Jake. He nodded and slipped from the room.

"I should collect my shawl," Amelia said and started for the door.

"You needn't leave the party on my account," Bibi said.

Amelia stopped to study her friend's pallor. Her cheeks boasted lots of color and pain no longer clouded her eyes. She couldn't be recovering already, could she?

"Don't be silly," Amelia said. "I would not feel right about staying without you."

"But you haven't spoken with Lady Eldridge or the duchess yet."

Nor did she expect either lady would deign to speak with her now. It was disappointing that she had been unable to secure more support this evening, but Bibi's welfare must be considered at the moment. "I will call on Lady Eldridge and Her Grace another day. There is still time to garner support before the board makes a decision."

Mrs. Hillary stepped forward. "Allow me to call for your shawl, dear. It was the beautiful gold embroidered one, was it not?"

Amelia nodded.

Mrs. Hillary and Jake met at the double-hung oak doors. Moving aside, he allowed his mother to pass.

"The carriage is driving up the street," Jake announced.

Captain Hillary swept Bibi into his arms again and carried her toward the entrance, taking care not to hit her foot on the door frame.

Amelia followed to wait in the spacious foyer for Mrs. Hillary to return with her shawl. "I will be along in a moment," she called after Bibi.

Jake halted on the fringes of the room and crossed his arms, assuming a brooding silence. She shifted her weight from foot to foot, increasingly uncomfortable with his change in demeanor. What had happened between their waltz and now to make him so surly?

"You are leaving," he said at last. A simple enough statement. So why did it sound like an accusation?

She inhaled sharply, preparing to give him a piece of her mind, to declare *he* was the one to leave first, but Mrs. Hillary bustled in with an expensive emerald green shawl belonging to someone else.

"Lady Audley, please accept my apologies. It seems your shawl has been misplaced. Please, take mine, and I'll have yours brought around when it is found."

Amelia restrained herself from snatching the offering and dashing out the door. "Good evening, Mr. Hillary."

"My lady," he said with an incline of his head.

Mrs. Hillary escorted her outside. "Now do not fret, dear. I have already spoken with Lady Eldridge and Her Grace. They are enamored with your project and will lend their full support."

"Thank you, Mrs. Hillary. You have been a godsend to the children."

Amelia didn't glance back to see if Jake watched her leave, but he hadn't followed them to the door. She did her best to ignore the sick feeling in her stomach.

Outside, Captain Hillary assisted her into the carriage and bowed. "Until we meet again, ladies."

He closed the door and secured the handle before the conveyance pulled away from Hillary House.

"Oh, thank heavens." Amelia sighed and sank into the cushions.

Bibi glared across the carriage; the shadows created by the light glow of the lamp made her features more severe. "I hand you Mr. Hillary on a platter and *you* leave the party?"

Amelia blinked. "Pardon?"

"I intended to strand you at Hillary House." Bibi tossed her head. "Honestly, Amelia. Mr. Hillary is too gallant to ignore a lady in need, especially one he desires. He would have escorted you home, and must I enlighten you on the rest?"

Amelia held up a palm. "Please, say no more." She leaned forward. "Are you deranged?"

With a huff, Bibi slumped on the carriage bench. "I'm beginning to question my sanity for giving up Mr. Hillary. Lucky for you, he has an equally handsome brother rendezvousing with me in an hour."

"And your ankle?"

Her friend threw her arms wide. "Amelia, have you not been listening? I have no injury." She chuckled in response to Amelia's jaw dropping. "I know. I should have been an actress. Bloody shame it's not a profession open to aristocracy."

Only Bibi would concoct such a harebrained scheme.

"Perhaps you should share your brilliant plans before launching into theatrics next time, dearest."

With a smile, her friend shrugged. "How was I to know you were such a noddy? I always thought you clever. I will do you no more favors."

"I'll thank you to keep your word."

"If you desire a tumble with that gorgeous man, you must do the work yourself."

Blessed be. Amelia closed her eyes and rubbed her temples. "And what makes you certain Mr. Hillary desires a tumble?"

"What else could he possibly want? He's a man."

A man who blew hot and cold with no predictability. Amelia would be a noddy indeed to hope for anything from Jake.

Five

Jake was sore, glum, and foul-tempered the morning after Daniel's party, proving unfulfilled desires made for poor bedfellows. They created the perfect frame of mind for boxing, however.

Daniel's pained grunt was the sweetest sound he'd heard all week. Jake repeated a jab to his brother's kidney to hear it again. The bones in his forearm shuddered with the impact. Daniel was massive and built like a bull. One solid hit from him could knock Jake into the afterlife. Fortunately, Daniel had sluggish feet, and Jake had no qualms about using his speed and agility to trounce his brother.

Jake leapt back when Daniel swung a clunky fist for his midsection, missing his tender parts by a fraction of an inch. He took advantage of his brother's unprotected jaw to nail him with a left hammer.

"Hellfire!" Jake's fist burned something terrible in spite of the protection of a muffler. He retreated, bouncing around the ring as he shook out his hand. "Your head is harder than a damned boulder."

"Not hard enough," Daniel said with a groan as

he slumped to the ground. He rested his forearms on his knees and panted. "Couldn't you allow me one hit today?"

"Not and live to speak of it. Do you yield?"

"Until next time, pup."

Jake tugged off his gloves and walked to where his brother sat bested. His mood had improved with the exercise more so than defeating his opponent. Despite Daniel's ability to aggravate, he was his brother, and on most days Jake was fond of him. Tucking one of the gloves under his arm, he offered Daniel a hand up.

"Much appreciated."

Jake accepted congratulations from the other gents en route to the dressing room.

"Did you mar my face?" Daniel tipped his jaw up to reveal the beginnings of a bluish bruise.

"Anything is an improvement to that ugly mug," he teased.

Daniel smirked. "The ladies rarely complain."

Jake shrugged on his shirt. "I would hardly classify them as ladies, and I don't believe it is your face that impresses them."

His brother snorted with laughter and snatched his own shirt from a chair.

Jake chuckled as well. "I meant they are attracted to your large purse."

"It's not only my purse the ladies enjoy."

Jake threw his discarded shirt at his head, but Daniel caught it.

They dressed in companionable silence then decided to walk back to Hillary House for further exercise. Jake adjusted his hat as they stepped into the bright sunlight. "You do realize," his brother said, "I'm not required to pay for my pleasure. In fact, I tumbled a proper lady last night."

Jake lifted an eyebrow. "A *proper* lady allowed you in her bed?"

Daniel shrugged. "I suppose I may have overstated the quality of the lady involved, but she is a lady in the strictest sense so I had to slip into her house undetected."

The clomping of their boots echoed in the ensuing silence. Daniel couldn't mean he had bedded Amelia, could he? She *had* been his intended bed partner last night. A tight twisting began in Jake's gut, moved into his chest, up his neck, and into his jaw until he felt fashioned of stone. It didn't stop with his body but invaded his mind to twist his thoughts. If Daniel had gotten to her...

Jake halted in the middle of the walkway. "Who the bloody hell was it?"

Daniel stopped as well. The corner of his lip inched up. "It wouldn't be proper for me to say."

Jake's fingers curled into fists. Perhaps they had ended their session at the saloon too soon.

"Let's just say she wasn't the one I truly wanted." Daniel winked. "Yet." He dashed ahead, laughing.

Jake's tension melted away. With a shake of his head, he followed at a stroll, recognizing that his brother teased him. Nevertheless, he would remind Daniel once they reached the town house that he lost the bet last night. Amelia was no longer an option, and though she didn't want Jake, Daniel couldn't have her either. That seemed a fair arrangement.

Lying in bed last night, Jake hadn't been able to

shake the memory of holding Amelia in his arms while they danced. She felt right with him, but he seemed to be the only one to recognize how they suited.

Just as he had gathered the wherewithal to ask her about his unanswered letters, she had dashed away. He couldn't help but to feel discouraged by her lack of curiosity over his desire to speak with her even as he admired her loyalty to her friend.

Never once had Amelia acknowledged his declarations of love or offer for her hand, which spoke of her feelings about him. She cared nothing for him. Selecting a wife from among the debutantes would serve him better. Unfortunately, they all possessed one fatal flaw.

None of them was Amelia.

On the day he had spied her shopping on Bond Street in preparation for her debut five years earlier, he had been struck mute in the middle of a sentence. David Audley had teased him without mercy, but he hadn't cared.

Jake's desire for her had only grown stronger as the season progressed. A generous heart resided beneath her ethereal beauty, and he had known with certainty she was the one for him.

And while he had attempted to work out the best way to court Amelia, for he had wanted everything to be perfect, his best friend played him false and wooed her in secret.

Shaking off his familiar anger, he entered Hillary House. The butler stepped forward to take his hat and gloves. "Captain Hillary awaits you in the blue drawing room."

"Thank you, Hogan." Jake headed for the drawing room to join his brother for a drink.

Daniel had already helped himself to a brandy and lounged in a chair with his foot propped over his knee. "What took you so long?"

Jake's brows rose. "Perhaps I was not eager for more of your company." Despite his words, he had missed his brother while he was at sea. The only true source of conflict between them was Daniel's cool treatment of their mother—that, and his brother's insistence on behaving like a first-rate scoundrel. He should show more respect for himself.

Crossing to the sideboard, Jake poured a brandy before assuming the adjacent chair. "Daniel, I'm curious. Why is it you rent that rat's nest when you have a perfectly good home on Curzon Street?" His brother's glass paused midair. He took his time contemplating an answer, and Jake sipped his drink while he waited.

"I don't entertain lightskirts at my residence."

The brandy went down the wrong way, causing Jake to sputter and spew his drink, sparking a string of curses from his brother.

"Sorry," Jake mumbled once he recovered.

Daniel jerked a handkerchief from his waistcoat pocket and blotted his face. "This whole sharing among siblings is overprized. I have my own spirits, thank you."

"I said I was sorry."

"And as I was saying, I confine certain activities to the appropriate settings. I don't wish to cause an uproar with the servants."

"I see."

"I'm sure you don't." Before Daniel could launch

into his usual tirade about Jake's tendency to adhere too closely to societal expectations, their mother glided into the room.

"Excellent. You have returned." She shook a fist of sheer fabric with gold edging at Jake. "The servants located Lady Audley's shawl. She may need it, so be quick about it."

Jake frowned. "Be quick about it? What is your meaning?"

She shook the shawl again. "The phaeton is prepared. I want you to deliver this to the lady."

"Send one of the footmen."

Her hands landed on her hips, the shawl cascading almost to the ground. "Send a footman? Darling, they are much too busy with their duties." She thrust the shimmering material at him again. "I ask very little of you, Jake."

"I would be happy to assist, Mother." Daniel set his glass on a side table and prepared to push himself from his chair.

Jake bolted from his seat and grabbed the fabric before his brother could stand. "She asked me."

If Daniel thought Jake would allow him to call on Amelia, he was deluding himself.

❦

Amelia spread orange marmalade on her toast and scanned the pages of *The Morning Times* as she ate breakfast alone. She had been following the same routine since moving to the Park Street town house after her husband's death. In fact, her routine dated back to the early days of her marriage.

Had Audley ever shared breakfast with her? Often he had remained in bed after a late night out, or he never made it home. Whatever entertainments he sought outside their marriage bed left her engaged in solitary pursuits, much like her childhood. After her mother's death, her father had become like an apparition floating in and out of her life as it suited him.

She frowned and turned the page, smoothing the wrinkles with her hand. Why Audley had bothered marrying her was still a mystery to her. She hadn't carried a large dowry, and there were more accomplished young ladies presented that season. Of course, he *had* professed to love her, which seemed a nice sentiment, one that had piqued Amelia's interest at the time. Yet, oddly, a man's love felt similar to his indifference.

Her butler entered the breakfast room, impatience flashing in his eyes. "Lady Kennell has come to call."

Amelia suspected Bradford found Bibi's early hours for visits improper, but she didn't mind. Her friend made certain she was never alone for long, and Amelia loved her for her efforts.

"Please, show her in."

Bibi burst through the doorway. "I *told* you she would see me, Bradford." Obviously, she had eavesdropped outside the breakfast room.

Strolling in, she took a seat as if she resided at Verona House, which she should, considering she spent most of her time there. "And I'll take eggs and toast with honey, crusts cut off."

"Yes, milady." Bradford's tone left little doubt her demands irritated him.

Bibi winked at Amelia. "Oh, and Bradford?"

Sweetness dripped from her words like the honey she had requested.

He halted with a sigh. "Yes, Lady Kennell?"

She flashed her white teeth in response to his dour expression. "I would appreciate a smile when *you* serve my tea."

"Thank you, Bradford," Amelia added, "but it won't be necessary for you to serve Lady Kennell. One of the footmen will do."

Poor Bradford. Bibi took pleasure in tormenting Amelia's servant.

After a stiff bow, he swept from the room.

"When he serves notice, you are finding his replacement," Amelia warned.

Bibi leaned against the white velvet seat cushion. "He'll never leave. He secretly loves me."

Amelia shook her head and chuckled. "As do all men, or so you continuously inform me. I didn't expect to see you here this early."

Bibi's gaze meandered around the room. "I have always adored the quaintness of Verona House."

Amelia loved her cozy home, too. After the move, she had thrown herself into redecorating every room in the house. The project had helped to keep her agonizing thoughts at bay after Audley's death, such as how repulsive must one be to drive a husband away?

A footman ambled into the room with Bibi's breakfast but left upon a single glance from Amelia.

Slumping against the chair, Bibi gave a heavy sigh.

Amelia suppressed a smile. She wouldn't be an easy quarry. If her friend wished to discuss whatever woe plagued her today, she would have to be forthcoming.

Arching her eyebrows, she made a show of studying Bibi's plate. "Has something gone awry with your breakfast, dearest? Cook trimmed the crusts."

Her friend wrinkled her nose. "There's nothing wrong with my toast."

"Your eggs are not to your liking?"

Bibi slapped the table. "Again, you toy with me. There is nothing wrong with my breakfast. Ask me what troubles me before I burst."

Amelia chuckled. "Or you *could* simply tell me."

"Where's the fun in that? I much prefer having you coax confessions from me."

Folding her arms, Amelia leaned on the table, attempting to hide her amusement, and suspecting she did so poorly. "Very well. Darling Bibi, you seem out of sorts this morning. Please, oh, please tell me what tragedy has befallen you."

Now Bibi laughed. "You mustn't be so dramatic." She took a bite of toast, her expression sobering as she chewed. "I have come to believe all men are the same. None cares a whit about pleasing a woman. They all do the same tired things, no creativity whatsoever. And *then* they only do it for a minute before they're ready for the main event."

Amelia sipped her tea. Assuming Bibi spoke of Captain Hillary, she experienced more than a little discomfort.

"I wish to find a man who takes his time. One who really cares if I enjoy myself, too," Bibi said. "Do you think a man like that exists?"

Her chocolate eyes searched Amelia's as if she had answers when it came to gentlemen.

"One can always hope," she replied with a slight shrug.

Bibi sighed and rested her chin on her upturned hand. "Hope for the hopeless. That's exactly what I need."

Amelia couldn't agree more.

A short moment later, Bibi perked up again. "Let's go shopping. A new gown never disappoints me."

Amelia swallowed, hesitant to reveal her plans. "I am afraid I won't be able to join you today."

"Why ever not? Do you have another boring meeting with your horrid solicitor? That man is as interesting as a box of rocks. No, I take it back. I have met rocks more intriguing."

"Hmm," Amelia answered and fiddled with the morning newssheet.

"Just reschedule. Please, please, *please*?" Bibi drew out the last please, earning Amelia's full laughter.

"I really must decline, Bibi."

"Then I will accompany you, and we can visit Bond Street afterward."

She sighed. Bibi never made anything easy. "I'm not visiting my solicitor."

When she offered no more, Bibi frowned. "Then what, pray tell, *are* you doing?"

Amelia busied herself with spreading marmalade on the other half of her toast, avoiding her friend's gaze. "I wish to call on Mrs. Hillary, to thank her for an enjoyable evening. Perhaps my shawl has reappeared as well."

Forming a temple with her fingers, Bibi smirked. "I see, how kind of you. Please, give my regards to *Mrs*. Hillary."

Amelia dropped her head to hide the blush she knew must be coloring her cheeks. "Yes, I'm happy to pass on your regards."

"Oh, and offer Jake Hillary my best, will you, Amelia?"

Her hands fluttered around her place setting, re-adjusting her silverware and turning her plate a quarter of a turn. "I-I doubt our paths will even cross."

Bibi's eyes narrowed as she leaned forward. "Lady Audley, what is it you are keeping secret? You've been acting bizarrely ever since last night. Is there something between you and Mr. Hillary?"

"N-no, don't be silly." Amelia attempted to laugh, but it came out strangled and transparent.

"There *is*," Bibi said in a rush of breath. "You are having an affair with him, aren't you?"

She bolted upright. "No! I-I'm not. We never, I mean we—"

A wicked grin spread across Bibi's lips. "Captain Hillary is wrong about his brother's experience in the art of pleasing a woman. No wonder you defended Jake Hillary with such vehemence."

Oh, dear. This was humiliating beyond the pale. How could she explain her association with Jake without appearing a pitiable sap? Perhaps she should allow Bibi to believe she was intimately involved with him.

What am I thinking? Bibi would then let slip something embarrassing in front of Jake, a subtle innuendo that would reveal her lie.

"I've left you with a false impression, I believe. Mr. Hillary and I are not involved." She sipped her tea, refusing to meet Bibi's curious gaze.

"You never were any good at falsehoods," she said. "Remember the time Mrs. Meriwether questioned who smuggled the kitten into the dormitory?"

"I'm sorry I gave you away. I froze when she threatened to expel us if we didn't come forward."

Bibi flicked her hand. "I forgave you long ago. Besides, you tried to lay claim to the act of mercy, which would have been more in line with your character. I'm still uncertain of the reason the headmistress didn't believe you, but it illustrates my point. You are a horrible liar."

"I'm telling the truth. Jake and I are not intimate."

"And yet his given name rolls off your tongue with ease." Bibi crossed her arms. "Tell me the truth now, or I'll be forced to go to *Jake* for answers."

Amelia gasped. "You *cannot*! I would die on the spot."

Her friend lifted an arched eyebrow. "Then I suggest you tell me."

Blasted Bibi! "Very well, but you may not laugh at my expense." She cleared her throat. "We kissed, only once, mind you."

Bibi's eyes rounded. "And you never told me? When did this happen?"

She was certain her friend wouldn't judge her. Bibi knew as much about being in a loveless marriage as she did, but Amelia hesitated. She had held that moment with Jake close to her heart for a year.

Bibi clicked her tapered nails against the edge of her plate.

Amelia took a deep breath and blew it out slowly. "I was in mourning. I couldn't make it known." She looked up at her friend, finding nothing but acceptance in Bibi's expression and her defensive stance crumbled. "After Audley's death, Mrs. Hillary began to send Jake by several times a week with various treats and sympathetic notes she had penned. I was taken aback by her kindness. We were hardly more than acquaintances. Yet, she reached out with more caring than people I had considered good friends."

Bibi had to know she wasn't included in that group. Her dearest friend had stayed with her for days until Amelia insisted she return to her home.

"Naturally, Jake and I spent more and more time together. At first, he would linger when he made his deliveries. Later, I invented reasons to have him stay, such as to advise me on a household task or help with my accounts."

Bibi rolled her eyes. "As if you need assistance with your calculations. Go on."

"He began to stay for meals on occasion, and sometimes our companionship continued into the evening. We would play chess or read together. One night it just happened. It seemed a natural progression of our association. He was bidding me farewell for the evening and then we were kissing."

Amelia's belly flipped as she recalled the delicious feel of his lips on hers. He had tasted of cinnamon and sugar from their dessert, and her knees had quivered as he'd held her in his arms.

"Yes? What happened next?"

Amelia shook her head. "Nothing. He said he would call the next day, but he never did. He disappeared without a word." Her throat grew tight and ached with unshed tears. She swallowed harshly. "I don't know what I did to drive him away. Maybe I was too receptive to his advances. Or perhaps I—"

Bibi slapped the table. "What makes you think

you are at fault? That's your problem, Amelia. You constantly accept blame for the failings of men. First there was your father, then your husband— followed by Jake Hillary, I now learn—and finally that scoundrel Forest."

It wasn't as if Amelia had been unaware the gentlemen in her life had discarded her, but to have them cataloged as such was a blow to her person. Her bottom lip trembled, much to her despair.

Bibi shoved from the table and hurried to her side, her skirts rustling as she rounded the table. "Please don't cry, dearest. Those men are fools for missing the treasure you are." She threw her arms around Amelia's shoulders and squeezed. "That horrid Mr. Hillary. He does not deserve you." To agree that Jake was horrid would give her no satisfaction. When he had approached her at the Eldridge ball almost a year ago, the moment had been awkward and tension-filled. Amelia had struggled with the desire to throw her arms around him, to beg him to come home with her. Thankfully, her pride had kept her from making a fool of herself, any more than she already had.

A few tears welled up in her eyes, and she blotted them with a pastel napkin. "After our dance last evening, I'm more confused than ever. There seems to be something between us still, or it had seemed so for a fleeting moment."

"Pfft!" Bibi flopped into the adjacent seat. "It doesn't take a scholar to recognize the attraction. The man practically pants after you. But don't you dare fool yourself into thinking it's love."

"But—"

"Amelia, if love is real, why have I never seen it?" Bibi held up a finger to silence her when Amelia tried to answer. "Don't offer your usual argument that I cannot see air either. I breathe, therefore I believe. On the other hand, I have never loved. Jake Hillary wants the same thing all men want, pleasures of the flesh. If you choose to take him to your bed, make it on your terms."

Bibi's cynical view of men hadn't always matched Amelia's own, but perhaps her friend had a point. She had been searching for love all her life and had nothing to show for it.

Bibi patted Amelia's hand resting between them. "Enjoy the encounter for what it is without hanging your hopes on it becoming something more. There are many gentlemen who will be happy to step into Mr. Hillary's boots once you tire of him."

Amelia balked. *Tire of Jake?* She couldn't see that happening.

"I suppose if *you* have no intention of falling in love," Amelia said, "then I shall give up the search as well. I will not be content unless you are."

"Splendid. I knew you would come around eventually."

Amelia took a deep breath. Well, she wouldn't sit around feeling sorry for herself. Maybe she and Jake had no future, but she deserved some answers to help her put their association behind her. And she would get them today.

Six

JAKE CLIMBED FROM THE PHAETON AND SIGNALED TO THE young boy who called out an offer to tend the horses. Dread crept over him as he took in Amelia's tidy residence. The last time he had visited Verona House had been a disaster. He had never properly apologized for his atrocious behavior that day, but at this point in time, he wasn't certain he should rehash the event.

Perhaps he should have allowed Daniel to deliver the shawl instead.

"The hell I should." He snatched a bouquet of flowers from the carriage seat and marched up the stairs. Shifting the lilies and shawl to one arm, he raised his fist to bang on the door just as it flew open.

Amelia's high-pitched scream scared the devil out of him. He staggered, tripped over his top boots, and landed on a large potted topiary flanking the door. The blasted plant snapped and the jagged trunk poked his side.

"Good heavens, Mr. Hillary! Are you all right?"

"I believe so." Righting himself, he examined the plant. *Hellfire*. He might be uninjured, but the tree was mangled beyond recognition. "Perhaps it's salvage-able?" He lifted the dangling top sphere, pulled his hand away, and cringed when it flopped back. He met Amelia's wide gaze. "My apologies for the damage. I'll replace it."

She waved a dismissive hand toward the injured sentry. "It's simply a plant, Mr. Hillary. I have warned the gardener repeatedly about it being positioned too near to the entry. Perhaps now he will listen."

Jake swiped at the cypress needles clinging to his jacket only to have them stick to his glove.

"Allow me to assist." Amelia captured his wrist and peeled the glove from his hand. Her light touch initi-ated a rapid beating of his pulse.

Egads. What had he been thinking? He wasn't broken in the least. Amelia set his body aflame simply with her nearness.

Her blue eyes lifted to meet his. "Would you like to come inside and remove your jacket?"

"Yes." His voice had grown husky. Beyond her shoulder, a footman loitered inside the foyer.

Amelia released Jake's arm and turned to the servant. "Thank you, Thomas, but I won't require your escort now."

"Yes, milady." The man left them alone on the front stoop.

"Please come inside, Mr. Hillary."

Jake swept his gaze over Amelia. She wore a lavender walking dress trimmed in yellow along with a matching bonnet. Everything she donned hinted at her curvaceous figure, the contours of which regret-fully remained unexplored by him.

"You're on your way out," he stated as he followed her inside and pulled the door closed behind them before removing his other glove.

"I was."

"I shan't keep you then. Mother found your shawl." He fumbled the flowers as he tried to free the swath of gauze from his arm.

"And the flowers? I don't recall leaving those behind." The sparkle in Amelia's eyes raised his spirits. Perhaps he had done something correct for once.

He held out the bouquet. "I saw them when passing a flower monger."

She accepted the offering with a chuckle. "A flower monger just happened to carry lilies in April?"

"Well, not the first woman I passed, or the second or third." He tugged at his cravat, which his damned valet had tied too tight again. "Did I say a flower monger? I meant the florist. You do like lilies, do you not?"

Her grin widened. "The pink ones are my favorite. How did you know?"

"I overheard you talking once."

He knew many things about Amelia, such as how much she had adored Angelica Catalani's portrayal of Susanna in *Le nozze di Figaro*. How she ate every bite of dessert if the hostess served bread pudding, but she refused it if the sweet was prepared with nuts. He also knew she possessed a beautiful singing voice, but performing for others made her nauseous. He'd actually discovered that by accident.

One evening, a few weeks after her debut, her father had implored her to sing for his guests. Jake's heart had squeezed as she clutched her shaking hands and her voice quivered. When she rushed from the room after her performance, Jake had followed her into the garden where she lost her meal. Amelia had cried while he fought the desire to go to her for fear she would be mortified. Instead, he had waited inside the glass doors, keeping watch over her until she returned safely to the house. What if he had followed his heart that day instead of his sense of duty? Perhaps their circumstances would have been much different than they were today.

She hugged the bouquet against her chest. "They are magnificent, Mr. Hillary."

Her butler stood at the room's edge, eyeing him. Likely, the man recalled the autumn morning Jake had almost knocked the poor servant on his arse as he barged into Amelia's home uninvited. He offered an apologetic grin, but the butler repaid his efforts with a haughty sniff.

Amelia carried the lilies to the servant. "Please have these placed in the drawing room."

"Yes, milady."

She turned to face Jake again. "Thank you for the flowers, and for returning my shawl. Now, remove your jacket."

Her crisp order made him chuckle. "Yes, milady."

He shrugged off his jacket and handed it to her. Amelia draped it over a chair standing beside an entry table then returned to stand in front of him. "You have needles on your waistcoat as well."

Before he could suggest removing that layer of clothing, she began plucking the greenery from his person.

His throat grew thick and heavy. He was uncertain how much longer he could remain a gentleman with her touching him, and feared she would notice his arousal any moment.

A small smile played upon her lips. "Mr. Hillary, would I be imposing if I requested your opinion on a matter involving the foundling home?"

Jake jumped at the chance to shift his attention elsewhere, at least until they weren't on display in the foyer. "I would be honored to lend my assistance."

"Splendid." She linked arms and drew him toward the drawing room. "Perhaps you would be so kind as to view the plans for the new wing to see if they appear sound. The board has commissioned an architect, but I fear I can't make heads or tails of the markings. Perhaps with your superior drafting knowledge, you could explain them to me."

Jake's chest puffed up with pride. Study of architecture and drafting had been his hobbies since he was a boy of twelve. "Indeed. I am happy to assist you, Lady Audley."

Gliding to a desk by the window, Amelia gathered several rolled-up pages. "Please, have a seat."

Jake chose the settee with the hope she would sit beside him, but she lowered into an adjacent chair instead, resting the scrolls across her knees.

"Thanks to the Mayfair Ladies' Charitable Society, I almost have the financial support required to convince the board to move forward with the renovation. I foresee nothing to halt the project as your mother assures me she has others interested in pledging to the cause." She frowned, a small crease marring her smooth brow. "Have you any notion the conditions the children must endure?"

"I fear I am woefully unenlightened."

"The children are sleeping at least four to a bed, and those are the more fortunate ones. The older orphans have been relegated places on the floor with nothing but threadbare quilts for comfort. The donations the foundling home receives pay for the food they eat and clothe the children, but there is nothing left to improve the home itself. It's a pitiable situation, but I am of a mind to correct it."

Jake smiled. How like Amelia to take up the charge for others. "I admire your dedication. I have yet to pledge my financial support, but I should like to donate to your worthy cause."

"Oh, Jake! Would you truly? I would be eternally grateful."

His heart skipped a beat. Had she meant to call him by his given name?

"Here," she said, holding the plans out to him. "Please, tell me your thoughts."

He took the rolled paper and spread it out on his lap. A quick perusal revealed sound engineering. Amelia's addition wouldn't fall down around her ears.

"Mr. Brown knows what he's about."

She leaned forward to peer at the draft. "How many windows has he incorporated? I cannot tell what is window and what is wall."

"There are four along this wall." He pointed to the lines indicating openings. "And four on the opposite wall."

She craned her neck. "Where exactly?"

"Come here so I might point them out better."

Amelia rose from the chair and settled beside him on the settee. Their heads bowed together over the plans. Her floral perfume was sweet and clean, and it brought to mind a clear summer sky as blue as her eyes.

Jake touched the places on the paper where windows would be. "Here. Here. Here. And here."

Her hand brushed his as she ran her finger over the places he pointed out. Pleasing tingles raced along his skin.

"It's exactly as I had hoped," she said. "I wish to create a cheerful place for the children, a haven from London's cruel streets."

Jake nodded, enamored with the way her face softened as she spoke of her aims. "You have a way of cheering up any place, Mia."

Her cheeks flushed a rosy hue. "Mr. Hillary, it is fortuitous that you came here—"

A loud rap on the outer door caused them both to startle.

"Good heavens," she muttered. "Now who is calling?"

The butler passed the drawing room door as he walked to the front entrance, his spine rigid and his upper lip stiff. The man truly lacked any lightness of character. From their position in the drawing room, neither Amelia nor Jake could view the caller.

"Please inform Lady Audley that Captain Hillary wishes an audience." His brother's boisterous voice echoed in the foyer.

Hot anger shot through Jake. He should have known his damned brother wouldn't keep his word to stay away from Amelia.

༜

Amelia's heart raced when Jake scooted closer to her on the settee. Bibi was wrong. What passed between them was more than lust. They shared a kinship she had never experienced with another gentleman. After his arrival with flowers, she felt certain his aim was to court her.

She gazed warily toward the door. Bradford appeared in the threshold and threw her a questioning look. She could deny the captain an audience, but it would be awkward explaining her refusal to Jake.

She gave a quick nod to grant permission before Bradford moved aside and directed the captain into the drawing room with a sweep of his hand. The gentleman's stride was a cross between a swagger and a march, commanding as he invaded her quaint living quarters. She had a brief vision of him onboard his ship.

"Jake, I expected you would have departed by now," the captain said.

Sitting as close as she was to Jake, she sensed the tremor flowing through his body. She stole a glance at him. The murderous glint in his eyes made her breath hitch.

She touched Jake's forearm to soothe him, and his gaze snapped to her. Offering a tentative smile, she prayed the men wouldn't come to blows. If Captain Hillary injured Jake, she would never forgive the brute, and Jake might come out on the losing end, given his brother outweighed him by a stone at least.

There was a brief flash of tenderness in Jake's eyes before he glared at his brother again.

"Captain Hillary, what an unexpected surprise."

Amelia's greeting to her unwelcomed caller sounded strained. "Do you seek out Lady Kennell?"

The captain smirked. "Does the viscountess reside here as well?" He stayed close to the entry, not venturing to approach them. "It is you, my good lady, I seek."

What in the world was Captain Hillary doing calling on her? He couldn't expect her to consider him a suitor, because men like the captain didn't court ladies. She pressed her lips into a straight line. His visit meant one of two things—Mrs. Hillary had sent him here on an errand, or the captain expected something from her she was unwilling to give. And he didn't seem a man to accept rejection easily. She leaned into Jake, his warmth lending her security.

His muscles flexed under her fingertips. "What possible reason would you have for requesting an audience with the lady?"

A surge of affection flooded over her in response to his protectiveness.

Captain Hillary shrugged. "Lady Audley promised to tell me more about her charitable work. In addition, it's a beautiful day. What better way to enjoy the weather than a stroll through the park with an equally beautiful lady?"

Jake shifted the drawings to the side table, stood, and assisted her to her feet. He cradled her arm in the crook of his elbow. "I'm afraid she is unavailable. The lady granted permission for me to take her for a turn around the park. We were just on our way out."

The captain grinned, not seeming the least bit discouraged. "An excellent idea. Shall we? Lady Audley could sit between us."

"There's no room, Daniel. Now off with you."

Jake's brother acted as if he hadn't spoken. "I hope our paths cross tonight at the Chickerings' masked ball," Captain Hillary said. "What is your costume, dear lady? Perhaps you will grant me a waltz?"

She wished to keep her costume a secret from him, but with the intensity of the captain's stare, she feared leaving him unanswered. He must make for a dreadful shipmaster.

"I—I will be costumed as Freya."

Captain Hillary clapped his hands once. "Brilliant choice, my dear. You will make an excellent goddess of passion."

Jake guided her toward the door. "We haven't time for chitchat."

His brother stepped aside to allow them passage. "I shall look forward to our dance this evening, my lady."

Jake mumbled something that sounded like "over his dead body" before whisking her through the foyer and out the door to the waiting carriage.

Once he had settled her on the bench, she slid over to make room. He paid the young man tending his horses then climbed into the conveyance.

"Thank you, sir," the boy called out then tore off across Park Street.

Amelia smiled, lifting her face toward the sun to soak up its warmth. "This was an excellent suggestion, Mr. Hillary."

"You aren't angry with me for delaying your outing? Now that my brother is no longer watching, I could carry you to your destination."

She glanced at him from the corner of her eye. His

handsome profile sent her heart into a lively beat. She was exactly where she wanted to be.

"In truth, I was headed to Hillary House to collect my shawl. Since you were kind enough to deliver it, I have no need to go anywhere else. Let's enjoy our turn around the park, shall we?"

Seven

JAKE COULDN'T HOLD BACK HIS SMILE AS HE AND AMELIA entered Rotten Row. After their clash months ago, he wouldn't have trusted Amelia to spit on him if he were on fire, much less accompany him to Hyde Park.

He tipped his hat to acquaintances as they traveled along the sand-covered avenue. Jasper Hainsworth, Earl of Norwick, loitered along the fence. His slack jaw suggested he was more befuddled than usual.

"Good afternoon, Lord Norwick," Jake called cheerfully.

Norwick's gaze followed them. "Lady Audley?"

"Good afternoon, my lord." Amelia's response was cool, and she turned her back to him.

Disquiet stirred inside Jake. He was well aware widows were fair prey when it came to seduction, but Amelia wasn't just any widow. She was… Well, she should be… *Damnation*! He loved her and that was how it was. "Are you well acquainted with Lord Norwick?"

"I'm more familiar with his sister, Lady Banner." And if Amelia's pursed lips were any indication, she didn't hold the baroness in high esteem.

Jake's tight grip on the ribbons eased.

"What do you suppose has the earl so perplexed?" she asked.

Amelia was the most beautiful woman Jake had ever encountered. One glimpse of her could conceivably turn any man into a simpleton.

"The better question would be what doesn't have the man bewildered on any given day?" Jake said. "Let's pay him no more notice and enjoy our time in the park."

"Agreed." Amelia sighed and wiggled her bottom closer toward him. Having her snuggled against him reminded him yet again he was alive, well, and foolish for having questioned his virility. Yet, he must have been born under a halfpenny moon for they were never in the appropriate setting to remedy his condition.

Spotting a grassy area close to the Serpentine, an image flooded his memory. He pulled the carriage out of the line of traffic, stopped the grays, and pointed. "I saw you there once."

"Saw me? What do you mean? When?"

"The first time ever, I believe." Three years before Amelia came out. "You were just a girl. I assume you were with your governess."

"Marguerite." Amelia spat the name as if it were bitter on her tongue, but when she glanced at Jake, her expression softened. "And what was it I was doing to draw your attention, Mr. Hillary?"

"The hysterical screeching from your governess first earned my notice, but then I understood the cause. It's a wonder you didn't tumble headlong into the water. You were teetering on an outcropping of stones, trying to capture a toy boat with a stick."

Amelia's brow furrowed. "I don't recall having a toy boat. Are you certain it was me?"

"Of course it was you." He recalled the vision with clarity. With the sunlight casting Amelia's hair in a glow, she had looked like an angel in white muslin. An *insubordinate* angel. "You are correct, however. It wasn't your boat. You were retrieving it for a boy weeping on the bank."

Pink colored her cheeks, adding to her attractiveness, if that were possible. "I recall the day now. His nanny scolded him for letting it go, and she refused to retrieve it. What a tyrant she was, telling him he didn't deserve such a fine toy." With a stubborn set to her jaw, Amelia added, "*I* disagreed."

"Yes, you did." He had admired her bravery that day. Amelia had possessed a healthy dose of mettle for one so young. Rarely did he witness daughters of the *ton* defying authority, at least under the censorious eyes of society. Amelia had pursued the morally correct path despite the consequences. He liked that quality.

"What else do you recollect?" she asked.

"Your governess was livid and bellowed warnings that she wouldn't save you from drowning if you fell in the water."

Amelia huffed. "I would have been rescuing her is more like it. She never learned to swim and trembled if she came within five steps of a puddle."

"A cowardly governess for the brave young Mia."

She wrinkled her nose, a smile lifting the corners of her lips. "Well, she is French."

"How dreadful."

Amelia touched her hand to his leg as she laughed,

seemingly oblivious to her action, but Jake wasn't. He stiffened and his breathing almost ceased. A simple touch sent his senses whirling like a tempest. Did she have any idea what she did to him?

She cocked her head to the side. "Mr. Hillary, please forgive my boldness, but I have wanted to ask you for some time what happened with Lady Delilah?"

Lady Delilah? Who in the devil's name...? "Oh! Do you refer to Lady Ramsden?"

Amelia offered a sympathetic cluck of her tongue. "I do hope I haven't opened an old wound by asking after her."

Jake blinked and readjusted his hat, searching his memory for any dealings with the baroness and recalling none. "I'm afraid I don't follow your meaning."

Amelia shifted toward him on the seat. Her compassionate gaze searched his face. "Were you terribly hurt when she rejected your offer?"

He laughed, thinking she was jesting. "Me? Marry Lady Ramsden? I mean before she became Lady Ramsden, of course."

His merriment faded quickly, however, when Amelia frowned.

"I thought you desired a match with Lady Delilah. Audley said it was a certainty she would accept your offer. He said she held a *tendre* for you and you for her."

Jake's heart began pounding in his ears, so that anything more she said became muffled and incomprehensible. Audley had said Jake held a *tendre* for Lady Ramsden? That was a blatant lie. He knew full well Jake had eyes for no one but Amelia.

"When did Audley tell you this?" Despite Jake's best efforts, anger lent his voice a harsh edge.

Amelia's gaze dropped to her gloved hands resting on her lap. "I'm sorry, Mr. Hillary. I should not have pried into your affairs. I've upset you."

He bit back an oath. Taking a deep breath, he forced lightness into his tone. "You're not prying. Please, tell me when he shared this with you."

When she glanced up, wariness swam in her eyes. "I refused his first offer of marriage, and he…"

Jake's nostrils flared. That damned blackguard. If Audley were still alive, he would pound him senseless. Jake had extolled Amelia's admirable qualities and professed his undying love to his closest friend. All the while, Audley had catalogued her shortcomings as if he did Jake a service. Then he had stolen her with covert meetings and lies.

The significance of what she said hit him. She had turned down Audley's first offer for her hand. "Did you marry Audley because you thought I wished a match with someone else?"

Her face drained of color. "No! Why would I?"

"I didn't mean to imply—"

"Audley used your association with Lady Delilah as an example. To illustrate a point. It was time he took a wife, too." She swiveled on the bench, her movements agitated. "I married him because he said he loved me."

His hope crashed at his feet. Of course Audley hadn't been her second choice. What had he been thinking?

She inched farther away from him. "I don't know what you take me for."

He'd made yet another mistake insinuating Amelia had married out of desperation. He had painted an unflattering picture of her in his haste to believe she held him in some esteem.

"Audley loved you, Amelia, as you loved him. I never meant to imply otherwise. I apologize." He lifted the reins, directed the horses back onto the avenue, and headed back toward Verona House.

They rode in silence, not even speaking as he escorted her up the front stairs. When she passed through the front door in a swish of skirts, he stopped at the entrance, unsure if she wished him in her home after the ghastly assumption he had made.

⁓

Amelia had never wanted Jake to know she'd accepted Audley's offer only after realizing Jake pursued another match. What a weak-minded ninny that made her.

Her stomach churned with humiliation and a growing resentment toward her deceased husband. She paused in her step. There had been something in Jake's eyes a moment ago. A lively flash when he had realized the truth. She hadn't been mistaken, had she? Perhaps she should take a chance and expose her true feelings for him.

She spun around to address him, but her sentiment stuck in her throat. Instead of following her inside, he loitered at the entrance, looking for all the world like he wished to run away.

She clamped her lips together and breathed deeply to steady her voice before she spoke. "Thank you for the lovely outing, Mr. Hillary."

He nodded. His expression was rigid and undecipherable.

"Perhaps we shall cross paths this evening at the masquerade," she said, hoping he might give her some encouragement to speak her heart despite the sudden chasm separating them again.

"Perhaps." His voice lacked conviction.

With a quick tip of his hat, Jake stalked back to the phaeton.

She hurried to the drawing room, pulling the doors closed before her tears fell and the butler witnessed her emotional outpouring and sent for a vinaigrette.

When the doors closed, fury swept over her and she trembled from head to toe.

Blast Audley for lying! Blast him! Blast him! What had possessed her husband to coerce her into marriage? Audley had known of her feelings for Jake. Somehow, he had ascertained that she favored Jake and used her tender feelings against her.

How dare he steal her chance for love? If Jake couldn't have loved her, then another gentleman might have held some affection for her. Because, truth told, Audley hadn't cared a whit for her. Not when he abandoned her after three months of marriage. How she wished he had revealed his true nature during their courtship, but Audley had been charming and determined in his bid for her hand, penning her love poems and whispering sweet words into her ear.

Amelia wandered the drawing room.

She had never hated anyone, not even her father, but perhaps she could make an exception for her husband. Even though her father had faults, he had never taken from her. Audley had tried. He had attempted to take her pride and her confidence. Perhaps even her one opportunity for love.

He would not succeed. She refused to embrace the bitterness pulsing through her veins, and she wouldn't abandon hope. Certainly not for him.

David Audley was in the past.

And he could stay there.

⤙⤚

Amelia adjusted the black feather cape to cover her décolletage as she and Bibi stepped into Mayfair's mythical world of Greek gods and goddesses, dominos, Roman soldiers, and even a pair of matching topiaries. The Chickerings' ballroom vibrated with excitement, causing goose bumps to pop up along her bare arms.

She enjoyed masked balls, but she approached the evening's event with trepidation.

Captain Hillary had indicated he would seek her out, and she was uncertain how Bibi might react if he did. In addition, she dreaded the talk she must have with him, but she couldn't avoid the unpleasantness. She would tell Jake's brother, so there was no room for misinterpretation, that she desired no association with him.

Bibi readjusted the snow-white mask covering the top half of her face and grinned, her red lips standing out in contrast. "Lively crowd this evening."

Merry voices intertwined and overlapped until nothing was distinguishable, aside from an occasional peal of laughter. The ballroom boasted low lighting, lending a wicked ambiance to the affair. Gentlemen and ladies stood closer than deemed appropriate, a subtle brush of hip against hip or gentle touch of hand to elbow revealing their secret desires.

Bibi's brown gaze swept over Amelia. "Signore Alberto surpassed all expectations with your costume. Reports of his superior craftsmanship were not exaggerated."

It was true the artisan had created a masterpiece, from her helmet and mask combination to the gold-plated breastplate, which shielded barely anything from view. Amelia felt overexposed and consequently grateful for the full cape of dyed goose feathers draped around her shoulders.

"Let's join the fray, shall we, Freya?"

Amelia hung back as Bibi immersed herself into the gay crowd, but soon hurried after her. Being alone in a social gathering was even worse than being surrounded by heavily perfumed bodies and the occasional wandering hand.

When Bibi disappeared among the taller guests, Amelia followed the golden asp's head rising into the air from her mask.

The snake slithered and bobbed, twisting until she lost sight of it. Jumbled bodies closed in around her. A light sheen covered her skin as a wave of dizziness engulfed her. She had to get out of there. Amelia gulped in big breaths of air to fight the suffocating sensation and shoved through the guests to escape to the sidelines.

Cooler air drifted inside through the opened French doors, the veranda beckoning to her. Amelia searched the crush once more for Bibi but didn't see her. Slipping into the night, she filled her lungs with fresh air.

A full moon illuminated the empty space, creating a magical world in the gardens beyond the veranda. She moved to the railing and leaned against the smooth marble. A welcome breeze washed over her heated skin, and she lifted her face with closed eyes.

"Freya, most glorious of the goddesses."

Jake. A smile pulled at her lips. She peered over her shoulder, her breath catching at the sight of the ethereal deity sharing the veranda with her. "Adonis, we meet at last. Rumors circulated that you were merely a myth, but I see everyone was mistaken."

Jake's chuckle warmed her blood, as did the glimpse of his strong calves peeking out from beneath the pristine robe.

"Should you be out here alone?" he asked.

She patted the sword at her side as she turned fully to face him. "I am armed for battle. Do you have need of a protector?"

"An armed escort as I walk the gardens might be wise." He stepped forward with a slight frown. "Amelia, could we go somewhere to talk?"

Eight

JAKE'S THOUGHTS FLED AS SOON AS AMELIA LINKED HER arm with his. Not that he had prepared a speech when he followed her to the veranda. He hadn't even formed a solid plan when the sight of her in the full moonlight had stolen his breath. Inviting her to walk in the garden had been impulsive.

They meandered along the path. The whispers of a set of lovers rendezvousing in the shadowed garden carried on the breeze.

Jake glanced down at Amelia on his arm; her silky tresses glowed almost white in the moonlight. Her hair fell to the middle of her back, tempting him to test its softness with his fingers.

He led her to a bench and urged her to sit before sinking down beside her. A warm breeze brushed his cheeks and the scent of lilac and rich soil permeated the air.

She tipped her heart-shaped face toward him, her almond eyes glimmering. He had recognized her the moment he saw her in the ballroom, and would have even if he hadn't known her costume. Jake had memorized every gorgeous feature: her pert nose turned up at the tip, eyes the color of the Mediterranean, and her luxurious pink mouth. He loved how her bottom lip was fuller and the way the top formed two perfect arches like the beginning of a heart.

"You said you wished to speak with me, Mr. Hillary?"

He snapped to attention. "May we dispense with formality, Amelia?"

Her lips puckered, and he could picture the tiny crease that formed between her brows when she was puzzled.

Opening and closing his mouth, he was unsure where to begin. Should he open with an apology or move directly to the point? The blasted trouble was he always had time to prepare prior to appearing before the court. He was meticulous in his study of the issues at hand and organized arguments thusly. Not so in spontaneous declarations of love.

After a while, she sighed. "Is that the whole of it? You wish to dispense with formality between us?"

"Yes. *No!*" he blurted, causing her to jump. *Damnation.* He rubbed his temples. This was going poorly. What a bloody travesty that a tiny woman could reduce him to a bumbling fool.

She hugged her arms close to her chest. "No, you do *not* want to dispense with formality?"

Jake shook his head to free it of cobwebs. "I would like you to refer to me by my given name, but that isn't the reason I asked to speak with you. I want…"

She looked expectantly at him.

"I want you…"

Amelia licked her lips, wrecking his entire line of thinking. The desire to taste her was highly distracting.

He longed to lay her in the bed of clover behind them and taste her all over, but that would never do.

"You want me?" Her voice sounded breathless.

"Yes," he said, enchanted with the rounding of her eyes. "I want you… t-to forgive me." Quite right, he should start with an apology. He jumped from the bench, warming to his topic and gearing up to present his case. "Yes, that's exactly what I am trying to articulate. I wish for your forgiveness."

"Oh!" Amelia blinked. "Forgiveness for what, exactly? Just so we are clear."

Did he really have to say it? He had been a deplorable cur last autumn and practically accused her of being a trollop. Very well, part of clearing the air required one to confess to wrongdoing. He took a deep breath. It was an uncomfortable conversation, his behaving like a jealous fool that day. "I never should have stormed into your home making ridiculous accusations. I had no right to—to lend commentary on your marriage or association with Forest."

Amelia winced.

He was fouling up his apology, hindering his chances of addressing the second half of the conversation. He did want her.

"Amelia, what I mean is—"

She leapt up from the bench, too. "Please, stop," she hissed, her gaze shooting wildly around the garden. "I don't want to discuss *him*."

Quite right. What if someone overheard?

"I made a mistake, but you wrongly judged me." She tried to rush past Jake and his world tipped out of control.

He grasped her arm. "Amelia, no. I didn't mean anything I said that day. You are a wonderful lady. I never should have said… You are correct, let's not discuss him, or that day. I want to discuss us."

She stared at him, her lips parted. "Us?"

"I know there is no us. Look, I am sorry for barging in and accusing you of being disloyal to Audley. It was stupid and improper and uncalled for."

She wiggled her elbow from his grasp. "I understand. You were coming to my husband's defense." Her eyes shimmered with unshed tears. "But, Jake, I swear I never was unfaithful to him."

"I don't give a damn about Audley."

Amelia's gaze snapped up to his, her mouth falling open in shock.

"I should have thrashed him from the start and been done with it."

"Oh!" She did it again. Her mouth formed a perfect pink circle and his body jerked to life.

"Amelia, I behaved like a lunatic that day. The truth is I wanted you to be with me. I wanted you in *my* bed."

Amelia stalked toward him, and he braced himself to receive her palm across his face. She stopped a mere inch from his chest. No blow followed. Good Lord, she had the sweetest scent, like that flower. The one that bloomed in the spring. What was it called? It came in pink or blue and resembled a spear.

"What is that flower—?"

"Be quiet and kiss me." She threw her arms around his neck and pulled him down to meet her soft lips.

To hell with flowers.

Jake wrapped his arms around her and breathed in her essence. Her luscious mouth moved beneath his as he kissed her back. When she brushed her velvety tongue across his lips, he moaned, opening his mouth and allowing her access before giving back what she offered.

Her costume breastplate pressed against his chest, the thin metal sheet preventing her ivory skin from touching him. He became acutely aware of the throbbing in his groin and that his hand rested so close to her beautiful, round bottom. He reached downward, eager to feel her beneath his fingers. She shivered in his arms, and knowing how inappropriate further exploration would be, he pressed his palm against her waist to hold it in place. Amelia deserved romance, not groping in a garden.

Without breaking their kiss, she removed an arm from around his neck and captured his eager hand and moved it lower to cover her bottom.

"Mia!" His fingers curled into the lush flesh. His shaft pounded with more vigor and grew harder than Carrara marble. She rose up on her toes as he dragged her against his hardened length. He wanted to bury himself inside her, to claim her once and for all.

A small cry passed from her lips.

Blast and damn! His enthusiasm was frightening her, but it had been so long.

Jake grasped her waist and gently pushed her away from him, breaking their kiss.

"No." She reached for him, her hips twisting to free herself from his grasp.

"We have to slow down, sweetheart."

She blinked at him, her breathing heavy and matching

his own. Her eyes grew round, and she stumbled back a step. "I-I'm sorry. I did not—oh, dear heavens."

He captured her around the waist as she tried to rush past, pulling her against him and setting his senses on fire again. He dropped his head close to her temple, his churning breath stirring the loose tendrils curling around her cheek.

"Please, don't be sorry," he implored. "I am only sorry for starting something I cannot finish here."

No matter how fiercely he wanted Amelia, he wouldn't treat her like a trollop. Bedding her in the gardens at a masked ball was too debauched by half.

His fingers trailed up her back before sliding into her silky hair.

"May I call on you tomorrow, Mia? Perhaps we could ride in the park again?"

She eased from his embrace, fluffing her shimmering skirt before reaching out to smooth his robe. "That would be lovely."

❦

Jasper Hainsworth, Earl of Norwick, struggled from the carriage. He tugged at his jerkin to keep from exposing his goods to the other guests also arriving at the masked ball. The skirt was deuced short, and his knees were showing. The hose stopping partway up his calves were ridiculous.

"Stop fidgeting," his sister scolded, her fingers digging into his upper arm. "Henry VIII was dignified."

With a frown, he pried her grip from his person. "You mustn't wrinkle the monarch's attire," he mumbled. "I shall have you thrown in the Tower."

Fiona ignored his comment and linked arms to pull him toward the entrance. "Don't become belligerent, Tub."

He wanted to shout at her to stop calling him that ridiculous nickname. He had lost at least two stones since she'd christened him Tubby.

He narrowed his eyes at Fiona. Was that the reason she had insisted he portray Henry VIII? "You realize I'm dressed as the younger, more handsome King Henry, do you not?"

"Of course you are," she responded in a condescending tone.

She thought him still rotund. Bristling, he lengthened his stride so she would practically have to run unless she wished him to drag her across the foyer.

Why had he agreed to attend this abysmal affair? He never attended balls and loathed escorting his sister any place, not that she required an escort. Fiona had a perfectly capable baron at home, who apparently had more sense than Jasper.

Lord Banner pretended his wife didn't exist most days, which meant Fiona spent more time at Jasper's Hertford Street town house than he desired. He should ban her from visiting for all the trouble she gave him, but how did one turn away the woman who had changed his nappies?

Fi was his half sister, actually. Her mother had died before producing an heir for their father, and then Jasper's mother died in childbirth. He sighed and slowed his step, a rush of affection for the woman he considered his mother softening his stance.

Nevertheless, he was head of the Hainsworth family,

a peer of the realm, a man of influence and prestige. He demanded respect.

"I don't intend to stay long," he said. "I'll leave you to summon a hack if you aren't ready to depart on my command."

One glance at his sister's pinched mouth took the wind from his sails. Perhaps commanding was a bit harsh. He would request she defer to his wishes, at least when in public.

As they entered the crowded ballroom, he smiled with sudden inspiration. Brilliant. They would never find each other again if separated in this crush.

Fiona's black eyes swept over him. "You will not leave early, Tub. It's high time you selected a wife. There is the matter of issue, as I'm certain you are aware."

He winced. "Lower your voice, Fiona." He didn't need everyone to know his affairs. Besides, he was still a young man of eight and twenty. He had plenty of time to marry and produce offspring. A wife wasn't on his agenda, but perhaps his sister had stumbled upon a solution to a pressing dilemma.

Since Maggie, his former mistress, had taken up with another gentleman, he had been frequenting the bawdy houses, but he missed the companionship a mistress provided. He desired an association with lasting benefits.

A widow would solve all of his problems. She wouldn't be an innocent or fancy herself in love. She likely wouldn't even entertain thoughts of marriage. And if that prig, Jake Hillary, could win the incomparable Lady Audley's attentions, surely Jasper was capable of attracting a widow half as beautiful.

"You're brilliant, Fi," he said.

"And you are hopeless." His sister yanked off her glove, licked her thumb, and reached for him.

Jasper slapped her hand away when her wet digit scrubbed his chin. "Egads! Have you gone batty, woman?"

"Chocolate," she stated with a smug gleam to her masked eyes. "I require refreshment now."

She didn't wait to see if he agreed to accompany her. With a frustrated shrug, he followed in her wake. He glanced at the obscured faces as he and Fiona weaved toward the refreshment room.

Blast! How was he to know the widows from the married ladies when he couldn't identify them? At least the innocents were easy to spot as they gathered in groups with their chaperones lurking in the background.

Lady Chickering boasted an extravagant spread. The white linen table was loaded with tempting sweets: strawberry tartlets, ratafia cakes, sugar cookies, marzipan. Jasper groaned and looked away before he drooled. Controlling his sweet tooth was difficult, but he wouldn't overindulge for fear of regaining what he'd lost, becoming an even larger target for his sister's insults.

"I'll meet you in the ballroom," he said.

Fiona loaded her plate with two of everything. He envied her ability to gorge herself like a man while retaining her scrawny figure.

She flicked her hand. "Off with you. I don't require an escort."

Now she didn't need an escort. She could have told him that an hour ago.

❧

Amelia danced the minuet with Jake. This was their second dance in a row, but with identities hidden, rules mattered less. Of course, in the light of day, she must be more cautious due to the foundling house renovation. She couldn't allow anything to destroy the support she had thus far received from the reputable ladies of the *ton*.

Her fondness for Jake would set tongues to wagging, and everyone would think she had become his mistress. After all, that was the only role fit for widows.

When the quartet stopped playing, Jake seemed reluctant to release her hands. Perhaps they could chance one more dance. The crowd seemed absorbed by their own machinations this evening.

"I suppose I shouldn't monopolize your time," he said, showing no signs of leaving her despite his words.

A caped figure appeared beside them. "No, you shouldn't, little brother."

Captain Hillary's crooked grin set her teeth on edge.

"Freya promised me a waltz, and I would be foolish not to hold her to her word."

Amelia forced a tense smile for the odious man. Very well. She would take the opportunity to set him straight and end this silly flirtation.

"Of course, Captain Hillary. I would be honored."

Jake's jaw tightened when she took his brother's hand. Her gaze followed Jake as he moved to the side-lines of the ballroom floor. She and Captain Hillary took position, waiting for the music to begin.

"Your costume is divine, Lady Audley."

Amelia's eyes flicked over him. He hadn't bothered with a costume, omitting even a mask. His only concession was the black cape, buff trousers, and open collared shirt. The dark bruise at his jawline lent a touch of realism to his rakish attire.

"Do you come as a pillager, Captain?"

"I take nothing by force, my dear." He winked, his cheek riling her temper.

When the music carried on the air, he led her into a turn.

She pressed her lips together in a thin line. "About that, Captain. I hope you will not take offense, but I'm afraid I have nothing to offer you."

His eyes hardened as his hand gripped hers tighter. "None taken, my lady. And may I express my wish not to offend you either. Nevertheless, I insist on knowing what game it is you play with my brother."

Amelia gasped, missed a step, and came down hard on his toe.

Her misstep barely registered on his face. "I will assume that was an accident, although I am beginning to suspect you are not as docile as you appear."

Now that she was recovering from shock, a hot flush inflamed her body. "How dare you," she whispered furiously.

The captain clamped her upper arm and dragged her toward the outer doors in the middle of the dance. She threw a desperate look over her shoulder for Jake, but she couldn't see him through the jumbled bodies.

Captain Hillary didn't pause as he marched across the veranda, down the stairs, and into the darkened garden. A scream bubbled up in her throat, but he released her before she let loose a howl.

"I'm not going to hurt you, Amelia."

She shrank back, trembling. Men didn't drag women to darkened gardens to play a friendly game of whist. "Please, let me go."

Captain Hillary exhaled loudly. "I didn't mean to frighten you. I promise you are safe. I only wanted to speak to you where Jake cannot overhear." He took a step forward but didn't touch her.

Amelia darted her eyes, searching for an escape, but he stood too close. He would grab her again before she moved.

"Speak to me about what, exactly?" she asked. "I'm not playing any games with your brother. I apologize, Captain Hillary, but I prefer him over you."

He scoffed. "I realize you care nothing for me, nor I for you. You passed my test."

"Your test?"

She sidestepped, but he matched her movement. His smug grin made her want to slap him.

"This afternoon you declared your interests. You chose Jake, so I feel confident you hold him in some esteem. However, if your interest is fleeting, I demand that you end your association now."

"My feelings for Jake are none of your concern."

Captain Hillary took a threatening step forward and Amelia backed into a shrub. "I will not see him suffer again. When you didn't answer his letters, it crushed him. And then taking up with that rake. Have you no sense of decency?"

"I know nothing about any letters. You are insane."

"That may be, but I'm certain you know the letters to which I am referring."

Amelia had had quite enough of his accusations.

She could scream and bring a host of gentlemen to her rescue. "When were these supposed letters to have arrived?"

He crossed his arms, his eyes boring in to hers. A shiver ran up her spine. Her scream might not deter him in the least.

"Jake wrote to you from Sussex. Don't pretend with me."

Her heart skipped a beat before accelerating to a rapid pace. Jake had written to her? "But I thought…"

She swallowed. She had never received any letters from Jake, but Captain Hillary didn't seem amenable to believing her.

"Of course, you're correct, Captain. I should seek him out at once." She reached out a tentative hand to plead with him to believe her, but she jerked it back when he snarled. "I have no intentions of ever hurting Jake. My feelings for him are heartfelt."

"See that they are. Don't disappoint him again."

His threat hung between them. She had no way to determine if he would truly hurt a lady, but he seemed sincere enough to set off another round of tremors.

Captain Hillary didn't try to stop her when she slipped by him to hurry along the gravel path toward the house. Through the lighted windows, she could see guests dancing a quadrille. The lively music drifted through the open doors. She dashed up the stairs and into the crush to search for Jake.

Nine

JASPER DOWNED TWO TUMBLERS OF BRANDY IN PREPA-
ration to approach a woman. Yet, the moment he took
a step toward the ballroom, he questioned the wisdom
of indulging in spirits. He wasn't foxed, but his eyesight
blurred a bit, which wouldn't help him separate out the
married from widowed ladies.

Although plenty of married women engaged in
trysts, the idea of an affair with another man's wife
soured his stomach. Aside from the risks of getting
oneself shot, Jasper didn't believe in being a party
to cuckolding a fellow gent. Just because he had no
desire to become leg-shackled yet didn't mean he
disrespected the sanctity of marriage.

Circling the great hall, he nodded to those he
thought were acquaintances. It was too blasted
hard to tell with all those masks and billowy capes.
Speaking of billowy articles of clothing, the fur-lined
robe he wore was going to kill him if he didn't catch
a breeze soon.

Again, he cursed himself for listening to Fiona.
Henry VIII? No wonder the ladies kept their distance.

Having a reputation for liberating others' heads from their necks tended to breed mistrust.

Beads of sweat formed on his brow, and he dabbed at them with the sleeve of his robe.

Jasper sighed. He needed a reprieve from the heat. Spotting a door opening onto a balcony, he hurried toward it and slipped outside. He closed the door behind him and welcomed the cool breeze on his damp skin. Still, the night was too warm for a fur-trimmed anything. He swirled the velvet cloak through the air as he removed it, tempted to toss it to the ground below. Instead, he draped it over the railing.

As if the robe wasn't bad enough, the revolting codpiece under his jerkin squeezed his shaft. Jasper lifted his skirts and jiggled to readjust himself.

"Ah, much better."

A chuckle startled him, and he spun around to locate the source.

"I thought to scold you for blocking my view, but then you are so very entertaining." The smoky female voice sent a jolt through his limbs. "What are you, the court jester?"

"Damned Fiona," he mumbled under his breath. "I'm King Henry the Eighth." He held his head high as if he were truly royalty, which was absurd given the lady had caught him with his breeches down. Or would that be skirts up? Blast! Either scenario was humiliating.

"You're not here to find wife number seven, are you?"

Jasper drew back. "Egads! No."

"Then you mustn't run off." The lady stepped from the shadows, her mask held in her hand.

He'd always been the luckiest bugger. Jasper

Hainsworth, Earl of Norwick, shared a balcony with the most notoriously libidinous widow in all of London. His gaze shot around the balcony. Where was her ubiquitous companion, Lady Audley?

"Lady Kennell, what brings you outside with all the activity in the ballroom tonight?"

"Likely the same as you, Lord Norwick. It's hotter than Hades inside. It was either step outside or shuck my dress."

Her lack of decorum delighted him. He'd heard rumors. "I suppose it was a difficult choice to make. Do you believe you followed the correct path?"

"Now, Lord Norwick, it is no secret I rarely follow the straight and narrow path."

Her melodious laughter made him tingle in the most wonderful places, naughty places that hadn't been entertained for several days.

"In fact," she said, "I haven't ruled out the complete removal of my attire."

Jasper's hand slapped over his hammering heart. "Indeed? Yet, you have no lady's maid to assist you."

A slight breeze carried a whiff of vanilla to his nose. Bianca Kennell smelled delicious. A ray of light shone through the glass doors, illuminating her midnight black curls and reflecting off the gold necklace around her neck.

"Hmm," she purred. "Yes, that is a dilemma."

A tremor of pleasure raced through him. Lady Kennell responded to him. She didn't run from the balcony or push him over the edge. What was the world coming to?

He attempted to clear his constricted throat. "M–might I offer my assistance?"

"I never would have mistaken you for a lady's attendant, my lord."

"I'm always willing to help a lady in distress."

Lady Kennell laughed again. "Chivalry is a wonderful thing, Lord Norwick. Perhaps I will require assistance later, but now, I desire refreshment. Will you escort me inside?"

Jasper sprang forward to open the double door for her, allowing her to precede him into the brighter ballroom. Without darkness blurring her features, her appearance struck him dumb.

He had never realized how delicate Lady Kennell was. And he was a large man, towering above her by a foot at least. She reminded him of a fragile porcelain doll. He shuddered at the thought of breaking her.

She pointed an elegant finger in the direction of the refreshment room. "I will join you in a moment, but first I must see to my dear friend. We became separated earlier, and I've been unable to locate her."

He nodded, trying his best to veil his disappointment. "Very well."

She was deserting him now that she had gotten a good look at him, and Jasper couldn't blame her. "It was nice conversing with you, Lady Kennell."

Her arched brows shot upward. "I'll see you in but a few short moments. Wait for me by the refreshment table."

"Of course." Jasper moved toward the adjacent room to seek out refreshments, the smile never leaving his lips. He joined the long queue waiting for the lemonade and hummed a happy tune under his breath. But after waiting an eternity without making any progress toward the punch bowl, his good mood began to fade. He stepped out of place.

Lady Kennell hadn't joined him yet either. He glanced toward the refreshment room entrance, but she wasn't anywhere in sight. The lady had probably run as soon as he turned his back. She was a clever one to use implied promises to send him away.

Grumbling, he returned to the ballroom to see if she came his way but couldn't locate her there either.

Jasper's shoulders drooped on a sigh. He might be lucky at the gaming tables, but he never won the lady of his choice. How could he have forgotten?

There was no point in staying. He would search for Fiona then leave, whether she cared to join him or not.

❧

Jake darted through the crowd, searching for Amelia and his brother. One minute they had been dancing and the next they had disappeared. Knowing Daniel, Jake had checked the veranda first. Relief washed over him upon the fortuitous discovery they were not there.

Thank goodness Jake hadn't found them outside. He generally frowned upon fratricide.

He considered searching the gardens but dismissed the idea. Amelia wouldn't slip away with Daniel as she had done with him. She wasn't that type of woman, unlike her friend, Lady Kennell. In addition, he and Amelia shared a closeness she didn't have with Daniel.

Nevertheless, as Jake rounded the great hall and refreshment room for the fourth time without spotting

Amelia or Daniel, doubts began to niggle at the back of his consciousness. He returned to the French doors opening onto the veranda. Standing in the doorway, half in, half out, he wrestled with whether to scour the gardens. His insides knotted.

Amelia wouldn't slip away with Daniel. Jake's weight shifted to his toes as if he prepared to plunge headlong into a canyon. His breaths came hard. But Daniel had no honor. He *would* slip away with Amelia.

Oh, blast and damn! Jake shot into the heavy night.

❧

Amelia hadn't located Jake in her search of the great hall or refreshment room. The foyer was the last place to look. She lifted to her toes and tried to peer over the guests' heads. She didn't see Jake anywhere, but Bibi's golden asp jutted above the crowd, headed her way.

Amelia pushed through the bodies to reach her friend.

"Have you seen Mr. Hillary?" she asked as soon as she and Bibi met.

"No, but I have been looking for you for the better part of half an hour. Where were you?"

Amelia shook her head. "It's an involved accounting. I shall tell you later, but I must find Mr. Hillary now. I haven't searched the foyer."

"Allow me to assist."

Together, they foraged forward, making slow progress. A group of ladies blocked their path from the great hall.

"Featherbrains," Bibi muttered.

Amelia cleared her throat. Lady Banner lowered her

mask and turned a cold eye on them before resuming the conversation with her companions.

Bibi stiffened in response to the obvious cut, and Amelia felt her pain. These petty women were no better than her friend was. In fact, Bibi outranked Lady Banner, but the baroness cowed her companions, Ladies Davenport and Clevedon.

Of course, Lord Banner was to blame for his wife's animosity. Months past, he had boasted to the gentlemen at White's that he and Bibi had become lovers. And like most gossip, the story had spread to the drawing rooms before the day ended. The baron was a liar, plain and simple. Bibi avoided him like the Black Death. His sojourn to Wales had been a welcome reprieve these past few weeks for it had afforded her friend a moment to relax her guard.

Amelia opened her mouth to confront the women when Lord Norwick appeared by his sister's side.

Bibi clung to Amelia's arm. The disdainful look on the earl's face urged Amelia to take a step back, bringing Bibi with her. Would he too treat them with scorn?

"For goodness' sake, Fi," he snapped at his sister, "move aside. Can you not see these ladies wish to pass?"

Amelia suppressed a wild laugh. The expression on Lady Banner's face when Norwick used her given name and called out her rude behavior was priceless.

The baroness pretended to gasp, her hand upon her chest. "Oh, dear. Please accept our apologies. We were unaware we were barring your path."

All three women scooted aside to create an opening.

"Thank you, *ladies*," Norwick said before following Bibi and Amelia to the foyer.

Bibi leaned close to speak in her ear. "Amelia, we should call for my coach. I feel a headache coming on."

"Oh, dearest, I am sorry. We should get you home immediately, shouldn't we?"

Norwick came up on Bibi's side. "Is something the matter, Lady Kennell?"

"I need to call for my carriage. I fear I am unwell."

Norwick nodded toward the open front doors. "It's congested outside. It may be half an hour at least before your carriage can be summoned. I have already called for mine. Perhaps you will allow me to assist."

Amelia thought it unwise to accept any more assistance from the gentleman. Although appreciated, his intervention in the ballroom would likely yield unpleasant consequences in the long term. Yet, when Bibi clutched her head and turned a disturbing shade of green, Amelia tossed aside her concerns. They would have to confront any possible repercussions later.

"Thank you, my lord. Your assistance is appreciated." She eased Bibi toward the exit and into the cooler air outside. "Goodness! I forgot about Mr. Hillary."

Bibi slumped against Amelia. "Try to find him. I can wait."

"No, you can't. I will send word to him later."

Bibi looked to Lord Norwick. "My lord, could you send word to Jake Hillary, requesting he call at Verona House this evening?"

"Of course." He dashed back inside as his carriage rolled up to the curb. In no time, he returned. "I didn't see Mr. Hillary, but he will receive the message. Or else," he added under his breath. "You look pale, my lady. Is your ailment worse?"

"I'm afraid so." Bibi's voice was little more than a whisper.

The footman opened the door to the Berlin.

"Are you certain we are not impose—ah!" Bibi pressed her fingers to her forehead.

The earl dashed forward to place an arm around her shoulders and guided her into the carriage. "It's no imposition."

Lord Norwick offered a hand up to Amelia next.

"You may take us to Verona House," she said.

The gentleman relayed instructions to the groom before climbing the stairs, the carriage listing under his weight. Bibi opened one eye as he assumed the spot across from them.

"Thank you, my lord."

"It's my pleasure, although I wish the circumstances were different."

Amelia regarded him with wariness. Despite his generosity this evening, she still worried it might be a mistake to accept his help.

Ten

A MANLY GRUNT BROUGHT JAKE UP SHORT. HIS BOOTS skidded on the gravel path and his ears perked up. Leaves rustled. With the moon higher in the sky, less light spilled over the garden foliage. He blinked into the darkness.

"Ahh…" The soft feminine moan sent his heart racing.

Dear Lord! What if he stumbled upon someone other than his brother and Amelia in the bushes? Interrupting a lovers' tryst seemed exceptionally rude.

This was madness. Amelia wouldn't steal away with Daniel. If the way she sought Jake's protection this afternoon was any indication, she disliked his brother a great deal. How nice it had been to have Amelia snuggled against him. Perhaps he should even thank Daniel for the positive developments this evening.

Jake scratched his head. Now that he considered it, Daniel's arrival at Verona House had been oddly timed. He knew Jake would be there.

What does it matter? He hadn't figured his brother out after all these years, and he didn't expect he would tonight either.

Jake turned toward the house, reassured by his earlier encounters with Amelia, and ready to give up his absurd hunt.

A high-pitched squeak pierced the air. "Oh, Cap'n." The sultry female voice flowed on an outpouring of breath.

His brother's laughter instigated a tidal wave of rage crashing down on Jake. With a deep growl, he barreled through the brush toward the noise. His brother had Amelia against a tree in a clearing, his breeches around his knees. The cape around Daniel's neck blocked Jake's view of much else, but they weren't playing tiddlywinks under there.

"You blackguard!" Jake tore across the clearing, grabbed Daniel's cloak, and jerked him off Amelia.

Her scream ripped through the night air, sending a chill tearing through him.

"What the devil?" Daniel's eyes darted around the space, unrecognizing the danger posed by his own brother.

Jake's fist slammed into his jaw and sent him crashing to the ground.

"Damnation!" Daniel rubbed his face and moved as if to stand up. "That hurt, you bloody bugger."

"Stay down or I'll knock you unconscious." Jake snarled and shook his fist, hoping his warning went unheeded. Another burst of rage made him quiver, and he drew back his fist to land another facer.

A battle cry hollered from somewhere behind him made him hesitate. Something pounced on his back and almost knocked him to his knees. Jake staggered with the extra weight, tripped over Daniel's legs, and slammed his shoulder into a tree.

"Hellfire and damnation!" He hugged the trunk to keep to his feet. A searing pain throbbed in his shoulder and shot down to his elbow.

A holy terror clamped steel thighs around his waist and tore at his hair, screeching like Morrigan.

"What the devil is on me?"

"Help! Thief!" Her howl blasted in his ears, and her claws dug into his forehead as if trying to draw blood.

"Stop that!" Jake spun in circles, trying to throw the tiny fury from his back.

She tightened her grip. Her high-pitched screeching pierced his eardrum. Disoriented, he careened into a prickly bush and scratched his bare calves.

"Get off me, you harpy!"

His robe's sleeve caught on a thorn. He tugged to release himself. Flinging his arms around his back, he tried to dislodge her with the same success a hunchback would have tossing aside his hump.

Daniel's hearty laughter rang out. "Ginny! Ginny! He's not a thief."

"Ginny?" Who the hell was Ginny? "Get her off me. She's ripping out my hair."

His brother bolted from the ground, pulled up his breeches, and snatched the hellion from Jake's back. "Come, luv," he said. "Jake is harmless."

She didn't release him. Instead, she yanked his hair again. He wouldn't put it past her to sink her fangs into him next.

"Good God, Daniel. Why are you hesitating?"

"I swear it, Ginny. He won't hurt us." Daniel spoke in a soothing voice as he reached for her.

She slapped the back of Jake's head once more

before releasing her legs from around his middle. Jake whirled to face the tiniest, most vicious woman he had ever crossed.

"Where did you find this horrible little harpy?"

Ginny growled and would have launched herself at Jake again if Daniel hadn't captured her upper arms. Her exposed chest rose and fell in rapid sequence as she breathed heavily through her mouth.

Daniel kissed the top of her head. "Promise you won't attack him, and I'll release you, luv."

She nodded once, but her glare was filled with hatred.

"She's lying. I see it in her eyes." Not that Jake had cause for concern now that he had his bearings, but he refused to strike a woman.

Daniel drew her against his chest and wrapped his arms around her waist. "Now, now. I would be displeased if you broke your promise, Gin."

"I gave my word," she snapped. When Daniel released her, she yanked her dress to cover her shoulder while he fastened the back of her gown.

"Ya bloody nabob," she said. "Wha' ya be thinkin' striking a man mid-shag?"

She had a vulgar tongue to match her violent temper.

Daniel chuckled, drawing her against his chest once more. "Shh, enough of that talk. I suspect it was a case of mistaken identity. No harm done."

She practically growled, showing her teeth. "'E struck ya."

His brother nuzzled her neck. "Yes, but he is my brother. He's allowed a blow or two upon occasion."

Jake had made a huge mistake. This harridan wasn't Amelia. She wasn't even a lady, which was somewhat of a relief in itself since voices headed their direction. He would feel awful being a party to ruining anyone's reputation.

"Hide her," Jake whispered before dashing through the foliage in order to head off the group. Waving his hands above his head, he approached the gentlemen heeding the call for help.

"Everything is all right, gents. The thief has been subdued. Um, he is on his way to Bow Street as we speak."

"A thief in the gardens?" Lord Getty asked. "Is no place sacred?"

Apparently not to Daniel. Jake tapped his toe as the men complained about the horrendous crime rate in Town, sharing the latest assaults by pickpockets and such. And men accused ladies of clucking like hens.

He glanced over his shoulder several times, unable to see anything. Had Daniel gotten the lightskirt to safety? And where had he found the blasted woman anyway?

At last, the group dispersed and returned to the house. Jake spun around and headed back to the spot where he had left his brother. Daniel appeared through the trees.

"You have an annoying habit of interrupting my pleasure, Mummy's boy."

Jake's body heated now that he had time to consider his actions. It was unlike him to behave with such irrationality. "Perhaps a different locale would be advisable next time. And a different caliber of companionship."

"I don't know. I like Ginny. She had no qualms about slipping through the back gate and waiting for me." Daniel slapped Jake's back. "If you don't trust the lady, you should direct your affections elsewhere."

Daniel didn't need to mention Amelia's name for Jake to know to whom his brother referred. "Yes, well... I do trust her."

"Splendid." Daniel didn't sound as thrilled as his word choice suggested. In fact, there may have been an undercurrent of sarcasm in his tone. His brother gave him a shove toward the house. "She is searching for you. Hurry before she finds a different gent to replace you."

Jake raced up the dark path toward the house and up the veranda stairs. A blast of heat washed over him as he passed through the doors. He made a hurried sweep of the great hall, but couldn't find Amelia. As he neared the foyer, a thin rail of a woman stepped into his path and planted her hand against his chest.

"Mr. Hillary, there you are."

Jake squinted at the masked woman blocking his way. Her shimmery gown and white wings indicated she was an angel, but the malicious glint in her eye spoiled the effect.

"It's Lady Banner. I see you do not recognize me in costume."

True, but her nasty sneer would have given her away if she hadn't provided her identity.

"I have a message from Lady Audley," she said.

Jake bent forward to hear her better. "Indeed?"

"She said to inform you she has left with my brother, and she wishes you well."

Jake drew back. "Norwick? Why would Lady Audley leave with Lord Norwick?"

A sardonic smile stretched the baroness's lips. "I would venture to say she fancies him. She could barely keep her hands off him from the looks of it."

Norwick? That was preposterous.

Lady Banner lowered her voice to a stage whisper. "Jasper calls on Lady Audley often. Have you not heard?"

He was woefully uninformed of Amelia's activities. Jake dashed for the front door. It took forty-five minutes for his carriage to arrive at the Chickering town house entrance, which provided him with time to stew over the unfolding events of the evening.

"To Verona House," he said before barreling into the carriage.

Jake wouldn't take Lady Banner's word that Amelia was with the earl. Daniel he could at least fathom, but not that bugger. He was finished listening to rumors involving Amelia.

❧

Lord Norwick supported Bibi's weight, almost carrying her to the drawing room.

"I will have a room readied for you," Amelia said.

Her evening shoes clicked against the marble tiles as she crossed the foyer. Each heel strike felt like a nail being driven into Bibi's head.

"I need to sit down," she said.

Lord Norwick helped her to the Grecian couch, lifting her legs and removing her slippers. "Where do you hurt, my dear?" His tender voice was soothing.

She grasped her head in both palms. "*Here.*"

"I see." Lord Norwick nudged her leg, wishing to sit beside her. She scooted over as far as possible, leaving him to teeter on the edge of the furniture. It couldn't be comfortable, but he didn't complain. "I am told I have a gift for healing. Shall I try to assist you?"

Bibi opened her eyes and scowled. "You are not the first gentleman to claim he has a magical touch, my lord."

He chuckled, his smile catching her by surprise. Norwick's countenance was pleasing, if not classically handsome. "I cannot fault any man for resorting to such trickery to touch you, Lady Kennell, but I assure you my intentions are honorable. May I?"

"Yes." Bibi allowed her eyes to drift closed again. At this point, it wouldn't hurt to try anything. If his methods failed, perhaps he would knock her over the head to render her unconscious.

Norwick placed her feet in his lap. "I must remove your stockings."

"My *stockings*?" She knew it. He planned to seduce her while she wallowed in excruciating pain. All men were unforgivable scoundrels.

He met her suspicious gaze, his expression innocuous. "There is a place between your toes. I cannot reach it with your stockings donned."

He pressed his thumb into the arch of her foot and massaged. Bibi's tension eased, and she sank into the plush couch.

"Very well," she conceded. "You may proceed."

Norwick slid his hands under her skirts, grazing his fingers along her calf and thigh until he reached her garter. A small smile played upon his full mouth.

"I believe you enjoy your ministrations too much, Lord Norwick."

A wicked twinkle lit his obsidian eyes. A lock of coal black hair stood up as if he had run his fingers through his curls in frustration, and she had an urge to smooth it. "I never claimed the act would bring me no pleasure, my lady."

Despite her pain, she laughed. She appreciated a man with a devilish streak.

He released her stocking from the garter and rolled it down her leg. His warm fingers brushed the inside of her thigh and brought a shudder of anticipation to her core.

Tugging her stocking over her toes, he studied her face. She wondered if he watched for signs of protest. Receiving none, he repeated the actions with her other stocking before grasping her foot in his hand and wedging his finger between her big toe and its neighbor.

Bibi moaned.

"Does that hurt?"

"A little," she admitted, but it also felt good.

"Then I have found the right place, but I will be gentle." He pressed against the area and held the pressure. "Close your eyes and lie back."

Bibi did as he instructed and forced herself to draw in even breaths. She received no relief at first, but with a longer period of applied pressure, the pounding in her head decreased. "I think it is working."

Lowering her foot, he gathered the other one to lavish the same attention to it. After several minutes, only a dull ache lingered behind her eye.

"It's a miracle. My headache is going away just as you promised. Are there any other spots?"

He offered her a hand. "Sit up, my dear."

Once he had hauled her to a seated position, he angled her away from him. Sliding his fingers along her exposed back, he stopped halfway in between her shoulders and neck then pressed.

She groaned again. "Oh, my. Right there is good, too."

"You are tense, Lady Kennell." His warm breath brushed her neck and fanned out across her upper back.

She swallowed, aware of her budding desire. "You may call me Bianca, or Bibi, if you like."

His strong fingers massaged in circles, causing her to melt against him. "Bianca is a lovely name. It suits you."

Her headache had peaked and was receding. "May I call you Jasper?"

"You may call me whatever you like." His fingers plucked the hairpins from her coiffure. "This is likely the cause of your pain."

He released her hair and nestled his fingers into her curls, creating lovely tingles along her scalp.

"How does that feel?" he asked.

Bibi sighed and leaned into his chest. "Heavenly. You *do* have a magical touch, Jasper."

He wrapped his arms around her waist and lifted her onto his lap. "I promised I wouldn't resort to trickery, but I find I cannot help myself."

Bibi wriggled around to look at him, placing her hands on each side of his face. She studied the slant of his slender nose, his rosy complexion, round cheeks. His skin heated under her touch, and he turned a darker shade of red.

"I'm not much to look at, Bianca." His long lashes rested against his skin as he closed his eyes. He had amazing lashes; any woman would be envious.

"Perhaps you would allow me to judge for myself," she said. "I find you pleasing to behold."

His eyes popped open, and she stared into their fathomless depths. Glorious eyes to match his lashes. "There is only one problem, sir."

"I know." He sighed. "I'm too large."

"No." Bibi shook her head. "I'm uncertain whether to keep looking at you or kiss you."

Jasper's lips parted on a gasp before stretching into a broad smile. "You may gaze upon me at any time, Bianca. Let's not miss this opportunity to indulge your curiosity."

His full lips covered hers, so warm and soft. He kissed her as a woman yearned to be kissed. The way Bibi had dreamed of being kissed, slowly. He didn't rush her, allowing her to drink in his kisses, focused only on the feel of his lips against hers.

Jasper Hainsworth, Earl of Norwick, was much more adept at kissing than she would have guessed.

Eleven

BEFORE JAKE'S CARRIAGE CAME TO A COMPLETE STOP IN front of Amelia's town house, he threw the door open and hopped to the ground.

His jaw dropped to his toes.

Lord Norwick's coach was parked in front of Verona House, just as Lady Banner had said it would be. Jake shook off his suspicions. There could be a hundred explanations for Norwick's presence. He only hoped for *one* that didn't involve Amelia and the earl locked in a heated embrace.

Jake prepared to dash up the front steps, but movement through the window drew his attention. He halted and moved closer to the house. Leaning over the iron fencing, he peered through the lace-draped window. What was that large bulk in Amelia's drawing room?

He squinted and tried to make sense of what he saw. Was it an animal? An elephant in the drawing room?

He craned his neck. Broad shoulders and dark hair identified the bulk as Norwick. His back was to the window. Nevertheless, Jake was having a blasted hard time making sense of what was draped around the earl's neck. He rested his hands on the fence and lifted to his toes to position himself for a better view.

A loud clearing of a throat caused him to jump. Amelia's butler stood on the front stoop and frowned down at him. "*Mr.* Hillary, what is it you are doing peeping into her ladyship's window?"

"Jake, you made it." Amelia slipped around the servant and froze on the second step. "What *are* you doing?"

Jake peeked through the window once more. *Egads!* Norwick was reclining on the sofa with Cleopatra in his arms. "Uh, I… I thought I spotted a thief… in your drawing room."

The butler sniffed. "Indeed, the only thief I see is the one stealing looks through the window."

"Bradford, you may go," Amelia said.

The servant's face puckered, giving the appearance of trying to eat itself. "Yes, milady." He spun on his heel and stalked back inside.

Amelia's hands landed on her hips. She had changed from her costume and into half-dress. "Were you spying on Lady Kennell?"

To admit so seemed foolish in the extreme, but it was preferable to admitting to spying on Amelia. What was he about, skulking around engaging in intrigue?

He released the fence and moved toward the stairs. "Forgive me. I didn't know what I saw at first, though that is no excuse."

She held her hand out in invitation. "Think on it no more. Come inside."

His forehead creased as he climbed the stairs and placed his hand in hers. "Why are Lady Kennell and Lord Norwick here again?"

Amelia drew him inside and closed the door. "Did you not get my message?"

"I received it, but apparently some details were missing. You left the ball with Norwick?"

"Yes, well, he was available and offered. We couldn't decline without appearing rude."

We? "You *and* Lady Kennell?" The buffoon possessed more prowess than Jake had given him credit for.

Amelia chuckled and shook her head as if he was dicked in the nob. "Of course Lady Kennell and me. Who else? I couldn't abandon her in her time of need."

Jake glanced over Amelia's shoulder at the butler glowering at him from his post outside the drawing room door. "But you are out here."

She turned a fetching shade of pink and lifted one shoulder. "The earl is assisting Lady Kennell's head-ache. His methods are a bit unorthodox, and I thought it wise to leave them undisturbed."

The butler's dark looks were trampling on Jake's last nerve. "Either dismiss your man or let us retire to a different area."

"Come this way." Amelia led him toward the back part of the house and paused in front of the breakfast room door. "Will this do?"

The room was dark except for the moonlight falling through the arched windows.

He took her upper arm and escorted her inside before closing the door with his foot.

"Do you not wish for a candle?"

He eased her around to face him, his eyes adjusting to the dark. "You didn't leave the ball with Norwick to—how do I say this? You and he are not on intimate terms, are you?"

Her already large eyes widened. "No! Good heavens, no! Whatever would leave you with that impression?"

The tension drained from his body, and he hugged her to him with a sigh. Her soft hair brushed his chin as her head fit snugly against his chest. "I knew Lady Banner lied."

"Lady Banner?" Amelia wiggled against his hold, tunneling her arms up between their bodies and digging her elbows into his ribs in the process. "What did she say?"

Jake grunted and loosened his embrace to allow her to pull back. "The baroness insinuated you and Norwick were involved. She said you left the party with him."

Her outraged squawk filled the room as she shoved away from him. "And *you* believed her?"

Jake captured her around the waist and tipped her chin up with his free hand. "I wouldn't have come if I had believed her lies."

Her body shook with violent tremors. "You did. You were looking through my window. You thought to catch us together."

"I did not. I swear upon my word as a gentleman, I knew she spoke a falsehood. I refused to make the same mistake I did last year and listen to rumors. I was simply caught unaware when I discovered Norwick's carriage outside."

"If there is ever any doubt, you will always believe the worst of me."

His hands cradled her head, his fingers twined in her hair. "Then clear up any doubts, Amelia. Promise me there will be no other gentlemen. Tell me you will be mine."

"Oh!"

"And blast it all, stop doing that with your mouth unless you pose an invitation for me to make love to you right here."

She gasped.

Damnation. He had gone too far. Dropping his hands from her, he moved back a step, preparing his apology.

"Oh!" she said, catching him off guard. A tantalizing smile spread across her lips. "Oh, oh, oh!"

Jake's blood forged through his veins, hot and hungry. "You *want* me to make love to you."

Her eyes glittered like jet. "Yes."

He required no further coaxing. His muscles tensed a fraction of a second before he sprang forward and gathered her in his arms. Their mouths collided. Her sweetness roused his appetite.

When she backed up a step, he advanced. She came up against the table and started. "Oh!"

"Good God, Mia." Every civilized part of him fled, and he lifted her to the table, pushing her skirts up on her thighs. Bare skin met his eager fingers and he drew back. She wore no drawers, stockings, or anything under her dress.

"Was this for me?" he asked, his voice a near growl.

A shiver raced through her. "I *was* expecting you. After the garden... Well, and then there was the dancing."

He raised her chin to look her in the eyes, his thumb

caressing her bottom lip. "Do you agree there will be no others?"

A wicked smile spread across her mouth. "I don't want anyone else." Her pink tongue licked the pad of his thumb and almost set him afire. When her searing mouth closed over his entire digit, he closed his eyes on a groan.

"Brilliant answer, sweetheart. Neither do I."

While she lavished each finger with attention, her hands fisted in his robes and dragged the hem upwards. She was about to receive a surprise of her own. Perhaps those bloody Scots knew what they were about running around free as the day they were born.

Her breath hitched before rushing out on a soft laugh. "Is this for me?" Delicate fingers walked down his skin and circled his shaft.

A raging fire ignited in his groin and fanned out to engulf his entire body. "Hell yes." With a low rumble in his throat, he crushed her against him and possessed her mouth.

Her silky tendrils threaded around his fingers as he slid his hand to her nape. He placed a kiss on her chin before languorously trailing his lips down her neck. Amelia arched, providing him with better access to her tender skin. Supporting her weight, he leaned her back farther and flicked his tongue over the swell of her breast.

She sighed.

Her feminine sounds stirred him as much as when she had touched him. His length jerked and grew thicker. Slowly, he raised her again before claiming her lips, delving his tongue inside her sensual mouth.

Damn, he loved touching and tasting her. He pulled back a fraction, their lips close enough to feel her heat still. Her labored breaths matched his. He covered her heart with his palm and counted each time it knocked against his hand. Amelia's heart pounded for him. Her half-mast eyes clouded with desire for him. And the faint scent of her arousal was all for him.

❧

A haze had descended over Amelia so that the only thing clear in her heart was giving herself to Jake. She had never behaved with such lack of inhibitions, but Jake awakened a side of her dormant until his touch.

"Remove your clothes," she commanded.

He released her long enough to drag the white robe over his head.

Her fingers traced the honed muscles of his chest before smoothing over the ridges of his abdomen. Her eyes followed her fingers as if powerless to do otherwise, dropping to his member before rising back to lock with his impassioned stare.

"My goodness, you are glorious to behold," she said.

His lips curved up in satisfaction. "Your turn." He lifted her from the table. When her feet hit the floor, he peeled her gown from her body.

She placed her palms against his chest and gently pushed him down in the cushioned dining chair. "Please, have a seat."

He did as she requested before hauling her to stand between his thighs, his firm hands cupping her bottom, his fingers kneading her flesh. "Are you directing our lovemaking this round?"

"M-maybe."

With one hand on her behind holding her in place, he slid a finger along the curve of her collarbone then drew lazy circles on her skin. "Splendid. Tell me how you like to be touched."

His husky voice heated her blood as his fingers raised goose bumps along her arms.

"Um, that feels nice."

Flicks of his tongue over the tip of her breast wrenched a pleasurable moan from her. He pulled back with a teasing smile. "That's not good enough, sweetheart. I want to hear what you want me to do to you."

A flush engulfed her, and she was grateful for the dark. Jake Hillary was much less proper than she had expected, and his daring excited her to no end. Nevertheless, she had never spoken of such improper things, even if she was engaged in the scandalous act.

Instead of speaking, she lifted his hand to her lips to place a loving kiss on his palm before lowering it to her breast.

"I like to be touched here, softly."

Jake rewarded her with a grin before meeting her lips. His fingers glossed over her nipple and she sucked in a quick breath. Tweaking the tip, he initiated a pulsing pleasure in her core then leaned forward to place a kiss on her skin.

Amelia gingerly grasped his head to keep his lips at her breast. When he took her nipple into his mouth, she released a loud sigh of pleasure. "Oh, yes."

Her nails grazed his scalp as she threaded her fingers through his dark blond hair. Jake licked and suckled until her legs quivered. If not for his strong arms around her waist, she would collapse on the floor. He found her lips again, lifted her off her feet, and placed her back on the table.

"Shall I discover all the other places you like to be touched on my own?"

Her heart slammed against her breast bone, threatening to break through and leap from her body. She nodded. "Please?"

Jake chuckled and kissed the tip of her nose. "Very good."

His fingers traveled from her fingers, up her arms and over her shoulders before trailing along her collarbone. Black fire blazed in his eyes.

"You are beautiful," he murmured. "So exquisite."

His adoration wrapped her in warmth and her affection for him grew.

He cupped her breast as he had done earlier, slightly pinching her nipple until it stood erect. Tingles raced along her skin, and when his warm mouth closed around her bud, she melted against the table linens. His tongue swirled the peak of her breast in excruciating slowness and heady pleasure.

"Oh, Jake. That's perfect."

He switched his attentions to her other breast while still stroking the recently lavished bud. Amelia shifted her hips, hungry for his touch lower. She covered his hand with hers and guided him to caress between her thighs. The light sweep of his finger across her sensitive spot brought a blissful cry to her lips.

He smoothed his finger over it again, eliciting the same enthusiastic response. "Right there?" His voice held a teasing quality.

"Yes," she said between panting breaths. "Right there and lower."

Jake carefully probed her swollen flesh, inserting the tip of his finger inside her. Amelia lifted her hips to take him in, but it wasn't enough. "I want to feel you inside me."

Jake issued a half groan, half gasp. "My pleasure."

Grasping her hips, he pulled her to the table's edge and filled her. His head rolled back and he closed his eyes on a sigh. Slowly, he thrust in and out, driving her insane with lust.

He smiled down at her, locking eyes as he slid his hand up her thigh and touched the hardened pearl between her legs. A few long strokes over her quivering flesh sent her careening over the edge where she tumbled into the most delightful world of pleasure she had ever known.

"Jake, oh…"

Perhaps it was the sound of her voice or her fingers grazing his waist, but he pumped his hips in frantic movement, reaching his own completion with an outrushing of breath. After a moment, his heat withdrew, but before she could protest, he gathered her in his arms and sat back in the chair with her in his lap.

They held each other, slick with perspiration, and gazed into each other's eyes. "I will never want another woman as long as I live, Mia."

She had no cause for argument, because she could never give herself to anyone ever again either.

A strip of light cut across the floor as the door swung open. "Amelia?"

She gasped and ducked her head as Jake wrapped

her in his arms. *Oh, dear heavens.* Let the earth swallow her whole now. Bibi would never let something like this pass without acknowledgment.

Jake didn't bother to look at their interloper. "Lady Kennell, have you ever heard of knocking?"

"This is the breakfast room, Mr. Hillary."

Amelia peeked over his shoulder to discover Bibi with her hand on her hip. "Just a moment longer, dearest?"

"Take your time," Bibi said with a wink. "Should I request my toast in my chambers on the morrow?"

Amelia had no doubts she changed a telling shade of pink from head to toe. "That is unnecessary."

"Very well. I wished to inform you I am retiring for the night." Bibi backed from the room, pulling the door closed as she left.

"Sleep well," Amelia called out then groaned and dropped her head against Jake's shoulder.

Twelve

BIBI REMAINED AT VERONA HOUSE THE NEXT DAY well beyond the time a hostess could expect her guest to leave. Not even Bradford, with his irksome condescension, could drive Amelia's stubborn friend from the town house this morning. Therefore, courtesy of Bibi's thickheadedness, Amelia accepted that she couldn't hide in her chambers all day to avoid an uncomfortable encounter and invited her to afternoon tea.

Bibi perched on the adjacent drawing room chair and nibbled a ginger biscuit. Her dark eyes penetrated, making Amelia wiggle in her seat.

"What a telling display of emotion," Bibi said with a lift to her thin brow and note of mirth in her voice.

Amelia sighed and set the cup of tea on the matching bone china saucer. "I do not wish to discuss last evening's events."

"I didn't inquire."

"Splendid." She prayed that would be the last spoken of her audacious behavior.

Bibi wrinkled her nose and chuckled. "But in the

breakfast room? Really, my dear, I never thought you had it in you."

Amelia broke into a light sweat and fanned her hands in front of her face. "Please, don't remind me. I am mortified you discovered us in such a compromising position."

With a cluck of her tongue, Bibi leaned forward to pat Amelia's knee. "There, there. No need to act priggish with me. You know I would never judge you. Mr. Hillary can tup you on the rooftop for all I care. Certain indulgences are a mistress's due."

"*Mistress?*" Amelia jerked upright on the chair as if a lightning bolt shot down her spine. "I'm not Mr. Hillary's mistress."

"Then what are you? Surely you will bed him more than once."

Amelia licked her lips and adjusted her position on the chair. She hadn't thought to label their relationship or their respective roles. But she didn't wish to be a mistress, even Jake's. She had always considered herself best suited for the position of wife.

"I am certain Mr. Hillary has no intentions of making me his mistress."

"Amelia, do not pretend you are ignorant to what gentlemen are about. We are widows." Bibi shook her head, her mouth turning down in a troubled frown. "What is it you expect from him, my dear? An offer for your hand?"

Amelia reached for the white teapot and busied herself with refilling her cup, even though it was almost full. When Jake had asked her to remain faithful to him and declared he wanted no other, she had assumed he wished to remain together forever. Marriage was the only alternative she would consider.

"Amelia." Sympathy saturated Bibi's tone. "Gentlemen do not exercise amorous rites with their wives any place besides the bedchamber. Only a mistress can drive a man to lose his head as Mr. Hillary did last night."

"You are mistaken about Jake." She spoke with complete confidence, but it was a falsehood. Amelia's judgment of men had been anything but exact over the years. She wanted Bibi to be wrong, but she feared her friend held superior knowledge of men.

"I hope you are correct about Mr. Hillary," Bibi said with a delicate shrug. "Nevertheless, becoming his mistress is hardly a reason to be glum. His pockets run deep, you know. Shall I casually mention your fondness for diamonds in the next encounter with the gentleman?"

"I will thank you to tend your own affairs."

Bibi sipped her tea. "It's no trouble."

Amelia cleared her throat, ready to change the subject. "About Lord Norwick…"

"What about him?"

She drank from her teacup to stall. Bibi had never been amenable to advice, no matter how well intentioned, and based upon the stubborn hitch of her chin, she wasn't about to welcome Amelia's opinion. Yet, she must try to reason with her friend.

"Perhaps you should take pains to avoid him."

"Whatever for? Norwick is delightfully refreshing. Granted, he is nothing like the gentlemen who usually capture my attention. For one thing, he is thoughtful.

How many gentlemen would alter their course to aid a lady in distress?"

Likely hundreds if there was a chance for a show of gratitude such as Bibi had shown Lord Norwick. Entering her drawing room to discover Bibi's bare foot in the earl's hand had been arresting, though a foot in the hand was unequal to the wild tryst she'd had with Jake. Even now, she blushed with the memory of her wanton behavior.

"Indeed, the earl is kind," Amelia said, "but it is no secret his sister wishes you banned from London."

"All of *England*, dear Amelia. Her ambitions are farther reaching than a mere town. Why, she would exile me to St. Helena with Bonaparte if she had her way."

"Precisely my point. What might she do in retaliation for dallying with her brother? She has him under her finger, from all accounts."

Bibi flicked a hand. "Lady Troll doesn't concern me, and neither should she concern you."

The sparkle in her eyes and knowing smile increased the tightness in Amelia's chest. Bearing witness to the direct cuts Bibi had received over the last months often made Amelia want to cry on her behalf. Her friend didn't deserve the cruel treatment she received at Lady Banner's instigation. Amelia must make one more attempt to deter her.

"Are you certain an association is wise? There are other gentlemen with less malicious relations."

"You fret too much." Bibi rose from the chair. "Now I must hie off to Kennell Place. I have correspondence awaiting my attention."

Jake shaded his eyes from the bright afternoon light as he exited Brook's. Judging by the sun's position, he had time to change his attire and visit the mews before calling on Amelia. The toe of his boot struck something—a trousers-clad leg lying across the pathway—and he stumbled forward, barely correcting his footing in time to save himself.

"Damnation!"

He whirled around to discover a thoroughly foxed Lord Ellis sprawled against the side of the building. The earl had left Brook's a few moments earlier, but clearly should have had an escort.

Ellis blinked up at Jake. "What're you doin' in my coach, Hillary?"

"You have taken up residence on the streets, my lord."

"Splendid. Call for a blanket." His head bobbed before his chin dropped down on his chest.

"Perhaps you should reconsider before your unfortunate circumstances are heralded in the gossip rags." Jake looked up and down St. James Street. "I don't see your conveyance. Are you on foot?"

Ellis's eyes drifted closed. "I am on my bum."

Jake kicked his boot, causing the earl to jerk. His eyes fluttered open a moment, but then he was asleep again.

Stooping to place an arm under Ellis's shoulder, Jake helped him to his feet and held on as he swayed forward. "Wake up, you rotter. Have a bit of common sense. I cannot leave you to the pickpockets. My carriage comes this way now. I'll give you a lift."

When the landau rolled to a stop and the footman

lowered the step, Jake assisted Ellis inside where he collapsed on the velvet seat.

Taking the seat opposite, Jake studied the earl. He had never known the man to be a Lushington, not any more than the average fellow.

"Minx'll make a match 'fore the week's out," Ellis mumbled and slumped on the bench.

Lady troubles. No more explanation was required. "Blasted minxes have been known to drive a man to an early grave."

Ellis cracked open an eye. "You've been stricken too?"

"I was, but everything has righted itself."

Memories of his passionate evening with Amelia crowded in his mind, and he turned his smile toward the window. It wouldn't do to flaunt his happiness when his companion was in despair.

"The lady won't even speak to me," Ellis said. "Put a toad in her bed once."

"You might try a bouquet next time. Do you know nothing of women?"

The earl glowered. "I was but a lad at the time. Didn't know how bloody beautiful she would become."

"Rotten luck."

Ellis grunted. The carriage rolled to a stop in front of his town house. The coachman opened the door and offered Ellis assistance. Once on the ground, the earl looked back over his shoulder as he clung to the servant. "Perhaps you're correct, Hillary. A toad is no gift for a lady. Get your lady something nice."

Jake supposed the man had a point. One must be thoughtful when courting a lady.

The servant delivered Ellis to his door then

returned to seek instruction. "Are you returning to Hillary House, sir?"

He checked his watch. "First I must visit Rundell and Bridges." He had arrived with flowers for Amelia yesterday. Today he would find something much better to express his adoration, and it sure as hell wouldn't be a frog. A stone to match her beautiful, blue eyes would give his proposal the perfect touch.

❧

Jake ignored the butler's soured frown as he took his calling card.

"This way, *Mr.* Hillary."

Bradford's manner of addressing him was galling, but Jake grudgingly appreciated the man's sense of protectiveness when it came to Amelia. He didn't like to think of her living alone without someone watching over her.

As he followed the servant to the drawing room to wait, he glanced at the surroundings. Amelia had created a cozy home here at Park Street, elegant and understated in warm shades that reminded him of peaches and cinnamon. If she wished to retain the residence after their vows were spoken, he could picture them residing at Verona House for the season.

A noise at the drawing room door made him turn around. A wide smile broke across his face. "Mia."

"Mr. Hillary." Her formal address and cool tone served as a reminder to be mindful of his manners with others present. She stepped inside the drawing room and pulled the doors closed behind her.

"At last." He strode across the room to sweep her into a much anticipated kiss. Her sweet lips parted beneath his on a small cry of surprise, but a moment later, her mouth grew supple and moved with his.

He had to be the luckiest fellow in London. Amelia, so generous of heart and beautiful, had given herself to him and promised to love only him.

Jake drew back, still holding her around the waist. "I have something for you, a token of my affection."

A shutter lowered over her eyes, denying him access to her thoughts. "What sort of token?"

He released her with a chuckle and dug inside his jacket pocket. "One that dulls in comparison to the sparkle that was in your eyes but a short moment ago. You will like it, I promise."

Pulling the handkerchief from his jacket, he laid the bundle in his outstretched palm. "Open it."

She reached toward the bundle, hesitated, and then unfolded the handkerchief with shaky fingers. The sight of the sapphire and diamond necklace wrenched a cry from her, and her hand covered her mouth as she spun away. "No!"

Jake winced. "No?" What lady disliked jewels? "I thought it a rather nice piece, but if you would prefer something different…"

She wheeled around to face him. "It is not the gift, but the intention behind it."

"The intention? What intention?"

Her delicate eyebrows rose, her lips parted as she waited for him to respond to his own question.

Egads! He adjusted his cravat. This was one of those riddles ladies posed to make a gentleman appear a dullard. Unfortunately, Amelia had him bested for he had no clue as to her meaning.

"My intentions are pure. You must know I hold you in the highest esteem."

Her hand landed on her hip. "Do you, Mr. Hillary? Do you possess the same regard for me as you would a mistress?"

Jake's jaw dropped. A thousand thoughts flew through his mind, but not a single word formed on his tongue.

"Well, do you?" She marched forward to plant herself in front of him. "Because gentlemen do not shower their wives with jewels or—" She flung her hand in the air, lowering her voice to a fierce whisper. "Or have relations with them on tables."

Jake tugged harder at his cravat. Damn Rupert and his blasted tight knots. "Er, yes. I take your meaning, I think."

Did he? He wasn't certain. Having never been married, he hadn't considered how a man might conduct himself in private with his wife.

"I enjoyed choosing a necklace for you. And you look lovely in blue."

A delicate crease appeared between her arched brows.

He had liked losing himself with her last night, too, casting off his tiring restraints and surrendering to his desires for once. But he could see she considered herself abused, though she had been shockingly unrestrained herself wearing nothing beneath her gown. It seemed unfair to assign all the blame for their delightful encounter to him. There must be some room for negotiation.

He held out his hand in invitation. "Shall we sit a moment? I believe we have some questions to sort through before we visit the park."

Amelia hesitated before she placed her hand in his and allowed him to lead her to the settee. She sat stiffly on the edge with her hands in her lap. Her almond-shaped eyes lifted to his. A flash of hurt in their depths pulled at his heart.

"Sweetheart, if you wish for our relations to be confined to the bedchamber, I will comply. Though I must be honest and admit I have never heard it said a husband and wife must confine themselves to the bed. Are you certain this is a rule?"

Her long lashes fluttered. "I beg your pardon?"

"Are you certain we are not allowed to… *experiment*? Just a bit? Nothing debauched, I assure you. Various locales on occasion. Perhaps a change in position…" He trailed off when faced with her wide-eyed gape and shallow, ragged breaths.

Blast and damn! He'd shocked her into the vapors. He searched for a fan on a nearby surface. Finding nothing useful, he sandwiched her hand between his and prepared to beg her not to faint. "Please, pretend I never spoke. The bedchamber is acceptable."

"D-did you say you wish to *marry* me?"

Jake drew back. "Of course I wish to marry you. I offered for you, did I not?"

She wrestled her hand from his grasp. "When is it you think you made an offer of marriage?"

"In my posts. Didn't you read them?"

"The letters from Sussex," she mumbled, speaking more to herself than him. "I never received them."

Jake crossed his arms over his chest, adopting the same expression he saved for witnesses in court when they perpetrated a falsehood. "And yet you have knowledge of the letters. How can that be unless you received them?"

She rubbed her furrowed brow as if this entire affair was giving her a headache. "Captain Hillary mentioned them last night. I thought he was mad."

"But you received my message, did you not? You knew a family matter called me away."

"No, there was nothing."

Jake blew out a long, noisy breath. Now *he* was getting a headache. "Are you certain there was nothing? Because I clearly recall penning the note."

"Jake," she said, an edge of irritation returning to her voice. "I promise I received no word at all."

Good Lord, she was telling the truth. No shadow of deceit clouded her earnest gaze. How could this be? "Amelia, I don't know what to say. I wrote to you every day in the beginning. When you didn't respond, I thought…"

She reached for his hand, entwining their fingers. "I would never dismiss you in that manner. I hope you do not have it in you to believe otherwise."

He lifted her hand to his lips and closed his eyes as he breathed in the floral scent gracing her wrist. What a fool he had been to think her capable of deception. "I sent a note before we departed. Mother needed me to accompany her to the country and stay until she recuperated."

"You were gone such a long time." Amelia splayed her fingers upon his cheek. "What terrible illness required your mother to take refuge in the country?"

Everything that was gentle resided in Amelia's touch, reaffirming his belief that entrusting her with his family's secret was safe.

"Mother has been afflicted for many years, before I was born. She has spells. Some might unfairly call it madness if they saw her."

A soft gasp slipped past her lips, but she didn't pull away. "I am so sorry, Jake. I can only imagine how challenging this must be for all involved. Your poor mother."

"Thank you, Mia." He leaned close to place a feather-like kiss on her cheek. "Your compassion touches me."

"I find it difficult to believe your mother suffers any abnormality. She has always been gracious in our encounters."

"We never allow others to witness her troubled state. If anyone knew…" He shrugged, his arms heavy and limp. A hundred lifetimes weighed on his shoulders though only five and twenty of those years could he claim as his own. "Please trust that I would never have left had I known you remained ignorant to my whereabouts or the reason I had to go."

She bit down on her bottom lip and stilled the slight quiver there. "I thought you left, that our kiss…" Her voice broke on the last word.

Jake captured both of her hands, caressing his thumb over her ivory skin. "Our kiss meant everything to me. I love you, Mia. My feelings haven't altered since that night."

Tears welled in her eyes and slipped down her cheeks. "How can you forgive me for what I did?"

"Shh, don't cry." He kissed each cheek, her salty tears damp on his lips. Amelia had suffered as much as he had, and he wouldn't allow her to carry the burden of believing she had betrayed him. His family, however, wouldn't be spared his anger. "I fault you for nothing. I am the one who should apologize. For my family. I'm certain they played a role in intercepting my correspondence."

"But why? Do they find me unfit?"

"No, sweetheart. Mother's illness…" How could he explain the lengths his father would go to in order to protect their shameful secret when he would never understand? What drove his father to commit a heinous act that led to the suffering of two innocent people?

She grasped Jake's hand. "I swear I will never speak a word to anyone. I would not see your mother hurt for all the world."

"I have no doubts in your sincerity, my love." Lowering to one knee, he held her gaze. "Amelia, would you pay me the honor of becoming my wife?"

She nodded, a fresh set of tears pooling in her blue eyes, which reminded him more than ever of the Mediterranean Sea. "I will."

He gathered her to him for another kiss, but nothing too passionate. They hadn't cleared up the bedchamber-only nonsense yet. When their embrace ended, he resumed his spot beside her on the settee. "If you will indulge me for one more moment, there is another matter we should clear up at once."

Thirteen

Jake alighted from the carriage as soon as it clattered to a stop in front of Hillary House. Without breaking stride, he stalked through the antechamber, tugging off his gloves and removing his hat.

Hogan approached and accepted his belongings. "How was your afternoon at the park, sir?"

"Very agreeable, thank you."

"Your sister inquired after you when she called on Mrs. Hillary."

Jake chuckled as he crossed the marbled entry floor with Hogan trailing behind him. "My apologies, my good man. I hope Lana did not make a nuisance of herself asking after my affairs."

"No, sir. Her ladyship is always a welcome sight."

"Indeed." Jake hadn't spent time with his sister since Daniel's dinner. Curiosity must be driving her mad. Lana would want to interrogate him on his waltz with Amelia. How pleased she would be to learn of the recent developments. Even though she thought herself subtle, her desire to play matchmaker on his behalf was transparent. Perhaps he would call on his sister later this evening, but presently a more important matter required his attention.

"Is Father home?"

"He returned from the club an hour ago, sir," Hogan said. "I believe he is in his study with Mr. Berg."

Jake wouldn't allow his father's man of business to deter him. He rapped on the oak door before letting himself in to the study.

Father looked up from his monstrous desk before nodding toward Mr. Berg. "I would like a moment with my son."

Rising from the burgundy leather chair, the man gathered his papers and mumbled a greeting as he passed Jake.

His father broke into a huge smile as he rounded the desk. "Allow me to be the first to offer my congratulations."

Congratulations? No one could know of his engagement already. Why, Amelia had accepted his offer only two hours earlier.

Grasping Jake's hand, he pumped it up and down several times. "Daniel needed someone to put him in his place, and it sounds as if you beat him regular like at the club. He still has the bruises to prove it."

"Oh, that is your meaning." Jake extracted his hand from his father's grip. "I am surprised Daniel is admitting to it."

"He admits to nothing. You know your brother. The gents at Brook's were discussing it. What did you think I meant?"

"My engagement to Lady Audley, though only the two of us are aware of our agreement. I thought perhaps you employed spies." His father had certainly engaged in subterfuge over the past few months. Jake sat in the chair Mr. Berg had vacated and crossed his ankle over his knee, drumming his fingers against his calf in agitation. "And now you know."

"I see." Father nodded. "Allow me to be the first to extend my best wishes. Lady Audley is a lovely young woman."

The storm brewing inside Jake grew in intensity, but he fought to harness his fury. Duty required him to defer to his sire as head of the family even when he wished to rail over the injustices done to him. "Will you pretend to know nothing about my message to Lady Audley last April never reaching its destination?"

"I deny nothing nor do I offer apologies."

"No apologies?" Jake's shouted words echoed in the spacious room.

Leaning against the desk with his legs stretched out in front of him, his father reminded Jake of Daniel. They possessed the same arrogance and insolence.

"You may despise me," his father said, "curse me for being a deplorable father, but I did what I deemed the best course of action."

Jake leapt to his feet. "How can you say that? Amelia thought I had abandoned her. We were kept apart for a year."

His father shrugged. "Yet you are reunited."

Jake's fingers curled into fists of their own accord. His casual dismissal of Jake's suffering was almost too much to bear. "Much to your chagrin, I take it."

With a sigh, his father pushed from the desk, returned to his chair, and lowered into it. "Someday you will find yourself faced with difficult decisions. You will do your best to make the right choices, but you'll realize sometimes there are no *correct* decisions. You must choose the best path and hope to minimize the damage your decision might cause."

Rage coursed through Jake's blood, making him tremble. "What are you saying? Have you grown addled in your advanced age?"

His father's eyes hardened. "Take. Your. Seat."

Jake met his stare, his jaw twitching. Neither of them looked away. Jake wouldn't surrender, not when his father's interference had caused undue heartache not only for him but also for Amelia. He and his father both knew Jake had sacrificed much to care for his mother. He had remained at Hillary House upon his father's request when his contemporaries enjoyed freedoms he didn't. He too could squander his inheritance, live a rogue's life, travel the world, but his allegiance had always been to his family. How disheartening to learn his devotion was one-sided.

His father blinked first and looked down at the papers on his desk. "Please. If you will sit, I will explain myself."

"I bloody well deserve some answers." He sank to the chair. A surge of blood flowed to his fingers as he released his fists.

"I never realized the depth of your feelings for Lady Audley," his father said. "I thought you would be much like your brothers and need to sow your oats as well. Look at Benjamin and Daniel. Neither has taken a wife, and Benjamin is one and thirty."

"Indeed? Well, now you are aware of my abiding affection."

His father leaned his elbows on the desk and scrubbed his hands down his face, stretching the skin under his eyes and making him appear gaunt. "Had I known of your constancy, I'm uncertain if I would have altered my decision, but I would have spoken to you about it. I couldn't risk the *ton* discovering your mother's troubles. There have been rumors, but no evidence of her madness."

Jake's spine stiffened. He was unappreciative of his father's callous manner when discussing his mother. "She suffers bouts of illness," he said through clenched teeth. "She is not mad."

"Yes, yes." With a wave of his hand, Jake's father dismissed him. "It matters little if she suffers bouts of illness or is simply batty. No one cares for the truth. If Lady Audley had received your forthright message, and she in turn spread the news to others—"

"Amelia is not one to spread rumors." Jake sprang to his feet. "Wait one blasted moment! You read my message?"

His father folded his arms on top of the desk and frowned. "Given the timing, I suspected you spoke of your mother, and I was correct."

"Damn you!" Jake hammered his fist against the desk, startling his father. "Your invasion of my privacy is unforgiveable, not to mention your deceit and interference in my personal matters. How could you?"

"I don't expect your forgiveness, son, but be reasonable. Lana was entering her second season. The Paddock disaster had shaken her confidence. I couldn't allow another scandal to hurt her chances of securing a fortuitous match."

Jake scoffed. "As if Forest would have cared…" His sister's husband adored her. And it wasn't as if Forest had been in possession of a spotless past either.

His father reclined in his chair with a rueful smile. "Yes, well, I never factored in Forest."

Jake supposed he hadn't either. "And my letters from Sussex?"

"Nicholas intercepted any further correspondence, but please do not hold your brother at fault."

Pinching the bridge of his nose, Jake sighed. All this cloak-and-dagger nonsense created a dull pain behind his eyes. Had the King enlisted his family's assistance in spying on France, the war would have been ended before it had barely begun. "If you would have trusted me…" he said. "I could have given Amelia another story. Our separation was unnecessary."

They sat in silence until Jake was ready to give up on his father speaking again, to forget about ever having any type of relationship with his sire. Disquiet rumbled through him.

"I *am* sorry you suffered, Jake. I didn't realize the impact of my decision. Perhaps you will allow me to make amends."

Jake doubted that was possible. His father reached into his waistcoat pocket to pull something from it and enclosed the item in his fist. Indecision flitted across his countenance before his jaw firmed. "This belongs with someone as cherished as its original owner." In his hand was a silver ring. His father placed it on the desk and slid it across to Jake. "I want you to give this to Lady Audley."

Jake picked up the ring and held it between his

thumb and forefinger. The violet gem caught the light, fracturing it into multiple points of shimmering color.

"It's beautiful. Who did the ring belong to? Grandmother?"

His father gave an incisive shake of his head. "It no longer matters. Isabel has been dead for a long time. I am certain she would like Amelia to have it." He adjusted the papers on his desk and picked up his quill. "If there is nothing more, I have tasks that require my attention."

Jake suppressed a frustrated sigh as he cradled the ring in his palm. This was all he would get from his father. To pursue the matter further would only result in more aggravation and unnecessary heartache. He had Amelia now, and he would spend every minute of his time celebrating his good fortune, not lamenting the past.

He opened his hand to look at the ring once more.

Long ago, Jake had heard rumors of a first marriage for his father. He had dismissed the story as nonsense as there had never been mention of a first wife in his household, no portraits or evidence to suggest another Mrs. James Hillary had ever resided in Hillary House. Until now. His father had kept her ring on his person, a testament to his abiding love.

Jake held the ring out to his father. "I cannot accept this."

His father looked up from his papers.

When he didn't take it back, Jake placed it on the corner of the desk.

"I am sorry for everything, Jake."

"I know." He did see his father was sorry, and

because of his sincerity, Jake would forgive him eventually. He would not, however, accept a gift that could cause more strife between his parents.

◈

Amelia urged Bibi to have a seat in the drawing room. They hadn't seen each other for two days because of a recurrence of Bibi's headaches.

"Would you like refreshment, dearest?"

Her friend sat on the tufted Grecian couch and rearranged her plum-colored skirts. "Madeira would be nice."

Wandering to the sideboard, Amelia held the crystal glass up to the candelabra then rubbed her gloved finger over an almost undetectable water spot. She reached for the decanter but sat it back down to recheck the glass.

"Do hurry, Amelia. I wish to arrive before the fireworks display."

"We have plenty of time." She checked the mantle clock and experienced a jolt. Actually, she had little time to prepare Bibi for Jake's arrival or share her news. She doubted Bibi would consider her marriage to Jake to be good tidings as Amelia did. Bibi likened marriage to imprisonment after her experience with Lord Kennell.

She glanced over her shoulder to find Bibi patting her curls. "I wonder if we will cross paths with Lord Norwick at the gardens."

Amelia repressed a sigh as she poured Madeira almost to the rim before carrying the drink to her. Bibi seemed in high spirits this evening. It would be a shame to spoil her good mood. Perhaps she should postpone this conversation until another day.

Taking a seat on the settee, Amelia rested her hands on her lap, one on top of the other.

"Are you not having a glass as well?" Bibi asked.

"Not this evening." Although a drink might help to decrease the progressive tremors running the lengths of her arms and legs. She cleared her throat and tried to affect a cheerful voice. "Do you recall our discussion the other day? When I said I had no intentions of falling in love unless Cupid shot his arrows your direction, too?"

"Yes, vividly." Bibi sipped her drink, her narrowed, dark gaze assessing. "Although I realized at the time you were not swearing an oath, nor would I ask that of you."

Amelia melted against the cushions. Thank goodness. Perhaps this was going to be much easier than she had expected.

"However, if you claim to love Mr. Hillary after one passionate night, I may very well be inclined to clout you with my reticule."

"Bibi!" It had been three nights of passion, to be exact.

Her friend set the glass on the diminutive side table. "Need I remind you of the gentleman's habit of disappearing after he samples your wares? Don't be a fool, Amelia."

"I am not a fool. There were legitimate circumstances surrounding his retreat to the country."

"Such as?"

"I cannot reveal them."

Bibi rolled her eyes. "Lies, I am sure. Why else would he ask you to keep his confidence?"

"How can you say such a thing? You are barely acquainted with Jake."

"He is a man. That's all I need to know." She lifted the hem of her skirts and pushed up from the couch. "Now, let's go before we miss all the excitement. By tomorrow, you will have forgotten all about Mr. Hillary."

There was a light knock at the drawing room door.

Amelia rose from the settee, a stiff smile straining her lips. "It will be impossible to forget Mr. Hillary by the morrow as he is our escort this evening."

Bibi whipped around with a gasp. Her expression was a perfect reflection of betrayal and outrage.

Amelia held up her hand to halt her friend's arguments. "I refuse to discuss this any further tonight. If you do not wish to join us, you may decline. But it would mean a lot to me if you accompanied us and tried to become better acquainted with Mr. Hillary. I am extremely fond of him."

"You should have given me more notice. I cannot leave now without insulting the gentleman."

Amelia smiled at Bibi's show of defiance. She would never admit to concessions of any kind, but she made them for Amelia.

"I suppose you are correct, dearest. Next time I will exercise more courtesy."

Fourteen

JAKE WAS READY TO ABANDON ALL ATTEMPTS TO DRAW Lady Kennell into conversation. The evening reeked of failure, and they had yet to cross Westminster Bridge en route to the pleasure gardens.

Amelia's troubled gaze met his when their companion turned her face toward the window. He concealed his frustration with a gentle smile. Last night Amelia had expressed her desire for Jake and Lady Kennell to become friendly with one another. The viscountess was like family to Amelia, the only real family she had since her father's passing two years ago. As much as Jake wished he could dismiss Lady Kennell from their lives, it appeared he was stuck with her. Therefore, he would make every effort to win her favor.

"This is lovely," he said. "The three of us enjoying an evening at Vauxhall together. Have you seen Madame Saqui's rope dancing? She is a marvel."

Lady Kennell sniffed. "I am convinced she is Old Boney in costume."

A sharp laugh burst from his lips. Madame Saqui

boasted a masculine countenance, and he could picture the resemblance. "Bonaparte posing as an acrobat? What a brilliant disguise. Should we notify the Home Office?"

A corner of Lady Kennell's mouth curved up, though she barely graced him with a glance before returning her attention to the sights beyond the carriage window.

Perhaps all was not lost if he could coax a begrudging smile from her. When Amelia looked his way, he winked. Her reward was more gracious and heartfelt. The steps he would take to make his love happy… He sighed, resigning himself to his fate.

When the carriage stopped in front of the gates of Vauxhall Gardens, the twilight sky hinted at the darkness to come. Jake alighted first before assisting each lady down the steps. He stopped to pay nine shillings for their admittance while the ladies wandered through the gate. Amelia linked arms with him, and the three of them walked arm-in-arm along the gravel path. A breeze stirred the greenery and sent the red hanging lanterns into a frenzied dance on their lines.

"What shall we do first?" Amelia asked.

She looked to Lady Kennell for a suggestion, but the viscountess remained silent until the moment passed awkwardness and approached excruciating embarrassment.

Jake cleared his throat. "I have always enjoyed the ruins."

"Fake," Lady Kennell declared. "I can spot a counterfeit at a glance."

"Bibi." Amelia directed them toward an outer

pathway marked with arches. Worrying her bottom lip, she darted her gaze between her friend and him.

Jake covered her hand with his free one to reassure her all was well. "No one has ever claimed the ruins were genuine, my lady. Nevertheless, they are interesting."

"The first time or two they have appeal, but one soon tires of them. Wouldn't you agree, Mr. Hillary?"

Amelia stiffened on his arm, alerting him that this conversation was about more than the garden ruins. He inferred the viscountess spoke of his association with Amelia, but he was unsure who the lady expected to tire of the other first.

"I can only speak for myself," Jake said. "But once I admire something, my sentiment remains constant."

"Indeed? I had the opposite impression."

Amelia stopped in the middle of the path. "That is enough. Mr. Hillary deserves an apology at once."

"Oh." The viscountess's dark eyes shimmered with tears as she looked between them. "Forgive me, Mr. Hillary. I am not myself tonight." She broke away to rush ahead on the path.

Amelia's hand on his arm stopped him from giving chase. She blew out a slow breath. "Please, allow us a moment alone."

He opened his mouth to protest the wisdom of two ladies walking the gardens unescorted. "We will not go far," she said. "Please, I realize her manners are deplorable this evening, but I know Bibi. Something is troubling her."

Jake pressed his lips together to contain the oath on his tongue. "Very well. But I insist on following at a distance."

"We need privacy, Jake. I will catch up to her then we will double back and meet you at the supper boxes."

Pulling a handkerchief from his jacket pocket, he dabbed at the sweat dampening his brow. The night had seemed pleasant a moment ago, but somehow the air had turned hellishly hot. "You promise to hurry back?"

"I promise. I only need a moment with her."

He gave a sharp nod then waited until she caught up to her friend and gathered her in a hug before he wheeled around to see to the supper box he had hired for the evening.

❧

Amelia held her friend at arm's length. "Bibi, what is wrong?"

"I just—" She shook her head and backed away from Amelia's hold. "You are falling for him. What kind of friend would I be if I didn't at least attempt to save you from further heartache?"

"Jake doesn't wish to hurt me."

"He already has. And I cannot for the life of me understand how you can forget."

Amelia brushed a stray strand of hair from her forehead. Her friend was unfairly judging Jake, and Amelia was to blame. She should have kept their past a secret rather than burdening her friend. "Jake has asked me to marry him."

"Marry him?" Bibi's eyes flew open wide. "But I didn't think he would—blast it all! What did you say?"

"I agreed to become his wife, of course."

"How could you?"

A spark of irritation flared inside Amelia. "You know I've longed for a husband and children. I thought you would be happy for me."

Bibi hugged her arms close around her body, her gaze directed away. "I *am* happy for you, Amelia. Please, forgive me. It is just..." She sniffed and dragged her sleeve across her eyes. "I will miss you terribly."

"Miss me? I am remaining in London, silly girl. When will you have time to miss me?"

"Nothing will be the same." Bibi's luminous brown eyes contrasted with her pale complexion. A cheerless smile graced her lips. "Mr. Hillary will not welcome me any time I wish to visit."

Amelia managed to suppress her amusement. "When has that stopped you in the past? Bradford is scandalized every time you arrive before noon."

"Yes, well, Bradford is not a husband."

When her bottom lip trembled, Amelia's smile faded. Poor Bibi had been exceedingly unhappy in her marriage to Lord Kennell. Ten years her senior, he had kept her isolated from everyone, even from Amelia.

"Jake will not attempt to keep us apart," she said. "He loves me and therefore will care for the ones I love." She wrapped her arms around her friend once again and kissed her cheek. "And I do love you, dearest. You are the sister of my heart."

Bibi groaned and wiped the tears from her eyes as she withdrew from Amelia's embrace. "You are a sentimental fool, Amelia Audley. If you didn't have me in your life, you would walk around spouting mawkish nonsense all the time."

Amelia smiled. "Then the matter is settled. You

are a necessity." She hooked her arm with Bibi's and turned her back toward the supper boxes. "You must remain close at hand to remind me not to fall prey to my sentimental foolishness. Now, let us reunite with Mr. Hillary and enjoy our evening together, shall we?"

"Oh, very well. If you insist." They hadn't passed through the arch before she squeezed Amelia's arm. "I rather like the type of fool you are. I don't wish for you to change in the least."

"Why, thank you. And you, dearest, are my most cherished ninnyhammer."

Bibi chuckled, her typical bright spirits returning. They entered the rotunda where the orchestra had begun to play and made their way toward the supper boxes. Fashionably attired ladies and gentlemen gathered in clusters, chattering with one another.

Amelia pointed to the farthest box. "I believe we are dining over there this evening."

A gentleman stepped from the crowd, startling them. "Lady Kennell?"

Bibi's fingers tightened around Amelia's arm and drew her closer.

"Lord Banner, we thought you were in Cardiff." Amelia greeted the baron on behalf of Bibi and tried to guide her around him, but he stepped into their path.

"I returned this morning. Where are you ladies off to in such a hurry?"

"If you will excuse us, my lord, we are late for dinner."

"Nonsense, it is early yet." He grasped Bibi's elbow and tugged her away from Amelia's side. "Let's stroll through the garden."

"I must decline, my lord," Bibi said, her voice quivering.

Instead of heeding her wishes, Lord Banner whipped her around and pulled her back toward the walkway. "Come with me, my dear, unless you wish to draw unwanted notice."

Amelia's heart quickened. She searched the crowd for Jake but was unable to find him. With only a brief moment of hesitation, she hurried after Bibi and the man who was the source of all her friend's troubles.

❧

Jake had waved to Amelia and Lady Kennell when he spotted them, but their view was blocked by Lord Banner's sudden appearance. After what seemed like a polite exchange, Lady Kennell allowed the baron to escort her from the area. Amelia looked around once then dashed after them.

Hellfire. Where were they going?

Jake elbowed his way through the crowd, mumbling his apologies when anyone protested his forward behavior. Leaving the clearing, he retraced their earlier steps, praying they stayed to the well-lit main walkway. If they traveled one of the winding trails, he might never find them. He spotted Amelia kneeling on the ground the moment he passed through the first archway. She braced her elbow on the bench beside her, stood, and took one hobbling step before lowering to the bench.

He rushed forward to assist her. "Amelia, what happened?"

She swung her head around toward him and blew

out an exasperated breath, lifting wisps of hair lying on her forehead. "I turned my ankle, but I am fine. Go after Bibi before she finds herself in trouble."

In the distance, Lady Kennell and the baron veered off the walkway and disappeared into the trees.

Blast and damn! The woman lacked common sense in spades. Banner was a lewd old goat, known for taking liberties with genteel ladies. To become entangled with the gent was proof of her poor judgment. He would speak with Amelia about the dangers of an association with Banner later. Right after he saved Lady Kennell's bacon.

As he neared the place where the couple had left the path, Lady Kennell's silky voice drifted on the air. "Please, Charles. Not here. Someone will discover us."

"Then tell me where. You cannot put me off again. I want to be with you, Bianca."

Her tinkling laugh rang a note just shy of hysteria. Banner had her backed against a tree, and when he leaned forward to kiss her, she turned her face away, her eyes squeezed shut.

Jake sprang forward; a branch cracked under his boot. "Lady Kennell, there you are."

Banner jerked back and ran a hand over his thinning hair before adjusting his jacket. "Mr. Hillary, what are you doing here?"

"I am watching out for my own, my lord. I wouldn't want any unpleasant rumors circulating about my betrothed's dearest companion. That would never do."

Lady Kennell pressed back against the tree and inched away from the baron.

Jake nodded encouragingly. "Come along, my lady. Dinner will be served soon."

When Banner made to grab her arm, Jake stepped forward, his fists raised from force of habit. The baron balked and moved away.

Lady Kennell lifted her skirts and ran the short distance to reach his side.

"Good evening, Banner," Jake said and tucked her arm in the crook of his elbow before tipping his hat.

Lady Kennell clung to his arm as if he were a log in a river that could save her from drowning. Perhaps this once he had succeeded in playing the hero, but her imprudent choices would eventually result in trouble from which no one could rescue her. And it was his duty to make certain she brought no harm to Amelia in the process.

"Thank you, Mr. Hillary."

"I wish I could say it is my pleasure to come to your aid, but I would prefer it if you would take better care with your decisions. Lord Banner is a rotter and undeserving of your attentions."

"Yes, I know."

They entered the walkway and headed in Amelia's direction.

"You are a careless young woman," he added, "and I do not wish for you to drag Amelia into any danger. Do you understand my meaning?"

She released his arm but stayed by his side. "I believe I take your meaning clearly, sir. You fear an association with me will sully your betrothed's name."

Damage to Amelia's name was the least of his worries. She would be inconsolable if any harm came to the viscountess. "Conduct yourself with more decorum. I would not like to see her suffer because of your recklessness."

"If you think I planned any of this—" She stood up straighter and tossed a glare at him. "Oh! Go to hell, Mr. Hillary."

She marched ahead, arms swinging and black curls bouncing.

Amelia rose from the bench when she saw them approaching. "Bibi, thank heavens. Are you all right?"

"Plumy."

Amelia placed her arm around Lady Kennell's shoulders and walked with her toward the supper boxes, glancing back at him once with a frown.

Jake sighed. Good Lord, watching out for his own was to be a near impossible feat. He could see that now. But there was no help for it. He would perhaps run himself ragged attempting to save the viscountess from herself, but both ladies were under his protection now. And it was obvious he could not afford to relax his guard.

Fifteen

Bibi dreaded the opera as one dreaded one's own execution. Some of the refined ladies of the *ton* were appallingly uncivil to her. Yet she couldn't adopt a hermit's life, and she couldn't expect Amelia to be her constant companion anymore.

Mr. Hillary's disapproving glowers and the reprimands present in his tone the other night were enough to make Bibi want to scream. Nevertheless, she wouldn't allow her problems with the man to become a hardship for Amelia. Her friend was obviously torn between remaining loyal to their friendship and her growing affection for her betrothed. Therefore, Bibi had taken the initiative and removed a vital source of conflict from the equation. Herself.

She entwined her fingers and squeezed them together on her lap. For the tenth time since her carriage had turned off Half Moon Street onto Piccadilly, she questioned her sanity in venturing out alone.

A chance meeting with Lord Banner without Amelia to shield her would be dreadful indeed. Bibi cringed. The baron disgusted her, and his boasting that they were lovers created all sorts of unkind sentiments toward her. *Lovers indeed.* She would never classify them as such. Even worse would be an encounter with his vicious wife this evening. Lady Banner was a horrid woman to be certain. The only decent thing about the baroness was her brother, Lord Norwick.

Bibi sank against the seat back with a soft smile. To look at the earl, one would think him a complete buffoon, but after the way he had touched her… Good heavens, the memories still brought her shivers.

When the carriage rolled to a stop in front of the opera house, exuberance bubbled up inside her despite her frayed nerves. Norwick was escorting his sister to the opera this evening. Seeking out the earl could be a monumental mistake, but it wouldn't be Bibi's first. Nor did she expect this to be her last.

A footman opened the door to assist her from the carriage. Bibi clutched her fan and pulled her Chinese silk wrap around her shoulders as she passed through the double doors of the Theatre Royal. A multitude of eyes turned her direction. Their faces blurred as her breaths came quicker. Willing herself to breathe slower, she waited until everything came into focus again before putting on the same performance she had been for the last two years. She straightened her spine, lifted her head, and pasted on a brilliant smile, maintaining this facade all the way to her box before almost collapsing onto the crimson velvet chair.

Retrieving her opera glasses from her reticule, she scanned the other boxes for Norwick. Lord and Lady Banner's box was filled with Lord Banner's associates, but neither Norwick nor his sister sat among the group.

How curious that Norwick was attending the opera tonight. He didn't seem the type. Bibi couldn't recall ever seeing him at the theatre, but sadly, the earl had been below her notice before the masked ball. Lowering the glasses, she tried to remember the location of the Norwick family box. It seemed his father had rented a spot on the second level across the way. Bibi raised the glasses again.

There was Norwick, peering back at her and grinning like a dolt. Bibi couldn't hold back her own version of a fool's smile. She gave a subtle wave, which he returned, but his friendliness was short-lived.

Norwick's troll of a sister smacked his arm with her fan as she scolded the earl. He lowered the glasses and looked away with a frown. The sting of his cut hurt even after the lights lowered. Bibi forced her eyes away from Norwick as the actors took the stage.

The imaginary world of *The Talisman of Oromanes* soon drew her in, and she pushed aside thoughts of the earl and his disappointing reaction to seeing her again. So lost was she in the performance, she experienced a pang of disappointment when intermission came, especially since it appeared Lord Norwick would snub her like his sister always did.

Still, she wouldn't cower in her box. With all the dignity she possessed, Bibi stood and pushed her way through the curtains.

A hulking figure outside caused her to jump. Captain Hillary cocked a grin. "Lady Kennell."

"Captain Hillary, I did not expect to see you again."

"And here I thought we'd had an enjoyable encounter."

He was a charming and roguish man but not one with whom she desired a repeat assignation. Bibi should send him away, but a formidable presence by her side possessed great appeal. She slipped her arm through his. "*Had*, Captain Hillary, as in the past tense."

He patted her hand. "Understood, my lady, but perhaps you could use an ally this evening given your usual companion is missing." He led her toward the foyer. "Are you behaving yourself so far?"

Ah, it seemed the captain was on a mission. "You may tell your brother I have run off with the gypsies. I don't require a keeper. He is marrying Lady Audley, not me."

"Now, now, my dear. We know how Lady Audley worries for you. Jake only wishes to keep her happy."

She sniffed. Mr. Hillary was too presumptuous. "I don't require an escort, Captain."

"You have no fear of swimming alone with the barracudas? You must possess a set of brass ballocks, my dear." He winked.

His off-color compliment pleased Bibi even though she didn't wish to show it. There was no reason to mislead him into thinking he might charm her. "Why, thank you, Captain."

He leaned close to speak in her ear. "Banner hasn't made a nuisance of himself this evening, has he?"

Her gaze darted toward him.

His earnest eyes stared back. "My brother feared the baron might inflict his unwelcomed company on you again without an escort. Banner altered his course when he spotted me outside your box."

Bibi's heart expanded, and warmth radiated through

her. Mr. Hillary *had* realized she wished nothing to do with Lord Banner after all, and he was concerned for her welfare. She almost could forgive him for speaking harshly to her.

"Yes, well, that was almost thoughtful of Mr. Hillary."

"I shall take the liberty of telling him so."

"Please don't."

The opera boasted an excellent turnout, resulting in a crush in the foyer. Her fingers curled tighter around Captain Hillary's arm.

"Shall we seek out refreshment?" her companion asked.

She nodded. Perhaps she wouldn't cross paths with Norwick given the size of the crowd, which would please her to no end. Of all gents to give her the cut direct… Her chest tightened. Lord Norwick was unlike any man she had ever considered in the past, and the only one she had genuinely liked.

⤎∾⤏

Jasper pawned his sister off onto a group of gossip-mongers to keep her occupied during intermission and left in search of Bianca. He'd had enough of his sister and her harping on the lovely viscountess. When would Fi realize he did not have to listen to her? He was an earl, and if he wished to pursue a nubile, younger, sensual…

Lord Almighty, there weren't enough words in his vocabulary to describe how beautiful Bianca looked tonight. She had chosen a delightfully revealing sapphire gown that hinted at the treasures beneath her fragile garment, and he yearned for a closer look.

Finding her in this mad crush might be a challenge, though. He weaved through the overdressed fops and gentle ladies, doing his best to avoid meeting anyone's eye for fear of someone detaining him. After several moments slipped by without locating the magnificent goddess, Jasper's frustration mounted.

Blasted clock, blasted crowd, and blasted Fiona! His sister wasn't a debutante in need of a chaperone. Inspiration struck. He would rush Fi back to her seat early then linger outside Bianca's box, and perhaps secure an invitation back to her town house.

Fiona grumbled when he insisted she return to her seat early, but Jasper gave her no choice. His fingers clamped around her upper arm and pulled her along to their seats.

"What is the meaning of this, Norwick?"

He deposited her at the box. "Sit down and hold your tongue," he said, "or else sit with your husband."

Fiona folded her arms across her chest and dropped onto a chair with a grunt, one of those fabricated little sounds that thin people made just to annoy the plumper ones.

"He does not wish for my company," she grumbled.

Jasper would like to say he could empathize with his brother-in-law, but he didn't wish to hurt Fi, no matter how annoying she could be. "You are welcome to sit here, but I must attend to a matter. I may not return either, but I will send the carriage to take you home." He dashed away before she could pose any inquiries.

With a skip to his step, he skirted the remaining patrons loitering in the foyer and ran up the stairs

on the opposite side of the opera house. He reached
Bianca's box and peeked through the parted curtains
to discover she hadn't returned. Taking up position to
intercept her, he waited.

Finely dressed ladies and gentlemen filed past him.
Some tossed curious glances his direction before
moving on without a word. After several moments
with no sign of Bianca, Jasper began to worry she had
departed already, but her laughter lifted his spirits and
brought an eager smile to his lips. He stepped from the
corner with a pleasant greeting at the ready and balked.

Bianca—*his* Bianca—strolled along the corridor on
Captain Daniel Hillary's arm.

"Norwick," she exclaimed on a rush of breath. Her
brown eyes widened. "What are you doing here?"

"Lady Kennell," he said with a bow.

Damnation. He was an unforgivable fool. Why
would Bianca, so perfect and delectable, have any
interest in a frumpy codger like him? She could have
any spirited buck of her choosing. Just look at her with
that smug bugger Hillary.

"Is the earl bothering you, my dear?" the captain asked.

"No, he is a harmless sort. You may leave us."

Hillary lifted her hand to place a kiss on her
knuckles. "Thank you for the honor of your delightful
company, my lady. I shall remain at the theatre until
you have no more need for me."

He ambled back down the corridor as if he owned
the bloody passageway then disappeared down the stairs.

"I asked what you are doing here, my lord."

Jasper fidgeted with his coat sleeves, unsure what to
do with his hands. "I wished to extend my greetings."

"Indeed." The lady cocked a hip, drawing his notice to her sleek body. "Did Lady Banner finally grant her permission?"

Jasper frowned at her sarcastic tone and jab at his manhood. Granted, he couldn't boast bulging muscles like Captain Hillary—the man was an unnatural phenomenon—but Jasper possessed what he needed to distinguish him as a man.

"I do not require anyone's permission to do anything," he snapped. "I am a lord of the realm."

The corridor was empty now, and music swelled on the air. Bianca took two steps forward. Her head rolled back as she tipped her pretty face up toward him. "It seems to me your sister has ample control over you, my lord, to the point of directing who you can and cannot ogle."

"I may ogle anyone of my choosing," he said through clenched teeth. His gaze roved over her body to illustrate his point. A flush rose up her chest. "And may I say, Bianca, your breasts look positively delicious in that dress."

Her breath hitched. "Lord Norwick!"

Bugger. Jasper might have taken liberties he shouldn't have. He thought to apologize at once, but a mischievous spark lit her eyes.

"Are you indicating you do *not* require your sister's permission to take me home for a tumble?"

This time Jasper gasped, but it transformed into a guttural growl. "The hell I would. I'll take you home right now and shag you every which way known to man."

Her delicate hand fluttered over her heart as color

flooded her cheeks. "Oh, my, Jasper. Do you truly know so many ways? Then please, let's not dawdle."

Jasper smiled. One thing he appreciated about Bianca was her directness. He needn't guess at anything she wanted, and the way she looked at him with her smoldering cocoa eyes said she wanted *him*.

His blood pounded in his ears and his mouth went dry. She had incited his temper and driven him to make such a bold proposition. But he had never bedded a beauty like Bianca, nor one as delicate. What if he flattened her like a French crepe?

Her hands went to her hips, and her arched brows pulled together. "Why are you hesitating? Is it your sister again?"

He would be mad to pass up this opportunity. Tempted to toss the lady over his shoulder, but knowing such action would set tongues to wagging and possibly wrench his back, he instead hooked arms and raced with her toward the theatre exit to call for his carriage.

The wait for his driver was torturous, and even though he was about to engage in the most intimate of acts with Bianca, he couldn't think of a thing to say. He had never romanced a lady before. Did they wish gentlemen to woo them first, perhaps reciting poetry?

He could do that. In a moment. Once something came to mind. He frantically searched his memory for anything—anything at all—but only a childhood rhyme came to mind. And it wouldn't blasted go away.

Ride a cock horse to Banbury Cross. Ride a cock horse to Banbury Cross.

"Ride a cock horse to Banbury Cross," he mumbled, "to see a fine lady upon a white horse."

Damnation. That wouldn't do.

Bianca squeezed his arm. "With rings on her fingers and bells on her toes, she shall have music wherever she goes." She laughed. "Norwick, what are you doing reciting children's rhymes?"

He broke into a cold sweat and ducked his head. But when Bianca positioned herself where she could gaze up into his eyes, her expression was one of delight.

"I thought to recite poetry," he admitted, his cheeks flaming even hotter. "But I could only think of this ridiculous rhyme."

The carriage rolled up, ending their conversation. The lady accepted the footman's assistance without hesitation. Once she and Jasper settled on the bench side by side and the carriage jerked forward, she took his hand in hers.

"That is the sweetest thing any man has ever done to impress me."

He had impressed her? Surely not.

Her face was lit with adoration when she looked up at him. He sank against the seat back.

"You make everything easy on me, Bianca. Thank you."

Sixteen

JAKE STOOD AMONG THE CHILDREN GATHERED AROUND the wingback chair where Amelia would soon perch to read the book she had brought for the occasion. He had been pleased by her invitation to accompany her for the weekly story time at the foundling hospital, but now that he was here, he wasn't sure what to do with himself. The drawing room was noticeably lacking in seating with only one upholstered piece and a ladder-back chair with a wobbly leg.

Amelia cooed to a rosy-cheeked babe in her arms and placed a kiss on his pale hair before handing the boy back to the nurse. At least Jake thought the babe was a male child. It was difficult to tell the difference when their nurses dressed them in gowns like ladies.

"Take your places, children," Amelia called. Her voice was merry and her eyes shone with animated light.

A smile pulled at his lips. She enjoyed her time with the orphans. He hadn't been certain of her affection for the children, though he had believed in her sincere desire to improve their living quarters. Many ladies took on charitable causes, but he always had the impression their involvement was a necessary drudgery.

Amelia gestured to the hardwood chair. "Would you like to have a seat as well, Mr. Hillary?"

He didn't dare sit on the rickety chair with his tendency toward clumsy displays at the most inopportune moments. "That's all right, my lady. I shall stand unobtrusively over there." He pointed to the wall behind Amelia's chair.

The slight crease between her arched brows appeared. "As you wish."

She picked up the book lying on the chair cushion then lowered to the seat. "This evening's reading is from *The Life and Perambulation of a Mouse* by Mrs. Dorothy Kilner."

The children sat on the wide, plank floor at Amelia's feet, which appeared too hard for their tiny bums by half. Perhaps he would send 'round a carpet on the morrow.

Amelia opened the book on her lap and began the reading. "Like all other newborn animals, whether of the human, or any other species, I cannot pretend to remember what passed during my infant days."

Her soothing voice lulled the children, and they settled in to listen to more of her tale, but only a little ways into the reading, the younger ones began shifting positions and their gazes wandered about the room. Mrs. Kilner was losing their attention. Jake wanted to assist his betrothed, but he was unsure on what to do.

"Impatient to use our liberty," she continued, "we all set forward in search of some food."

Jake pretended to shade his eyes from the sun, crouched low, and scanned the area, all with a silly expression, eyes being crossed and all. His dramatic interpretation earned several giggles, drawing the notice of some of the other children.

Amelia paused briefly to study her audience before returning to the story. "Or rather some adventure…"

Lifting his hand into the air, Jake lunged as if engaging in swordplay. More ripples of laughter traveled the half circle at Amelia's feet.

She read on. "…as our mother had left us victuals more than sufficient to supply the wants of that day. With a great deal of difficulty, we clambered up a high wall on the inside of a wainscot."

He pantomimed scrambling up a ladder then wiping the sweat from his brow with an exaggerated, though silent, huff of breath.

The children's delighted response buoyed his spirits. Perhaps he had a knack for tots after all.

Amelia lowered the book to her lap, palms on the pages, and leaned forward. "Children," she said in a loud whisper, "what mischief is Mr. Hillary up to behind me?"

Jake placed his finger over his lips as if to beg their silence, which caused a high-spirited uproar.

Turning in the chair, Amelia caught him in the act of misbehavior. He shoved his hands behind his back, looked up at the ceiling, and whistled nonchalantly.

Her soft chuckle warmed his insides and drew his gaze. How strikingly beautiful she was when she was happy, her eyes more brilliant, her mouth pliable, her perfect complexion radiant. At that moment, he vowed to keep Amelia happy for the remainder of their lives together, perhaps even beyond.

"I believe we have a thespian in our midst. Pray, Mr. Hillary, do continue. The children are enchanted by your performance."

He bowed with added flourish. "At your command, my lady."

As Amelia continued the story, his actions became larger and more outlandish until all of them laughed, he and Amelia included. When the time came to end their reading for the evening, the children protested.

"I am sorry, my dears, but you must all be off to bed. I shall return next week and we will continue with the mouse's adventures."

"Will you bring Mr. Hillary again?" one of the older boys asked.

"Please, please, please," the other children called.

Amelia glanced at him in question.

"Nothing could keep me from returning next week." He lifted his imaginary sword. "Not vicious dragons, nor wild beasts of the forest, nor—"

"That is quite enough for tonight, sir." Despite her reprimand, Amelia grinned at him over her shoulder.

The nurses ushered the children from the drawing room to prepare them for bed. Their noisy chatter faded as they moved farther away. He and Amelia were alone and would see themselves out.

He offered her a hand up. She stood and wrapped her arms around his waist, laying her cheek against his chest.

"You shall be the finest of husbands, Mr. Hillary." Her warm breath penetrated his waistcoat.

"I shall try to be," he promised then placed a kiss

atop her silky hair. He would cherish her, love her with reverence, and protect her as a doting husband should. Nothing would stop him.

Not dragons.

Nor wild beasts.

No creature great or small.

∽

When Amelia and Jake arrived at Verona House, she led him toward the veranda, winding through the town house, and outside through the French doors.

The cloying scent of honeysuckle hung on the air, reminiscent of the happier times of her childhood playing in the gardens at the finishing school with Bibi. They had plucked the small trumpets from the vine, pinched off the ends and then, as carefully as a glass maker, pulled the delicate stamen to release the translucent drop of nectar. Nothing had seemed sweeter than those halcyon days of innocence, until now.

Jake was the most endearing gentleman. If only Bibi could see what Amelia witnessed tonight with the children, she would understand Amelia's devotion. Bibi would also realize he was unlike Lord Kennell. Jake was protective, not overbearing. Amelia recognized the difference.

A footman followed Jake and Amelia to the garden to light the torches, lending an incandescent ambiance. "Will there be anything else, milady?"

"Make certain we're not disturbed," Jake answered.

"Yes, sir." The servant bowed before gliding back inside and pulling the glass doors closed.

Amelia stepped into Jake's embrace, resting her

chin against his chest. She looked up at him and smiled. "Don't keep me waiting any longer."

Jake snuggled her close and kissed the tip of her nose. "You're an impatient young woman."

"I grow more impatient with each moment you stall. Now, tell me your news, as I'm becoming cross with you." She tipped her head to the side and smiled. She was anything but cross with him.

"First, I have a surprise for you." Lifting her by the waist, he sat her on the wide stone railing enclosing the veranda before digging inside his coat pocket. "You must close your eyes."

She shook her head slowly as if put out with him, but lifted her face up in expectation and did as he requested. He touched his lips to hers just as she had hoped.

"I thought we agreed to no more gifts," she said.

"I agreed to nothing of the sort." Grasping her hand, he removed her glove then glided a ring onto her finger.

Her breath hitched.

"Open your eyes."

Amelia's eyes flew open, and she held her hand in front of her face. The round, aqua gem glittered in the torchlight when she wiggled her fingers. "Oh, Jake. It's beautiful. Is this a blue diamond?"

He nodded, looking pleased with himself. "It was brought to my attention recently that I should give you a token of my love, a ring to remind you how much I cherish you."

His ever-expressive eyes, softly glowing with love, would be the only reminder she ever needed. She had never had anyone regard her so.

"I shall never remove it, my love." She looped her

arms around his neck and drew him closer. "Now allow me to present you with a token of *my* affection."

She intended to place a chaste kiss on his lips but his hand slipped to her nape and held her in place while he possessed her mouth. She melted against him; her lips parted on a sigh, their tongues brushing against one another.

Just as her ability to think on anything besides him was on the brink of extinction, he broke the kiss and rested his forehead against hers. "I love you, Mia."

Mia, Latin for mine. A trill of pleasure swept over her every time he called her by the pet name.

"And *I* love you." She placed her palm against his chest and imitated a severe look as she recalled the true reason she brought him to the veranda. "Now, do stop distracting me with beautiful gifts and lovely kisses. What is this pleasant development you mentioned in the carriage?"

He reached into his pocket to procure a folded document. "A pledge for the foundling hospital renovation project. Lord Ellis has agreed to donate the last two thousand pounds needed to secure the board's approval."

She issued a tiny squeal as she snatched the parchment from his hand.

"You truly have no patience at all," he said with a laugh.

"How am I to have patience when you delight me so?" She opened the paper to find the Earl of Ellis's bold signature. The earl remained a bachelor with no female relations Amelia could approach to speak with him about the project. "You amaze me, Jake. How did you enlist Lord Ellis's assistance?"

He shrugged. "I presented the facts, and he agreed to contribute to the cause. Although he may have been swayed somewhat when I mentioned Lady Gabrielle Forest was enchanted with the idea of a new wing for the foundling hospital. I believe he has a *tendre* for the duke's daughter."

"But Lady Gabrielle has no involvement with the Mayfair Ladies Charitable Society."

"Truly?" Jake drew back, a wicked twinkle in his hazel eyes. "I could have sworn you mentioned her name once or twice."

"You, my dear husband-to-be, are as crafty as your younger sister."

"Where do you think I learned such trickery?" Jake accepted the parchment she held out and slid it back into his pocket.

Amelia reached up to trail a finger along his chiseled jaw, his freshly shaved skin smooth to the touch. Light reflected off her ring, reminding her how fortunate she was to be loved by him. Jake's appearance had always had the ability to take her breath away, but the beauty he allowed her to see inside him tonight made her feel like laughing and crying and behaving in all sorts of mad ways.

"Thank you, for everything."

A slow smile spread across his lips. "I'm incapable of denying you anything. Promise you won't use my weakness against me."

"I promise."

Inching her skirts over her knees, his fingers grazed the sensitive spot above her stockings. She sucked in a sharp breath and shot her hand out to still his.

Amusement flickered in his dark eyes. "Are you ticklish, sweetheart?"

She refused to answer when he obviously knew the answer.

"My apologies." He nuzzled her neck as his other hand skimmed her waist. His fingers brushed the underside of her breast, and Amelia closed her eyes on a sigh.

"What about here?" he asked then lightly tickled her ribs.

"Jake!" She squealed and nearly toppled from the wall, but her fall was stopped by contact with his solid chest. His arms went around her and held her securely, his heat pleasant and welcome. She swatted him. "You are a horrible tease."

He laughed and snuggled her closer. "No more teasing. I know what you want, and as we've already established, I'm powerless to deny you anything."

"Splendid." Amelia looked up at him and offered her most mischievous grin while her hands wandered to the fastenings of his trousers. "Because you owe me a tumble in the gardens."

Stealing her hand inside the front fall of his pants, she caressed his firm length with the backs of her fingers before curling them around him. He leaned into her touch and closed his eyes on an outpouring of breath. "Never let it be said I dishonor my debts. Don't I owe you a good shag on the Persian rug in the drawing room, too?"

"I believe you paid that debt yesterday." Grasping the waistband of his trousers, she shoved them low on his hips and freed him. "But you have yet to take me in the library."

"An oversight I will remedy soon."

When he grazed his mouth over hers, she wrapped her arms around his neck. Her tongue flicked across his bottom lip, but she pulled back with a smile when he would have deepened their kiss.

"You wicked minx." With a playful growl, he buried his fingers in her hair and held her in place while he claimed her mouth. She abandoned toying with him and surrendered to his kiss.

❧

Jake released her as Amelia eagerly returned his kisses and inched her skirts above her knee before sliding his hands beneath her to cradle her bottom, cushioning her seat upon the hard wall surface. Amelia's skirts rode higher on her thighs as she wriggled to the edge and guided him to stand between her legs. A hiss of hot breath escaped him as his shaft bumped against her feverish skin. She had foregone drawers again this evening, as all ladies had before the invention of the blasted undergarments.

"I love an old-fashioned lady."

She chuckled. "I'm not old-fashioned, simply practical."

Stealing into the neckline of her gown, he lifted each mound from the confines of her corset. He fingered the tip of her breast until it stood erect before bending to sweep his tongue over the bud. She quivered when his lips closed around her.

"Oh, Jake, yes."

Soon, she was writhing on the wall as he nibbled her sensitive flesh. Her warm breath mixed with the sultry air and feathered over his face. Her head fell back on a pleasurable moan when his hand skated along her inner thigh and sought out her curls. He lavished her other breast with the same detailed attention while his fingers stroked the moist heat between her legs.

She was close to begging him for more, but he delved a single finger just inside her, tempting her. A low groan sounded at the back of her throat.

"Jake, *please.*"

He stood between her legs, touching the crown of his shaft to her, but held back from sliding inside. Kissing her, he invaded her mouth, their tongues wrestling in frenzied movement. His heart beat heavily, a hard drumming vibrating throughout his body.

"Tell me what you want, Mia."

"I want you," she whispered. "Now, inside me."

Fire washed over him and he buried himself to the hilt in one movement. Amelia was warmth, pleasure, and joy surrounding him. He slowly eased back before pulling her flush against him. It never seemed close enough when they made love, and yet, never had he felt so intertwined with another.

She held his gaze as he filled her over and over again, her eyes dark mirrors reflecting the torchlight. When he sought out her sensitive spot to bring her to completion, she sighed as her head lolled back. His lips found hers and they paused, tenderly, reverently kissing one another.

"Tell me you love me," he murmured as he began stroking her once more. Her breath hitched and grew ragged. It seemed a lifetime he had waited for Amelia to love him in return. He never tired of hearing her speak the words.

"I… love… you." She gripped his shoulders as passion consumed her, her cries of pleasure muffled against his waistcoat. Her sweet scent carried on the spring breeze, wrapping around him and heightening his arousal.

His fingers tightened on her hips as he drove into her with great urgency, chasing after his own ecstasy. Her hands stole into his waistcoat and caressed his chest over his fine lawn shirt, quickening the flow of his blood and breath. A burst of light rendered him blind to everything, oblivious to sound. His only awareness was of Amelia's loving touch, the one constant that brought him slowly back to life.

She leaned her cheek against his heaving chest when he enfolded her in his embrace. Her mussed hair tickled his chin.

"I love you, too, Amelia. More than life itself."

She hugged him tighter then lifted her face up to receive another kiss. He gladly complied before fastening his trousers then attempting to set her back to rights and finding there was no way to return her to her corset.

He removed his jacket and draped it around her shoulders. "You look thoroughly ravished."

She sighed, an easy smile on her plump lips. "I've *been* thoroughly ravished."

Jake pulled the jacket tight around her, kissed her forehead, then lifted her from the wall. Finding a seat on a nearby bench, he settled her on his lap. "I know I must go soon, but I don't want to leave you."

She worked her arms into the jacket sleeves, which were at least two inches too long for her, and pushed them up to her elbows. Capturing his face in both hands, she feathered her thumb across his cheek, her lips turning down slightly. "I wish you could stay, too. Maybe once the board has approved the project…"

"I understand, sweetheart. Soon." He placed his hand over hers, intertwining his fingers with hers.

"Jake, do you go home when you leave me at night?"

He drew back to see her better. "Where else would I go?"

"I'm not naive to the habits of gentlemen, but I don't have it in me to tolerate unfaithfulness. Once we are married, I wish you to be home with me every night."

He couldn't help but to feel pleasure over her admission, but he also heard an undercurrent of worry. "Amelia, I asked you to pledge your fidelity, and I gave my word that I too will remain faithful."

A shadow passed over her face. "Gentlemen don't always keep their word."

He nodded. "No, I suppose we can be deplorable scoundrels at times. But not every gentleman marries his one true love either."

"I don't wish to repeat the mistake I made in marrying Audley. I was unhappy in the extreme."

Reflecting on Amelia's past relationship with Audley stirred the darkness slumbering inside him. The blackguard hadn't deserved her. "Make a list of every distasteful habit your former husband possessed," he said, pushing his anger for Audley aside in favor of basking in Amelia's presence, "and I'll do the opposite."

A hint of a smile crossed her lips. "It would be a long list, sir."

Jake wrapped her in his embrace, feeling helpless to remedy the past, but wishing more than anything that he could take on the burden of her memories. "It's hard to stomach knowing he mistreated you."

"Then let's not speak of him again. He's no longer an impediment to our happiness."

As she snuggled against him, he welcomed her warmth and softness. Amelia would never be hurt again, not by his hand or anyone else's. He wouldn't allow it.

Seventeen

JASPER WHISTLED A LIVELY TUNE—ALBEIT AN ORIGINAL arrangement and off-key to all but the tone deaf—as he entered Norwick Place. He had been loath to leave Bianca's bed this morning, especially after a rousing send-off, but he did have responsibilities.

His butler stepped forward for his beaver hat, gloves, and walking stick. "Greetings, my lord."

"And greetings to you. What a fine morning it is." Jasper resumed his whistling and headed for the stairs.

"Is that Tub coming in at this hour?" Fiona's shrill voice came from the drawing room. "Present yourself at once."

"Damnation," he mumbled, tempted to dash up to his chambers, but it was best to confront her anger over his abandonment last night and be done with the matter. "Coming, Fi."

He headed for the drawing room.

"Sir?" His butler advanced, pointing a slim finger toward Jasper's middle.

"What is it?"

The servant swept his finger in the air from Jasper's neck to waist. He looked down.

"Egads!" Jasper's waistcoat was fastened wrong, lending him a lopsided appearance. He fumbled with the buttons until his butler stepped forward to assume the task. Once he was set to rights, he squared his shoulders and approached the drawing room.

Fiona was perched on the settee edge with a pinched look about her mouth. Her expression made her appear older than her years.

"Why are you awake this early, Fi? You need your rest."

Her frown deepened. "How am I to sleep knowing you are cavorting with whores?"

Jasper flinched and rubbed his temple. Perhaps his sister didn't realize he had left the opera with Bianca after all, though he was surprised to hear Fiona speak of whores and brothels. "Forgive my lack of sensitivity to your status as a lady, but since you introduced an inappropriate topic... When did you start losing sleep over my gentlemanly pursuits?"

She pushed herself up from the settee. Hellfire and brimstone couldn't be hotter than the fire shooting from her eyes. "How could you leave the opera with that trollop? Have you no shame?"

Good Lord. It was too early for his sister's nonsense. Jasper sauntered to the sideboard to pour himself a drink. If he must endure one of her tantrums, he deserved alcohol to dull his hearing.

"Lady Kennell is not a trollop or a whore. I would thank you to remember she is a lady of higher rank than you and address her as such." He sloshed a healthy portion of brandy into a glass and downed half the contents in one swallow.

"She is disgusting. I loathe her very existence, but to think of her and you…" Fiona wrinkled her nose and spat on his carpet.

"I say! You are behaving like a rag-mannered hoyden." He pointed a finger at her. "What type of lady spits? And on a Persian rug? Do that again and I will demand your husband replace it."

She puckered her lips and for one moment, he thought she would defy him.

"Have you eaten?" He moved toward the call bell. "You can be a bear when you're hungry."

"I am not hungry," she screamed and stomped her foot. "I'm furious with you."

He pulled the cord anyway. Perhaps a mouth full of food would derail her tirade.

She marched over to the cord and jerked it repeatedly. "Happy, Tub? How can you enjoy a meal when I'm miserable?"

He pried the cord from her fingers and grabbed her upper arm to lead her back to the settee. "Sit."

She crossed her arms and glared at him, but at least she was confined to the settee for the moment.

He ran a hand over his brow. "What has gotten into you, Fi? You are raving like a lunatic. If anyone heard you, you would be locked up. Explain your obsession with the lady."

Fiona's jaw jutted forward. She had inherited their father's stubbornness.

"Very well. Keep your lunacy to yourself. I care not."

A footman presented at the drawing room door.

"I will break my fast in the breakfast room. Lady Banner may join me if she wishes."

The servant bowed and left to do his bidding.

Jasper turned to his sister, who continued to sulk upon the settee. "Consider this fair warning: If you bring up Lady Kennell to me again in a negative light, you will no longer be welcome at Norwick Place. Whatever misinformed opinion you have of the viscountess, you should take pains to have your facts checked. Lady Kennell is a kind and generous soul. Why, I'll have you know, she has given a sizable donation to the foundling hospital renovation without seeking any recognition."

He stalked to the door but wheeled around once more. "She gives out of the goodness of her heart only. You and the other ladies of that pompous charitable society cannot say the same."

He didn't wait to see if his sister had a reply. He had heard enough from her for one day.

❧

Amelia clutched the deplorable missive from the foundling hospital board against her chest. Since receiving it that morning, she had read it enough times to memorize it, but the words still made no sense. "We have the funding to move forward with the renovation. How can they postpone the project?"

Mrs. Hillary stopped pacing and swung to face her. "Let me read it again." She stalked forward, holding out her hand.

Amelia surrendered the letter.

Mrs. Hillary's face flushed as she held the parchment up and scanned the contents. "Poppycock!"

With a flick of her wrist, she snapped the letter back to Amelia. "Jake will get to the bottom of this nonsense."

Jake had left Hillary House nearly three hours earlier. Had Amelia realized his errand would take this long, she would have returned to her own house to wait. Surely Bibi had called on her at Verona House by now and would wonder where she was. Perhaps Mrs. Hillary would allow her to send Bibi a message.

Before she could act on the thought, Jake sailed into the drawing room.

"Good heavens!" Mrs. Hillary hurried forward to grab his arms and pull him toward the settee. "I thought you would never return."

Jake's dark brows sank low over his eyes, hinting at the bad tidings to come. "Colburn had a late showing at the club." He gently extracted himself from his mother's grasp and assumed the spot beside Amelia. His knee brushed against hers, and she longed to hold his hand.

Mrs. Hillary stood over them, twisting her fingers together and swaying.

Jake looked up at his mother, seeming to follow Amelia's line of sight. A soft smile graced his lips. "Mother, would you like to take a seat while I share what I learned?"

Mrs. Hillary's eyes flew open in alarm. "Is everything truly that bad? Should I recline on the fainting couch?"

Jake stood, tucked his mother's arm through his, and escorted her to a chair. "Nothing is beyond repair. There's no need for swooning."

Once he had settled her, he placed a kiss on her cheek before moving back to the settee. Amelia's gaze had followed him, noting each kindness he showed his mother. Her eyes misted as love for him flowed over, around, and through her with every breath. The intensity of her feeling sometimes bordered on madness, a heart-pounding, energizing obsession that had been her companion day and night these past few days. How had she survived this last year without him?

Jake took her hand in his when he lowered to the settee. "A complication has arisen, but it is not insurmountable."

Amelia dropped against the seat back with a soft sigh. "I knew you would know how to make sense of everything. What must be done so we may get on with the renovation?"

He grazed his thumb over the back of her hand. "As you may or may not know, Mr. Ettinger, the board president, is related to Sir Davenport."

"Yes, and Sir Davenport made a large contribution to the foundling house renovation. I would think his involvement would help our cause unless—" She sat up straight. "Oh, dear. They aren't engaged in a family feud, are they?"

"Quite the opposite. From all accounts, Mr. Ettinger holds his older brother in high esteem, so much so that he allows his brother's opinions to color his judgment. Sir Davenport has insisted on a halt to the project as new information has come to light that causes him grave concerns." Jake issued a weary puff of breath. "I am quoting Colburn, mind you. Sir Davenport's concerns are ridiculous in my estimation."

Mrs. Hillary bolted from her seat. "If Lady Davenport has anything to do with this, she is in for a proper scolding." She slapped her upturned hand against the palm of her other hand. "The children will *not* be attired in tiny matching hats and made to sing and dance for our entertainment at the dedication ceremony. Her suggestions grow more outlandish with each meeting."

Jake drew back, his mouth opening once before snapping shut. If the situation were less dire, Amelia might laugh.

"She did not..." He glanced to Amelia as if seeking confirmation.

"She did. It was one of her better ideas."

He pushed aside a lock of hair that slipped down on his forehead. "I see. Well, you may rest assured the children will do no such thing, Mother. If I may beg your indulgence, I would like to speak in private with Lady Audley. I'll share the details with you later."

"Of course." If Mrs. Hillary was offended by Jake's dismissal, she exhibited no outward signs as she bustled from the drawing room.

Once they were alone, Amelia turned back to Jake. "Are you saying Mr. Ettinger can hold up the renovation indefinitely simply based on his brother's opinion?"

"I'm afraid that is the crux of it."

"He is but one man. The board can overrule Mr. Ettinger, can they not?"

"The man's temper is legendary. He will make the board members' lives as unpleasant as possible. No one wishes to cross him."

"What are they, sheep? Do they have blasted wool for brains?"

A corner of his mouth inched up. "I would not be

the least bit surprised to discover this is true. Don't be discouraged, sweetheart. I promise your project will come to fruition."

"But how long must the children be kept waiting?" She sat back and crossed her arms. "Tell me what concerns Sir Davenport has."

"Apparently, he has learned of Lady Kennell's involvement in the project, and he is making a show of disapproval."

"Disapproval? Whatever would give him cause for disapproval? She has made a generous donation. More than he has pledged."

Hooking a finger between his cravat and neck, Jake yanked to loosen the knot and cleared his throat. "Sir Davenport has it in his mind that Lady Kennell is wanton and proposes she intends to exert her influence over the children. He is also fearful his wife's reputation will suffer if it becomes widely known she has joined in a venture with Lady Kennell."

"How preposterous! Bibi has no interest in the children beyond funding a decent place for them to sleep. And Lady Davenport has done nothing worthy to attach her name to the project. What is Sir Davenport thinking?"

"Gentlemen rarely believe themselves required to engage in logical thought when it comes to ladies." He tapped a finger against his head. "You know, wool for brains and all."

His attempt to lighten the situation had little effect. Ire buzzed around in her mind like a thousand bloodthirsty mosquitoes. "What does he propose?"

"It matters not what he thinks."

"Tell me, Jake."

He sighed, his shoulders sinking on the exhale. "He has insinuated the project could move forward if Lady Kennell distances herself."

"She's a silent partner, or was a silent partner. How much more removed could she become?"

Jake frowned and rubbed his forehead. "He has suggested the matter could be put to rest if the project leader distances herself from Lady Kennell as well."

"In other words, he wants me to abandon Bibi, to give her the cut direct." Amelia jumped up from the settee, grabbed her reticule from the side table, and marched for the drawing room door. "Lady Banner is behind this and I won't allow her to win."

Jake caught her by the shoulders before she escaped and turned her around to face him. "Where are you going? We need to discuss this further."

"There is nothing to discuss. I won't do it."

Her bottom lip quivered and she bit down on it. Dreams of building the new wing for the children had kept her sane when she had longed for Jake with a pain so gaping and deep she never thought anything could fill it. How could she abandon everything now? But to betray Bibi...

Jake trailed his fingers along her cheek and over her traitorous lip. "You do not have to choose between Lady Kennell and the children. I will find another solution. I swear it to you, Amelia."

❧

Bibi was toying with the lace curtains draping Amelia's drawing room window when a phaeton carrying Amelia and Mr. Hillary rolled to a stop outside Verona House. Why must the man be Amelia's constant shadow?

Bibi frowned. This afternoon had been allotted to her, and alternating time with Amelia had worked wonders in her ability to get on with Mr. Hillary tolerably well.

She headed toward the foyer to snatch her dear friend from Mr. Hillary's sticky clutches, but skidded to a stop the moment she spotted Amelia's expression.

"Whatever is the matter? You look horrendous."

"I attribute it to my new bonnet." Amelia's grim smile did not lighten Bibi's concern.

"Are you ill?" she asked, stepping forward.

"Simply tired. Will you allow me to bow out of shopping today, dearest?"

Bibi scrutinized Amelia's pale complexion and red-rimmed eyes as Mr. Hillary led her to the drawing room. She trailed close behind.

"Your well-being is more important than Bond Street."

Amelia's butler presented at the drawing room entrance.

"Bring tea," Bibi and Mr. Hillary said at the same time.

"And biscuits," Bibi added to prove her higher level of devotion to Amelia. It was petty, she knew, but she felt bereft in their presence and didn't know where she belonged anymore.

Bradford closed the door behind him as he left the room.

When Amelia lowered to the Grecian couch and said nothing, Bibi looked to Mr. Hillary for answers. "Tell me what has happened."

"The renovation project has met with resistance, but it is not insurmountable."

Amelia offered a halfhearted smile. "Everything will be fine. It may just take some time."

Amelia and Mr. Hillary exchanged a lingering look. Bibi glanced between them, her eyes narrowing. They kept something from her, a secret shared by the two of them. A burning lump formed within her belly, and acid climbed the back of her throat.

"I want to know what it is you both are privy to." Her voice was rising, growing louder. "I'll not be left in the dark."

"Please, have a seat." Mr. Hillary stepped forward and reached for her arm. She jerked away.

"And I will not be herded like a stray lamb." Crossing her arms, she lifted and squared her jaw.

Amelia sighed. "Very well. I will tell you, but you cannot run off half-cocked. We will figure out a solution."

When Amelia nodded toward a chair, Bibi complied with her unspoken request then shot a defiant glare at Mr. Hillary. She wanted to blurt, *See? We have a secret language, too.* The depth of her immaturity hit her, and she lowered her head.

Amelia filled her in on the situation with Mr. Ettinger, the board chairman, and his brother, Sir Davenport. Bibi's fingers gripped the armrests as the account drew to an end.

Amelia's blue eyes flamed and her face hardened. "Sir Davenport's veiled threats will have no bearing on my allegiance."

"And if you refuse, the children's wing will not be built?" The room was closing in on her. This could not be happening. She could not be responsible for spoiling Amelia's dream, but to be all alone again... Holding tight to the anxiety trying to uncoil inside her, she took a deep breath.

"The renovation will be completed," Mr. Hillary said, inserting himself uninvited into their conversation. "I'll find another way."

The pompous man. Always thinking he could come to the rescue.

"You must do as Sir Davenport demands," Bibi blurted.

Red infused Amelia's ivory skin. "I will not. Sir Davenport and the entire foundling board can go hang."

Bibi waved her hand dismissively, but her hand shook. "Do as he asks and get on with the project. Would you deny the children a place to sleep to avoid insult to my person? What do I care what others think?" Her bravado was slipping fast.

"I'm sure you care not one whit," Mr. Hillary said, a soured expression of disapproval transforming his usual handsome face into one she was growing to loathe, "but Amelia would not betray your friendship. She has integrity."

"And I do not." She jumped at a chance to shift her attention from the looming threat of being alone in the world to anger at the man partly responsible for her fate. "Is that your meaning?"

He scoffed. "Is there truly any comparison between the two of you, Lady Kennell? You flaunt your promiscuity like a ship flies her colors. It is no wonder you're a target to sanctimonious boors like Davenport."

"You mean sanctimonious boors like you?" She

bolted from her seat, prepared to do full-out battle since he was willing to engage her. "Perhaps I should be more like *you*, Mr. Hillary, and allow my lovers to compromise me on the table where guests dine."

Amelia gasped, drawing the gentleman's swift attention.

"Mind your tongue," he warned through gritted teeth.

"Or what? You will throttle me? Or worse, subject me to more of your tiresome lectures?" She turned toward Amelia. "This man is churlish beyond the pale."

Amelia rubbed her temples. "Stop it, please."

Bibi couldn't stop herself. She was like a team of runaway horses on a collision course. "If you consent to marry him, you belong in Bedlam."

Mr. Hillary crossed his arms over his chest. "*I'll* be the one sent to Bedlam if I'm forced to endure your company day after day."

She jabbed a finger at him. "I knew you wished to tear us apart. Why don't you speak what is truly on your mind? You want to forbid her from being my friend."

"I said nothing of the sort."

Amelia stood. "Stop bickering. You are both acting like children."

"Go on," Bibi goaded. "Dare to forbid our friendship, Mr. Hillary."

"This is ridiculous," Amelia mumbled and started for the door.

Bibi took a step toward him, every ounce of defiance within her vibrating through her body. "Come now, sir. You know you really want to ban me from your household. So go ahead. Show some ballocks for once."

"Fine!" He threw his arms wide, his face redder

than she had ever seen it. "From the moment Amelia takes my name, she is forbidden from continuing an association with you. No wife of mine will ever foster a friendship with a foul-mouthed wanton with the God-given sense of a chestnut. Is this what you wish to hear?"

The actual words spoken aloud were like a blow, and she stumbled back a step. It wasn't until several moments later that they noticed Amelia had quit the room.

"Oh, hell," Bibi grumbled. "Look what you have done now, Mr. Hillary."

Eighteen

JAKE HAD TOLERATED ALL HE COULD OF LADY KENNELL and her defiance. If anyone needed a keeper, it was that woman. A generous heart did not make up for her lack of good sense. Since their argument in Amelia's drawing room the other day, the viscountess had been badgering Amelia nearly every hour to toss her on Davenport's sacrificial alter.

When he had arrived last evening to escort Amelia to the theatre, her sunken eyes and sallow complexion struck him with the power of a left delivered by Gentleman Jack himself. The entire affair was taking an alarming toll on her. If Lady Kennell would leave well enough alone, Jake would have the renovation matter settled before the end of the night. By introducing the topic of Sir Davenport yet again while she and Amelia had been shopping, the viscountess had stirred the bees' hive. Of course, Jake hadn't helped matters when he had taken the lady to task on the ride and instigated another heated row.

Jake rubbed his temple in an attempt to erase last night's memory. Amelia's expression had been miserable when she had dashed inside the Royal Theatre, leaving him and Lady Kennell in the carriage to tussle like dogs vying for the same bone. It was no wonder Amelia had ended their evening early. He had behaved with a deplorable lack of restraint.

His carriage turned onto Park Street, headed for her town house. If he were fortunate, Amelia would forgive him the lapse in manners and allow him another chance to prove he could accept her dearest friend, though the viscountess tried his patience beyond what any man should have to tolerate. Still seething a bit over Amelia's impertinent companion, Jake climbed from the carriage and marched up the stairs of Verona House. He took a cleansing breath, attempting to set his irritation aside, then knocked on her door with calm assurance.

When there was no evidence of anyone answering his call, his patience began to leach away. Jake raised his fist and pounded on the door. Still, there was no immediate response.

What is taking so bloody long?

His foot tapped an erratic rhythm as he waited.

And waited.

As Jake prepared to hammer on the door, the lock clicked and it drifted open.

The butler's craggy visage greeted him, stern and annoyed. He lifted his nose and sniffed. "*Mr.* Hillary."

His derision fanned Jake's irritation. "I would like an audience with Lady Audley."

Bradford didn't move aside to allow him access. "I am afraid that is impossible. Good day, sir."

Hellfire and damnation! Who was the butler to decide

if Amelia would see Jake or not? "Now see here." Jake stepped forward, sending Bradford scurrying behind the door as if to throw his slight weight against it. "*First* you must take my card to my betrothed before turning me away. I'll wait in the drawing room."

Bradford's eyes rounded and his fingers gripped the door's edge. "Sir, her ladyship is not in residence. I cannot present your card."

Jake scowled. Amelia wasn't one to play coquettish games. She must truly be out this afternoon. "Very well, but when Lady Audley returns, inform her I wish to speak with her."

Bradford nodded, wary relief showing in his eyes. "As you wish, Mr. Hillary." When Jake stepped back, the man seized the opportunity to slam the door in his face.

He growled in frustration. Bradford deserved a thorough thrashing. Thumping his fist against the door once, Jake spun on his heel and returned to the sidewalk.

What now?

He checked his watch. His brother-in-law was meeting him at Brook's in an hour. He supposed he could arrive early and have a brandy. He needed one with the week he was having.

But after tonight, things would turn around for the better, and he had his sister's husband to thank. Forest had been a first-rate scoundrel prior to his marriage to Lana, and while he had abandoned all forms of depravity in favor of Jake's sister, he retained his sly charm. The man was undoubtedly an asset when it came to duping another.

Earlier this morning, Jake and Forest had reviewed the plan they had set into motion several days ago. A scheme that would have Sir Davenport giddy with his desire to support the foundling house renovation, as it would be the lesser of two evils. Forest had flashed a downright wicked smile when he had made that pronouncement, and Jake hadn't questioned his assertion. He figured Forest knew all about the evils that could befall a man.

Jake shook his head. He almost pitied Sir Davenport. It was a shame what became of henpecked gents, but in this instance, Lady Davenport's tyranny gave Jake an edge, and he would show no mercy at the gaming tables tonight.

But first, he had an argument to stage with Forest.

⁓

Jasper wanted nothing more than to wallow in bed all night with the charming Bianca Kennell, but duty beckoned. His close confidant was calling in a favor. Jasper owed Forest for forgiving his gambling debts a time or two over the years, though his friend had lost to him on occasion as well. They mostly considered themselves even, except when Forest required a favor, which was less often now that he had married a certain spirited redhead.

"Come back to bed," Bianca cooed, teasing Jasper when she knew he couldn't comply. Wrapped up in the tangled sheets, her eyelids drifted at half-mast and her black curls lay in disarray against the brilliant white pillow.

A rush of affection flooded through him, and he

leaned to kiss the tip of her turned-up nose. "You are temptation incarnate."

His Bianca proved every bit as lively as Forest's wife was reputed to be. Perhaps that was the secret to a successful union: marry a peppery chit. A smile spread across his lips. Bianca Hainsworth, Lady Norwick. He liked the ring of it.

"Why are you smiling?"

"You please me, B." He kissed her once more then straightened to adjust his waistcoat. Any more lip sampling and he would be back in bed. Then he'd have the devil to pay. "I must go. I promised to meet Forest and Sir Davenport for a rousing game of loo."

Bianca scrambled to a seated position, holding the sheet against her chest in a rare display of modesty. Her dark eyes clouded over. "Are you well acquainted with Sir Davenport?"

"I've never cared much for the man." Jasper curled his top lip as he shrugged on his jacket. "Gads. Davenport allows his wife to lead him around by the nose. Can't stomach a gent with no courage to stand up for—"

He slanted a look at Bianca, heat creeping up his neck and spreading to the tips of his ears. He had allowed his sister to dominate him at one time. That seemed even more pathetic than tolerating a wife's browbeating. Bianca was courteous enough not to mention Fiona. In fact, her thoughts seemed to travel in another direction. At least he hoped her wrinkled brow and severe frown had nothing to do with him.

"Did I say something to make you cross, my dear?" he asked.

"I don't approve of Sir Davenport. I wish you did not entertain an association with him."

Jasper moved back to the bed and perched on the side, the mattress dipping under his weight. "I cannot foresee any further cause for an association beyond tonight. Can you keep a secret?"

She nodded, her mouth still turned down in displeasure.

"Jake Hillary has a score to settle with the man, so he called on Forest to assist. I'm afraid it's a sordid affair, and for that I am sorry, but from all accounts, Davenport deserves any troubles that come his way."

Her frown lines softened and she reached for his hand. A feathery sigh passed through her lips. "Mr. Hillary loves my Amelia so very much, does he not?"

Jasper squeezed her hand. "I suppose he does."

He wanted to tell Bianca he was falling in love with her as well, but the words faded to nothingness before he could speak. She had made him promise to want nothing more from her than physical affection. He had thought it an easy promise to keep at the time.

"I suspected you might have knowledge of Davenport's interference with Lady Audley's foundling project," he said, "but I didn't want to upset you if you were unaware. You understand, I hope."

"Of course." She released his hand and crossed her arms. "Do his accusations trouble you? I admit I cannot boast a sterling reputation, but I would never attempt to corrupt children."

"His accusations?"

"Blast," she muttered, unnecessarily smoothing the wrinkles in the sheets. "I spoke too quickly."

He scowled. "Perhaps you did, but I'm bothered that you would keep something from me. What did Davenport say, and what do you have to do with the halt in the renovation?"

She slapped her hands against the bed, her eyes flaring. "I have nothing to do with anything. *He* is the cause of the project's troubles. I made a donation for the children and wished to remain anonymous, but Sir Davenport learned of my involvement."

Unease rippled through him, raising goose bumps along his skin. "How did he learn of your involvement?"

"How should I know? I've barely spoken more than a word to the gentleman in all the time I have been in society. Yet, he has it on good authority that I am a wicked, wicked woman set on corrupting the children at the foundling house. It's ridiculous, really. Hardly a matter deserving my attention. I told Amelia to do as he demands, give me the cut direct in public, and move forward with the renovation, but she is steadfastly stubborn on the matter."

Jasper's mouth pinched as a slow stream of breath flared his nostrils. *Fiona.* His sister knew of Bianca's involvement in the project. She boasted an intimate association with Lady Davenport. And she despised Bianca with a vigor that defied reason.

"This is my doing," he said through gritted teeth. "I shall repair the damage at once, and I will wring Fiona's skinny neck in the process."

"Your sister cannot be responsible. I would never tell her of my donation and neither would Amelia."

"But I would. I *did*." He clutched his forehead and

groaned. "Good Lord, what is Fiona about these days? I don't recognize her anymore. She has become an unmitigated shrew."

Bianca raised her eyebrows as if disputing his claim that his sister had *become* a shrew, and she was correct. Fiona had been ill-tempered since Father refused to pay Banner her dowry or acknowledge her any longer. But Jasper had made amends once he had inherited, which should have smoothed her ruffled feathers.

"I've had enough of Fiona's foolishness," he said and rose from the bed. "I'm getting to the bottom of her animosity toward you at once."

"No!" Bianca clambered from the bed, tripping when the sheet caught her foot.

Jasper caught her around the waist. "Gads, woman. Don't break your neck."

"Please, don't go to your sister. I'm untroubled by her and you should be too."

He set Bianca away from him, dread churning in his guts. "B, why do you tolerate her mistreatment?"

Reaching for a curl, she tugged and twirled it around her finger. "Lady Banner is of no consequence." She almost sounded nonchalant, but her voice broke and gave her away. "Please, don't waste your time speaking to her on my behalf. I care not if she holds an unfavorable opinion of me."

Jasper studied her. He had heard the rumors about Bianca and Lord Banner, but he knew his brother-in-law well. The man couldn't be trusted to speak an honest word about anything. And his claims that Lady Kennell welcomed him in her bed had rung false. The beauty would never accept the likes of Banner, or so

Jasper had thought. But she had become *his* lover, and he had no more to recommend him than the baron.

"Is it true about you and Lord Banner?"

She released her curl and faced him squarely. "Good Lord! Have you lost your mind? I wouldn't have the revolting mongrel if he was the last man on earth." She spit out the words with vehemence, convincing beyond question.

A flood of relief rushed through his body and released him from his torturous imaginings. He held out his arms. "Come here, darling. I apologize for being an unpardonable fool."

She hesitated before capitulating, but once she was in his arms, she melted against him. "You are not unpardonable," she mumbled into his waistcoat.

He chuckled and drew her closer. "Just a fool then?"

She tipped her head up to gaze at him with unfathomable cocoa eyes. "I shouldn't like to argue with you any further, my lord. I concede you're a fool if you say as much."

"There is my submissive little lover."

Jasper grunted when he received a playful blow to his ribs.

Nineteen

Sir Davenport grinned at Jake. "I suspect you and Lord Andrew have a score to settle after the row I heard about at Brook's."

Jake shrugged and settled back in the crimson cushioned chair, ready to get on with matters.

"If you choose firearms, Lord Andrew will come out the victor," Davenport said, nodding to Forest on his left. "You, Mr. Hillary, excel at fisticuffs, and you are equally matched at blades."

Norwick, seated across from Davenport, sniggered. "They both swing their blades like ladies."

"Don't concern yourself with my *blade*." Jake glared at the earl, playing his role admirably.

Davenport laughed and showed off brown teeth chipped away by age. "True gentlemen allow the cards to settle their differences."

A waiter entered with a tray of tumblers and a decanter.

Davenport turned in his seat. "You may pour a brandy for my companions then leave the decanter on the sideboard."

Forest picked up the deck sitting between him,

and Davenport then absently flipped through the cards. Pushing the deck toward their host, Forest touched his eyebrow to signal to Jake that it was indeed marked.

Forest had been playing cards with Davenport and his marked deck in his private card room at The Den of Iniquity for the past three nights. Jake's brother-in-law had made it clear earlier that he expected to recover his losses tonight. Playing the flat didn't sit well with a gent accustomed to winning.

Fortunately, the odds were in their favor three to one. He, Norwick, and Forest would split the pot at the end of the night. But first they must play with an honest deck.

Davenport shuffled the cards. "Shall we play loo, gentlemen?" Without waiting for consent, he began stacking chips and pushing them to each player. "Thirty chips worth twenty pounds apiece. Or is that too rich for your tastes, Mr. Hillary?"

Jake picked up the stack and tested its weight in his palm. "Make it one hundred pounds a chip and you've sparked my interest."

Davenport's eyes lit like a child's in a sweet shop. "One hundred it is." He glanced at Forest and Norwick. "Gentlemen?"

An insolent smile spread across Forest's face. "I'll gladly pay such a steep price to see Mr. Hillary weep like a baby."

The smug lift of one corner of Davenport's mouth indicated he expected victory. "Lord Norwick, are you in?"

"Nothing would bring me more pleasure, sir."

The earl's cold stare seemed lost on Davenport. "Splendid."

They cut to see who would act as the first dealer. Davenport naturally had the lowest card and earned the honor. "Ante in, gentlemen."

Jake tossed three chips in the middle as did everyone else.

Davenport flicked the cards around the circle with speed and efficiency then turned over the trump card. "Spades it is."

Jake fanned out his cards. Nothing but red. And his highest card was a ten.

"I'll play," Forest said and tossed two more chips into the pot.

"Not me." Norwick laid his cards face down on the table. "I fold."

Jake matched Forest's two hundred pounds and tossed his cards toward Davenport. "Give me a new hand." His new cards were just as useless.

Davenport won two thirds of the pot. Play continued with Davenport taking the majority of the stake the first hour. If one had no knowledge of his cheating, one might be impressed with his intuition. Davenport knew exactly when to fold and when to press the bet.

"Gentlemen, it appears my good fortune is holding out," he said as he raked his winning chips from the middle.

Forest drummed his fingers against the table before snatching up the deck and shuffling. This was Jake's cue to change the game's course.

Pulling at his cravat, Jake bolted from his seat. "I

need another drink." At the sideboard, he looked back over his shoulder. "Would anyone else care for a refill?"

Forest lifted his empty glass in salute.

Jake left the crystal bottle stopper lying on the sideboard and carried the open decanter back to the table. As he neared, he pretended to trip on Davenport's chair leg then unintentionally rammed against the table, losing control of his actions. The brandy sloshed from the decanter, splattered all over the cards, and doused Forest. Jake pressed his lips together to stop the burst of laughter bubbling up in his chest.

"Hell's teeth!" Forest leapt from his chair and ripped a handkerchief from his jacket to blot at the spirits soaking into his waistcoat. "You bloody idiot. Your sister will think I'm foxed."

Sir Davenport slammed his fist against the table. "Forget about your wife. Look at my cards. They're ruined."

"No need to go into hysterics," Norwick said as he reached inside his jacket. "I carry a deck on my person."

Davenport's eyes narrowed when the earl slapped down the deck. "If it's all the same to you, I will call for another from the house."

"What are you implying?" Norwick leaned forward, his head dropped in challenge. "There's nothing wrong with my deck. Only cowards cheat."

Davenport stiffened, his eyes darting to Forest, Jake, and then the exit.

Forest clapped a hand on Davenport's shoulder to push him down in his seat when it appeared he might run. "Davenport's not a coward or a cheat,

Norwick, so let's continue our game. Pass the deck." He took the cards from his friend and held them out to Davenport. "Inspect them to be certain."

He accepted the deck with a frown, rifled through the cards, and then passed them back with a shaky hand. "E-everything appears aboveboard."

"Grand." Jake scooped up the soggy cards and carried them back to the sideboard along with the empty decanter.

When he returned to his place at the table, Forest was dealing the next hand. Jake's chips made a dull clink against the other chips when he threw his ante on the pile.

"Queen of hearts," Forest said when he turned up the top card.

Jake peered at his hand. He had the ace of hearts, jack of hearts, and a spaded knave. He would at least win a third of the pot this hand.

Norwick decided to play the cards dealt and raised the bet by three hundred pounds.

"I'll see your three hundred and raise another two," Jake said.

All of them looked to Davenport. His Adam's apple bobbed. "I-I fold."

Playing it safe became Davenport's strategy, and he folded the next four hands. *Hellfire and damnation.* They could be here all night chipping away at his winnings.

Forest pushed away from the table after a fifth round passed with Davenport folding each hand. "Pardon me, gentlemen, I feel the need to stretch. Sir Davenport requires a moment, too."

He grabbed the man's arm and hauled him from the

chair. Davenport squealed and scrambled to keep his footing. Huddled in the corner, Forest's angry whispers carried across the room. "You led me to believe you're an expert at loo. What are you about?"

Davenport's mumbled response was impossible to decipher.

"Well, get in the game. I want my pound of flesh as promised."

When they were seated once again, the game resumed. Jake didn't bother holding back a grin when he took the entire pot that round.

Davenport's play continued to be conservative, and though he won a portion of the round on occasion, his chips dwindled at a faster rate. When he was left with two chips, he picked them up and rubbed them together. "P-perhaps we should end our evening, gentlemen. My coach will be calling in half an hour."

Jake allowed shock to show in his expression. "Sir Davenport, you've lost close to three thousand pounds this evening. Don't you wish for a chance to win back your blunt?"

Davenport swallowed, his eyes bulging. "Three thousand pounds?" His voice was a hoarse whisper.

Jake pushed all of his chips into the middle. "Play me for my entire winnings. One hand for five thousand pounds."

Forest grunted in disapproval. This wasn't part of his plan, but Jake had his own version to execute. He focused on Davenport.

"But I don't have five thousand pounds to match your bet, Mr. Hillary."

"Perhaps there is something else you can offer."

He leaned forward, his face hard. "My five thousand pounds to your renewed support for the foundling hospital renovation. If I win the hand, you instruct your brother to approve the renovation."

Davenport shook his head. "I can't."

"Very well," Jake said, slouching on the chair. "I'll call on you tomorrow to collect. You do have three thousand pounds at your disposal, do you not?"

Sweat appeared on the man's forehead, and his face flushed pink. "Of course I have the funds. But it may take a while to-to gather that amount."

Jake waved his hand. "Don't worry overmuch about the money."

"Truly, sir?"

"Please, don't give it another thought."

Davenport wilted upon his chair. "Mr. Hillary, you are too kind—"

"I'm certain you have belongings of equal value in the home. Perhaps a piece of Lady Davenport's jewelry. I will require an appraisal, of course, but we shall find a way to settle your debt. I imagine your wife can advise me on which piece she believes is worth the amount you owe. I'll come by when Lady Davenport is receiving callers tomorrow."

"No!" Davenport jumped to his feet. "Please, you cannot intrude on Lady Davenport and her guests."

"Then what do you propose, Sir Davenport?" Forest said. "Mr. Hillary's offer sounds more than generous to me."

"I suppose I could improve upon the offer." Jake looked to his brother-in-law. "How much did you lose to Sir Davenport?"

"Four hundred pounds."

He blinked. "Four hundred? Does Lana know?"

"I intended to recover my losses," Forest said through clenched teeth.

"There's no need to get in a temper." Jake returned his attention to Davenport. "Let's forget about playing another hand. You ensure the renovation is approved, and I'll return two thousand pounds to you. Your wife will never know you almost lost her property."

"Wait one moment," Norwick said. "I'd like to add something to the negotiations."

Jake gestured to the earl. "By all means. Please, say your piece."

"Not only will you make certain the renovation goes forward, you'll escort your wife to a dinner my sister will be hosting in a show of support for the project."

"Lady Banner is hosting a dinner in honor of the renovation?" Forest asked. "I was unaware she held such good intentions."

"As is she," Norwick said.

Davenport shrugged off his jacket. Sweat rolled down his face and soaked into his cravat. "Lady Davenport will be furious if I go back on my word."

Jake raised an eyebrow. "Will she be pleased when I arrive on the morrow to collect her jewelry?"

Davenport shook his head. He looked as if he might burst into tears at any moment.

Forest stood and slapped his back. "Davie here is no henpecked husband, if that's your meaning. He's a man of influence, power. He isn't one to be dominated by the fairer gender. Tell him, Davenport."

The man glanced up at Forest. "N-no. I'm not."

Moving behind his seat, Forest grabbed Davenport's shoulders. "Ol' Davenport is going to march into *his* home and remind *his* lady wife that *he* makes the decisions. No clinging to the skirts for this fellow."

"Yes," Davenport said in a voice growing stronger. "It *is* my house. I won't cling to the lady's skirts."

A mischievous glint in Forest's eye spoke of his devilish side. "Why, Davenport will tell his wife just how it's going to be from now on. She will do *his* bidding, submit to *his* wishes."

"Yes, she will."

"He'll not have it any other way."

Davenport hammered his fist against the table and rose from his chair. "No, I won't. Martha is going to listen to me for once. And by God, she *will* honor her wifely duties, or else."

Forest balked. "After you woo her, of course."

"Well, yes," Davenport agreed, peering at his companion. "I suppose wooing is important?"

"Immensely," Jake said. "You may wish to start with a bath."

Forest sniffed the man and drew back. "Egads." He put distance between him and Davenport. "Brilliant suggestion. Listen to Hillary. And you mustn't forget to compliment Lady Davenport."

"On what?"

"Why, on her hair and eyes. They are her most pleasing features."

Jake nodded. "Bring her flowers at least once a week, then a trinket on anniversaries."

"And be gentle," Norwick said. "No need to rush in like a Norman storming a castle."

Davenport's head swung to each of them as they spoke. "Should I be writing this down?"

"Perhaps," Forest said, unable to hold back a grin.

By the end of the negotiations, Jake had exactly what he wanted. Amelia's project was saved. Forest had his four hundred pounds returned. Norwick acquired Sir Davenport's promise that his wife would attend his sister's dinner. And Lady Davenport was in for more than one surprise. Hopefully, at least one of those would be pleasant.

Jake stood and stretched. It was too late to share the good tidings with Amelia, but early on the morrow he would visit Verona House and bask in her joyful appreciation.

When he reached Hillary House, however, his good mood vanished. Waiting upon his desk was a letter written by Amelia's hand.

My dearest Jake,

   By the time you read this, I will have already left London. I must sort through the complexities present in my life now. While I do not doubt my love for you, I am uncertain if my feelings will be enough to overcome the obstacles that accompany becoming your wife.

   I understand the reasons you dislike Bibi. Yet she has sustained me through the hardest moments of my life. I need her as much as she needs me.

   Following the disagreement outside the theatre, I realized the truth. You will never be able to tolerate Bibi, because she will never allow it. Therefore, our days will be filled with endless arguments and hurt feelings. I cannot continue in this manner.

I wish it could be otherwise, that you and Bibi could respect each other even if you cannot foster a fondness for one another. But I fear it will never come to pass. This is my dilemma. How do I choose between you when you both hold equal value in my heart? Do I choose a husband, a father for the children I so desire, my lover, or do I choose undying loyalty and a friendship that has brought me much happiness? I have no answers, so I must seek them away from both of you.

Please respect my need to be alone. I will contact you when I have reached a conclusion.

Yours truly,
Amelia

"No." Jake threw down the offensive letter. She couldn't do this to him. She couldn't deny him the chance to prove himself. He wouldn't allow it.

The sky hinted at a sunny day as he stalked from Hillary House to find the steed he had ordered readied for him. Amelia's childhood home, the estate left to her by her father, was a short distance from Town. She had to be at Merrimont, because she had nowhere else to go. In less than two hours, he would plead his case before her. She would see she had judged him wrongly. And Amelia would know whomever she loved, Jake would also make room for in his heart.

Twenty

WARMTH ENVELOPED AMELIA AS SHE SLIPPED OUTSIDE into the twilight. She breathed in the earthy, country air. Fireflies danced on the breeze, beckoning her to join in their merriment, but her heart was too heavy for celebration.

After two days with nothing to do besides ruminate on her troubles, she hadn't sorted out anything. How to save the renovation project. What to do with Bibi.

And then there was Jake to consider.

Amelia missed him with a wretched hunger that made her dream of him at night, to reach out for him in a drowsy haze only to remember moments later where she was. The Audley family home, occupied by the current Marquess of Audley, his wife, and Amelia's precious niece and nephews, couldn't compare to being with Jake.

How would she ever let him go? She didn't know if she could any more than she could give up Bibi. There was, however, something she needed to release.

Her husband had been dead for over two years, but his hurtful words and disdain lived on in her mind, casting shadows over her ability to judge the sincerity of others. Part of her feared his lasting influence might be driving her to push Jake away, and she refused to allow Audley to hold power over her.

She headed for the cemetery where she would leave her bad memories at his grave, as she should have done long ago. The family plot rested a little ways from the house. Earlier she had stood at the garden's edge and watched the shadows move across the graveyard. The larger stones had served as unintended sundials, reminding her of the precious hours she had wasted on him.

A sugary, sweet scent filled the air, courtesy of the white moonflowers spreading their petals under the approaching night. Reaching the garden's outer boundaries, she picked her way down the gentle incline toward her husband's fenced resting ground and that of his predecessors.

Crickets chirped and blended to create a strident, yet soothing, whir in the air. At various intervals, a deep-throated frog croak punctuated the night, a soloist in nature's symphony. A breeze brushed her cheeks, expanding the branches of the ancient oak standing sentry by the entrance, the swish of leaves eerily like whispers. The iron gate groaned but swung inward with ease.

Amelia hadn't been allowed to see her husband after the accident. It seemed as if he lived on, hunting the land he had favored over her. She wondered if it was difficult for Thomas Audley to believe his brother was gone, too. If not for Lord Henley witnessing the fire, Thomas would have been unable to identify his brother. Did it seem as if he had buried a stranger?

She took a tentative step, careful with her footing on the sloping ground. Audley's resting spot lay on the edges of the cemetery, closer to the house. She weaved through the tombstones toward his grave. The cemetery's desolation seemed both peculiar and fitting. Close to a hundred spent souls lay all around her. Yet, there was no sensation of anyone dwelling there. Perhaps this wouldn't fulfill her needs after all.

Her husband's simple, arched stone stood in contrast to the ostentatious monuments, avenging angels, and towering crosses. Audley's understated marker acted as testament to his eye for refined detail and high quality. As his spouse, Amelia had owed him authenticity at least.

She walked over to his gravestone to run her hands along the rougher edges before skimming her palms along the smooth surface. Her finger traced the etching of his name, the letters' deep grooves within the impenetrable stone.

She hadn't cried when she had learned of Audley's accident. She hadn't cried when he was buried. For weeks, she had tried to evoke any fond memories or feelings to foster some show of emotion, but she had few of either in relation to her marriage. She had castigated herself for shedding no tears for her husband. A steadfast wife should feel something when losing her spouse, but she hadn't. And she didn't now, either.

But what if it had been Jake? There was a sharp pinch in her chest. She pressed her hand over her heart to subdue the panic welling up inside her. Closing her eyes, she took a slow, deep breath. It wasn't Jake. He was alive in London, perhaps frantic over her absence.

Her eyes flew open again in realization. *This* was her answer, this feeling deep inside her heart. Her body had been speaking the truth for days, but she had foolishly relied on her thoughts, believing logic had anything to do with love.

She no longer had anything to say to Audley and turned away from him forever. She was going home.

❧

Amelia hadn't been residing at her country home. The servants were unable to shed any definitive light into where she may be staying. The housekeeper had speculated she might be in Yorkshire visiting an elderly aunt and distant cousins, but it was too far to travel without some guarantee Jake would find her at the end of the journey.

Upon his return to London, he set off for Kennell Place directly from the mews. After hours in the saddle, he welcomed a brisk stroll. If Lady Kennell knew of Amelia's whereabouts, he must convince her to tell him.

As he hurried along the walkway, the occasional yipping of a pampered canine sounded from the houses he passed. The playful laughter of children wafted on the air. Carriages drove by carrying well-dressed ladies on their way to make calls. Everyone went about their daily tasks with no sense of how bleak London had become without Amelia.

He noted a phaeton resting in the circular drive as he neared the viscountess's residence. The carriage's red wheel was visible through the manicured hedges beyond the iron fence enclosing Kennell House. A groom spoke of his Sunday plans, presumably to the horses since his conversation appeared to be one-sided.

What a bloody nuisance to find Lady Kennell entertaining when Jake needed to speak with her. He debated approaching the mansion, but chose to wait outside the gate until her guests left. Leaning against a stone pillar flanking the gate, he wiped perspiration from his forehead with a handkerchief.

He never paid calls himself, seeing as how the activity was within the domain of ladies mostly. He imagined visits as long, drawn-out affairs. After all, his sister could be long-winded once she warmed up to a topic.

Jake settled in, wishing he had something to help pass the time, but no sooner had he returned his handkerchief to his pocket than a feminine giggle floated on the air. Peering around the pillar to see which lady called upon the viscountess, he discovered it was no lady paying a call.

The Earl of Norwick peeled off Lady Kennell's glove, leaned over her hand, and lavished it with kisses that made Jake blush on the earl's behalf. Norwick behaved like a besotted fool. Jake could only imagine the gent would suffer a broken heart in the end.

He ducked behind the hawthorn hedge before they spied him. Lady Kennell's yellow skirts provided patches of color just on the other side of the greenery.

"Don't collect me late for the Pennyworth ball tonight," Lady Kennell said.

"Never."

The carriage groaned as Norwick climbed to the seat.

Jake pressed his back against the iron fence as a footman allowed the phaeton to pass through the gate before closing it again. Once Norwick's carriage disappeared down the cobbled street, and Jake guessed the servant had gone inside, he entered the property. The well-oiled gate swung open, and he stalked across the drive. He lifted his fist to knock, but the door flew open and two heated, brown eyes pierced him.

"What, pray tell, are you doing lurking outside, Mr. Hillary?" Lady Kennell's hands landed on her hips. "I suppose you are here to apologize for the other night. Well, be quick about it. I have much to do."

"You wish *me* to apologize? You haven't exactly been above reproach."

"Oh, do be quiet." She blew the hair from her forehead. "I have no patience for your foolishness. Follow me."

Jake held his ire in check. Arguing with Lady Kennell was the cause of his troubles to begin with and would solve nothing.

The viscountess whirled around and marched across the foyer. For a small woman, she moved quickly. Jake scrambled to catch up, uncertain as to the reason he allowed a woman less than half his size to order him around as if he were a wayward child.

"I'm seeking Lady Audley," he said.

"Try Verona House."

"She left London yesterday."

Lady Kennell stopped without warning, causing Jake to ram into her. He grabbed her shoulders to steady her before she fell to the floor. Once she had regained her balance, he realized he was touching her person and dropped his hands to his sides.

"My apologies, Lady Kennell."

Instead of yelling as he expected, she looked over her shoulder with a slight smile. "My, but you are a clumsy one. I suppose Amelia finds this quality endearing, but I'm afraid I would grow tired of doctoring your cuts and bumps and listening to your apologies."

Jake ducked his head. Really, how did one respond to such frankness?

Her frosty demeanor returned. "Did you say Amelia has left London?"

"I received a letter from her saying as much. Yesterday her butler refused to admit me, stating Amelia was not in residence. I rode to Merrimont, but she wasn't there either."

"She rarely returns to that horrible place. It holds nothing but bad memories."

Jake nodded, at once aware that Lady Kennell was more sensitive to Amelia's feelings than he was. He hadn't considered that the home where she had lost her mother at so young an age might be the last place she would go. "Could she be in Yorkshire?"

"No." A small crease formed between her brows. "Follow me to the rose drawing room, Mr. Hillary, but do keep your distance this time."

Lady Kennell floated along the corridor and disappeared through a doorway. Jake took care to leave adequate space between them this time in case she had a notion to halt abruptly again. Entering the room behind her, he paused. Everything delicate and breakable known to man filled the room. He feared breathing.

She gestured to a pink chair more suited for a chit than a man. "Please, have a seat."

The viscountess knew how to emasculate a gent,

but he'd had enough of her high-handed ways. Selecting a chair that fit him better, he sank into it. "Do you know of my fiancée's whereabouts or not?"

Lady Kennell shook her head. "I'm afraid I had no knowledge of her departure much less her destination." She paused, her dark eyes boring into him. "For heaven's sake. Where were you, Mr. Hillary?"

Jake started, caught unawares by her shift in topic. "I was outside your gate—"

"Not *now*. Really, sir, you try my patience." Lady Kennell crossed her arms. "Where were you all those months when Amelia ached for you?"

His whereabouts were none of Lady Kennell's concern; at least this would have been his stance as of yesterday. But he recognized the anxious concern written in the lines of her face. He and Lady Kennell had at least one thing in common.

"We both love her, my lady. Must we fight over which of us possesses the stronger sentiments?"

"You *behave* as if you love her now, but how can I be certain of your constancy?" Lady Kennell paused, her eyes downcast. "I cannot watch her hurting again, Mr. Hillary. I think my heart shall rip in half."

She appeared as a lost child in that moment. Jake wanted to reach out and hold her hand for reassurance. Instead, he chose to trust her as Amelia placed her faith in her. To love every aspect of Amelia meant accepting Lady Kennell and hope she would accept him in return.

"I never intended to hurt Amelia. I've always wanted to marry her, but certain forces conspired to keep us apart." He shared with her about his mother's illness and the measures his father had taken to keep it hidden.

Lady Kennell listened, her expression unreadable throughout the telling of his story. At the conclusion, she rose from her seat and walked to the sideboard. "Perhaps you would care for a drink, Mr. Hillary?"

He accepted her peace offering, for that was how he chose to view her invitation. It might require many instances of creatively seeking the positive in Lady Kennell's actions and biting his tongue to forge an amiable association with her, but this was what he must do to make Amelia happy.

With drinks in hand, she carried one to Jake. He accepted the goblet and sipped the bitter concoction while Lady Kennell returned to her chair.

"Please, if you know where she might be, reveal her whereabouts," he said. "You must realize I truly love her."

Lady Kennell glanced away. "Indeed, Mr. Hillary," she murmured. "And I've never believed a man capable of love."

Twenty-one

AMELIA HELD HER BREATH AS HER NIECE AND NEPHEW teetered atop that atrocious bull her husband's family erroneously referred to as a dog. "Oh, do be careful."

Her sister-in-law laughed at the children's antics. "You mustn't worry so. Rachel and Paul take a good spill at least once a day. Children are resilient."

Amelia and Louisa sat on a blanket the servants had spread for their picnic. The newest addition to the Audley family lay between them. Baby Howie's attempts to swallow his foot failed to ruffle Louisa any more than her older children cavorting with a dangerous beast. But Louisa's nonchalance did nothing to reassure Amelia.

What if the horrid animal gobbled up the children? The mastiff turned his head to stare at her as if he knew her thoughts were on him. A shiver raced down her back.

While her niece and nephew had provided a pleasant diversion during her sojourn to the country—when their actions couldn't lead to their dismemberment—Amelia was anxious to return to

London. Unfortunately, when she had raised the topic over dinner last night, Louisa had insisted she remain at Crossing Meadows at least until the end of the week. It hadn't helped matters that Rachel and Paul had pleaded with her to stay when she paid a call to the nursery earlier that morning to say good-bye.

Louisa waved her fan with a lazy flick of her wrist. "Rachel, stop tugging Alistair's ears, love."

The dog appeared to smile at the sound of his name, quivering strings of slobber dripping from his jowls. Amelia wrinkled her nose and looked away. She wasn't envious of the children's nurse. Her niece and nephew would require a good scrubbing once they returned to the house.

Baby Howie's cooing drew her attention, and she looked down at his plump, sweet face. His blue eyes brightened when he flashed a toothless grin, and his arms and legs windmilled in a frantic burst of excited screeching.

Amelia offered her finger and his chubby hand closed around it. "Howie, you've stolen my heart."

"Careful or he might steal the ring from your finger." Louisa sat up straight and shaded her eyes. "Someone is coming up the lane."

Amelia glanced over her shoulder at the dust cloud slowly rising above the trees lining the winding lane. "Had I known you were expecting a guest, I would have insisted on leaving today. I don't wish to impose."

"You are not an imposition, Amelia." Louisa's mouth pinched slightly as she pushed to her feet. "Thomas failed to mention he was expecting anyone. Sadly, I expect we are in for a dry evening of political commentary. Come along, children. We have a guest."

Amelia took in the children's bedraggled appearance and questioned Louisa's judgment, but since Amelia was no longer the lady of the house, she held her tongue. She gathered the baby against her chest before his nurse could claim him and rose from the blanket.

Rachel and Paul slid from the dog's back while clamping his fur in both fists. Alistair uttered no complaint but exacted his revenge when he barreled past the children and knocked Rachel to the ground.

"Oh, dear," Amelia muttered.

Her niece pushed herself up and ran after her brother. Amelia could drive herself to an early grave worrying about these children.

As she reached the drive, the travel coach turned onto the lane leading to Crossing Meadows. It navigated the circle drive and rolled to a stop in front of the house. No markings on the door indicated who the guest might be. A coachman alighted to open the door, and a black boot emerged. Her breath caught when Jake stepped out into the sunlight.

She hugged the baby closer as her stomach knotted. Whatever was he doing at Crossing Meadows, and how had he found her?

Jake's head swung around until his gaze landed on her; his dark brows sank low over his intense, green eyes. They were always greener when he was in a passion. He held up a folded sheet of foolscap. "Amelia, what is the meaning of this?"

He took one stride toward her, but Alistair jumped

between them and issued a deep-throated growl. The hair along the beast's back stood on end, and his muscles tensed as he crouched low.

The air around Amelia vanished. She couldn't breathe.

Alistair paused for one still moment where she hoped she misread his intentions before he sprang through the air. His front paws struck Jake's chest and knocked him to the dusty drive.

Louisa screamed, the veins standing out on her forehead.

The animal's ragged jaws went for Jake's throat, but his arm shot out in time to absorb the blow. The mastiff sank his teeth into Jake's arm and shook him as if he were a child instead of a man.

"Stop him!" Amelia's shout startled Baby Howie and sent him into a high-pitched wail that jagged its way through her frazzled nerves.

The nurse rushed forward to take the baby from her arms.

Amelia looked desperately to Louisa. "He's killing him!"

"Alistair!" Amelia's brother-in-law dashed from the house, shouting nonsense as he raced down the stairs. "*Zuructreten! Zuructreten!*"

The beast released Jake and withdrew to Thomas's side as his master reached the drive. Sitting on his haunches, Alistair offered another slobbering grin as if attacking a guest was all in jolly good fun.

"Jake!" Amelia hurried to his side and dropped to her knees. She stroked his forehead, pushing aside the dampened hair from his eyes. "Dear heavens, are you injured?"

He stared up at her, unblinking, his complexion chalky. "Please, say something."

Jake sucked in a deep breath then met her gaze. "Amelia? *That* dog speaks German."

A sobbing laugh burst from her chest, and she bent forward, almost kissing him before remembering they weren't alone. She jerked her hand away from his face and rocked back on her heels. "Yes, well. It appears you haven't suffered any lasting damage, Mr. Hillary."

Jake pushed up to his elbow and examined his torn sleeve. "Gads, this is a new jacket."

Amelia's hands landed on her hips. "You are mauled by a great beast and your concern is for your jacket. Whatever is the matter with you?"

Thomas stepped forward and helped her to her feet. Louisa and the children had already been rushed inside. "My apologies, Hillary. We keep Alistair penned when we expect visitors."

"Yes, well, I should have sent word." Jake stood and dusted off his clothes, casting a distrustful glance at the dog panting at Thomas's feet. "If I might have a moment of Lady Audley's time. The first Lady Audley, that is. Well, not the *first* obviously—"

He sighed and rubbed his temple. "Perhaps I hit my head for I cannot express exactly what I mean. Just one moment of privacy, please, my lord, and then we shall be on our way back to London."

We? Surely Jake didn't include her in his travel party without consulting her first.

Thomas smiled, affable as always. "You may have an audience with Amelia in the yellow drawing room, but I'm afraid we cannot allow you to leave Crossing

Meadows so soon. You must remain as our guest, at least until the morrow."

"That is kind of you, Audley, but my betrothed and I don't wish to overtax your hospitality."

Amelia flinched.

"Betrothed?" Thomas's brows shot to his hairline.

A flash of heat licked up her neck and into her cheeks, and she averted her gaze. She couldn't say the reason she had kept her betrothal a secret from Thomas and Louisa. They had been encouraging her in that arena for some time, claiming she was too young to remain a widow. Yet, she was concerned as to how they might interpret her choice to move forward with her life.

When she didn't answer Thomas, he stepped forward and clapped Jake on the back. "Well done, Hillary. I believe you may have come out the victor in the arrangement."

Jake accepted the marquess's congratulations with a good-natured laugh. "We are of like mind. I shall strive to deserve her good favor."

His twinkling hazel eyes and smile cooled her temper by a degree.

Amelia's touch was light on Jake's forearm. "Come inside so I may examine your arm."

"You may use the yellow drawing room if you like," Thomas said. "Clive will provide whatever you require to tend Mr. Hillary." He snapped his fingers at the dog. "Alistair, *kommen*."

The animal bounded behind him as he sauntered around the side of the house.

Jake offered his uninjured arm and smiled when

Amelia slanted her head to meet his gaze. "You didn't sic the dog on me, did you, Mia?"

"Of course I didn't."

They climbed the stairs arm in arm and entered the double-hung front doors.

"I wouldn't blame you if you did," he said, "not after the way I behaved."

She pressed her lips together as if in contemplation, but more so to hold back a grin. "Excellent argument, Mr. Hillary. Shall I have Thomas bring the beast back to finish you off?"

Jake chuckled. "Please don't, sweetheart. At least until I have been given a chance to speak with you."

"Very well. This way to the drawing room." Amelia called out instructions to the butler as they passed him in the foyer. "Have a bath drawn for Mr. Hillary."

Jake trailed behind Amelia as they crossed the foyer. She glanced over her shoulder and caught him in the act of sniffing himself. He dropped his arm quickly when he realized she was watching. A splash of red colored his cheeks. "You ordered a bath for me?"

She bit back a smile. "To protect against infection. If that beast has broken your skin, you must cleanse it thoroughly with lye soap."

"Lye!"

"I'll hear no arguments, Mr. Hillary."

Dutifully, he ceased his complaints and followed her through a set of double doors. "Good Lord! What happened in here?"

Amelia squinted as she took in the lemon yellow paint covering the drawing room walls. The color spilled over onto the furnishings and carpet. "Be grateful Thomas didn't suggest the green drawing room. The color reminds me of something unpleasant the baby sometimes produces."

She laughed when Jake's lip curled in disgust. Leading him to the settee, she urged him to sit then sat next to him. "I cannot examine your arm unless you remove your jacket."

"Oh, yes, I suppose." He shrugged out of his garment, revealing a rip in his shirt sleeve as well.

Amelia rolled his sleeve up to his elbow. She twisted his arm gently to view the puncture marks then rubbed away a dirt smudge with her thumb. Touching him sent tingles from her fingertips to her toes.

"Alistair didn't draw blood, thank goodness. Still, you should clean the area well to ensure you do not catch some horrible illness from him."

Jake shuddered. "Is drooling contagious?"

"I hope not." Amelia grinned, removed her gloves, and placed them on a low table in front of the settee. "No one in polite society would tolerate such deplorable manners."

"Amelia, please come home." He captured her hand and held the back of it against his lips. Her pulse skipped like a leaf caught in a gust of wind. "Lady Kennell and I have reached an understanding. I give my word that I shall never argue with her again."

She pulled her hand free; a slight frown wrinkled her brow. "You shouldn't make promises you can't keep. I am not blind to Bibi's ability to incite others to anger. She tries my patience on occasion, too. All I ask is that you try to see the good in her, because it's there."

"I know it is." He reached for her hand again,

gently pressing the pad of his thumb into her palm and restarting the fast tempo of her heart and breath. "I shall make every attempt to live peacefully with her. The lady is loyal to you, Amelia. I can find no fault with this quality."

"What do you mean?"

"Lady Kennell realizes how much I love you, and she urged me to come for you."

Amelia rolled her eyes. "Now I know you never spoke with her. Bibi would never say anything of the sort."

His fingers threaded with hers. His gaze was intense and unfaltering. "Because she doesn't believe men are capable of love?"

A soft gasp sounded at the back of her throat.

Jake leaned forward and brushed a strand of hair from her cheek. His gentleness made her tremble with suppressed emotion. "Please, Amelia, allow me another chance to prove my devotion. Upon my honor, I will not disappoint you again."

For a fleeting moment when his mouth skimmed over hers, seeking her permission, she wondered if she was surrendering too easily. But forgiveness was too sweet a dish to pass up, and faith in the one she loved, divine.

"Yes," she whispered against his lips. "Take me home."

"I wish to take you here." Jake's arms shot around her waist and lifted her onto his lap. A small cry passed her lips.

"What if someone discovers us?"

"No one will." His rough voice made her insides quiver. Would he truly make love to her here?

He adjusted her so she straddled his thighs then plundered her mouth. His hands slid up her waist and molded to her breasts, his thumbs rubbing circles over her nipples. A strong pull between her legs made her gasp.

Any concerns about possible discovery leached away as his lips played with hers. Amelia resettled herself, making contact with his already hard shaft. She drew back. "Were you thinking of tumbling me *before* I even forgave you?"

An unrepentant smile spread across his face. "I'm sorry, sweetheart, but I can think of little else most of the time."

His grin was infectious, the crinkling around his eyes endearing, and the obvious pleasure he took in her warmed her heart. "I suppose I can make certain allowances this once."

She eased her arms around his neck and leaned forward to kiss him, but a scratch at the door sent her scrambling for the far end of the settee.

She fluffed her skirts and folded her hands. "Come in."

Jake groaned, snagged a pillow, and plopped it on his lap. The butler entered and offered a slight bow to him. "Sir, your bath awaits you."

"Splendid," Jake grumbled under his breath.

⤜⤛

Jake sat up tall in the tub when the dressing room door clicked behind him.

"Damnation! What is it now?" This was the third interruption since he'd climbed into the warm water. The boy assigned to serve him during his stay at Crossing

Meadows had officially become a nuisance. Jake twisted at the waist, ready to take the young servant to task, but his angry words died away. "Amelia."

She tightened the belt of her wrapper and moved toward the tub, revealing a flash of inner thigh as the garment parted. "How is the water? Is it warm enough?"

It would be boiling once he had her in the tub with him. His shaft gave an excited jerk. "The water is adequate. What are you doing here?"

"I came to see if you are using the lye soap."

His eyes darted to the untouched bar resting in a dish on the wash stand.

"I knew it," she said with a smile and withdrew a pale, yellow bar from her pocket. "I decided my edict was too harsh, so I brought a bar of chamomile."

He sank down in the water and rested his head against the rim. "Oh. Is that all?"

Amelia knelt beside the tub and picked up the cloth draped over the side. "I also decided if I allow the use of chamomile, your wound will need extra attention." She dipped the soap in the water, lathered the cloth, and touched it to his arm.

His heart launched into his throat as she circled the cloth over his minor cut, something he could have done for himself. "My arm isn't my only part that would like extra attention."

"Then I shan't leave any part of you feeling neglected." A sensual smile eased across her lips as she swept the cloth slowly up his arm and across his chest before heading lower. As she leaned over the porcelain side, her wrapper gaped open, revealing a smooth strip of her bosom. He sucked in a sharp breath when she touched his shaft and ran the cloth along the length of him and back.

He closed his eyes while she stroked him. "I—" His voice came out gravelly, and he cleared his throat. "I should warn you, the whelp assigned to assist me has a habit of entering without advance notice."

"I turned the lock. He won't be disturbing us." She smoothed the cloth over Jake's abdomen and inner thighs.

He cracked one eye open. A pink flush colored her neck and cheeks, and the robe flapped open to her waist. He traced the underside of her breast with his wet finger and followed the path of a water droplet with his gaze as it slid down. "If anyone saw you like this in the corridor, I would have to thrash him."

"The chamber adjoining yours is vacant. No one saw me."

"How clever." Slipping his hands inside her wrapper, he pushed the silk off her shoulders. As she pulled her arms from the sleeves, the robe dropped from her body in a shimmering cascade but caught at her waist and hung there. "Release the belt so I may see all of you."

She draped the cloth over the side of the tub, stood, and untied the sash. The garment slid to the floor, revealing the perfect curve of her hips and slender waist. Her pale pink nipples had hardened, and she absently brushed across one as she reached to smooth a strand of hair behind her ear.

"Beautiful," he murmured.

Instinctively, he gripped his shaft and ran his hand over it to ease the ache. Amelia's lips parted on a soft gasp, and her eyes grew round. He let go of himself, a wash of heat spreading up his face.

"Forgive me. I forgot myself."

"No," she said on a breath. Pink infused her cheeks and her lashes fluttered, but soon she met his gaze again. "I like it."

A wide grin spread across his mouth. He loved that there were pleasures yet unknown to her, and that he would be the one to introduce her.

As he ran his fingers up and down his arousal, he couldn't tear his gaze away from her. Her eyes became a night sky, her lips swollen and irresistible. "Touch yourself, Mia."

She crossed her arms over her breasts and looked away. *Perhaps another day.* He held out his hand. "Then come here so I may touch you."

Her fingers overlapped his, and he curled his to create a link, urging her closer. She shuffled forward until her thighs bumped against the tub. "But there's no room for me."

"I'll make room." He pulled her into the tub so that she straddled his chest. Amelia braced her elbows on the tub's sides as he cupped her bottom and urged her closer to his mouth. With one hand, he parted her curls and flicked his tongue across her glistening skin.

Her breath caught in a hitch. He glanced up to gauge her reaction. Her eyes drifted at half-mast as he caressed between her legs. "Is it all right if I kiss you here?"

"Yes," she whispered. When he placed his mouth on the most intimate spot a man could kiss a woman, her fingers slid into his hair and drew circles on his scalp. He lovingly stroked his tongue over her, igniting a tremor in her legs. Each pass elicited more violent quivers, and she struggled to hold on to the edges of the tub.

When he pulled back, she whimpered. "Let's move to the bed. Then I'll kiss you more."

A jagged breath tore through her before she climbed from the tub. Jake hauled himself to his feet and stepped from his bath while she retrieved a towel, but instead of handing it to him she rubbed it over his chest and abdomen. She bent over and dried each leg before pausing at his erection. Her deep blue eyes lifted and locked with his. His stomach tightened as he waited to see what she would do. Slowly, she leaned forward and placed a kiss on the tip of his shaft.

He drew in a sharp breath, whistling softly. Triumph lit her face and an enticing smile eased across her lips. Holding his gaze, she lowered to her knees and circled her fingers around him. She kissed him again then touched her tongue to his scalding flesh. Jake jerked in her hold. Emboldened by his reaction, she licked him with long strokes as she would an Italian ice. She swirled her tongue around his shaft and nibbled until he couldn't take the exquisite torture any longer.

"Hold me in your mouth," he pleaded.

Amelia looked up at him, her lips forming an O.

Jake released a tense chuckle, more like a strangled breath, and smoothed a hand over her head. "It's all right, sweetheart. You don't have to—"

"I want to kiss you here like you did for me." Her sweet lips closed gingerly around him, so loving, simply cradling him with her tongue. She raised her eyes, seeking reassurance.

"Yes, that's perfect, my love." He gently clasped

her head, her soft hair twining around his fingers, and guided her movements. Her heat engulfed him, and he closed his eyes, existing only in this moment and in the heavenly sensations she created within him. Every touch was reverent, the sweep of her tongue adoring. Never had he been loved or loved another so deeply.

"Mia," he said softly, emotion making his voice shaky.

She withdrew from him and looked up, her eyes overcast and shaded by desire. Jake captured her hands, helped her stand, then led her to the bedchamber. Once Amelia reclined on the bed, he settled between her thighs to show her the same adoration she had lavished on him. Her sighs became more pronounced and came more frequently as he loved her with his mouth, his tongue circling her hardened pearl.

She tensed and pushed against his head when an especially strong tremor raced through her. Her eyes were wide and uncertain.

He placed a gentle kiss on her thigh. "Allow me to complete you." He massaged her legs until she lay back and sank into the bedding. Her fingers curled into the covers when he touched his mouth to her again. She surrendered to his ministrations, trusting him to undo her, opening herself up to vulnerability. Her breath came in shallow gasps, and she gripped the counterpane. A barely audible cry fell from her lips as she neared her peak. Jake carried her over the edge. Louder, more heartfelt sounds broke from her as shudders wracked her body over and over. As all tension left her and she dissolved against the bed, he simply watched her, his blood pounding through his vessels. Her chest rose and fell heavily, the dips slowing as she recovered.

Unable to wait any longer, he kissed his way up her stomach and chest then entered her. His lips met hers as Amelia rocked her hips to counter his thrust, making him smile against her mouth. He brushed the hair away from her eyes and drove into her again. With each push, she moved with him, following his pace. Her hands traveled his back and brushed his buttocks. Cupping him, she pulled him closer until he couldn't go any deeper then possessed his mouth. He kissed her back with the same fervor.

Good God, she aroused him like no other and shattered his control. Desperate, he pumped into her fast and hard until he hovered on the edge of splintering into a thousand fragments, every part of him madly in love with her. She held on tightly as he climaxed, her legs hugging his waist. Her embrace was warm and welcoming; he wanted to stay this way with her forever. His heart battered against his ribs, slowing by minuscule degrees.

Burying his face in her hair, he breathed in her scent. The strands tickled his cheeks and nose, but he still held on. He caressed her side down to her hip and back again in languid movements. Her skin was as soft as rose petals.

"I love everything about you," he whispered in her ear.

She smiled against his cheek before she kissed him. "I love everything about you, too."

Twenty-two

AMELIA HAD BEEN UNABLE TO CONTAIN HERSELF WHEN Jake had told her the renovation had been approved by the board. Yet, it was learning of Lady Banner's desire to host a dinner in a show of support for the project, along with an invitation for Bibi to attend the affair, that nearly caused Amelia to faint.

She still had no real notion as to how Jake and Lord Norwick managed to right everything, but she chose to leave the matter unexplored after a vague mention of loo and the power of persuasion.

Bibi clutched Amelia's hand as the landau carried them to Lady Banner's town house. Jake had suggested she and Bibi might enjoy some time alone and planned to meet her at the dinner. Bibi and Jake had gotten on splendidly ever since he and Amelia had returned to London.

Amelia patted Bibi's arm. "You have no cause for worry, my dear. I won't leave your side even for a moment unless you bid me to do so."

Bibi's worry lines softened. "Amelia, I cannot thank you enough. That troll is more than I can stomach."

"Lady Banner is serving troll *again*?"

Bibi's peal of laughter warmed Amelia's insides. "Oh, Amelia. She is worse than beastly, is she not? What *is* worse than beastly? The devil's spawn?"

Amelia squeezed her hand. "We mustn't attend if you would rather not. I could feign a sudden illness."

"No," Bibi said on a sigh. "Unfortunately, I'm fond of the devil's kin. I promised Norwick I would attend this evening."

"Lord Norwick is a different sort."

Bibi extracted her hand from Amelia's hold. "Do not judge him. He's a kind gentleman."

"I'm not judging him. I am acknowledging how different he is from his sister."

When Bibi didn't respond, Amelia frowned. "I'm surprised you have maintained an association with him when you've proclaimed no desire to settle with one gentleman."

"So you judge *me*. How charming." Bibi turned her face toward the window. "I'll have you know I—" She swung around and jabbed a raised finger Amelia's direction. "*You* have no faith in me, do you?"

Easing back against the squabs, Amelia offered an apologetic smile. "I have nothing but the deepest affection for you and applaud your change of heart. I never thought you would alter your position on love."

"I haven't!" Bibi's hands fluttered to her hair to smooth her perfect coiffure. "Don't be a ninny. Love is for fools…" Her voice trailed off and she looked out the window again.

Refusing to allow her friend to hide her true feelings, Amelia moved to the seat across from her, spying

Bibi's wide smile before she tried to hide it behind her fan.

"You *have* changed your mind," Amelia said. "Admit it."

Bibi laughed. "No, I haven't. Leave me be."

Amelia leaned across the carriage and captured Bibi's wrists, pulling the fan away from her face. Her friend boasted a happy glow. "You are in love with Norwick, aren't you?"

"Oh, Amelia. I don't know." Her luminous eyes spoke of her sentiments. "Jasper is hopelessly clumsy in polite society, and he's not handsome like the gents I typically like. He dresses a mess and needs reminders not to overindulge at meals, but he is… *kind*."

A tremor shook Bibi's petite frame, and she squeezed her eyes closed. A beatific smile spread across her lips. "Jasper cares about pleasing me. He treats me like a precious possession." When she opened her eyes again, they sparkled. "I think I *may* love him. Does that make me mad?"

Amelia moved back to the spot beside Bibi and gathered her in a hug. "You're not mad, dearest, and I'm happy for you."

The carriage rolled to a stop at Lord and Lady Banner's town house.

"Are you certain you wish to go inside?" Amelia asked.

Bibi nodded. "I have no choice really."

Amelia smiled and followed her friend.

Lady Banner's face pinched when they entered the drawing room, and she didn't approach to receive them. Her husband performed the honors in her stead.

"Why, Lady Kennell, what a pleasure to see you

at last." Lord Banner's last word was slurred, his tone petulant.

Bibi's fingers dug into Amelia's forearm. While Lord and Lady Banner's estrangement had been the latest *on-dit* months ago, it was passé now. Yet one rarely spotted them at the same engagement.

"I was beginning to believe you were taking pains to avoid me, Lady Kennell." The baron's soured breath assaulted Amelia's senses.

He captured Bibi's free hand and attempted to draw her away, but Amelia planted her heels and tightened her grip on her friend. Lord Banner shot her a venomous glare and jerked on Bibi's arm. Amelia tried discreetly to draw her back to her side. Her gaze darted around the room. The game of tug-of-war had begun to earn curious stares, so she released Bibi. Where was Jake?

Bibi lightly touched her fingers to her throat. "M-my lord, I must beg your forgiveness, but I am a bit under the weather this evening. Perhaps you would be so kind as to retrieve a drink for Lady Audley and me?"

A shadow fell over Bibi's face. Lord Norwick saluted them with two glasses of lemonade. "No need to trouble yourself, Banner. I have refreshments for the ladies. You may tend your other guests."

"Norwick." Bibi's voice softened to a caress. "How happy I am to see you."

Lord Banner's complexion drained of color, and for one breathless moment, Amelia thought he might keel over on the worn drawing room rug. A light sheen appeared on his forehead. He cleared his throat. "I see you are in good hands, ladies."

Bibi turned a brilliant smile on Norwick, genuine and full of affection. "The best hands in London, my lord."

Amelia might have felt sympathy for Banner upon witnessing his stricken expression if he were any other man. But he wasn't. She held no compassion for the blackguard.

Norwick returned Bibi's smile, his rosy cheeks shining. Her attention affected him as it did most gentlemen, but there was something in Norwick's manner that hinted at deep affection and protectiveness.

"Will you allow me to make an introduction?" he asked Bibi.

"Go on," Amelia whispered, surrendering her to his care before retreating to a corner. Norwick escorted Bibi around the room, stopping to speak with other guests along the way and making a show of her special status in his life. Everyone greeted Amelia's friend differently this evening with the earl by her side. Bibi *was* in good hands with Norwick.

A soft touch on Amelia's elbow drew her attention. "Hiding in the corner, my lady?"

"Mr. Hillary. You have arrived at last." She tried to train her gaze straight ahead, mindful of the gossips milling about the room, but she couldn't resist stealing a quick look.

Jake's hazel eyes were a dark green this evening, the color enriched by the emerald and gold embroidered waistcoat he wore under his black jacket. "I missed you, too," he murmured.

A footman clanged a miniature gong, the tinny sound rippling through the room. "Ladies and gentleman, dinner is served."

Jake offered his arm and pulled her closer than proper while escorting her to the dining room. Pointed stares and whispers followed them. There had been no official announcement of their intentions, so she could only imagine as to their speculations. *Let the gossips think what they like.* Soon enough everyone would learn of their betrothal and the whole *ton* could eat crow.

When she tested the soup Lady Banner served moments later, Amelia reconsidered crow's appeal. Perhaps she had unfairly judged it. She scrunched up her nose and gingerly maneuvered the soggy chunks of lamb around her bowl.

Mr. Tucker, the American heir with a connection to the architect who had sketched the plans for the foundling house renovation, sat to her left. He leaned toward her and wrinkled his nose. "What is this meat in my soup?"

She stifled a chuckle. "It is lamb, sir. Do they not serve such delicacies in America?"

A lock of blond hair slipped down on his forehead when he shook his head. "Tragically, no."

"What is it they serve in America?"

"Similar fare on the east coast, I imagine, but I hail from New Orleans. Dishes feature more rice and fish." He lowered his voice. "And I daresay they are tastier than tonight's first course."

Jake peered around her and joined the conversation. "My elder brother speaks highly of the cuisine. His ship sails to the Port of New Orleans."

"He's the master of a merchant ship," Amelia added in a show of solidarity with her betrothed. Jake's brother had made a scandalous choice to follow in his grandfather's footsteps.

Fortunately for Captain Hillary, there were hostesses who prided themselves on inviting the most infamous gentlemen to their soirees, finding the lure of a possible scandal titillating. Although Jake's brother might consider it *unlucky* to receive so many invitations, given his tendency to sneer at society.

"New Orleans is a wonderful city," Mr. Tucker said, "but it cannot boast the impressive architectural structures found here and on the continent."

"Do you have an interest in architecture?" Jake asked.

When the women retired to the drawing room, he and Mr. Tucker talked animatedly about their shared passion. Amelia was happy to excuse herself from the topic of architectural design, as it had exhausted her interest half an hour earlier, and reunite with Bibi.

Amelia joined Bibi on the gaudy patterned settee. "How was dinner, Lady Kennell?"

Bibi folded her hands in her lap. "Very pleasant, thank you."

Her restraint impressed Amelia, especially when a lively twinkle in her eyes spoke of her exhilaration.

Ladies Eleanor and Lydia approached them. "May we join you?"

Bibi blinked up at the ladies. "Oh… certainly. Please, have a seat."

They lowered into the vacant seats across from the settee as gracefully as two swans gliding in to land on the Serpentine. Amelia braced herself for unpleasantness, but both young women regarded them with guileless, wide eyes.

"Lady Kennell, please do not think me forward," Lady Eleanor said, "but your gown is divine."

Lady Lydia nodded. "Yes, truly divine. Cousin Jasper boasts it's at the height of fashion in Paris."

Bibi returned their eager smiles. "And you believe your cousin to be an expert in ladies' fashions?"

Lady Eleanor giggled. "You do have a point."

"But your dress *is* magnificent." Lady Lydia bit her lip as if she contemplated saying anything further and must have decided it was safe to proceed. "Could I persuade you to divulge the name of your modiste?"

"Perhaps I could do even better and accompany you to Madame Girard's boutique. I think you will be pleased by her designs."

Lady Eleanor clapped her hands. "Splendid! Have you any engagements on the morrow?"

"Nothing that cannot be addressed on another day."

Amelia sat back with a satisfied sigh as Bibi formulated plans with the young women. Lord Norwick was opening doors for Bibi that Amelia had been unable to unlock. Perhaps Bianca Kennell was being afforded a new beginning.

Twenty-three

BIBI'S EVENING WAS GOING WELL. SO SPLENDIDLY, IN fact, she had sent Amelia away with Mr. Hillary a few moments earlier before the gentleman forgot himself and tossed Amelia onto the dining room table and scandalized everyone.

Bibi floated into the retiring room, chuckling. Ladies were crowded around the dressing tables and a queue had formed to make use of the necessary hidden behind an Oriental folding screen. A few glanced at her in wry amusement, but no one spoke. As she approached the dressing tables, Mrs. Lamport and Lady Saribury closed their reticules and turned for the door.

One by one, the ladies filed from the retiring room as if in a great hurry, leaving Bibi alone. She plopped onto the tufted stool and sighed.

In the looking glass, Bibi caught the maid's reflection. "There must be a fire."

"The ladies did seem in a hurry. Perhaps they fear the cordial will run dry."

Bibi caught the gleam of mischief in the young girl's eyes. "What's your name?"

The servant lowered her head. "'Tis Mae. Please forgive my impertinence."

Bibi laughed. "I value impertinence myself. Does your employer appreciate your cleverness?"

"I don't imagine so, milady."

Bibi checked her reflection. A few curls had fallen from the diamond pins in her hair. Her lady's maid had a devil of a time fashioning a lasting coiffure.

"Come demonstrate your other talents, Mae. One cannot earn her keep providing clever observations alone."

"Yes, madam." The young woman positioned herself at Bibi's back. Releasing her hair from the pins, the maid twisted it deftly before reinserting the glittering fastenings.

"Do you know who I am?" Bibi asked.

Mae's cheeks pinked. "From the ladies' reactions, I'm guessing you are Viscountess Kennell."

"I appreciate your forthrightness." Bibi sighed and groped in her bag for her lip rouge. She would miss Amelia when her friend married Mr. Hillary. Although he was becoming a likable gent, Bibi doubted he would allow Amelia free rein to run about London with her as they had done the last year. She must resign herself to more evenings such as this one and endeavor to develop tougher skin.

The maid dropped her hands at her side and stepped back. "There you are, milady. You look even more ravishing than when you entered."

Bibi turned her head different angles to view the girl's work. "Saints alive. I do look splendid." She twirled around on the stool to face the servant. "Whatever are you doing working for Lady Banner?

You obviously do not attend the lady for it looks as if a rat has taken up residence in her hair."

Mae giggled into her hand, her cheeks aglow.

Bibi winked. "See? I'm impertinent, too." She closed her bag. "I do so enjoy impertinence and talent in one package. Do you have any desire to change employers? I have need of a new lady's maid."

The girl's eyes expanded. "Oh. Yes, milady. I would find such work pleasing indeed."

"Very well. Come around tomorrow morning to Kennell House."

Mae curtsied. "I know the place."

The door flew open and banged against the wall.

"Oh!" Bibi and Mae cried.

Lord Banner weaved in the threshold. He clutched the doorjamb to steady himself while he pointed a shaky finger at Mae.

"Get out." His bleary eyes glinted with wildness.

Mae hesitated, looking between Bibi and Banner.

"I said get out!"

The girl dashed for the door, ducked under his arm, and escaped into the corridor.

Bibi stood and squared her shoulders. "You've managed to stumble into the ladies' retiring room, Banner. I was leaving, so you may enjoy your privacy."

She tried to move past him, but he snatched her arm and dragged her back inside.

His lip curled, baring yellowed teeth. "You're not going anywhere."

Bibi attempted to pry Banner's fingers from her upper arm, but he dug his nails into her skin.

"Unhand me at once." Her voice cracked.

"Norwick?" He slammed her against the wall. His hand circled her neck, pinning her there. Bibi's heart pounded and a scream rose up in her throat.

Brandy laced Banner's breath as he shoved his face close to hers. "You chose that bastard over me?"

Bibi clawed at Banner's twitching fingers, fearful he would lose all sense and murder her while his wife and thirty guests partook of charades in the drawing room. Despite her tendency to court scandal, this was not one with which she wished to be associated. Crimes of passion were so bourgeois.

"Please, Charles. Release me."

"No!" He smashed her head against the wall; a shooting pain fanned outward from the point of impact.

Bibi cried out, but he paid her no mind. Really, the man was inconsiderate, to say the least.

"You spread those pretty legs for every man with an erect cock. Yet you deny me repeatedly. Do you endeavor to torture me?"

"Think of your marriage, Charles." Her fingers worked to loosen his grip.

"My wife is a wretched shrew."

"Well, there is that slightly disagreeable quality about her, but surely she has many good points."

"I would as soon toss her in the Thames as to look at her."

This tack was not working. Perhaps if she offered to lend her carriage?

Banner leaned so close, she thought she might toss up her accounts from the stench on his breath. "I want you, Bianca. And by God, I will *have* you."

The retiring room door slammed against the wall,

and Banner flew backward, crashing into a dressing table. The mirror shattered. Bad luck, that.

Bibi's knees quivered, but Jasper's arm went around her and held her up.

"Did he hurt you, love?"

One glance at his concerned expression made her burst into tears. She should have told the truth about her association with Banner when she had the opportunity.

Lady Banner stormed into the room, her face ruby colored. "What, pray tell, is all the commotion? We can hear you in the front room."

Jasper snarled. "Your husband was assaulting Lady Kennell."

Lady Banner glared at Bibi then turned her fury on her husband sprawled on the floor among the mirror fragments. He looked more addle-brained than usual. A trickle of blood dripped from a cut on his forehead.

"Assault?" She laughed bitterly. "Is that what they call it these days? Since when is bedding a married man in his own home considered assault?"

Jasper puffed up with anger. "I saw him, Fi. His hand was around her neck."

Lady Banner marched across the room to tower above her husband as he picked glass from his palm. "Is this true, Banner? Were you also assaulting Lady Kennell that time in the library?"

Jasper's black eyes turned on Bibi. Fire blazed in their depths. She would have stepped away from him, but he held her against his side. "You had an affair with Banner?"

Nausea swept over her.

"I'm sorry," she whispered.

His jaw hardened and his gaze turned to ice.

"We'll take our leave now, Fi." His expression softened when he looked at his sister. He was taking her side against Bibi. But what did she expect given the circumstances? "I'll take Lady Kennell out the back. I do hope we haven't spoiled your evening."

Bibi sniffled as Jasper escorted her into the darkened corridor. The young maid, Mae, hesitated outside the retiring room, wringing her hands. Had she collected Jasper? Bibi must thank her if she dared to arrive for their interview tomorrow after this debacle.

Jasper propelled Bibi outside. The cooler night air swept over her and made her shiver.

In the carriage, he took the spot across from her and turned his gaze out the window. Silence was a stone wall as high as heaven erected between them.

"Jasper, please allow me to explain."

"Hold your tongue. I'm in no state to discuss anything at the moment."

Bibi squirmed against the seat. Her throat burned with unshed tears. She had destroyed everything.

When the carriage stopped inside the gates of Kennell House, Jasper lumbered from the vehicle then turned to assist her.

"I had expected honesty from you, Bianca, if nothing else."

She dropped her head. "I'm riddled with regret, but I cannot change what has occurred."

"No, I suppose you can't." He walked her to the door. "Don't you believe in the sanctity of marriage?" His question held a curious inflection rather than judgment. She had expected censorship, and his response left her feeling more vulnerable. She had no defenses against *this*, whatever it was. A passing interest? Apathy?

She looked away to hide her hurt. "*I* was unmarried at the time."

"Interesting way of looking at it, I suppose."

He ushered her inside and handed his hat to the butler before leading her to the violet drawing room. Pulling the doors closed, he wheeled around. A frown marred his face.

"Allow me to rephrase my question. Have you no qualms bedding another woman's husband?"

The room flickered as unwanted tears filled her eyes. She had never felt so ashamed, so deplorable. "You wouldn't understand."

He took a step toward her. "I will try, B, but you must tell me the truth this time."

He wanted to forgive her. His eyes were glittery with hope, and she would disappoint him.

She swallowed hard, wishing she had protected her heart against Jasper and knowing it was too late. "Your sister has always treated me with disdain, as if I'm not good enough for the likes of her. My aim was to exact a small amount of revenge by engaging in a harmless flirtation with Lord Banner."

The corner of Jasper's mouth lifted, but he wasn't smiling. "Fiona can be a dragon. I don't imagine you are the first to wish to seek vengeance. But I cannot condone adultery."

He wandered to the sideboard and poured two glasses of Madeira then offered one to her. "Marriage is a sacred vow that shouldn't be broken. When I marry, I shall take no mistresses. And I will expect the same promise of fidelity from my wife."

Bibi nodded, miserable at the thought of Jasper marrying and ending their association. She accepted the glass he held out, lowered to a chair, and sipped the liquor. The burn on her tongue reminded her of that evening. She set the crystal tumbler aside.

"Tell me what transpired the night Fiona discovered the two of you."

Bibi squeezed her eyes closed. She didn't want to remember, but she couldn't hide from Jasper. Or herself.

"S-several months ago, I attended a soiree your sister hosted. Amelia left early. She'd had enough of Lady Banner's haughtiness and urged me to leave too, but I recognized the opportunity to put your sister in her place. Banner had been flirtatious throughout dinner, and his attentions paid to me irritated her. I decided it might be retribution to make her squirm longer."

Bibi looked down at her hands. How minuscule she seemed, so insignificant. So very petty.

"Banner retrieved drinks for us when the dancing began. I knew he had laced the punch with spirits on the first sip, but I liked the threat of scandal. The possibility of anyone discovering I partook of a man's drink was titillating. I drank all of it at his urging."

She hugged herself. "I didn't anticipate the effect it would have on me. When Banner asked me to dance, my head felt light and my eyelids itched to close. I begged off, but he assured me a turn around the floor would revive me."

Jasper's jaw hardened. "Go on."

"During the waltz, my legs began to feel weak. Like

they were made of butter and were slowly melting. I told him a sudden illness had come upon me. He suggested we retreat somewhere so I might rest. I couldn't argue. My tongue felt swollen and too dry."

Her palms grew moist and she wiped them against her skirts, forgetting she still wore gloves. "Everything else is hazy from the moment he led me from the floor. I was in a dream state when he lifted me to the library table. I remember tipping to the side and almost tumbling to the ground, but he caught me. I thought him kind. Then his hands were under my skirts, and I tried to push them away, but my arms were so heavy."

She shook her head, trying to clear her mind of the fog enveloping the rest of that night. She recalled the sound of screeching and the crash of glass, but nothing else before waking in her bed. Her head had pounded with such intensity, that she had thought it might burst.

Jasper's eyes burned blacker than ever. "He drugged you."

Bibi drew back. "No. Well, he gave me brandy, but I knew what he'd done."

He sat his drink aside and approached her. "Bianca." His voice was intense yet tender. It vibrated in her chest. Made her want to cry.

He didn't need to tell her brandy would have no such effect. His grim expression said everything.

"He put a sleeping potion in my drink?"

"Likely laudanum." Jasper's fists tightened at his sides and his mouth thinned. "I'll call him out for his trouble."

"No, please." She grasped his hand with both of

hers. "Don't risk your life for me. I'm to blame as much as he is. I shouldn't have teased him. I shouldn't have accepted the drink."

Jasper knelt before her and took her face between his hands. "You are not to blame. Banner rendered you almost unconscious. He took advantage of your incapacitation."

"Be that as it may, it would be foolish for you to challenge your kin to protect my honor." She had no honor any longer. She hadn't for a long time.

"Stop it."

She met his steely gaze. "Tell me what it is I should stop and I'll do it."

"Stop implying you are nothing to me," he ground out. "You've never been *nothing*."

What could she possibly mean to him? She had become his lover, perhaps his mistress, but given his convictions, they had no future once he took a wife. A sharp pain seared her heart. She hadn't entered this affair with any expectations for commitment, and if she had, tonight would have shattered her hopes. No gentleman would desire a wife like her.

"It has been a long evening," she said. "May we please forgo this conversation?"

Jasper dropped his hands from her face with a loud sigh. "For the moment, we shall postpone our discussion." He stood and urged her to her feet. "Shall we make our way to the bedchamber? I grow weary for bed."

Bibi suppressed a gasp. "Yes. Of course."

She had expected him to walk away from her tonight.

Jasper placed his hand on the small of her back as

they climbed the stairs. "Are you certain he didn't hurt you, my dear?"

Love for her darling earl swelled within her chest. "I'm fit enough for now." That is until he would end their association and trample her heart.

Twenty-four

AMELIA GRASPED HER HORSE'S REINS TIGHTER AS Clarabelle pranced and tossed her mane as if preening for the two stallions that flanked her sides.

"Whoa." A firm voice and strong hand proved useful in settling her mare. Soon Clarabelle walked serenely beside her companions along Rotten Row.

"You handle your horse well, Lady Audley," Mr. Tucker said with admiration in his voice. Americans were oddly transparent; everything they felt announced in their expressions, everything they thought spoken aloud.

She smiled with polite detachment. "Thank you, sir."

"Lady Audley has always been an excellent equestrian," Jake said.

He grinned, his white teeth shining like pearls, as if Mr. Tucker had paid him the compliment. Good heavens, how she'd love to drag Jake back to Verona House and snuggle under the counterpane again.

Amelia's cheeks heated at the shameful direction her thoughts traveled, and she dropped her eyes to the reins in her hands. She had become as wanton as Bibi, allowing Jake to stay the night. But who could fault her? Jake Hillary was handsome, passionate, and considerate.

She had been pleasantly surprised when he'd insisted she join him and Mr. Tucker for a ride in the park this morning. Jake never treated her as if she were a nuisance, as the gentlemen of her past tended to do.

He winked at her, making her flush with pleasure. "A few years ago, Lady Audley challenged another gentleman and me to a race. You should have seen her."

"Mr. Hillary, please." Amelia had been a bit less refined as a young lady.

"I have always been puzzled by how she missed the boisterous protests of her chaperone," Jake added. "But she seemed to hear nothing of the lady's cater-wauling, although all of Northamptonshire must have heard her. Was it the wind in your ears, my lady?"

Amelia chuckled at his teasing tone. She supposed she had been a handful for Aunt Chloe.

Mr. Tucker raised his eyebrows. "Do tell, my lady. What was the outcome of the race?"

"I cannot recall now," she said with a shrug, not wishing to embarrass her betrothed.

Jake laughed, a hearty, heartwarming sound that sent tingles all the way to her fingertips. "Don't allow her coyness to fool you, sir. She shamed us both."

"Lot of good it did me," she said. "Aunt Chloe whisked me away from the house party before I could savor my victory. And I received an impressive scolding for my unladylike behavior." The entire journey home, to be precise.

"Ah, the trouble with chaperones," Mr. Tucker commiserated. He glanced back over his shoulder before offering a cocky grin. "Of course, we have no one telling us how to behave today. What do you say to a rematch with Mr. Hillary? I could stand in for the other gentleman."

Amelia smiled politely. "You Americans are sadly uninformed when it comes to the *ton*. Just look around. We have more people watching us now than ever. The gossips nearly swoon from holding their breath in anticipation of the newest scandal."

"Is that the cause of all the swooning?" Mr. Tucker flashed a good-natured grin. "And you uptight English refer to us as silly."

The gentleman really was a likable sort. He conversed on many topics with ease and possessed a good humor. She could understand Jake's desire to further their acquaintance.

A rider entered the track ahead and stopped his horse, appearing to scan the area. As their party rode closer, Amelia recognized the gentleman as well as the tension in his rigid posture.

"It's your brother-in-law," she said softly to Jake. "Something is amiss."

"Please excuse me a moment, Lady Audley. Mr. Tucker. I shan't be long." Jake tapped the sides of his roan stallion, riding ahead to reach Lord Andrew.

From the gentlemen's expressions, one might never realize something was wrong, but Amelia had always been more in tune to others' moods. She sensed disquiet in the air.

Jake turned his horse and met her and Mr. Tucker as they rode his direction. He eased his horse alongside Amelia's to speak softly. "It seems Forest could use my assistance. It's Lady Gabrielle. The groom lost her on the morning ride."

"Oh, dear," she whispered in return. "Your sister must be beside herself."

Jake's gaze landed on Mr. Tucker and he offered a pleasant smile. "Could I impose upon you to provide escort for Lady Audley, sir? I fear I have a family matter to attend to without delay."

"It is no imposition, Hillary. Go about your duties. The lady will remain safe in my care."

Jake tipped his hat. "I'll return as quickly as I am able."

Amelia worried her bottom lip as Jake rode away. Lana had enough to occupy her without adding concern for her husband's sister to the list.

Mr. Tucker shifted in his saddle and adjusted his hat to cast a greater shadow over his face, blocking out the intense morning sun. "I'm beginning to understand the need for chaperones in this country," he teased. "You English girls are a reckless bunch, but your secrets are safe with me."

"I suppose you couldn't help but to overhear. Allow me to caution you against forming an opinion on my story alone, sir."

"Never, Lady Audley. I'm privy to other stories. I assure you I have formed my opinions based on *those* tales."

"You must have a talent for compelling others to confess their reckless acts. How long have you been in England?"

"A few weeks, but I cannot pretend to have said talent. I have an acquaintance in New Orleans who recites anecdotal stories for entertainment. He is an

English gentleman, nobility I suspect, although he has never admitted to it."

Their horses continued a slow lope along Rotten Row, the warm sun now at their backs.

"Of course, I'm skeptical of his outlandish tales. They are always told with exaggerated flair, and only when he is foxed."

Amelia smiled in encouragement, hoping he would choose to share one of these outlandish tales with her.

"He recounts a story about a house party, too. I do wish for the opportunity to attend one of these notorious soirees. They sound positively wicked."

"That depends on the company you keep, Mr. Tucker."

He chuckled. "I have no doubt which crowd I would gravitate toward. The wicked are much more entertaining."

Having grown accustomed to Bibi's frank talk, her escort's lack of propriety didn't offend Amelia. His manner emboldened her instead. "Tell me the story, Mr. Tucker. I'm beyond curious now."

"At your insistence, my lady. My gentleman acquaintance tells this story about his wife." Mr. Tucker scratched his head, nearly knocking his hat off before setting it to rights again. "Now that I think on it, he never has said what happened to her. I suppose he is a widower." Mr. Tucker waved a hand in the air. "But his marital status has no bearing on the tale really. To hear him tell it, his wife was a young girl of thirteen, not yet old enough to participate in adult entertainments. Are you certain you aren't easily offended, Lady Audley?"

"I assure you my sensibilities are not easily disturbed."

Mr. Tucker nodded, his brow wrinkled with uncertainty. Nevertheless, he continued the tale. "The girl wasn't old enough to take part in the festivities, but she was in residence. Her aunt and uncle planned a house party to celebrate Christmas. There was nothing debauched intended, I assure you."

A slight sense of uneasiness churned in her belly, but she dismissed it as the effects of a disagreeable breakfast. As Mr. Tucker had mentioned earlier, England boasted many country parties. Surely more than one involved a thirteen-year-old girl visiting relatives during Michaelmas.

"Go on," she urged.

"The day the party guests arrived at the manor, the girl's female cousins stole into her chambers and took her dresses while she bathed."

Amelia's head spun slightly, and she gripped the reins tighter to steady herself in the saddle.

"My lady, are you unwell? You appear pale."

"I–I'm fine, sir. Perhaps too warm is all."

Mr. Tucker frowned. "Let's rest in the shade."

She followed him to a sprawling oak, the cooler shade making no difference in the fuzziness of her thoughts or rate of her heartbeat.

"Should I try to find something to drink?" he asked.

Amelia shook her head. "Really, I'm fine. Please, finish your story."

A fine line formed between his brows as if he questioned the wisdom in continuing. "If you are certain you're not easily offended, my lady," he said at last. "Actually, the cousins didn't leave her with *nothing* to wear. They had placed a maid's uniform in her wardrobe."

"Indeed?" She tried to force a swallow down her dry throat. Could there truly be two such similar occurrences in England?

"Oh, and I forgot to mention that the precocious duo sent the servant attending her away and informed all the other servants to ignore her call as they were engaged in a game of pretend.

"When the girl climbed from the tub without assistance—the servant didn't answer her call, of course—she discovered her clothes were missing. She pulled the bellpull repeatedly, but no one ever came. Finding only the maid's attire in her wardrobe, she knew the mischief-makers were her cousins. She was upset."

Upset was an understatement. Amelia had been furious with her haughty contemporaries. "Did she put on the maid's dress?"

Mr. Tucker chuckled. "I think you might see where this story is headed. Yes, she did don the outfit and marched from her chambers to find her cousins. She intended to give them a piece of her mind. Before she could locate them, an older maid, with some authority it seemed, waylaid her. She scolded the poor girl for her sloppy appearance then shoved linens in her arms and ordered her to prepare one of the chambers. The curmudgeon wouldn't allow her to explain. She swatted her on the backside and pushed her toward the chambers."

Amelia's chin lifted. She was still indignant over the shabby treatment she had received from the servant.

"Not knowing what else to do, she hurried to follow the older woman's orders. She completed the task, but before she could return to her own chambers, the woman snatched her and gave her another chore." Mr. Tucker cocked his head. "Only I never understood how the older servant didn't recognize the young woman."

"She was hired special for the party."

His eyes rounded. "You know this story?"

Did she know it? It was *her* story. One she had only ever repeated once, to her husband, but he'd obviously betrayed her confidence. That was the only explanation for some gentleman being in possession of her story.

"It's a common practice. Mr. Tucker, who is it that told you this tale?"

"All is saved," Jake called as he rode toward them.

Thank goodness, she didn't have to endure the part of the story where the lecherous gentleman had attempted to become better acquainted with her in his guest chambers. Amelia had barely escaped unscathed, and then only because the overbearing maid had come to investigate what was taking her so long.

Once Jake reached Amelia's side, he dismounted his horse then assisted her from Clarabelle. "Unless Lady Audley protests, I would like to walk Sinbad for a bit."

She glanced at Mr. Tucker, desiring one more moment alone to ask him a few questions about his friend, but that wasn't to happen.

The gentleman tipped his hat before gathering his horse's reins. "Very good. I'll take this opportunity to bid you both farewell. I depart for Edinburgh on the morrow and won't return to Town for several weeks."

No! She had to speak with him before he disappeared. Where was it he was staying again? "Do you know your way back to the Clarendon, Mr. Tucker?"

Confusion flitted across his features. "I'm staying at the Pulteney, and I believe I can find my way back."

"Indeed. What am I thinking?" Amelia shrugged as if self-conscious. "I suppose a world traveler would have no trouble finding his hotel."

The gentleman offered a kind smile. "Your hospitality is much appreciated, all the same. Good day, Lady Audley, Mr. Hillary."

With a jaunty wave, he urged his dappled gray into a trot and soon disappeared from the park.

Jake led both horses while Amelia walked beside him. "We needn't walk the entire way," he said. "I didn't want to discuss Lady Gabrielle in Mr. Tucker's presence."

"I don't mind walking."

"Lord Ellis found Lady Gabrielle by the lake and kept her safe until her brother arrived. They are both fortunate no one saw them together, and Ellis is lucky Forest didn't issue a challenge. He's protective of his sister."

"Thank goodness Lady Gabrielle was unharmed," Amelia mumbled, knowing this was expected of her, but unable to focus on the girl's narrow escape from ruin.

Jake sighed. "Lana is reported to be beside herself. Lady Gabrielle has been their guest for the last week, and Lana is holding herself responsible for granting permission for the outing with the groom."

Amelia made the appropriate sounds and nodded,

but her thoughts were elsewhere. What type of gentleman stole a story belonging to someone else and presented it as his own? Well, not his own, really, but that of his wife. She needed to speak to Mr. Tucker again to clear up the ridiculous notion that the story was about her. Surely, there were other details to set it apart from her experience, and if he'd had time to finish, her mind would be at ease.

Jake didn't seem to notice her distraction. "I'm reminded I haven't seen my sister for a fortnight. Perhaps I should pay her a call."

Amelia snapped from her fog. "Yes, you *should* see to her welfare. I imagine this has been a troubling day for her." And Amelia had her own business, that of locating Mr. Tucker and hearing the rest of his tale.

Twenty-five

AMELIA FRETTED OVER WHAT SHE WOULD SAY TO MR. Tucker, if he even responded to her request to call on her at Verona House. Her message had simply stated she had an urgent matter to discuss with him post haste, and although she believed it to be life or death, he might disagree.

When a knock sounded at the drawing room door, her heart paused before beating at an ungodly pace.

"Enter." Her voice wavered.

Bradford appeared in the doorway and glided across the room with a tray in his gloved hands. A cream calling card with black script barely registered against the polished silver. "You have a caller, milady."

She plucked the card from the tray. *Mr. Isaac T. Tucker.* "Please show the gentleman in."

Bradford's slightly pinched face revealed his disapproval, but as with all good servants, he performed his duties without comment. She conceded that her behavior might raise his suspicions about her character. First, she had allowed an overnight gentleman guest and now she not only welcomed a different gentleman, she had summoned him. Nevertheless, Bradford's suppositions were beyond her concern at the moment, and he had proven himself capable of keeping household gossip at a minimum.

Mr. Tucker followed her butler into the drawing room and stood at a respectable distance.

Amelia gestured to a chair farthest from the settee where she sat. "Please, come in and have a seat, sir."

The gentleman nodded curtly and strode to the leather wingback before gracefully lowering his lanky frame. "Thank you, my lady."

Bradford took up position at the room's perimeter, doing his best to appear unobtrusive.

"Thank you for coming on short notice, Mr. Tucker."

His brows lowered as he leaned forward. "Your message indicated you had something urgent to discuss. Has a problem arisen with the design for the foundling house? I can relay a message to Mr. Brown."

"No, no. Everything is perfect. The children will be pleased with their new home." She twisted her hands together, unsure how she should broach the subject, but it wouldn't do to waste his valuable time. "I wish to ask more about your friend in New Orleans." At his dubious expression, she rushed forward. "It may seem an odd request, but I assure you I have my reasons. You say your friend, Mr…?"

"Mr. Canaan," he supplied.

"You say Mr. Canaan told you the story you shared today, that it was about his wife."

Mr. Tucker nodded.

"There was more to the story, wasn't there?"

He sat up straight. "What makes you think there is more?"

She folded her hands together to keep from picking at her Indian muslin skirts. "The story sounds familiar, but I may have Mr. Canaan's tale confused with another I've heard in the past." Lying didn't sit right with her, but she had never revealed the story to anyone besides her husband. Because of the humiliating nature of the situation, she would rather keep her role a secret. "Please, tell me what happened to the girl."

Mr. Tucker made a show of adjusting his jacket and avoided her eyes. "I apologize, Lady Audley, but I never intended to share anything more. It is inappropriate for polite company."

He was correct, but she had to know.

"Did a gentleman…" she paused, not sure how to word her question. "Did he ask for a special favor?"

His eyes rounded. "My lady, I—"

Amelia shuddered as she recalled the hideous sight of a grown man, well beyond his prime, soaking in a tub. Why, there should be a law requiring gentlemen of such *distinction* to bathe in full dress. "You may simply confirm with a nod of your head, Mr. Tucker. The girl was saved from the indignity of assisting the gentleman when the head maid searched her out."

Mr. Tucker's face flushed crimson. "Is this one of those Banbury tales I've heard gentlemen speak of in coffee houses? I must look like a wet goose."

"Not at all, sir." Amelia wished that were the case, and although she would like to hand the designation of royal ninnyhammer over to Mr. Tucker, it was her crown to wear. "Does Mr. Canaan ever mention his wife's name?"

"He rarely speaks of her, but once he mentioned the name Mia."

Mia? This couldn't be true. Audley had betrayed her; he had told another of her humiliation. Had he laughed when he retold her story? Had he called her a stupid girl who deserved ill treatment for being so foolish? He had spoken similar words to her when she had told the story to him years earlier. And she *had* been a fool, foolish enough to believe sharing would build a bond between her and her husband.

But why would this other gentleman desire to pass this tale off as one belonging to *his* wife? Who was Mr. Canaan?

"And the gentleman has never mentioned anything more about his wife?" she asked.

"Lady Audley, I am puzzled by your line of questioning. What is it you desire from me?"

"I believe I know your friend's wife. *Knew* her. We… we were childhood companions."

Mr. Tucker's eyebrows lifted. "So she *is* deceased?"

Amelia nodded rather than speak one more lie, although she was developing a talent for it despite Bibi's claims that she was a horrible liar.

"Was it a tragic death?" he asked.

How could she respond? Since he waited for her reply, she offered a sharp incline of her head and held her breath, hoping he would not ask for details. Perhaps she was not as gifted when it came to deception as she thought, because her mind was blank.

Mr. Tucker slumped against the chair back with a

thoughtful look. "It's no wonder he wanted to start over, leave his past in England. He must have loved his wife a great deal."

She made a sympathetic sound and encouraged him to continue.

"David always has a sad look about him when he speaks of her."

Amelia's spine stiffened. "David?"

"Yes, that is Mr. Canaan's given name, although I always thought he resembled a Herbert." Her thoughts dashed in different directions. The gentleman in New Orleans knew her story, one she had never told another soul. What were the chances his name was also David? And he was an Englishman, probably nobility, in Mr. Tucker's estimation.

"No!" She bolted from the settee.

Her sudden movement startled the American, and he stood too. "Pardon, my lady? Is everything all right?"

She raced through her catalog of memories. Did David have any identifying marks Mr. Tucker would notice? Heavens, she couldn't remember. At this point, their separation was longer than their marriage had been.

Her husband died in a fire, at least two years ago, in Durham. Surely, her thoughts were too fanciful. She took a deep breath. "Could you provide a description of the gentleman?"

He scratched his head. "I was never any good at this sort of thing," he mumbled to himself. "Let's see. He is a *man*." Mr. Tucker drew out the last word, looking expectantly at her as if they were playing a round of Yes and No, her least favorite parlor game.

"I had gathered as much, sir."

"Oh, quite right." He cleared his throat. "Hmm. This is difficult. Had you asked me to describe a building—"

"Mr. Tucker, *please*."

"Very well, but I cannot say I ever studied Mr. Canaan's person. He is medium in build. With brown hair."

"And eyes?"

"Yes." Mr. Tucker gave a sharp, decisive nod. "Mr. Canaan most assuredly has eyes."

She sighed. "Never mind, Mr. Tucker." He was only slightly less skilled at providing a recitation of another person's features as the average gentleman. She shouldn't have expected much assistance in this area.

"Do you believe he is your friend's husband?" he asked.

"Perhaps." But how could that be? David *had* died in that fire. His brother had received his body and buried him at Crossing Meadows. She had visited his grave, for heaven's sake.

Mr. Tucker fidgeted with his jacket again. "Do you wish to send Mr. Canaan a message?"

"*No!*" Amelia closed her eyes and breathed out slowly. "My apologies, Mr. Tucker. I simply meant I would not trouble you with relaying a message. Perhaps I will send a greeting at another time. However, if he wishes to start his life over, he may desire no contact with anyone from his past."

She certainly wanted no contact with her husband if he were still alive. *Stop, you silly goose! It isn't Audley*. She was allowing her imagination to run away with her.

Amelia had a good life now. She had Jake. He loved her, and they would marry in two days. They would have children, lots of strong and happy issue to fill her family home. She wouldn't allow Audley's memory to haunt her. This other gentleman—this Mr. Canaan— could continue his sick game on the other side of the world. It mattered little to her.

An image of Audley's ring, the one passed to him from his father, flashed into her mind. Her husband had refused to remove it, *ever*. His brother, Thomas, didn't wear the jewelry, so she had assumed the ring had been buried with Audley.

"Does…" She took a deep breath. Better to push forward and learn what a ninny she was being by believing her husband might still be alive. "Does he wear any jewelry? A ring?"

Mr. Tucker's mouth turned down. "He wears a ring, but nothing more. Jewelry wise, that is. He has always been fully dressed on the occasions I have seen him."

"The *ring*, Mr. Tucker?" Typically, she was a patient person, but the man had a way of testing her fortitude.

"The band is gold and in the center is an onyx."

Her heart quivered. "And is there an eagle on one side?"

"Yes, and a stag on the other."

A rush of dizziness made her pitch to the left. Mr. Tucker caught her when her knees buckled and lowered her to the settee.

"Get the smelling salts," he barked.

Amelia waved away her butler, who had hurried forward to assist. "No, I am fine, Bradford. Just a glass of lemonade, please." Her servant moved toward the doorway. "And bring a sheet of parchment and my charcoal."

He didn't hesitate in following her directives and spoke discreetly with another servant waiting outside the drawing room.

In a short time, he returned with the items she requested. She moved to the table, both men hovering like nervous nannies, and sat down to sketch the ring as best as she could remember it. She checked her drawing once more before handing it to Mr. Tucker. "Is this the ring?"

"It looks similar. I can't be certain." He held the sketch closer. "Yes, I believe it is. There is an A imbedded in the stag's bridle, just as you have depicted."

Bitterness rose in the back of her throat. Audley had faked his death. *The dirty, lying blackguard.* If Mr. Tucker were not present, she might let loose an unladylike string of curses she had learned from Bibi.

"Thank you, sir. Your assistance is much appreciated."

He frowned. "I feel as if something significant has happened, but I am kept in the dark."

She patted his hand and offered a sympathetic smile. "I am certain it is a familiar locale for you, sir."

"Yes," he agreed, his golden brows forming a vee.

Poor Mr. Tucker. She owed him some explanation, but she couldn't tell him the truth. No one could ever learn her husband was still alive. Audley wanted everyone to believe he was dead, and to her, he was.

"I suppose I can reveal this much to you, since my friend no longer lives to be troubled by a possible scandal. You see, Mrs. Canaan believed her husband to be dead when she passed. She would be shocked to learn otherwise."

Mr. Tucker blinked. "I see. I suppose David has a good explanation."

"I am sure he does, sir. Please do not mention anything about this conversation to him. It sounds as if he has suffered enough."

He nodded thoughtfully. "I'm certain he has suffered greatly."

"Thank you for your assistance, Mr. Tucker. I hope this does not cast a shadow over your travel. If you have never visited Edinburgh, you will find the city to your liking."

The mention of his destination brought a slight smile to his lips. "I am looking forward to my stay. And I am honored to have been of service to you, Lady Audley, although it pains me to have revealed troubling information."

"You are a kind man, Mr. Tucker." It wasn't until after the gentleman left Verona House that she wondered as to the identity of the body buried in the Audley family cemetery.

Twenty-six

JAKE PASTED A FRIENDLY YET SLIGHTLY BORED LOOK ON his face as he entered the Duke and Duchess of Foxhaven's great hall for another ball in a lineup of endless societal events for the season.

He liked his sister's in-laws, having furthered his acquaintance with them years earlier in Northumberland. Nonetheless, it wouldn't do to appear too satisfied with life. Otherwise, the gossips would begin their wild speculations.

There were already many whispers about his association with Amelia, but after this evening, the *ton* would have the truth. He loved Amelia, planned to marry her, and he wasn't interested in their eligible daughters.

Having gained the duke's consent, Jake's father would announce their engagement and subsequent wedding to be held in two days. He and Amelia had decided on a quiet ceremony at Hillary House with family and friends then making the announcement at dinner that evening. But he didn't like anyone assuming the worst about his betrothed, even if it was for only two more days. He needed to inform Amelia of the slight change in plans, but she hadn't arrived with Lady Kennell yet.

He ignored the quiet voice in the back of his mind that pointed out ulterior motives. Why should he fear her changing her mind? Amelia had demonstrated the constancy of her feelings for the past few weeks.

Across the room, Daniel was chatting with Lana's attractive friend, Lady Phoebe, and earning dark looks from her husband. From the slight flush of Lady Phoebe's cheeks, Jake guessed the nature of their discussion trod on dangerous ground. Before his brother developed lead poisoning from a well-placed ball to his person, Jake crossed the room to interrupt.

Lady Phoebe smiled gratefully as he neared. "Mr. Hillary, how nice to see you this evening. Your brother was just entertaining me with tales from America."

"You mustn't believe a word he says. Daniel has been known to exaggerate."

Daniel clapped him on the back. "Finally, you make an appearance. I arrived thirty minutes ago."

Lady Phoebe's gaze flickered to her husband and her eyes lit with amusement. "I hope you gentlemen will excuse me. I must mingle. I wouldn't want anyone to feel slighted. Enjoy your evening."

Alone, Jake pulled Daniel toward a far corner. "You take your life into your hands if you consider dallying with Lady Phoebe."

His brother chuckled. "I'm hurt by your harsh judgment of my character. I was simply complimenting her on her lovely gown."

"Indeed? I hope your comments were limited to the *color* of her lovely gown."

Daniel shrugged before taking two glasses of champagne from the tray of a passing footman. He handed one to Jake and sipped from the other.

"Of course," he said. "Why would I mention anything else, such as how the cut displays her assets to great advantage, or how magnificent it must be to place one's lips against the pearly shimmer of her luscious skin?"

"You didn't," Jake whispered harshly, ready to throttle him.

Daniel winked. "No, but I thought it. I am aware of Lord Richard's reputed bad temper, and I would like to avoid anything that might delay my departure for New Orleans."

Relief washed over Jake. "I suppose death *would* be a nuisance."

"For me, anyway. It is bad enough I must wait to witness your nuptials before sailing. I will be perturbed if the good weather doesn't hold out for a couple more days."

"You need not stay for the wedding. I know you are anxious to set off on your voyage."

Daniel grinned. "I wouldn't miss the blessed event. It's about time." He nodded toward the doorway. "Your betrothed arrives."

Amelia had entered the room with Lady Kennell by her side, infusing Jake with a rush of ardor. "Good God, how I love her."

"As if anyone cannot read it on your face, you must declare your devotion to the entire room?"

Jake cringed. Had he just spoken his feelings aloud?

"Don't worry," Daniel said. "No one overheard."

Amelia glanced Jake's way and smiled.

"I have more important things to do than listen to you blather on," Daniel teased. "Go ask the lady to dance before her card is filled."

❧

Amelia's stomach tumbled when Jake started in her direction. She wished she could forget her conversation with Mr. Tucker, but it preyed on her thoughts.

"Good evening, Lady Audley."

Her heart expanded as she gazed into Jake's tender eyes. *This is what it means to be loved.*

Bibi cleared her throat, a smirk twisting her full lips.

Jake winced. "*Oh*, and good evening, Lady Kennell."

Flashing her famous smile, Bibi tapped her fan against his arm. "I see I am an afterthought this evening. I will leave you two lovesick fools alone to admire one another."

"Forgive me, Lady Kennell, I didn't intend—"

Bibi whipped around and stalked away from them.

Amelia chuckled at Jake's stricken expression. "She is teasing. She spotted Lord Norwick a moment before you approached. I am afraid she is not above making you squirm on occasion."

He fiddled with his cravat. "Are you certain I didn't offend her?"

She threaded her arm through his and squeezed. "She is unoffended."

His Grace, the Duke of Foxhaven, took center stage and waved over his wife to join him. "Ladies and gentleman, Her Grace and I extend our sincere gratitude for your presence this evening." He lifted his flute. "May every left cross turn be performed with grace, and may all the ladies' toes remain intact."

"Hear, hear," the crowd responded with enthusiasm, lifting their glasses as well.

Their hostess took position for the quadrille with the Duke of Sagehorn to begin the evening's festivities.

After the first dance concluded, Jake led Amelia to the floor and bowed while she responded with a curtsy before they took their places for a minuet. The grand piano plunked out a lilting melody. Soon the cello and violin lent their voices, melding in harmony.

When Jake's fingers touched hers, a thrill shot down Amelia's arm straight to her heart. They drew close while their hands lifted above their heads then they pushed apart again. Jake's gaze locked on her, hungry and possessive. They circled.

Repeating the pattern, Amelia's body hummed in anticipation of him taking her in his arms. She longed for the warmth of his touch, the excitement he generated. When the time came, Jake was as light as the music on the air, swirling her around the space, intoxicating her with his nearness and light citrus scent. Amelia lost awareness of time and place, unaware of when the music ceased.

Jake grinned, breaking her from her trance. "Would you care for some refreshment, my lady?"

Her dry mouth made speaking difficult. She nodded.

Tucking her hand into the crook of his elbow, he guided her toward the back of the room where Her Grace had set up the refreshment table. Handing her a glass of lemonade, he ushered her to a quiet corner housing several potted palms.

"You look stunning this evening," he murmured. "Please dance every set with me."

She laughed. "I am afraid everyone would notice you hold a *tendre* for me if I did."

He returned her smile. "Let them notice. I am finished sharing you. Besides, in a few moments, it will no longer matter."

Her brows lifted in question.

"I spoke with His Grace earlier. He has granted permission for Father to announce our impending nuptials."

His revelation sent a frisson of fear rippling along her limbs. "Tonight?"

"Tonight."

A horrible thought invaded her mind. What if someone else knew Audley was still alive? What if someone called her out, accusing her of bigamy? Her hand fluttered to her chest to calm her galloping heart.

Jake frowned. "What's the matter, Amelia?"

"We agreed to wait until we had spoken our vows. There are only two days remaining. Why must we change course?"

"Our course is the same. We will still marry as planned. Father will simply announce our intentions before we join in matrimony." He lowered his voice even more, his concern saddening her. "Sweetheart, what troubles you?"

He leaned closer, his hazel eyes cloudy.

How could she have considered risking his heart anymore than she had already done? If her husband ever returned, her marriage to Jake would be void. And if she spoke her vows to Jake knowing her husband was still alive, how could he ever forgive her? He wouldn't. And she would never forgive herself.

"Call off the announcement," she choked out.

"Pardon?"

Amelia caught sight of Mr. Hillary approaching the raised platform. "Please, there is no time to explain. You must stop him." She shoved Jake toward the stage and prayed he would reach his father in time.

Jake shot across the ballroom, bumping into Lady Hollister on the way. Offering a hasty apology, he pushed through the crowd to capture his father's arm as he stepped one foot onstage. They whispered together for several moments then parted. Jake turned back to her. Much to her alarm, Mr. Hillary proceeded onto the platform, drawing all eyes to him.

Jake wandered back to her side.

She hugged herself, her fingers digging into her upper arms. "What is he doing?"

Mr. Hillary bowed slightly to the duke and duchess before addressing the crowd. "Ladies and gentlemen, I would like to take this moment to thank our gracious host and hostess for what promises to be a lovely evening. To the Duke and Duchess of Foxhaven, may you enjoy many years of continued prosperity and good health."

A polite smattering of "hear, hears" rippled around the room intermingled with whispers and curious stares aimed at Jake and Amelia.

Jake feigned a smile as he spoke between clenched teeth. "Do you care to explain yourself?"

She lifted her fan, waving it to cool her heated face. "Not here. Come to Verona House in an hour. I will tell you everything."

❧

Jake expected the usual disdainful looks from Amelia's butler, not pity.

"Her ladyship awaits you in the blue drawing room, sir." The sympathetic note in Bradford's voice triggered a surge of frustration tearing through Jake. What did the servant know of Amelia's thoughts while she kept him in the dark?

He held his temper in check and followed, fighting the urge to push past the man and burst into the drawing room. When they entered, Amelia glanced up. Her expression was neutral.

"You may leave us, Bradford."

A quick bow and then the servant backed from the room.

The carpet muffled Jake's footsteps as he strode to where she perched on a tufted chair. He extended his hand. "Come. Sit with me on the settee."

She didn't place her hand in his. Her gaze dropped to the floor. "I must keep you at a distance. Otherwise I will never have the courage."

Her answer was a punch in the gut, knocking the wind from him. He dropped onto an adjacent chair and rested his forearms on his knees.

Courage? Why must Amelia have courage to speak with him?

"I would never hurt you," he said.

"I know." She didn't look at him.

Jake examined the carpet below his boots and followed the intricate pattern of loops like a maze that could lead him out of his confusion.

"Jake, I am so sorry." Amelia's voice broke.

His gaze snapped to her face. Tears shimmered in her blue eyes. His heart felt a tug. "Please, tell me what's wrong. Whatever you say, we'll figure out how to make it better."

She shook her head and swiped at her tears. "There is nothing to be done. We cannot marry."

He shot to his feet and crossed the space separating them. "Of course we can. We have a license. The vicar is coming Friday morning." Jake pulled her up into his embrace. She wilted against his chest and wrapped her arms around his waist. His anxiety disappeared as she nestled closer. She just had a case of the nerves.

"You mustn't tease me like that, Amelia." He caressed his hands along the gentle curve of her back. "Do you have any idea how much I love you?"

With his finger, he gently lifted her chin and lowered his mouth to hers to kiss away whatever doubts she had about their suitability.

"No." Turning her cheek, she shoved her palms against his chest. He released her immediately, caught by surprise.

She stumbled backward, recovered her footing, and fled behind her chair. Her hand rested on the barrier between them.

"Jake, please. Y-you cannot hold me like that, or… or kiss me… anymore."

His irritation flared. "What nonsense is this? I cannot kiss you anymore? You are to be my wife."

"No." She gripped the seat back; the color drained from her face. "I can't marry you. While you called on Lana, Mr. Tucker visited Verona House—"

"Tucker came *here*? What did he want?"

"He didn't come of his own accord. I requested his presence."

Fury flew over him. Every muscle in his body ached for release. He longed to beat the man bloody, or to bellow toward the ceiling. Or break every precious piece of porcelain in the room. "Damnation, Amelia! Are you vulnerable to every scoundrel within your vicinity?"

How could this be happening again? Was she tossing him over for Tucker just as she had done with Audley and then Forest? He stalked to the sideboard, considered pouring a generous drink, and changed his mind.

He whipped around ready to chastise Amelia, but her misery extinguished his hot temper. She trembled and looked as if she might collapse to the floor. He flinched. "Good lord. This *isn't* about Tucker, is it?"

She shook her head. "Only in the sense that he is the bearer of devastating news."

"Egads." Jake ran a rough hand through his hair. "I'm the most deplorable jackass alive."

"No," she said on a breath.

"I am. At least in the top ten of first-rate jackasses. I promised to listen, but instead I have been ranting like a madman."

"Truly, it's all right."

"No, it isn't." He moved away from the sideboard, closer to her. "What I said was crude and undeserved."

She studied him, her brow wrinkled, as if weighing whether to confide in him. Her doubt ripped open his chest. He had done this, made her frightened to trust him.

"Amelia, *please*. I should have controlled my temper. Forgive me." He returned to his seat and gestured toward the chair she had vacated. "I want to keep my word. Let me assist with finding a solution to whatever dilemma you are facing. Won't you have a seat?"

Amelia skirted the chintz chair and sat, demurely folding her hands in her lap. "I think I should simply blurt it out. Then I may give the details." She drew in a shaky breath. "My husband is alive."

Jake listened, waiting for the problem to present itself. Her words didn't penetrate his understanding for several seconds. "Pardon, but did you say Audley is alive?"

"I'm afraid that is the truth of it. Yes."

Jake almost melted with relief. He didn't wish to patronize her, but he had some experience with a woman's intuition. And it didn't prove to be as accurate as the fairer gender often claimed.

"But he no longer calls himself Audley," she said. "He has adopted the surname of Canaan, and he no longer identifies himself as nobility. David owns a bookshop in New Orleans."

A corner of Jake's mouth quirked upward. Audley working as a tradesman? Did Amelia know nothing about her deceased husband? David Caine would rather die a thousand times than lower himself to do anything resembling labor.

"Mr. Tucker toys with you, sweetheart. Perhaps I should challenge him to fisticuffs as a just reward for his deceit."

"Mr. Tucker doesn't know about Audley or our marriage. Even now, he has no inkling what I coaxed him into revealing." She leaned forward, her eyes darkening. "In the park this morning, he repeated a story he had heard from an acquaintance in New Orleans. It was a story from *my* childhood. I never told anyone except my husband."

Jake rubbed his forehead, trying to absorb what she was saying. "And this is your proof Audley is living in America and passing himself off as a tradesman?"

"It proves nothing, I know. Audley could have told my story to someone else. This is the reason I summoned Mr. Tucker. I needed to gather more information. The bookstore keeper is named David too—David *Canaan*. He kept the same initials."

Good Lord. Amelia was grasping at straws. Did marriage to him frighten her so that she saw evidence where none existed?

She frowned and dropped back against the seat back. "Even that does not prove anything, I realize, so I questioned Mr. Tucker further. Do you recall Audley's ring, the one given to him by his father?"

"The black one. Yes, I recall it."

"This gentleman wears his ring. Audley never would have parted with it. How would this gentleman have his jewelry unless it was him?"

"Do you realize how ridiculous this sounds? Audley's grave is in Sussex. His brother received his body. Don't you think Thomas would know whether he buried his brother?"

"But Thomas admitted the body was too badly burned to identify. He took Lord Henley's word for it, but what if David promised Lord Henley something for his silence?"

Jake crossed his ankle over his knee. "There is still the matter of a badly burned corpse buried at Crossing Meadows. How do you explain this fact?"

Amelia twisted her fingers together. "David traveled with two companions, I was told. Lord Henley accompanied the body back to Crossing Meadows, but no one has heard from, nor seen, Lord Patterson since his departure for Glasgow."

Jake's spine stiffened. "Are you suggesting foul play?"

"I don't know what to think. But I know in my heart my husband is alive, and he's living in New Orleans."

"Do you still love him?"

"No! How could I love him? Audley was a deplorable husband, and he left me long before he faked his death."

"He abandoned you?"

Amelia's face flushed pink. Jake sensed her humiliation as deeply as if it were his own. What else had he done to her?

He forced himself to speak his fears. "Did he harm you?"

She shook her head, much to his relief. "He never lifted a hand toward me, but he never loved me." She finally met his gaze. "Not like I have been loved by you. Truly, not at all. So why should I be tied to him? It is unfair."

Jake fought the urge to gather her to him again, wanting to avoid upsetting her further by doing what she'd asked him not to do. He rested his elbow on the armrest and rubbed his chin. Audley couldn't possibly be alive, but until Amelia reached the same conclusion, Jake must respect her wishes, or he was no better than Audley.

"If I told you I wanted to be with you anyway, would you allow me?" he asked.

"Please, don't ask me to make that choice. I am not strong enough to deny you anything for long."

"Then help me to understand. As far as England is concerned, David Caine is dead. There would be no penalties imposed upon you if he returned one day."

"Yet, *our* marriage would become void, Jake. Our children would be illegitimate. Whether I like it or not, I'm already married. I cannot practice bigamy simply because England thinks Audley is dead. *I* know he's not."

Jake would be damned if he surrendered her without a fight. Rising from the chair, he walked to her carved oak secretary. "We'll send a post to Thomas on the morrow, requesting his immediate response. He will confirm that either he is in possession of the ring, or else the ring rests with his brother. Then you will see you are free to marry."

He didn't wait for her consent before procuring a sheet of foolscap and dipping the quill in the inkwell. Hastily, he scribbled a brief missive before folding the foolscap and sealing it using her wax and seal. "There. If it goes out first thing, we could have an answer before the end of tomorrow."

A small crease formed between her brows.

"Don't worry, Amelia. Soon we will put this entire affair behind us."

Later the next day, Jake's confidence faltered as he read Thomas's response. The ring *hadn't* arrived at Crossing Meadows with Audley.

He tossed the letter on the table. "This only proves his ring was stolen."

Amelia picked up the letter and stared at it. When her gaze met his again, sadness glimmered in the depths of her eyes. "You cannot believe that to be true. Jake, we must accept that Audley is alive. I'm not free to marry."

"No!" He shoved from the table. "I refuse to believe it. And if he *is* alive, he left you." He stalked from Amelia's breakfast room headed for the front door. Her skirts rustled as she hurried after him. "Where are you going?"

"Daniel sets sail for America on the morrow. Begin preparations for departure. We will be on that ship."

"Whatever are you talking about? I can't go to America."

"Your marriage to Audley will be dissolved even if I have to *drag* him to the courts. He doesn't deserve to be your husband."

Twenty-seven

"WHAT DO YOU MEAN YOU AREN'T GOING?" BIBI launched from her seat, startling Amelia. "You *must* go. Have you lost control of your faculties?"

Amelia sipped her tea and tried to appear calm, although her insides were running riot. No good could come from a confrontation with Audley. A man who had taken such pains to disappear was not likely to return to England to divorce her. The entire affair was costly and could take years, and in the end, Audley could successfully sue her, forbidding her from ever remarrying. He might be spiteful enough to try it, too.

"Jake doesn't want to face the truth, so I must be the voice of reason," Amelia said. A divorce was tantamount to social death. She would no longer be welcomed in most circles, and neither would Jake or their offspring. "What kind of life could we hope to have?"

"The kind where you can be together."

Amelia shook her head. "He deserves better, but he refuses to listen to logic."

Bibi marched over to her, grabbed her by the

shoulders, and shook her hard. She was surprisingly strong for such a tiny woman. "Perhaps you are the one not listening. Or maybe you have finally lost your mind. The man loves you."

Amelia pried Bibi's fingers from her person and rubbed her shoulder. "Need I remind you that you never wished for me to marry Jake?"

"Really, Amelia, can you think of no one but yourself?"

"*Me*?"

"See! There you go again." Bibi's hands landed on her hips. "Me, me, me. I'll have you know I put considerable effort toward liking your gentleman, and this is no way to show your appreciation. Tossing the poor man over."

"You barely put forth *any* effort until recently."

"But when I did, it was a lot." Bibi threw her arms out wide to illustrate the magnitude of her sacrifice. "A. *Lot*."

Amelia set her jaw. "I see no cause for me to sail halfway around the world. Mr. Hillary could face dire consequences if our association continues. It is better to sever our connection now."

"Mr. Hillary." Bibi scoffed. "You cannot hide behind propriety forever, Amelia."

"I'm not hiding. And I do not take your meaning."

"Yes, you are. I know you well. You are not unaffected by the prospect of living without him, so cease with pretending you don't care."

Amelia's gaze dropped to her lap. Of course she was affected, but how much worse would it be to watch him lose everything?

She squared her shoulders and met Bibi's dark stare. "I am needed in London. The renovations for the foundling hospital will begin in a few weeks, and with no one to oversee the project... I've made up my mind."

"Well"—Bibi wagged a finger in her face—"I demand you change it."

Amelia drew back. "You cannot demand for me to change my mind."

"And as for the project," Bibi continued, ignoring that Amelia had spoken, "I'm just as capable of overseeing everything as you are. In fact, I want to do it. I *need* it. Call me selfish, but I don't care."

"But I—"

"How many times must I state this, Amelia? Not everything is about you. Allow others to reap the benefits of your good works for once. All those warm feelings and such."

"Bibi—"

Her friend nailed her with a determined glare. "You *will* be on that ship tomorrow, even if I must arrange for your abduction."

Amelia closed her eyes, shook her head, and released a forceful breath. "I wish I could dismiss your ranting as that of a madwoman, but I learned long ago never to put anything past you."

"Splendid, then you are not such a noddy after all."

❧

Amelia squirmed under Captain Hillary's intense glare. He occupied the better half of one side of the table in his ship's quarters while she and Jake sat side by side across from him. The imposing man appeared even larger in his cabin than he had in the ballrooms.

The way his eyes narrowed as he leaned on his forearms made her stomach quake. She couldn't rule out the possibility of him tossing her overboard any moment. The tense silence became too difficult to bear. She searched her surroundings for something to compliment, perhaps to win his favor.

"Y-you have a nice boat, Captain."

The man's jaw tightened and his teeth flashed when he sneered. "The *Cecily*. Is. Not. A. Boat."

Jake crossed his arms over his chest and returned his brother's glare. "You are acting like a blasted arse. Amelia isn't a seaman." He glanced toward her. "The *Cecily* is a ship, sweetheart. Anything over three masts."

"Oh." Her cheeks heated. She had insulted Captain Hillary, the opposite of what she had intended.

"I'm aware Lady Audley isn't a seaman," the captain snapped, "which is the reason she doesn't belong on my ship."

"She is a passenger," Jake said. "You carry passengers all the time."

Captain Hillary jabbed his finger against the table. "Not women. A ship is no place for women."

Amelia wished they would stop discussing her as if she weren't there.

"Damnation, Jake!" Captain Hillary banged his fist, startling her. "What are you thinking bringing her to New Orleans? Look at her." He swept a hand in her direction. "She's as delicate as a flower."

"I am not." Amelia bristled over his assessment of

her fortitude. "And I won't stay behind. If you refuse to carry me to America, I'll find another way."

Her outburst earned another severe glower from the brute. "The hell you will." A thick finger pointed toward her. "*You* will abide by every edict I lay down. Do you understand?"

When had the man become such a stickler about rules? As far as she knew, he broke every edict society handed out. Why, she wouldn't put it past him to have broken a few laws of nature either.

Jake placed his arm on her chair back. "Amelia is under my protection. You needn't trouble yourself with giving her orders."

Captain Hillary's fierce stare landed on Jake. "Very well, Brother. She's your responsibility, and God help you if you don't keep her under close watch." He returned his attention to Amelia. "And as for you... Never let me catch you alone on this ship. You are to be with Jake at all times or safely in your cabin with the door barred. In the event we encounter a storm, you are to extinguish the lanterns and stay put. I will not have you swept overboard, am I clear?"

Storms? Amelia swallowed hard. She hadn't stopped to consider any dangers of traveling by sea. "I understand, Captain Hillary."

His expression softened. "You and Jake will take your meals with me. I have assigned you both to the cabin below my quarters."

"We are to share a cabin? But Jake said they are small. My trunks and lady's maid alone will..."

One raised eyebrow from the captain made her trail off.

"I don't have the luxury of space, Lady Audley. My first mate gave up *his* cabin to make room for you. Everyone must share quarters. I had assumed you would prefer to share with Jake. If that's not the case, I'll make arrangements for you to share with someone else."

"That wasn't my meaning, sir."

"And your lady's maid stays behind."

"I need her." She looked to Jake to speak up on her behalf, but he offered a sheepish shrug.

"I'm sorry, Amelia. I promise to make it up to you later."

She turned an angry scowl on the captain. "Why can't she travel with us? Surely there is a place for her."

"There isn't, so either your lady's maid stays behind or your trunks. Better yet, we could leave you in England where you may continue to enjoy the luxuries you cannot do without."

"Enough, Daniel." Jake's tone was sharp. "Amelia is coming with us. Her maid will return to Verona House."

Amelia crossed her arms and huffed. No lady's maid, indeed. It would serve the gentlemen right if she wore the same dress the entire voyage.

৵

Jake escorted Amelia below deck and pointed out the limited amenities in their quarters. At least the cabin boasted a small window to allow in some natural sunlight, but it wouldn't open to welcome fresh air. The space was tidy, but plain. She stopped at the foot of the bed, gaping at the straw mattress as if staring into the pits of hell.

"It's more comfortable than it appears," he offered as he came up behind her to place his hands on her shoulders. He kneaded her tense muscles, happy that she allowed him to touch her. Two nights ago, she had forbidden him from kissing her, but that was before Jake had promised to help free her from her disastrous marriage, *if* Audley was even alive. "We could try it out."

The thought of Amelia pressed against him caused his pulse to jump.

She shrugged away from him. "I'll take your word for it." Her clipped tone made him frown.

Surely she understood they must do without the luxuries of home for the time, but their sacrifices would be worth it. If there was any other way, he wouldn't insist on her traveling with him, but he needed her present if she wanted to end her marriage. Unlike England, New Orleans was governed by the Napoleonic Code, which allowed for divorce by mutual consent.

At least the blasted French had one thing right, two if he counted their wine. And their pastries weren't so bad either. Not to mention their ladies tended to be less inhibited in the boudoir. *Damn.* He almost envied the rotters. Although he had no cause for complaints. Amelia was a pleasant surprise between the sheets.

He sank onto the hard chair while she inspected the quarters further. After a brief glance at the folding screen in one corner of the room, she turned to him.

"How does the captain expect me to spend my days if I cannot leave the cabin?"

"We'll take daily strolls around the deck. As often as

you like." He snapped his fingers and jumped from his seat. "I almost forgot. I have a gift for you."

Crossing the room in two strides, he loosened the fastenings on his trunk and lifted the lid. He dug through his belongings until his fingers grazed the book spine. He lifted his offering from the trunk and held it out to her.

Amelia accepted the leather-bound volume and reverently ran her fingers over the gilded letters. "*The Plays of William Shakespeare.*" Her eyes shimmered with tears when she looked up again. "I don't deserve such a beautiful gift."

He frowned as he pulled her into his arms. "Of course you do."

She buried her face against his chest and sniffled. "No, you are the deserving one. I'm so sorry, Jake."

When a loud sob burst from her, he held her at arm's length. "Amelia, whatever is the matter? Why are you crying?"

She shook her head and wiped her tears with the back of her hand. "I don't know. I just am."

"I see." In truth, he didn't see at all, but he had learned a couple of important rules when it came to ladies and their sensibilities. Never ask a lady why she is angry. You'll only increase her fury for not knowing what you did wrong. And when a lady cries, offer her a handkerchief and hold your tongue. Soon enough the storm would pass.

Jake pulled an embroidered handkerchief from his jacket pocket, gave it to Amelia then tucked her up under his chin again. This time she laid her cheek against his chest and circled his waist with her arms.

He held her tightly, swaying back and forth, until her tears subsided. Once she had quieted, he still embraced her, grazing his hands over her back.

"Is everything better now?"

She nodded and touched the handkerchief to her face.

He released a pent-up breath. "Perhaps you would like to read to us after dinner. I'll act out the parts."

Her giggle caught him by surprise and eased the tension that had been building up in his chest. She looked up at him with a tentative smile. "You *would* make a striking Katherina."

Long, even tones of a sea shanty wafted from the half deck as the seamen worked the capstan to raise the anchor. "Would you like to go topside?"

She stepped from the circle of his arms and placed the book on the crude table beside the bed. "I don't think Captain Hillary wishes to be reminded of my presence."

"Pay him no mind. He believes a woman's place is in drawing rooms or ballrooms."

"And bedchambers," she added with a touch of surliness.

"I suppose he does, but in his defense, life at sea is rough. Daniel has been a seaman for ten years. I trust him with my life." More importantly, Jake trusted him with Amelia's life. "Follow his directives, love, and we will arrive safely in New Orleans."

"I'll listen to the captain, but only because *you* ask it of me."

"Fair enough."

She yawned, her shoulders drooping on the exhale. "Do you mind if I lie down for a while? I'm not feeling myself today."

She didn't seem quite herself either. If a nap would facilitate a return of her usual cheerful demeanor, he fully supported one.

"I'll see if Daniel could use my assistance while you rest."

❧

Amelia struggled to keep her eyes open during dinner despite a long nap. The cumulative effects of the salty mist and sunshine had the same effect as a large meal, a glass of wine, and a lullaby. Even on the archaic bed waiting for her in their cabin, she expected to have no problems with falling asleep. She couldn't recall a time when she'd been this exhausted.

She picked at the boiled pork on her china plate. The delicate dinnerware was out of place in the stark surroundings. One feminine touch in an all-male domain. The dishes reminded her of how out of her element she was. She missed Bibi already.

Unfortunately, the pink flowers on the plate rim did nothing to enhance the meal. The tough meat required excessive chewing, tiring her even more. Saltiness filled her mouth and the back of her throat. She fought against the urge to gag, setting her fork beside her plate.

Captain Hillary narrowed his eyes. "We waste no food on the *Cecily*."

"She's eating," Jake said, coming to her rescue again. "What would not be a waste is a practice in civility while in the lady's presence. Perhaps it would prove handy when we return to London."

"I have no time for ladies."

Amelia's gaze darted between the men. She disliked being the cause of conflict between them.

"The fare is more than adequate, Captain." She picked up her fork and skewered a piece of meat then popped it into her mouth. Her stomach roiled. Closing her eyes, she breathed in deeply until her stomach settled. "Mmm. My compliments... to... your cook."

Her stomach rumbled again. Another bite and she would toss up her accounts.

Jake pushed his empty plate aside. "Whatever you leave, I will gladly eat. I'm famished and didn't get my fill."

Amelia shot him a grateful look and passed him her meal. "I've had more than enough. Please, help yourself."

Jake accepted her offering and cleaned her plate. Wiping his mouth with his napkin, he leaned back in the chair. "What do you say to a reading this evening?"

She would prefer going to bed, but it seemed rude to excuse herself so soon after their meal. "Reading sounds lovely."

"Allow me to retrieve your book." Jake hopped up before she could protest being alone with Captain Hillary.

When he left the cabin, the captain's gaze bore into her. "You must eat whether you enjoy the fare or not."

She sat up straight. "Oh, no. You misunderstand. The food was superb—"

"Enough. I don't require false flattery. Either eat well, or you will not survive. Simple as that."

Amelia blinked, shocked by his bluntness. "I understand, Captain Hillary. I promise to consume all of my next meal."

He nodded, a slight smile erasing some of his sternness. "See that you do, my dear."

They sat in silence until Jake returned with her book of plays.

"Will you read tonight?" she asked.

Taking his seat again, Jake flipped the book open and leafed through several pages before settling on a play.

"Now, fair Hippolyta, our nuptial hour draws on apace; four happy days bring in another moon: but, O, methinks, how slow this old moon wanes!"

Amelia's body heated and she averted her gaze. Was it a happy coincidence he had chosen this play? Their own nuptial hour would have been yesterday, and it was her fault they remained apart. She never should have married Audley.

Jake seemed unaware of her discomfort and continued reading, changing to a falsetto when he recited Hippolyta's lines. She chuckled in spite of feeling wretched.

Jake peeked over the book's edge. A smile lit his eyes. Finding her response encouraging, he adopted different voices for Egeus, Hermia, Lysander, and all the characters of *A Midsummer Night's Dream*. Soon he stood and added movement, silly, overly dramatic gestures and fluttering eyelashes as he had to entertain the orphans.

His interpretation of the mischievous Puck made her laugh until tears rolled down her cheeks. Even Captain Hillary chuckled on occasion, much to her surprise. He had seemed incapable of merriment earlier.

At the end of the evening, she stretched out on

the straw mattress in the cabin and fell into a dead sleep before Jake had finished readying for bed. It was hours later when waves of nausea jolted her from sleep and sent her scrambling to locate the chamber pot in the darkness.

She careened into the side table, knocking something heavy to the floor and waking Jake.

"Amelia?"

She couldn't answer with anything other than a moan as she felt around in the black night for the folding screen. She stumbled into it, hitting her elbow, before a light flickered in the lantern. Dropping to her knees before the chamber pot, she tossed up her accounts, certain she was dying.

Jake came around the screen, knelt beside her, and supported her weight as she emptied her stomach.

After her retching ceased, he brushed the hair from her eyes. "Are you all right?"

A cold sweat saturated her night rail. "I'm uncertain," she eked out.

He lifted her weak body, carried her back to the bed, and laid her upon it with care.

"I'll retrieve the surgeon," he said.

"No, please. I-I think I might be seasick. Allow me to rest. I'll feel better on the morrow."

His brow creased as he studied her. "Are you certain?"

She offered a half smile and closed her eyes, unable to speak. Jake moved about the cabin then closed the door as he left. She was asleep before he returned.

When she next woke, a sunbeam thrust its way into their cabin through the pristine glass window. Jake was stretched out beside her, his arm draped across her waist. Her mouth was as dry as day-old bread, and her body ached. She stirred to relieve some of her discomfort, hoping not to wake him, but he shot upright.

"What do you need?"

"Water."

He pushed from the bed and moved to the small table to pour from a serviceable pitcher. Returning, he placed the cup on the side table then helped her sit up on the edge of the bed. He joined her on the mattress and kept his arm around her for support. The tepid liquid washed over her parched tongue as she drank every drop, easing the scratchiness in her throat.

"I think I am better now."

Jake didn't release her.

Her stomach heaved again, and she dashed for the chamber pot, unable to keep down water even.

As Jake assisted her back in bed, he frowned. "I'm collecting the surgeon."

Twenty-eight

AMELIA SIZED UP THE GENTLEMAN DESIGNATED AS THE
ship's surgeon standing in her cabin. He looked more
distinguished than she had expected. When Jake had
declared his intentions to summon him, images of a
raving madman wielding sharp instruments led her
to protest.

But now that the surgeon established his sanity, she
was thankful Jake had retrieved the man. Although
her stomach had settled over the last hour, and she
was convinced whatever ailed her had passed, Jake
remained skeptical. Perhaps the surgeon could help
her persuade him she was well now when he allowed
Jake back in the cabin.

"As you can see, I am fine. Whatever ailment
plagued me earlier, it has passed."

"Uh, huh. Open wide." Amelia did as Mr. Timmons
instructed, but she gagged again when he poked a stick
in her mouth.

She almost knocked him down in a rush to reach
the chamber pot, but all she did was dry heave.

"Hmm. Interesting," the man said from the other

side of the screen. "Once you've set yourself to rights, I have a few questions."

Tentatively, she peeked around the folding screen. "Yes?"

He waved her forward. "Come along. My exam is incomplete."

She moved to the chair he indicated.

Pushing her sleeves up to her elbows, he squeezed both wrists, turning each arm this way and then that, studying her skin, or perhaps her veins. Amelia was uncertain what he meant to accomplish. He took her face between his hands and swooped closer as if he might kiss her but stopped mere inches from her lips.

"Look up," he ordered, spreading her eyes wide with his fingers.

Amelia looked up, hoping her compliance would end this ridiculous encounter.

He stepped back. "I think I know what ails you. Yet I can only be certain one way."

"What way? What is wrong with me?"

His lips puckered and twisted to the side, as he seemed deep in thought. "No," he mumbled. "Perhaps there is a less improper way. Lady Audley, when were your last courses?"

Amelia's hand flew to her chest. "*Sir*, that is a delicate matter not discussed in mixed company."

"You mustn't consider me a mere man. I practice medicine. That places me in a different category, like a bishop. It makes any confessions acceptable conversation topics."

"*Confessions?*"

"Poor choice of words. I was trying to illustrate a point. Now think. When was your last menses?"

Amelia's entire body flushed with intense heat. He thought her with child. How ridiculous. Why, she had just had her last monthly… She searched her memory. Three—was it four? Oh, dear heavens. Six weeks ago?

"No!" She bolted from the chair. "This cannot be happening." Whipping around, she nailed the surgeon with a furious glare. "You are wrong. What *really* ails me? Do I have cholera? The plague? It's scurvy, isn't it? Yes, that must be it."

The man drew back with a puzzled frown. "You would prefer a horrid disease to carrying a child?"

She burst into tears.

"Yes," he mumbled, "my diagnosis is accurate. You are already suffering from the hysteria associated with bearing a child."

Amelia frowned at him through her tears. "I am not hysterical." The good Lord knew she wanted a child more than anything. And not just any man's issue. She wanted a child with Jake, but her divorce would never be granted in time. The thought of their child legally belonging to Audley made her nauseated all over again.

Instead of running from the cabin in fear of her sudden ill temper, the surgeon put his arms around her and led her back to the chair. "You mustn't cry, milady. The Almighty never gives you more than you can handle."

Amelia wanted to shout, "Ha!" or deliver a clout to the side of his head. What manner of idiot made such a comment? He seemed as qualified for his position on ship as the cook.

Of course, Mr. Timmons would think it was easy. *He* wasn't about to destroy the life of someone he loved or ruin his child's life. He probably thought birthing a fabulous way to spend an evening, too.

In fury, she glared at the simpleton. "Don't you dare tell *anyone* of my condition, or so help me... you... you'll walk the plank."

The dreadful man laughed.

"*I'll* keep your secret safe," he said, "but the child will give you away in time."

"Yes, well that is none of your concern. It's your duty to convince Mr. Hillary that I am fit."

His gentle smile infuriated her even more. Honestly, where had Captain Hillary found the charlatan?

"Eat smaller meals more often and get plenty of sleep to manage your nausea," he said. "The sickness will go away on its own."

"Please, leave me." She waved him away with an irritated flick of her hand, but before he reached the door, she added, "Thank you."

Under different circumstances, his diagnosis would have overjoyed her.

❧

Jake paced Daniel's quarters while his brother studied navigational charts and made calculations. "I should have heeded your warnings," Jake said.

"Hmmph." Daniel didn't look up from his maps.

"I shouldn't have brought her along."

His brother glanced up briefly before returning to his work without comment this time.

"What if she's really ill? What if she *dies*?"

Daniel's quill clattered against the desktop. "Has anyone ever told you that you babble more than a shallow brook? Timmons will be in shortly, and you'll realize what a ninny you are."

A knock at the door interrupted Jake's pacing.

"Enter," Daniel barked.

The surgeon meandered into his brother's office with a smile. "Good news, gentlemen. Nothing serious ails Lady Audley."

Jake's breath came out in a noisy whoosh. "Are you certain?"

"No need to fret in the least."

Jake did not need to hear anything more. He flew out the door and hurried below deck. Without knocking, he burst into the cabin.

Amelia jumped to her feet, her hand covering her heart. "Good heavens, Jake."

Before she could say another word, he crossed the small space and swept her into his arms, lifting her from her feet. He wouldn't let her go, no matter if she protested or not.

"Thank God you're not seriously ill." For a long time, he held her, swaying to the music in his heart. "Everything will be all right, Mia. You will see."

❧

Lord Banner had died a sudden death. Heart trouble, the doctor had said, but Jasper knew the doctor had lied. The blackguard hadn't possessed a heart. Jasper hadn't expected his sister to mourn Banner's death with any real conviction, so her stony expression and dry eyes at his wake hadn't been cause for alarm.

What did cause Jasper concern was how she continued to show no change in affect three weeks after Banner's burial. It was as if the sister Jasper had always known had slipped into herself and disappeared.

He studied her across the dinner table. Her face had grown gaunt, and her widow's weeds hung on her already rail thin frame. She'd barely eaten a bite of her meal, even though Cook had prepared her favorites.

When she pushed her plate away, Jasper followed suit, rose from his seat, and went to her side. "Let's retire to the drawing room. I wish to speak with you on a matter of importance."

He assisted her from the chair and linked arms. "I'm concerned for your welfare, Fiona."

She patted his arm and offered a wan smile, the first glimmer he'd seen of his sister for weeks. "It's my role to worry over you, Tub."

"Fuss over me is more like it," he teased. "Or perhaps fuss *at* me."

He saw her settled into a chair in the drawing room before he took a seat.

"You need to find someone else to fuss over you," she said. "It's high time you married. I cannot look after you forever."

Jasper adjusted his position on the chair. He had hoped to ease into this conversation, but since the opportunity presented itself... "I believe you are correct. It is time I took a wife and filled the nursery."

Fiona's smile widened. "The sounds of tiny footsteps would lend an air of cheerfulness to this dreadful place. We could use some cheer."

His sister had been unable to carry a child, which he

suspected added to her bitterness. She'd been a doting mother to him. It seemed a shame she'd been denied her own offspring.

He bestowed a tender smile on his sister. "I'm certain the pitter-patter of tiny feet will liven up Norwick Place. The children shall be fortunate to have such an attentive aunt."

Fiona preened, looking more like her old self. "Yes, well, I knew you would come around eventually. Have you anyone in mind? Lady Eloise is a lovely young woman, or perhaps the Duke of Foxhaven's daughter, Lady Gabrielle."

Jasper snorted. "Lady Gabrielle? We wouldn't suit in the least. She's still a girl."

"There is that. Well, Lady Eloise is not a green girl, but she is young enough to provide a houseful of issue."

"I'm not seeking a breeder, Fiona." He rubbed his forehead. "Perhaps we should change the subject."

"To what, pray tell? What is more important than discussing an heir?"

Gads, she was a single-minded creature.

"Indeed. An heir is important." He cleared his throat. "I would like to ask something of a personal nature. About Banner."

Her face hardened and she looked away. "He's no longer a factor in my existence. I have no wish to think on him."

"I understand, but there's something that has troubled me these last few weeks. Something I fear may have happened to you."

Her gaze snapped back to Jasper's face.

"What were the circumstances surrounding the night Banner ruined you?"

Fiona stood. "That is *highly* personal, Jasper Hainsworth. And I care not to discuss my ruination with my younger brother."

He jumped up and captured her arm gently. "I mean no harm. I simply wish to know if Father misjudged you. I always considered it unfair that he disowned you."

Fiona jerked from Jasper's grasp and turned her back to him. "Father was a tyrant. I've no desire to discuss him, either. Besides, you righted the matter when you returned my dowry."

"I think you were deeply wronged, Fi. Not just by Father." Jasper feathered his hand over her back as she'd done to soothe him as a child. She didn't shrug away as he'd suspected she might. "Did Banner bring you something to drink that evening?" he asked in a soft voice.

She spun around with a gasp.

"Did he give you a sleeping potion to render you incapacitated?"

"Oh!" Fiona's hand flew to cover her mouth as tears swam in her eyes.

"Fi, I'm sorry." Jasper wrapped his arms around her emaciated frame, absorbing the violent tremors that shook her. "I had no idea. Father couldn't have known, either. The matter would have been settled on the field if he had."

His sister held herself rigid, unwilling to accept any more comfort. "*Tell* me how you know."

He released her and scrubbed a hand over his face.

She wouldn't like the answer. "Lady Kennell had a similar experience with Banner."

Fiona stared at him, tumultuous emotions churning across her face. She said nothing. She didn't move. Silence and stillness stretched for what seemed like hours.

"Fi, did you hear me?"

Her earsplitting screech gave him a start. She dropped her head back and howled at the ceiling. "No!"

Thunder an' turf! His sister had the devil's own temper. Jasper backed away from her, but she struck out.

"You lie. You horrid, horrid liar!" Her fists glanced off his chest.

"Stop this nonsense at once. I wouldn't lie to you." He blocked her next blow by capturing her wrists. She twisted like a fish caught on a line, and he released her for fear of causing her injury. She caught herself against the side table, but not before sending an Oriental jar crashing to the floor.

"It's untrue," she cried. "Charles took drastic measures because he loved me. He was desperate to have me for his wife. He knew I'd never go against Papa. He did it for us."

"Fi, you must realize I speak the truth. How else would Bianca know of these circumstances?"

Veins bulged at Fiona's temples, her face an alarming shade of plum. "She's a lying whore. A lying, despicable trollop."

She stormed to the sideboard. He looked the other way as she poured herself a brandy. His sister deserved a nip after everything she had endured as Banner's wife. Still, he couldn't overlook her insults to B.

"Please don't speak of Lady Kennell in that manner. I've grown to care for her."

"Damn him to hell!" With an animalistic bellow, Fiona flung her arm and raked everything to the floor—crystal decanter, stemware, and a priceless vase. Jasper winced as the pieces broke against the marble floor.

She threw her tumbler to the ground then seized two figurines from a nearby side table and hurled them at the fire grate, severing the head of one and devastating the other.

Jasper stood rooted to his spot, making no attempt to impede her destruction. Objects were replaceable, but his sister's sense of reality had been shattered forever. Besides, she was making her way to that hideous vase inherited from Great-Aunt Gertie he had always considered an eyesore.

"I hate him," she railed. "I hate him, hate him."

She threw back her head, fists thrust down at her sides, and screamed. Her body quaked as rage and hatred coursed through her veins and escaped through a wretched screech that rattled his bones. Fiona should seriously consider portraying a banshee at the next masked ball. She had the howl down perfectly.

When his butler peeked through the doorway, Jasper issued one sharp nod to reassure the servant, and the man eased from the room, looking less than confident in Jasper's directive. Not that he could blame the servant. This was Fi's most impressive fit to date.

She screamed until her voice grew hoarse, and then she collapsed on the settee. Her chest heaved. Nothing but the sounds of her heavy breathing filled the room for a long time.

Jasper stood at a distance until she proved to be done with her outburst. It wouldn't do to take another blow to his person. Her tiny fists were like incessant mosquitoes, too annoying by half.

When she looked up, tears glittered in her eyes. "Do you think Charles loved her?" Her conversational tone was oddly incongruent given her furious display.

Assuming it was safe to approach her, he moved to the place beside her on the settee. "No man capable of love could do what he did to either of you."

"Yes, I suppose you're right." A small frown turned down her thin lips. "But *you* love her."

Jasper touched her forearm. "As much as I wish to avoid hurting you, I can't deny I love her. Bianca is the only woman to accept me for who I am, to make me satisfied with the man I've become. I wish to marry her."

Fiona closed her eyes and said nothing. She shifted away.

He rubbed his jaw, noting he needed to shave. "You needn't witness the nuptials. But be aware that I expect we will have children, hopefully soon. If you wish to be part of their lives—of my life—you must come to accept Bianca and treat her with kindness. I won't have it any other way."

"I see." His sister nodded before issuing a ragged, drawn-out sigh. "Very well, Tub. I will endeavor to be civil, for the children's sake."

"Thank you, Fi. Your acceptance, even given reluctantly, means a lot to me."

She pursed her lips. "Yes, well, the good Lord knows the children will need a proper influence in their lives. It's the least I can do."

Jasper suppressed a smile. He anticipated a rocky road ahead for all of them, but at least there would be a future with his sister. And what a bright future he would have with Bianca by his side.

Twenty-nine

As the surgeon had predicted, Amelia's nausea lessened, although it did not go away completely. The blasted illness plagued her at all hours of the day, unpredictable and inconvenient. And, as the surgeon also foretold, she wouldn't be able to hide her condition from Jake much longer. Especially if he continued to fuss over her like a mother hen.

Today in his bid to cater to her needs, Jake had arranged a bath for her where she now soaked and ran her hands over the telling roundness of her belly. A smile pulled at her lips. She had begun to feel tiny flutters inside, like the beating of butterfly wings. With this sign of Jake's child growing in her womb, her love for him grew.

She wished so much for their baby. No matter the circumstances of his birth, she would ensure he had more love than any other child in London. All of England, in fact. He would grow to become dashing, like his father, and a gentleman in behavior if not station. And he would be graceful on, *and off*, the dance floor, unlike his sire.

She chuckled.

"What's humorous, love?"

"Oh!" Amelia drew her knees to her chest, her head slipping under water. Scrambling to sit up, she coughed and sputtered.

Jake peeked around the screen, his forehead wrinkled with worry. "Are you all right?"

"Jake!" She tried to shield herself with her hands, not wanting him to learn of her pregnancy in this manner.

"Sorry," he offered before disappearing behind the screen again, but his mischievous grin had given him away. He wasn't sorry in the least.

She stood in the copper tub and snatched the towel draped over the folding screen. "Are you spying on me?"

"I came in for another pair of boots. I thought you heard me." The chair legs scraped against the plank floor. "Why were you laughing?"

"I was thinking of the time you nearly fell on poor Lana at Captain Hillary's welcome home soiree."

"Ouch. Not again." Despite his groan, merriment sounded in his voice. "Do you intend to ridicule me forever?"

She wrapped the towel around her middle and stepped from the tub. The wood planks were surprisingly smooth beneath her feet. "Perhaps."

"There may be something wrong with me, but I look forward to many years of your mockery, my dear." There was the thud of a boot hitting the floor.

Amelia's smile wavered. He should know the type of future they would be facing. Perhaps he had no cares about their standing in society, but having his child legally belong to another? No man would take the news easily. "Once I'm dressed, could we walk the upper decks again?"

"I'm afraid not, love. We are heading toward a storm."

Her stomach clenched. "Indeed?"

"It's several miles away yet. Daniel plans to sail around it if possible, but I need you to prepare the cabin in case we must ride it out." A second boot hit the floor. "Extinguish the lantern as soon as you dress and pack away any fragile items. I'll be topside assisting the men."

A tremor shook her whole body. How dangerous that sounded. "You're going topside in a storm?"

"I'll return before they batten down the hatches. Don't forget the lantern. I'll be back soon."

"I won't forget." She shoved her arms into the sleeves of her wrapper and pulled the tie around her waist before hurrying from behind the screen. "Jake, wait."

His hand stilled on the door handle, and he looked over his shoulder.

She wished to tell him many things, but she had no time to say them all. *I love you. I'm with child. I can't live without you.* Instead, Amelia forced a slight smile. "Be careful."

"No need to fret. I'll return before you even notice I'm not underfoot."

Then he was gone.

Amelia hurried to extinguish the lantern and packed her toilette set. She wanted to finish her tasks before Jake returned. Yet, once she completed everything, she didn't know what to do with herself. She tried reading in the dim light from the window, but even if she could see the words on the page with better clarity, her concentration was poor.

As the sky outside darkened, her disquiet increased. Visions of Jake tripping on a rope or that wooden swinging object knocking him from the deck filled her with fear. *Good heavens.* Topside with a storm approaching was the last place her clumsy darling should be.

When the ship lurched and creaked, she tossed her book aside. She had to see to his safety or go mad. She dashed out the door and scrambled up the ladder.

As she came topside, wind whipped her damp hair against her cheeks and plastered her gown to her body. The ship teetered and knocked her off balance. She stumbled hard into the railing and gripped it as her feet slipped on the wet decking. Men scurried about turning winches, tying down sails, and doing heaven knows what else.

Amelia clung to the rail.

"Jake." The wind swept her voice away. He would never hear her calling in this gale.

The nose of the ship dipped low before a wave thrust it back up. Great fountains of white shot into the air and rained down on the deck. Amelia hugged the rail when her feet slid out from under her.

Once she'd regained her footing, she released her hold and staggered forward. She drew in a deep breath to yell for Jake again. A force slammed against her ribs.

"Oomph!"

Her feet left the deck, stunning her into silence. A man tossed her over his burly shoulder and carted her below deck. Realization dawned on her and she screamed. She kicked and beat against her abductor's back, but it was like hitting rock.

He carried her to her cabin, knocking her ankle against the doorjamb. Pain shot up to her knee and her bone throbbed. He kicked the door closed. Giant hands circled her waist, surprisingly gentle given the rough treatment she'd received so far, and lowered her to a chair.

Her head snapped up. Captain Hillary's rage-filled face demanded her attention. She shrank back. He was scarier than any storm.

"I issued two rules," he said. "No wandering the ship alone and stay in your cabin during a storm. What the hell possessed you to venture topside?"

Amelia trembled. How could this barbarian be related to her kind and loving Jake?

"Do you have any idea what it would do to Jake if he lost you? You would destroy him. Dammit, Amelia." He jabbed his finger against his temple. "*Think*. And in your condition."

She gasped. "Timmons told you?"

"Timmons didn't need to tell me anything. I see the signs for myself."

"You can't tell Jake, please, Captain Hillary. He must hear it from me."

"Tell him soon before he discovers it for himself."

"I'll tell him today. I promise."

He issued a heavy sigh. "I didn't cause you injury, did I?"

She shook her head.

"Forgive my rough treatment, but you try my patience at every turn," he said. "We cannot keep you safe if you won't observe my rules. You must know how Jake adores you. His suffering would be unending if any harm came to you."

He turned to leave, but Amelia grasped his hand. "Captain Hillary, where *is* Jake? I didn't see him on deck."

"He can take care of himself as long as he doesn't have to worry about you. Stay put and I will find him."

⤨

At Daniel's insistence, Jake went below deck. The storm was mild at this point, and he had argued he could still help the crew, but Daniel wouldn't hear of it. He thought Amelia might be frightened and encouraged him to go to her. Jake had given in without a fight, but only on account of her.

He opened the cabin door. "I'm back, sweetheart. Is everything—?"

Amelia launched herself from the chair and flew into his embrace. The impact caught him by surprise, but she was a slight creature and didn't upset his balance.

"Oh, Jake. I was so worried. You said you would be back before I realized it, but you've been gone two hours."

I was? The excitement of man against nature had made him unaware of the passage of time. He cuddled her against his chest, reveling in her floral scent and silky hair against his cheek. "No need to fret. As you can see, I'm unharmed."

For once, she didn't pull away and dash for the chamber pot, which frankly had begun to hurt his pride, Amelia tossing up her accounts every time he tried to kiss her. He touched his lips to her temple. How he longed to make love to her. He missed the brush of her luxurious skin against his and the taste of her kisses. His fingers slid into her tresses, cradling the nape of her neck and caressing the slender length with his thumb. Ever responsive to his touch, she lifted her face and licked her lips.

"Ah, Mia."

With a hunger he had never known, he possessed her mouth, taking from her in his furious need. He devoured her; his heart launched into a heavy rhythm. She returned his passion, parting her lips to welcome the sweep of his tongue.

When his kisses trailed down her neck, she arched her body into him.

"I love you," she whispered. "I love you. I love you."

How many times had he asked her to say those words while he made love to her? He swept her up into his arms and laid her on the mattress. Ripping off his soaked shirt, he flung it toward the chair, unsure if he hit his target or not. Not caring.

Amelia's breath quickened, her chest rising rapidly, drawing his attention. With her hair fanned upon the pillow, she appeared to have a halo. His sensual angel swept her eyes along his torso and back up to meet his gaze. Her blue eyes turned sapphire as passion burned in their depths.

Jake stretched out beside her then hauled her to lie on top of him, chest to chest. His hands grasped her bum, which felt delightfully fuller than he recalled, and they kissed with abandon until her wriggling caused him to groan.

"Let's rid ourselves of these pathetic clothes," he said.

Amelia stiffened and stilled in his arms. "Oh, Jake." She dropped her head against his shoulder.

"What's wrong?" He lifted her chin. Her bottom

lip quivered and color leached from her face. "Egads! Are you going to be sick again?" He scrambled to help her climb off him, but she didn't fly from the bed.

"No, I'm not sick. I…" She put a hand to her head and sighed. "There's something I must discuss with you."

"Now? Can't it wait?" He reached to wrap his arms around her middle, but she leapt from the bed and rounded on him.

"No! It most definitely cannot wait."

Jake flopped on his back and growled his frustration toward the ceiling. When he opened his eyes, he discovered her troubled expression. "Agreed, but I'm in no state to listen with any attentiveness. Do you have any bathwater left?"

"Yes, but it is cold."

"Perfect." He swung his legs out of bed, stood, and dropped his trousers in one fluid movement. When he reached the folding screen, he glanced back at her with raised brows. "Are you certain we can't postpone our discussion, just for a bit?"

She flashed a grin. "It's tempting, but sadly, later will be too late."

"Splendid," he grumbled before rounding the screen and climbing into the chilled water. "Egads! It's freezing."

"I warned you."

"No gloating, love. It is your doing I'm in here."

Her light footsteps padded to where he soaked in the tub. She stood in front of him, biting her bottom lip and lacing her fingers together. "Jake?"

"Yes?"

"I have something to tell you. Something, um, *momentous*."

He sat up straighter. "Go on."

She didn't meet his eyes as she took a deep, shuddering breath. "It seems I am with child. We're having a baby."

Jake's heart tripped as all the air rushed from his lungs. On the next heartbeat, he shot from the water, splashing half the contents on the floor, and grabbed her up in his arms. "Amelia, my God. That's amazing."

She squealed as he hugged her even closer. "Yes, well, procreation has been happening for millions of years. Don't dislocate your shoulder patting yourself on the back."

He kissed her again, partly to quiet her but also to express his absolute joy. He was going to be a father. Holding her aloft, he kept her captive even after the kiss ended.

"You have soaked my gown." She didn't release her arms from around his neck despite her complaint. "Would you consider dressing now, Mr. Hillary? This is what landed us in this mess in the first place."

He set her on her feet and frowned. "I don't consider a child to be a mess. Do you?"

Her smile faded.

Yanking the towel from the screen, he scrubbed the rough cloth over his chest and legs before making his way to his trunk.

Amelia followed. "Under normal circumstances, no. But you must admit these circumstances are less than ideal."

"You don't wish to have my child?"

"It's not a choice I've been given. I am with child whether I like it or not."

His muscles went rigid. She didn't see this as the joyful event he did. "How long have you known?"

❦

Amelia winced in response to the chill in Jake's voice. She hadn't meant to insult him, and having his child would be an honor if they were already married and their child would have his name.

"Jake, please understand. I cannot think of this pregnancy as a blessing right now."

Every muscle rippled as he jerked on a dry pair of trousers. "I can *only* think of our child as a blessing. You didn't answer my question. I take it you have known for some time." He donned a shirt and tucked the tails into the waistband of his trousers. Stalking to the chair where his dry boots rested, he plopped down and shoved his foot into one.

"Are you leaving again?" she asked.

He glanced up briefly before returning his attention to his other boot. "The worst of the storm has passed. It seems Daniel managed to avoid the center."

She had failed to notice the violent rocking had ceased or the brightening of the sky. "But why must you leave?"

"You haven't responded to *my* question yet, Amelia. Do not expect any answers from me." He stood and stomped toward the cabin door.

She rushed forward. "Wait. Mr. Timmons told me. Our first day onboard."

Jake's jaw tightened and his furious glower caused

her to shrink back. "All this time you have known and kept it from me. You really see carrying my child as a curse, don't you?"

"I don't, but—"

"Save your explanations. I'll have your meal delivered to the cabin. Daniel will find another place for me to sleep." Before she could protest, he exited the room, slamming the door as he went.

She considered chasing after him, but her experience with Captain Hillary gave her pause. With Jake angry with her, she would rather avoid his overprotective older brother. Instead, she lit the lantern and pulled out her book to wait for Jake to come to his senses.

An hour later, she questioned if the man even had any senses to return to him. She placed Shakespeare on the side table.

Devil take it. Captain Hillary or no, she was going after Jake.

She marched to the door, flung it open, and screamed.

A giant boulder with human features stooped over outside her door, too tall to stand upright. "Shh, miss. Don't scare me like that. Captain Hillary sent me to guard you."

Amelia's heart pounded dreadfully hard.

"You see, miss. No one comes in your cabin, and—"

"No one comes out," she finished with hands on her hips and a soured expression.

The man scratched his head. "How would anyone get out when I've let no one in?"

"Let me rephrase. I cannot leave my cabin, correct?"

He squinted as he appeared to contemplate what she said. "You don't wish to come out of your cabin?"

"Of course I do," she snapped. Really, wouldn't her appearance in the doorway make her intentions obvious? And if Captain Hillary thought to stop her with some beast of a man—

Her gaze ran across the expanse of his shoulders and down his ridiculously bulging arms. Well, she supposed she would have to capitulate this time, but if her guard dozed, she would sneak past him. She eyed his forearm, which was the size of her thigh. *Maybe.*

"My name's Patch." He offered his arm. "I am to escort you when you leave your cabin."

"Oh." Actually, that was thoughtful of Jake's brother. She would have taken Patch's arm, but there was no way they could move side by side in the cramped space. "Perhaps I should follow you?"

"Yes, miss. Or is it milady?"

She suppressed a sigh. "Either will do. It matters little to me at this point."

Once topside, she linked arms with him and moved toward the captain's quarters, but Patch stopped, almost jerking her arm free from her person. "My apologies, milady, but you may not enter the captain's cabins."

"Why?"

"I don't question Captain Hillary's orders."

Oh, for heaven's sake. "Well, *I* am under no such obligations." Without her escort, she marched to Captain Hillary's door and banged with the side of her fist. Heavy footsteps approached before the door flew open.

"Patch, what the hell is going on here?" Captain Hillary glared past her shoulder at the man who had slunk up behind her.

"She don't listen too well, Captain."

"Then cart her below deck."

She'd had enough of this ill treatment. "I demand to speak with Jake, *now*."

Captain Hillary stepped from his quarters and pulled the door closed behind him. "He doesn't wish to speak with you, Lady Audley, so kindly find your way back to your cabin."

She stood toe to toe with him, returning his glare with every ounce of fire she could muster. Neither of them backed away.

"Allow him some time to calm down, Amelia. I will speak with him on your behalf."

When she still refused to budge, Captain Hillary spoke to Patch. "Use caution when you carry her below deck."

Patch moved toward her with regret heavy in his posture.

"Oh, very well," she said and slapped away his hands. "I will go, but inform Jake I will be back tomorrow, and the next day and the next until he speaks with me."

She spun on her heel and strode to the hatch with her bulky shadow trailing behind her.

Thirty

JAKE SAT ACROSS FROM DANIEL IN THE FLICKERING lantern light, uninterested in the mush in front of him. "And you say Amelia is still served meat?"

His brother grunted, which might have been an affirmation, but more likely meant Jake should stop chattering.

Their supplies were low at this point in the journey, and Jake couldn't thank Daniel enough for giving his usual fare to Amelia. He tried to repay his brother's kindness by being quiet, but before he raised the spoon to his mouth, another question tumbled out.

"And your man continues to report she is well?"

The corner of Daniel's lip lifted as if amused. "You seem uncommonly interested in the welfare of someone you don't care to speak with any longer. Perhaps four days has changed your mind."

"No, it hasn't." Jake shoved a piece of stale bread in his mouth, but couldn't even wait to swallow before asking his next question. "How did she respond when you sent her away today?"

His brother scooped the thick oatmeal with his spoon and grimaced. "She didn't try to see you today."

Jake's pulse quickened. "She didn't? Did you see her on deck? You don't think she's unwell, do you?"

"I saw her. She is causing a stir with the men, allowing her hair to flow freely." Daniel nailed him with a sharp glare. "*Someone* should take her to task, but I tire of playing the tyrant."

Jake ignored his brother's chiding and swallowed another spoonful of the cold fare.

Stretching his arms above his head, Daniel yawned. "It appears Patch and Lady Audley have formed a fast friendship. She has taken to inviting him into her cabin in the evening."

Jake almost choked, coughing into his napkin. When he recovered, he blurted, "Whatever for?"

"I told you, they have become friends."

He bristled at the thought of another man enjoying Amelia's company.

"Out of curiosity, how long do you plan to sulk?" his brother asked.

"I'm not sulking. I simply... I want her to..."

Blast it all. He was sulking, wasn't he? But he would be damned if he would admit to such a pathetic endeavor. "You tell me. How is a man to interpret a woman's despair over carrying his issue?"

Daniel scraped the bottom of his bowl and ate the last bite. "She appears serene for a married woman carrying her lover's child."

"I am *not* her lover. I'm... I'm her..."

"Yes?"

He hated when Daniel was smug, smirking as if he knew some secret.

"But I never intended to be her lover," Jake argued.

"I believed we were betrothed, as did she. I intend to be her husband."

"See where impatience will get you, little brother?"

"Sod off."

Daniel chuckled. "Of course any man who has waited as long as you have for the lady is granted some leeway."

He sat up straighter. "I *did* wait a bloody long time, and I will be damned if I lose her now."

His brother leaned back, balancing the chair on two legs. "Have you stopped to think about what you will do if Audley is alive and refuses to cooperate?"

"I will make him cooperate." Jake sprang from his seat, prepared to fight.

"But what if he cannot be forced into divorcing her? What if Amelia chooses to stay with her husband?"

"She wouldn't. Why would she?" He threw his arms wide as his voice grew louder. "Audley abandoned her. What woman would align with a man who doesn't want her?"

Daniel shrugged. "Maybe Audley had no choice but to leave. Men make mistakes, and avoiding detection may have been the only way to save Amelia from disgrace."

"What a ridiculous piece of fiction," he spat.

"But let's say it's true. Suppose Audley wants Amelia to stay with him. What reason would she have for refusing? She is with child and alone in England."

"She isn't alone. I will remain by her side forever. I don't require a legal document to prove my commitment."

Daniel raised one eyebrow in that pompous way he

had about him. "And Amelia will know you will stay by her side how exactly?"

Hellfire and damnation! Why did his brother have to be so damned sensible all the time?

Jake stalked to the cabin door. "I need fresh air."

"Take all you like." Daniel's sardonic laughter trailed him onto the deck, riling him even more.

Jake hurried to the hatch and scrambled down the ladder, stopping outside Amelia's door. Her laughter mingled with the deep voice of that dimwit Daniel had assigned to protect her. When a delighted squeal pierced the air, jealousy shot to the pit of Jake's stomach. He flung the door open, startling the occupants.

Amelia recovered from her surprise and scowled before scooping two dice in her hands. "Do you ever knock?"

Patch glanced over his shoulder. "Mr. Hillary, do you care to rattle the bones with us?"

"What are you teaching her?"

Amelia lifted her chin, her demeanor chilly. "It is called hazard, Mr. Hillary. Surely, you are familiar with the game. From what I have heard, you are a fair player at Brook's." She smiled at Daniel's lackey as if they shared a private joke. "Brook's is a gentleman's club in London."

"Filled with deuced aristocrats, milady?"

Jake had an overwhelming desire to thump his bald head.

"Mr. Hillary is not nobility, Mr. Patch. He simply has the arrogance of one."

Jake stalked to the table. "Your services are no longer required."

Amelia blew on her cupped hands, shook them in the air, and tossed the dice. "Oh, zooks!" She glanced at Jake. "*I* will decide if Mr. Patch's services are needed or not."

The hulking giant pushed from the chair, towering over Jake by several inches. "I think it's best to listen to the gentleman, milady."

"I understand if you feel you must abide by his wishes. I am under no such obligations. And I should still like to see you on the morrow, Mr. Patch. You promised I could watch the sunrise."

Jake gestured to the door. "Take the morning off."

"Yes, sir." Patch threw a sheepish glance toward Amelia. "Maybe another morning, milady?"

"It would be my pleasure, sir."

Once they were alone, Amelia snatched the dice and rolled them repeatedly, refusing to look at Jake. A deep frown furrowed her brow.

Finally, he cleared his throat, gaining her attention.

Her fierce glower, however, gave him pause. "Who are you to dictate who I may associate with and when?"

His Mia was more than sweetness and compassion; she possessed a healthy dose of mettle, not that he should have forgotten after their last big clash. He preferred being in her good graces.

"I'm the arse who loves you, Amelia."

His blunt response earned a slight lifting of one corner of her beautiful lips. "Castigating yourself does not make up for your horrid treatment, Mr. Hillary, but it's a good start."

"Will you please stop referring to me formally?"

He slumped into the seat across from her. "I'll admit I never stopped to think how you might view being with child. When you told me, all I could think was how thrilled I was to become a father. I could not fathom why you would not be happy, but I understand now. Things are a bit out of order."

"Reaching a point of understanding does not excuse your previous behavior."

Amelia wasn't going to give him an inch, and he loved her even more for her strength. "Excellent point. Understanding *doesn't* make up for my previous behavior. I won't pretend there is an adequate excuse. I was wrong and I am sorry." He reached his hand across the table, palm up, urging her to meet him in the middle. "Can't we put this behind us? Soon we'll be married and raising our child together."

"How can you be so naive?" She jumped to her feet. "Marrying me will turn your life topsy-turvy. *If*"—her hand sliced through the air—"Audley even agrees to return to England. Our child will be born long before the divorce is completed, which will help prove Audley's case against me, but hurt our poor child who will be deemed illegitimate. I cannot do this."

"Amelia—"

"It was a mistake coming with you." She rounded the table, headed for the door. "It's all too much to ask. You deserve a wife with fewer complications. I'm wrong for you."

Jake reached out, snagged her arm, and pulled her onto his lap. A cold knot lodged in his chest. How long had she been suffering under this mistaken assumption? "Shh, listen for a moment." She tried to break away, but he held her in place. "You are the only thing right in my life."

She shook her head and attempted to climb to her feet, but he wouldn't allow her to run away. Besides, there was nowhere to go.

"Amelia, I apologize. It never dawned on me you thought we were bringing Audley back to England."

"Then what *are* we doing?"

"Everything is different in New Orleans." As much as he wanted her, he would never put her through the hell of a divorce in England. He smoothed back loose tendrils of hair curling at her temple. "Audley has opened a door for us by establishing residency there. I promise, before we leave, you'll be free, and we shall marry."

"Truly?" Her bottom lip quivered, and Jake brushed his thumb across it.

"Truly. But take heart, perhaps Mr. Canaan is exactly who he says he is."

She scoffed. "Then we would have made this trip for no reason."

"Oh, come now. It hasn't been all bad."

"Hasn't been bad?" Amelia jabbed a finger against his chest. "Perhaps *you* should carry our child and spend most of your time in intimate conversation with the chamber pot."

He laughed. "Now that you mention it, I'm growing jealous of the time you spend with that fellow. Every time I get close, you run off to meet him."

Her worry lines eased but didn't disappear. "Your life would be easier if you forgot about me."

"Never." They had been separated long enough for him to know nothing was easier without her.

He rested his head against hers. "We belong together. If hardships stand in our way, we must hold tight to each other. We'll survive this. I promise."

She snuggled against him, her warmth penetrating his thin shirt. "If you promise, then I believe you."

"Does this mean you've forgiven me for being an arse?"

"If you will forgive me for hiding my condition. I wanted to tell you, but…"

He caressed her soft cheek with his fingertips. "I've already forgotten it, sweetheart."

"Then so have I."

Now that their quarrel had ended, curiosity was killing him. All he'd been able to think on these past few days was his child growing inside her. "How far along are you?"

"Twelve weeks, I believe."

He grinned. Sometime around the masked ball.

"Stop looking proud of yourself." Her smile softened the reprimand. Taking his hand, she placed it over her stomach. "I won't be able to hide my condition much longer."

He circled her belly with his palm. "Is he moving yet?"

"Not where you can feel. And what makes you think we're having a boy?"

"Do you sense you carry a girl?"

Her Mediterranean blue eyes filled with affection. "No, I've been thinking of the babe as a he myself."

"Splendid." Jake hugged her. In truth, he held no preference. Son or daughter, he would love the babe, every bit as much as he loved his child's mother.

His blood heated with her soft body pressed against

his. It had been too long since he'd made love to her. His lips brushed hers then applied more pressure. How many oceans would he cross for a lifetime of her sweet kisses? He could willingly let her go as easily as he could give up breathing.

His hand slid up her neck and pulled her closer, his mouth eager for her taste. She softened in his arms and returned his kiss, but when his fingers grazed the underside of her breast, she scrambled from his lap.

"Wait!" She bumped against the table in her haste, but instead of dashing for the folding screen, she stared, her hand resting lightly over her chest. "We can't."

"Pardon?"

"This." She swirled her hand as if performing a sleight-of-hand trick. "We can't do *this*."

"A magic act?"

"No!" she said and scowled. "We can't tempt fate."

Gads. This didn't sound promising. "Please explain, because you lost me at 'we can't.'"

She sighed and leaned against the table. "Don't you ever wonder if this would have come about if we had waited until we were married? I mean Audley. Not our child. If we had done everything in the proper order, maybe Audley wouldn't have resurfaced."

"Huh…" Was it just him, or was Amelia speaking nonsense?

"I want everything settled first. I want Audley to agree to the divorce. I want it all behind us, so everything is right."

He rubbed his forehead. "Are you saying if we had never become intimate, Audley would still be dead?"

"Yes. No, not really. But"—she scooted around the table—"how can we ever know?"

Applying reason and logic might be the first step.

"I don't wish to take any chances," she said. "It may sound like superstitious foolishness, but we can't be too careful. Our child's future is more important than anything, wouldn't you agree?"

"Well, yes—"

"Thank goodness." She collapsed onto the vacant chair. "I feared you might think me mad. Then we agree. Until everything has been put back to rights, we must remain celibate."

Celibate? Hellfire and damnation! When had he agreed to such an arrangement? "Isn't it a bit late at this point?"

She crossed her arms and her jaw jutted forward. "We must do what is best for our future *now*. You know I'm right."

Jake sighed and shoved his fingers through his hair. This wasn't good, not good at all. She obviously had a case of female hysteria. Thankfully, he retained sense enough to keep his observations to himself. Pressing the issue seemed unwise at the moment, but tomorrow was another day.

He offered a smile so as not to give himself away. "So, you play hazard?"

Thirty-one

BIBI CUDDLED AGAINST JASPER AND SIGHED WITH contentment as the Berlin carriage carried them back to Kennell House. She still missed Amelia, but she had done the right thing in encouraging her to travel with Mr. Hillary.

Amelia had an opportunity for love and marriage, something Bibi would never have. And never realized she had desired until recently. Instead, she had settled into a pleasing coexistence with her lover, trying not to think overmuch on the inevitable ending of their affair.

If anyone had asked her at the start of the season if she could imagine embracing a domesticated life, she would have laughed. Yet here she was living as one half of a couple deep into their dotage.

She and Jasper ventured out every evening, attending balls, dinner parties, or the theatre, but they also returned home early. Of course, their entertainments behind closed doors couldn't remotely resemble those pursued in old age.

Jasper drew her closer against his side. "Did you enjoy yourself this evening, B?"

"Oddly, yes."

"Oddly?"

"I hadn't expected Forest and his wife to be so amiable, although Amelia had warned me that I might like Lady Lana if I gave her a chance."

His body shook with a throaty chuckle. "As long as you were duly warned."

"Indeed. I believe Lady Lana and I could become friendly given time."

"Excellent."

Jasper sounded pleased by her admission. In fact, he had been rather enthusiastic about her forming new associations over these past few weeks. He often encouraged her to extend invitations to his cousins, Lady Eleanor and Lady Lydia, practically penning the notes on her behalf. His eagerness in arranging her social life gave her pause. One might think he wished to have her out from underfoot.

The carriage eased through the iron gates of her town house and rumbled to a stop.

"Ah, we return," Jasper said, his voice taking on a strained quality.

When he didn't make a move to exit the carriage when the door opened, Bibi glanced up. He pressed his lips together and cleared his throat.

"Do you not wish to come inside?" she asked.

"Yes, I do wish it, but…"

Bibi's eyes rounded a fraction before she could school her features. "But what, sir?"

"We cannot go to the bedchamber," he mumbled. "I have a matter I must address with you, and I cannot be distracted from my purpose."

Her heart paused for one horrible moment. This was it, the end of their lovely association. He had reached the conclusion it was time to take a wife. The season would end soon, and he needed to make an offer before the available young women returned to the country. Perhaps playing house with *her* had eased him into the idea of matrimony more quickly than she had hoped.

Her eyes narrowed. Was this the reason he had encouraged her to go on so many outings? Had he been courting his future bride while Bibi had traipsed all over Bond Street spending blunt like a fool?

"Speak your mind here, my lord," she said with a definite chill to her voice. "Then you may be on your way."

Jasper shifted his weight and climbed from the carriage. "I am afraid there is not enough privacy in the carriage, nor enough room."

Bibi hesitated to take his hand, but did so out of necessity. Had she not donned the most treacherously high heels in order to appear taller in his presence, she would have shunned his offer of assistance. Once safely on the ground, Jasper didn't release her hand, but pulled her close to his side and escorted her through the double doors.

He had been attentive, loving, and solicitous the entire evening, which irritated her to no end. If he had exhibited any aloofness, she would have known to steel her heart against this moment. As it was, she felt as vulnerable as a newborn kitten.

"Shall we retire to the violet drawing room, my dear?"

"The location makes no difference," she snapped.

Jasper gazed at her in surprise. "Indeed? I wish I had realized as much earlier. Perhaps on Forest's veranda would have been preferable."

Now he really had her back up. "In a place where we might be overheard? Are you mad?"

He released her hand and stepped back to rub his chin thoughtfully. "No, I suppose you're correct. This matter is best discussed without potential eavesdroppers or untimely interruptions."

With a spine fashioned of iron, Bibi walked to a lavender wing armchair and perched on the edge. "Do get on with it, Norwick."

His Adam's apple bobbed, and his gaze shot to the crystal decanter sitting on the sideboard. "Might I partake of a brandy first?"

She crossed her arms and glowered. "Do you require spirits for courage?"

"Well, this is new to me, Bianca."

That admission didn't buoy her morale in the least. A man who had likely always been on the receiving end of the disappointing news a relationship had run its course endeavored to end his association with her.

"It is novel to me as well," she said.

A bewildered look crossed his features. "Really? How peculiar," he mumbled to himself before looking up.

"For heaven's sake, Jasper. Spit it out."

"Have I angered you in some way?"

Bibi closed her eyes and took a deep breath. This was undignified. She had always known their association would end, and she had imagined it as a friendly parting. She had promised herself she would respond with something witty, such as... Maybe something like… Oh, for the love of God, how was one supposed to be clever at a time such as this?

"Pay me no mind, Jasper. I am simply caught unawares, but I am not angry."

He eyed her warily.

"Please, help yourself to a brandy," she said, waving a hand toward the decanter.

He didn't move. He stared in puzzlement, his face darkening to that pleasant red color it always did when he was emotional. Straightening his waistcoat, he stepped forward.

"No, you are correct. I don't require libations for what I am about to do. I have never been as confident in my decision as I am at this moment."

A choking lump formed in her throat. Her surliness had solidified his decision. He would toss her aside with no regrets.

"Bianca, it should come as no secret that I must—"

"Take a wife," she said on a wail. "Yes, I know."

"Mercy! Will you allow me to finish?" Jasper jerked on his waistcoat and stretched his neck. "This is *my* moment. Please, wait for your lines."

She procured a handkerchief from her reticule and blotted her tears. "Sorry."

"Yes, well. Allow me to try again." He shoved his hands in his pockets, a most uncouth behavior that made him all that dearer to her. "As you have stated, I must take a wife. I have considered it a distasteful duty until recently but now find my attitude toward matrimony has come more in line with what is expected of me as the seventh Earl of Norwick. Do you understand?"

Bibi nodded miserably.

"Brilliant. Then we understand one another." He beamed. "I must warn you, I not only *require* children, I find myself unexpectedly desiring them."

Warn me? What a bizarre choice of words. Of course, she knew he would require issue, but how would that affect her in any way? It wasn't as if she would be taking tea in his nursery, being forced to look into their chubby faces and large, obsidian eyes. Imagining tiny versions of Jasper toddling about choked her up again.

"Do you agree to children?" he asked.

Bibi's gaze snapped to his face. "Whatever are you saying, Norwick? Why would you seek my approval? I have no say in the matter. This is a question best posed to your future wife."

"My future wife?" He blinked. "Oh, bloody hell. I mucked it up, didn't I?"

Before Bibi could respond, he knelt before her and pulled his hand from his pocket. The glint from what appeared to be a million diamonds encircling a ring band with an obscenely larger diamond in the middle stole her breath.

"What is this?"

"A token of my affection. It worked well enough for Hillary," he said, an edge of defensiveness creeping into his words.

Bibi placed her hand over his. "It is beautiful, darling. You did well."

"My dearest, Bianca. I would be greatly honored and pleased if you would consent to be my wife."

"Me?"

Jasper frowned. "Who else would I wish to marry? We have been inseparable for weeks."

"But I thought you considered me your lover, not a candidate for a wife."

"Can you not be both?"

Bibi chuckled as tears slid down her cheeks. "Yes, Jasper Hainsworth. I can indeed be both a lover and wife to you."

"Then we have reached an understanding?"

She captured his face between her palms and kissed him soundly. "We have reached an understanding."

His smile left her legs weak. He slipped the ring on her finger, stood, and whisked her up into his arms. "By George, I *can* lift you without throwing out my back."

She swatted his shoulder. "Jasper!"

"Not now, my dear. I must concentrate if I am to navigate the stairs without killing us both."

He hurried from the drawing room and carried her to the bedchamber without the slightest threat of injury to either of them. He laid her on the bed and climbed up beside her. His eyes glittered in the candlelight as he gazed at her, caressing his thumb over her bottom lip.

"There is one more thing I neglected to tell you, Bianca."

"What might that be?" Her voice sounded airy.

"I love you."

Thank heavens Bibi had stolen to the balcony that night at the masked ball. Otherwise, she might have missed the greatest gift of all: a bumbling yet endearing man who challenged her false notions that love was simply a myth.

"I love you, too, Jasper."

Thirty-two

Amelia gaped at the surroundings marking the entrance to the Mississippi River. She supposed some might describe it as desolate with the banks of almost black mud, but there was an odd beauty to the area. The saturated earth shimmered in the sunlight, and the smooth texture from water having washed over it reminded her of a looking glass.

The place where no life should exist teemed with groups of pelicans. They huddled together as if gathered for a crude ball, issuing deep grunts that sounded like a cross between a swine's snort and an old man's snoring.

Jake leaned on the railing beside her and pointed at another bird wading along the shore. "It's a white ibis. See the black wingtips?"

The long-legged bird dipped his hooked beak into the shallow waters.

"How are you familiar with the bird species?"

Jake twisted his upper body toward her. His dazzling smile turned her insides to mush.

"I thought you knew I had sailed as part of

Daniel's crew a few times," he said. "Grandfather considered it part of our education. Benjamin had his stint as well, but Daniel was the only one to fall in love with the sea."

"What an unorthodox education."

"Agreed, but there was some logic involved. To protect one's investments."

She tipped her head to the side and glanced up at him. "Why must one know about sailing to protect one's investments?"

"There are many factors involved with a ship making her destination. To run a successful shipping business, it helps to be familiar with those factors. You want to hire the most qualified shipmaster, the one with the best chance of arriving with the shipment. Knowing what it takes to accomplish this task will guide you in choosing the best man."

"Oh."

She had never considered what a son might require as he grew into a man. A son needed a father to guide him, and Jake was the best man for the task. Tears pricked the back of her eyes, and she turned away before he noticed.

What if Jake was wrong about the laws governing New Orleans? Even he had admitted they would require counsel from a solicitor familiar with the divorce laws. What if the laws didn't apply to her? She was English, after all, and so was her husband. If that were the case, Audley would have to return to England, or she would never be free to marry again. And what if her husband refused, or demanded she stay with him?

Jake's hand grazed her elbow. "You're worrying again."

She tried to smile, but it felt tight and false. "I never expected to see my husband again. What will I say when I see him?"

Jake placed his hand over hers where it rested on the railing. His fingers fit snugly in the spaces between hers. "When I woke this morning, my first thought was of Mr. Canaan." He frowned slightly and shook his head. "Not true, he was second. You were first. You always are."

She laid her head against his shoulder for an instant, unable to resist touching him.

"If Mr. Canaan is not Audley, will you consider the matter settled?"

"Of course." A lump formed in her throat. She wanted to believe they had made a mistake more than anything, but she couldn't. Her instincts told her Mr. Canaan was a fraud.

"Are you tired, sweetheart? Do you want to go below deck?"

She shook her head. "I've missed civilization."

He chuckled. "I'm uncertain I would deem this area civilized, but I understand your meaning. Here comes the pilot."

Amelia craned her neck to view the longboat rowing in their direction. The man would help guide their ship over the sandbar, or so Jake had explained earlier.

"I never realized how difficult it would be to reach New Orleans," she said.

"Only the more daring attempt it."

Progress through the shallow, muddy waters was

arduous, but Amelia stayed by the railing, unwilling to miss any sight. The beds of mud eventually gave way to lush vegetation, untamed and mysterious. Ahead, a smattering of huts huddled together as if grouping the fragile domiciles might lend protection against Mother Nature.

She pointed. "Who lives there?"

"Fishermen, pilots, and their families. We've reached Balize Island. We will wait here until permission is granted to proceed."

"How long?"

He offered that heart-stopping grin again. "Don't worry. You'll eat well tonight. Are you hungry?"

"A little." *Blasted ravenous is more like it.*

"Splendid." His eye twinkled as if he knew she misrepresented her true state. Her appetite had become a demanding beast over the last couple of weeks, and much to her embarrassment, Jake appeared to have noticed.

She cleared her throat, ready to deflect attention from her expanding figure. "I want to accompany you to the bookshop when we dock. Perhaps if I speak with him—"

"Not until I've had a chance to see him."

"Why not? He's my husband."

Jake's jaw twitched. "Because I'm going to beat the gentleman senseless if he's truly David Caine. No man worth a shilling would leave you, Amelia."

She smiled despite her worries and the seriousness of his threat. "I promise to step outside if a thrashing becomes necessary."

～❦～

Once the *Cecily* reached the mouth of the Mississippi, Amelia had thought their journey at an end, but they'd still had a difficult leg ahead. Uncooperative winds left them sitting for more than half the day at times, making her question if they would ever reach their destination. Yet, now that they had arrived in New Orleans, and Amelia left the Dauphine Orleans on Jake's arm en route to Mr. Canaan's bookshop, she wished they were back on ship.

The harsh New Orleans sun seared her skin, and she raised her parasol in search of a reprieve. Whoever said ladies did not sweat had never worn the ridiculous layers favored by her contemporaries in a place where clothing should be banned all together. As they hurried along the walkway, there was little time to appreciate the charming ironwork balconies, not that she was in any state to enjoy the sights. All she could think on was the coming confrontation with her husband.

Her stomach whipped itself into a frenzy when Jake led her down a narrow passageway between two buildings. A wooden sign swung in the slight breeze, the metal links creaking with the effort of holding its weight. Black scrolled letters announced their location.

"Carlyle Book Shoppe," she whispered. Her legs trembled as they neared the entrance. Carlyle Manor had been in the Audley family for four generations, the home where her husband had reportedly lost his life.

She froze at the large shop window, fighting the urge to run away.

Jake looked to her, his brows drew together in concern. "Do you want to return to the hotel?"

She swallowed hard, her heart pounding, and then

she saw him. His hair was darker and longer, and held back with a tie. A tailored coat skimmed his narrow shoulders, and his breeches fit to perfection. Her husband was nothing if not immaculate in his grooming.

Audley conversed with a patron, his back to the window. Fury flared inside her, and she broke away from Jake to confront the horrid man she had been fool enough to marry.

"Amelia, wait."

She pushed through the door, setting off a jingling of bells.

Audley didn't turn to investigate. He spoke softly to the exotic young man in front of him.

"Mr. Canaan," she called, her voice reminiscent of a cracking whip.

"Yes?" He spun around and gasped. "Lady Audley?"

All her pluck and anger slipped. It wasn't her husband. *Thank God.* Jake wrapped his arm around her waist to keep her from sliding to the floor. A small smile played about his lips.

"Lord Patterson, I can't tell you how happy I am to find *you* here," Jake said.

The gentleman snarled. "Sorry I cannot say the same, *Hillary*."

Amelia drew back. Jake's smile slid from his face. She sensed his hesitation, the stiffening of his limbs.

"M-my lord, what are you doing in New Orleans?" she asked.

Patterson turned back to the gentleman aiming curious looks their direction and whispered something in his ear.

"Why must I leave?"

The men argued back and forth in a flurry of hissed words.

"As you wish." The man brushed past Patterson and bumped hard against his shoulder before stalking from the shop. The door slammed behind him.

"I take it he didn't find the book he wanted," Jake mumbled.

With a sigh, Patterson rubbed his temple. "Who sent you? My father? No, he can't wish to see me again."

"No one sent us," Amelia said. "We came here seeking my husband."

Patterson's hand fell to his side, and he scrutinized her with eyes narrowed. "Your husband is dead."

A flash of heat burnt her cheeks. "Well, yes. I can see how that might sound a bit peculiar, but we thought there might have been some mistake."

Jake offered his arm. "And now that we see there has been no mistake, we won't take up any more of your time." He directed her toward the door.

"You are seeking answers, Amelia. Not your husband."

Jake spun on his heel and thrust a finger at him. "Don't you dare address her by her Christian name. Have you any idea the suffering your little charade has brought us?"

Patterson frowned. "I shouldn't think any more than Audley's did."

Thirty-three

"WHAT DO YOU MEAN BY AUDLEY'S CHARADE?" Amelia's grip tightened on Jake's arm. "Are you indicating he *is* alive?"

"No, Lady Audley. I can assure you he's gone." Patterson pinched the bridge of his nose and squeezed his eyes closed. "I had the misfortune of bearing witness to his demise, and you are fortunate to have been spared the sight."

Jake pulled Amelia closer, tucking her up under his arm. There was no need to make her relive the past. Audley was dead. That was all the answers he needed. "Perhaps we should go and leave Lord Patterson, or Mr. Canaan, in peace."

"Peace," the gentleman spat. "What an abstract concept. I'm more likely to stumble across fairies or leprechauns."

"Fairies and leprechauns," Jake repeated under his breath. Patterson had always been an odd sort.

Jake tipped his hat. "Well, we wish you luck in your search for peace, fairies, and such."

A wry smile twisted Patterson's lips. "Your husband had no intention of returning to you, Mia. Were you aware?"

Amelia's breath caught. "How do you know that?"

Jake stepped between them, his shoulders squared. He didn't know what riled him more, the man's brazen use of Amelia's pet name or his insensitivity. "Recall your manners, sir."

The gentleman's lip curled. "David ruined the lady's life. Don't you think she deserves to know the reason?"

"My life hasn't been ruined."

"Not in the least." Jake offered his arm and directed her toward the exit. "We needn't stay any longer. We've discovered everything we need to know."

"Not everything, correct, my lady?" Patterson called after them. "You remain in the dark about the reason David married you."

Amelia halted.

Damnation! If Patterson was toying with her…

"Allow me to close the shop, and we may speak in my apartments above stairs," Patterson said. "I promise not to take much of your time."

Jake wanted to tell him to go to the devil, but Amelia released his arm. "Did my husband tell you he was leaving me?"

"In a manner of speaking. I can explain once there is no risk of anyone intruding."

Her blue gaze was uncertain as she looked to Jake.

He tamped down his frustration. If Amelia required something more to put her past behind her, he couldn't interfere.

"If you wish it," he said. "I won't leave your side."

She nodded.

Patterson moved to the shop door and turned the lock. "Follow me."

A weighty silence hovered on the air as they wound through the tight aisles between bookcases, the musty scent of old volumes familiar. Nothing said awkward quite like an encounter with an impostor posing as the husband of one's betrothed.

When they reached a staircase nestled in the back of the shop, they braced their hands against the walls in absence of a railing. The stairs creaked with each footstep.

They stopped on a landing outside a paneled door, and Patterson glanced back at them. "It's smaller than what I had in England."

"We shall endeavor to hide our shock behind masks of apathy," Jake said. Really, the man could live in a cave as far as he was concerned.

Patterson twisted the tarnished brass handle and pushed the door open. Afternoon sunlight filtered through the arched windows. Disjointed shadows marked the scarlet upholstered settee and sagging chairs, lending an air of wretchedness to the space.

The size of his lodging should be the least of Patterson's concerns. He should be demanding an apology from his decorator.

Patterson motioned toward the furniture grouping. "Please, have a seat."

Jake and Amelia moved in unison to the settee.

She cleared her throat. "You said Audley wasn't coming back to me. How do you know this unless he told you?"

"David rarely spoke of his thoughts or feelings, but he kept a journal. After the accident…"

"A journal?" Amelia leaned forward. "Is that how you knew of the house party? Please, I wish to see it."

"I'm afraid that's impossible." Patterson's Adam's apple bobbed and his gaze flicked toward a doorway. "I threw the diary away."

Jake narrowed his eyes. *A liar and a thief.* Apparently Jake's education at Eton had been lacking for he had missed those courses, unlike his classmates, Audley and Patterson. "I believe you know exactly where the journal is. Retrieve it for the lady unless you would like to discuss the matter further outside."

Patterson scowled. "You're a suspicious sort, Hillary. And insulting. To accuse a gentleman—"

"Retrieve the damned journal," Jake said, rising from the settee. "I haven't traveled halfway around the world to play games."

Patterson's lips thinned and defiance sparked in his eyes. Jake clenched and unclenched his fists, sorely tempted to thrash the man even if he did give over the journal. He could imagine at least thirty different ways to spend his afternoon. Decidedly more pleasant ways. He glanced back toward Amelia. And his imagination was rather vivid.

"Now," Jake snapped.

Patterson bolted from the chair. "Very well." He held himself erect as he disappeared into a back room.

Jake sat again, listening for Patterson's hurried movements, but the man moved at a speed that would make a tortoise appear fleet of foot by comparison.

His gaze slid down Amelia's legs and rested on the delicate curve of her ankle peeking beneath her skirts. He adjusted his position on the settee. "What's keeping you, Patterson?"

He reappeared in the doorway with a worn leather

book in hand. Instead of passing the object to Amelia, he lowered onto his chair and hugged it close to his chest.

"This belonged to David," he said. "I think he never meant for anyone to see it."

Jake lifted a brow. "No one?"

"I had no choice," Patterson snipped. "You should thank me for taking it."

Amelia sharply inclined her head. "You also possess his ring, I see. It's a family heirloom."

Patterson held a shaky hand out in front of him and studied the black stone. Placing the journal on his lap, he tugged the ring from his finger and held it out to her. "My apologies, Lady Audley. I had no right to keep it."

"Do you also keep a stash of Audley's drawers some place?" Jake said. "You seem to have taken everything else."

Amelia's fingers closed around the solid piece of jewelry. "Jake," she chided, but the corners of her mouth curved slightly. "Lord Patterson, what are you doing here? No one has seen you since the fire at Carlyle Manor."

His gaze flicked toward the windows. "How did you find me?"

"We share a mutual acquaintance, Mr. Isaac Tucker. He's a chatty fellow." Amelia recounted her discussion with the American.

"I see." Patterson scrubbed his hand over his face. "Tucker was never one to keep his own counsel, but I suppose I'm to blame. David wrote about the incident at your relatives' country home. Had I known the tale would travel halfway around the world, I never would have repeated it."

"That hardly excuses your lie, sir. Why on earth would you claim I was your wife?"

A telling blush crept up Patterson's neck, and he pulled a handkerchief from his pocket to dab at beads of sweat popping up on his forehead. "I had need of a wife. Since I've remained unmarried and lack imagination, I modeled my fictional wife after you, from the things David wrote about you. Do you think anyone else knows I'm here?"

"I wouldn't know. Is someone searching for you?"

Patterson shrugged and began tapping his fingers against the armrest.

Amelia blew out a long sigh. "Lord Patterson, what is it you wished to tell us?"

Jake captured her hand and rubbed it between his larger palms. Her pale complexion stirred his concern for her well-being and that of his child. "Yes, man. Get on with your explanation. Can't you see the lady tires from this conversation?"

Patterson aimed a pointed look at their joined hands. "What a desperate fool David was, unwilling to accept that his love would never be returned. His obsession held him prisoner."

Amelia entwined her fingers with Jake's and held on. "Your estimation is wrong, sir. I have come to the conclusion Audley never loved me."

The man stared at her, his lips parted as if he debated his response.

Amelia shifted on the settee and pulled her hand from Jake's hold. "I *said* my husband never loved me."

"No, he didn't," Patterson agreed in a quiet voice.

"But you indicated my husband was a desperate fool in love. You speak in riddles."

And they weren't even clever riddles, in Jake's opinion. More like the nonsensical jokes Amelia's niece had peppered him with when they had visited Crossing Meadows.

Why did the mother hen travel to Bath? She likes ham and cheese. Jake chuckled under his breath. Complete balderdash.

Patterson's unblinking eyes settled on him. "I apologize, Amelia, but I was referring to David's attachment to Mr. Hillary."

Jake laughed, a loud barking sound amplified in the small space. He had underestimated the man's ability to amuse. He stood and offered a hand up to Amelia. "Shall we? He knows nothing of value."

The man flipped the book open. "A reading from David's journal. 'I have committed the unforgiveable today. I offered for Miss Barton's hand. I do not know what came over me. As she spoke of Jake, I could see it in her eyes and my heart sank. She loves him, as much as he loves her.'"

Jake froze.

"'I could not catch my breath as I imagined the two of them together. I have never known such intense sorrow. I felt as if I were dying, a drowning man clutching on to anything to keep from slipping under the dark waters of despair. I begin to lose hope of him ever becoming mine, but I cannot stomach the thought of my love with any—'"

"Give me that." Jake closed the space between himself and Patterson and jerked the journal from his hands. "Dark waters of despair," he mumbled as he read Audley's script. What a melodramatic twit!

As he read further, fire began to churn in his guts. Audley's deception and disdain for Amelia set off a tremble that traveled down his arms and legs. Jake tossed the offensive book back at Patterson.

"He married me to keep us apart?" she asked.

Patterson made a sympathetic sound at the back of his throat. "I'm sorry, but you deserved the truth. David wasn't the man I thought he was. He excelled at hiding his true self."

Audley wasn't the man any of them had believed him to be. Early on, Jake had considered him a friend. Later, a traitor. But he had been more than that. Audley had been a selfish blackguard who had misused Amelia cruelly and played Jake for a fool. Worse, Jake had *allowed* him to hurt Amelia.

One glance at her pale face compounded his shame. "How will you ever forgive me?"

She lifted her head, a determined set to her jaw. "You have no reason to apologize."

"I failed to protect you. I walked away."

"No, you are a man of honor." She rose from the settee and wrapped her arms around him. "Audley lied to us both. I won't allow you to take on the burden of guilt."

Patterson crossed his leg over his knee and jiggled his foot. When his eyes grew misty, he looked away.

Amelia followed Jake's gaze. She worked her bottom lip with her teeth. "My lord, it appears we are not the only ones who suffered at Audley's hands."

Patterson shook his head and flicked a hand across his cheek.

Amelia released Jake and moved to stand in front of Patterson. "I hope you understand that I must take the journal. I assure you, no one else will ever view the contents."

Patterson's arms hung limply at his sides as she retrieved the journal. She held it close. "If my husband named you in his journal, please don't fret."

He turned watery eyes on her. "There's not a single mention of me. Just your Mr. Hillary."

She reached out to touch the man's shoulder. "You loved him and he wrote nothing about you."

Patterson shook his head and used his fists to wipe away his tears. "I shouldn't speak of this." He struggled to get out of the chair, forcing Amelia to step back. "You should go, Lady Audley. And please tell no one of our conversation."

"Of course I won't."

Patterson looked to Jake.

He shrugged. "I'm content to forget we were ever here."

"Perhaps Audley only wrote about the parts of his life that made him unhappy," Amelia offered.

"Perhaps." Patterson turned his back on them and moved to the window.

Amelia nodded. "We should go."

Jake escorted her to the door and down the stairs. They wove through the bookshelves to reach the exit. Outside on the sidewalk, they paused.

Fine lines appeared on Amelia's forehead. "Are you all right?"

He considered her question. If he had been privy to the same information several months ago, he would have answered with a belligerent no. But then he'd not had Amelia. Now, everything he had always wanted was within his reach. He wouldn't feed a resentment that no longer served anyone.

Looking down at her, he pretended to frown. "I'm afraid I will never be all right again."

Her eyes expanded. "Oh?"

"I've been struck by a serious illness," he said with the appropriate level of graveness. "And I hear there is no cure for love sickness."

"Love sickness, you say? That is serious." Amelia slanted a delightfully wicked smile at him. "But you're in luck, Mr. Hillary, for I hear the treatments for this particular illness are rather pleasurable."

"I fear I shall require many."

She chuckled softly, a warm blush coloring her cheeks. "I just bet you do, Mr. Hillary."

With Amelia by his side and a bounce in his step, he guided them away from the bookstore and toward the future that should have been theirs years ago.

Thirty-four

JAKE LED AMELIA INTO THE HOTEL CHAMBER AND closed the door. She removed her bonnet and gloves then placed them on the gilded entry table. Turning, she looked up at him with resplendent blue eyes. Her tentative pink tongue wet her lips, igniting the passion that had been a smoldering fire inside him for the past few weeks.

"Come here, sweetheart." His voice had taken on a rough quality.

She walked into the circle of his arms and laid her cheek against his chest. He caressed her from hip to nape before searching for the pins securing her hair. One by one, he pulled them from her silken locks until her curls tumbled down her back.

Pressing her hands against his chest, she eased from his embrace. "I should lock the door."

Jake released her, but immediately regretted the loss of her warmth. He followed in her path and trapped her against the smooth surface of the door as she turned the key. Fitting their bodies together, he splayed his hand across her belly. Amelia trembled in his arms; the splendid curve of her bottom lightly cradled him.

"Mia," he said on an exhale.

He trailed one hand over hers, along the underside of her arm, brushed his knuckles against the side of her breast, and continued to her hip. How he hungered for her, to once again explore her silken skin beneath her gown. To slide his fevered flesh against hers.

Her gossamer hair wisped over his cheek as she turned her head. Sweeping her curtain of hair aside, he grazed his lips along her tender neck and took her velvety earlobe between his teeth. She sighed and melted under his touch, molding her body more firmly to his.

"I love you," he whispered. His kisses elicited a shiver and sensual moan from her that almost undid him. She arched her back on another sigh, dropping her head to rest against his shoulder. Desire streaked through his limbs like lightning and with as much impact.

Allowing his lustful urgings free rein at last, he captured her breast and buried his face in her fragrant hair.

Hyacinth. That was her scent, sweet and intoxicating.

Her breath caught in ragged gasps, and she squirmed; each movement shot pleasurable waves through him. He closed his eyes on a groan as he smoothed his hand over the swell of her breast, her corset barring his access.

She turned in his embrace and twined her arms around his neck. His fingers tangled in her hair and he lightly pulled to tip her face up. Amelia's lips parted on a gasp, and he kissed her, sliding his tongue into the moist sweetness of her mouth. She lovingly met his kisses and caressed his tongue, battering the last of his restraint.

Sweeping her into his arms, he carried her to the bed and placed her on the edge. He lowered to one knee and removed each slipper before inching her skirts over her thighs to seek out the ties of her drawers. His breath came in hard pants as he fought back the urge to take her as he wished. Barely controlled lust battled with his desire to be tender.

Holding her hands, he coaxed her to stand and turn her back to him so he could work the fastenings of her gown. Each newly bared inch of skin received a soft kiss.

"Too slow," she said on a breath.

His fingers tightened on her dress. "Patience, my love." He placed another teasing kiss on her back before easing the gown off her shoulders. The muslin floated down her body to land at her feet.

"I don't want to be patient. *Hurry*."

Her command broke through his control, and he tugged on the strings of her corset, unlacing her with increasing fervor.

Once she wore nothing but her chemise, she spun in his arms and grabbed at his cravat. "Come here."

Her eyes darkened to a stormy sea blue as she played his harried valet. Shoving his jacket down his arms and grasping at his waistcoat, she met him in a battle of lips. Her unbridled kisses tasted of desperation as her tongue darted into his mouth, bold and determined. He followed her lead, entangling his fingers in her locks and slanting her head to accept his exploration. Good Lord, she couldn't have been more welcoming if she had thrown a party in his honor.

The feel of Amelia, her passion. This was what he had been missing. Partly.

He broke the kiss, both of them panting. When she reached for him again, he held her back. "Tell me you love me too." Desire saturated his voice, making it deeper. He needed to hear her speak the words.

"I do," she whispered before showering his face with kisses. "I love you, Jake. I have always loved you."

Her lush frame shuddered in his arms as their lips met again. He swallowed her sweet sentiments, his heart beating with revived energy.

As he lifted her, she wrapped her legs around him, binding them together. Jake collapsed on the bed, catching his weight on his elbows with Amelia entrapped below him. The soft cotton of her chemise brushed against his chest, but he wanted to feel her skin.

Hauling the hem of her undergarment, he shimmied it up her body, peeled it over her head, and bared her breasts. Her arms became bound above her head, ensnared by the material, and Jake took full advantage of her position. His tongue feathered across her nipple, eliciting a sharp intake of breath. He smiled and blew across the hardened flesh.

"Jake." She wriggled beneath him.

"Not now, sweetheart. I'm preoccupied," he teased before drawing his tongue slowly across the tip until a soft whimper slipped past her lips. Her hips twisted and her soft curls brushed against his belly.

"Good God," he groaned. His shaft ached with desire, and he pressed his hips into the bedding to ease his pain. He had missed her so much over these last weeks, and he wished to be like this with her for as long as possible, drawing out their lovemaking, but he didn't know if he could hold himself in check much longer.

Closing his mouth over her breast, he circled the hardened bud until soft cries of pleasure emanated from her as musical as a siren's song. He pulled back to admire his beautiful wife-to-be. Her body shimmered under the late afternoon sunlight, her skin dewy and luxuriant.

She squirmed free of her bindings and buried her fingers in his hair, guiding him back to her breast. Jake chuckled as he kissed a trail to her other breast and lavished the nipple with the same heart-stopping results. Amelia's lusty murmurings ignited an inferno inside him. His fingers sought out her hot center and brushed across liquid silk.

"Are you ready for me, Mia?"

"Yes," she gasped as he dipped a finger inside her. When she tightened around him, a soft moan rose up in his throat.

Amelia captured his face, urged him closer, and kissed him. Their mouths lingered together, sharing the same breath.

"I want you," she whispered, "under me."

Jake's smile widened. "You shall have me however you wish, my love."

⚜

Amelia's heart pounded looking into Jake's lush blue-green eyes, his love for her unguarded and offered without conditions. She ran a gentle hand across his shadowed jaw, the roughness so pleasant beneath her fingers. "I love you, too," she whispered.

Grasping both wrists, she shoved his arms above his head and leaned her weight against them when he halfheartedly strained against her. "Amelia!"

"No, I shall have you as I wish."

A wicked grin stretched across his handsome face as he relaxed into the bedding. "Yes, milady."

Easing her leg across his waist, she perched atop him. His hardened ridge pressed against her sensitive flesh, and Amelia closed her eyes on a sigh. She slid her body along his, drawing out the moment, intent on driving him to the brink as he had done to her.

When she looked down, his chest heaved with rapid breaths, and his eyes had darkened to a midnight sky.

Jake broke free of her hold and seized her hips. "I'm sorry, but I must have you now."

He guided her on him and quaked beneath her. Amelia's heart beat against her breastbone. Smiling down at him, she set a steady rhythm, and then, at his urging, raced faster. He sat up, drawing her against his chest, his hands cupping the back of her head and bottom to move her with him. She clung to him, kissing him wherever her lips wandered—his forehead, his cheek, his strong jaw, his corded neck.

His hand covered her breast, his thumb rubbing across the rigid plane of her nipple. A spark of pleasure shot to her center, and she dropped her head back to savor the feeling. Warm tingles infused her body as he continued his play with her breasts and his lips found her neck.

"Are you close?" he murmured.

Amelia swallowed hard and nodded. Everything coiled tight within her as Jake slid deep inside her then withdrew in short strokes. A haze of lust clouded his gaze.

"Come with me," she urged.

A low rumble sounded in his chest, the erotic sound pushing her over the edge. She cried out as she soared upward, Jake with her, his voice intertwined with hers. As they reached the apex, they held tightly to one another, neither letting go as they stilled, every ounce of breath rushing from them, before unhurriedly drifting back to solid ground once more.

Even then, they held on to one another. Jake stretched out on the bed and curled her against his side, his warm limbs tangled with hers.

"Never let me go," she pleaded as sleep threatened to overtake her.

He nuzzled her hair and placed a kiss there. "Never again."

❦

The next morning Amelia lowered into a cushioned chair and blinked against the bright sunlight pouring through the window of the sleeping chamber. The cheerful room with its yellow walls and floral paintings reflected her hopeful mood. She was free to marry the man she'd loved for so long.

Last night, she and Jake had remained intertwined in each other's arms and basked in their joy at beginning a new life together. They had spoken of their child and dreams for his future. The last thing she remembered was the midnight chime of the clock on the mantle before blissful oblivion overtook her. Jake lay tangled in the sheets, his bare limbs lax while he still slumbered.

Audley's journal rested on the side table and caught her eye. Lifting it, she brushed her palm over the worn cover. Such an innocuous object from the looks of it, but the words inside provided a glimpse into her husband's troubled soul.

Many times during their marriage, and for some time after his death, she had wished to read Audley's mind. Now that she had the opportunity to understand him better, she no longer cared.

She lifted the journal and tested its weight. It was odd how things that had once seemed of great importance had lost significance with the passing of time. Pushing up from the chair, she carried the book to the fire grate, placed it inside, and retrieved a tinderbox. The pages caught slowly, the edges turning black and shrinking, until the flames grew and began to devour Audley's words inch by inch.

"Good morning, sweetheart."

Amelia turned with a smile at the sound of Jake's voice.

This was all that mattered now: Jake, their growing family, and her freedom to love and be loved in return.

Thirty-five

JAKE PRESSED HIS CHIN AGAINST THE STACK OF BOOKS balanced in his arms as he teetered up the gangplank. Amelia had chosen more than enough reading materials to last throughout the return voyage, which meant one thing. Her flood of tears and guilty conscience last night were not a fleeting symptom of her being with child.

In a desperate attempt to calm her, he had agreed with her suggestion to wait until they married to consummate their relationship again. Although he had agreed they deserved a fresh start, the one they would have had if not for Audley, he had made his pledge based on the belief she would be rational today. Apparently, he had learned nothing in his five-and-twenty years. Women were unpredictable creatures.

Had Daniel's New Orleans connections been able to procure a marriage license, he would not be in this predicament. And since his brother had his own matters to attend to before they sailed again, Jake hadn't asked for assistance. Now he wished he had imposed on Daniel.

Jake groaned under his breath. There was no way he could survive the return voyage without making love to Amelia, especially with her emerging curves. Gads. He had lost all concentration and stopped speaking midsentence at dinner last night when she had leaned forward and revealed her newly enhanced bust. He would find a way to convince her to reconsider.

He glanced up as he navigated the wooden walkway. Amelia stood at the top, her brow wrinkled.

"You won't drop them, will you?" she asked. "I'm looking forward to reading each and every one. I will require *something* to keep me occupied on this long, long voyage."

He didn't require any reminders as to the length of their journey. "I won't drop them," he bit out.

Amelia tossed her head before waving her hand in the air. "Oh, Mr. Patch, would you lend your assistance?"

Jake scowled at the mention of the other man's name. It seemed the bloody giant followed Amelia everywhere these days like a loyal puppy. He had been escorting her on shopping trips in which Jake had been excluded—likely selecting the largest books they could find—and the two disappeared for hours. The sooner they reached London, the better. Otherwise, Jake might abandon all good sense and challenge the brute to a round of fisticuffs, which would surely end badly for him.

He shifted the stack to Patch's waiting arms once he stepped aboard the *Cecily*.

Amelia smiled. "Please carry them to my cabin, Mr. Patch. You know the way."

With the man out of earshot, Jake gently grasped

her arm to guide her to the quarterdeck. "You needn't make it sound as if the man has visited your cabin repeatedly."

Amelia tilted her head and gazed at him with innocent eyes. "But he *has* visited my cabin repeatedly. Do you not recall the voyage over—?"

"*Yes*, and please keep your voice down, sweetheart." The hurried movements around them didn't cease, so he doubted anyone overheard their conversation, but it was the principle of the matter.

"I don't wish to give anyone the impression you... How should I say this? Well, that you are not mine."

Amelia chuckled and swatted his arm. "Oh, that is ridiculous."

Her infectious laughter melted his tension, and he too laughed at his show of jealousy.

She shrugged one shoulder. "To say I am *yours* as if I were an object to own, like a new cravat or waistcoat. You are a silly man."

Jake's jaw dropped, but before he could utter any protest, her attention shifted elsewhere.

"Oh, look. Ladies and a young boy."

He turned toward the gangplank where she pointed and spotted a young woman dressed in mourning clothes holding the hand of a boy half her height. A willowy woman of regal bearing and expensive attire followed behind them.

Amelia clapped her hands and issued a delighted squeal. "It seems my presence onboard has loosened Captain Hillary's strict standards of no women on the ship. I do hope the ladies are friendly. I have much need for female companionship on the trip."

"Don't we all," he grumbled.

"Pardon?" She dismissed him with a wave of her hand. "Oh, it matters not. I shall make the young women's acquaintance before going below deck for a rest. You will be all right up here alone, won't you?"

He spread his arms wide. "I'm not a child, my dear. Do I not seem perfectly fine to be alone?"

Amelia patted his lapel and clucked her tongue. "You seem a bit surly, actually. Perhaps you should have a rest in Captain Hillary's quarters." With that said, she whisked away to speak with the newest travelers.

Hellfire and damnation! The situation was worse than he had imagined. Amelia no longer viewed him as a man with certain urges and needs, but had begun to see him as a child prone to tantrums and in need of naps. He spun on his heel and stormed into Daniel's cabin.

His brother glanced up from his logs, a half smirk twisting his lips. "Where's Amelia?"

Jake helped himself to the liquor decanter. "Greeting the passengers." He sloshed the amber rum into a tumbler and sipped, studying Daniel over the rim of the glass. "You've allowed a lady and her child to travel on the *Cecily*?"

His head snapped up. "She's here?"

"If you refer to a female dressed in all black and a raven-haired slip of a boy at her side, then yes, they have arrived."

Daniel shoved from the table and stalked to the door. "I should see the passengers safely to their quarters."

For the love of God, even Daniel had changed in New Orleans. It was as if someone had placed a voodoo curse on his betrothed and brother. Neither of them resembled the people they had been when the ship had sailed from London.

Jake made his way to an armchair that hadn't been in Daniel's quarters on the first leg of the voyage and plopped down. His eyes felt gritty, so he leaned his head against the seat back and closed them, listening to the noises outside. Through the jumble of voices, the haunting call of the seagulls floated in the background, soothing his ruffled temper.

A gentle breeze drifted through the open window and caressed his hot cheeks, lessening his irritation even more. The ship swayed gently back and forth. Back and forth. Back and forth.

A loud bang startled him and Jake jumped from the chair. He glanced around, unsure where he was.

"Wake up, you pampered mama's boy," Daniel called from the doorway.

Jake blinked as he realized where he was and that he had indeed drifted to sleep.

The ship's rocking was more pronounced and steady.

"We've lifted anchor?" Jake asked.

"Three hours past."

Jake's gaze landed on the windows along the ship's aft where overgrown vines outside tried to choke out the trees and trailed toward the water. New Orleans was long behind them, it seemed.

He stretched his arms overhead and uttered a groaning sigh.

Daniel lifted a brow. "For God's sake, Jakie, you stink. Get cleaned up. You haven't much time."

"Time for what?" he grumbled.

"Amelia is serving luncheon in her quarters. So,

either you can make yourself presentable, or I will drag your smelly arse below deck as is. Either way, you *are* attending."

"Ha, ha. You are hilarious."

Daniel snatched a cloth from the table and threw it at him. "I'm serious about the luncheon. And consider it a favor that I advised you to wash up ahead of time. There is a basin with fresh water in the sleeping chamber."

Jake trudged toward the door to the sleeping chambers. "But in her quarters? It's minuscule compared to here."

"She wishes to surprise you. Will you please get a move on it? And act surprised or else."

Jake shrugged, the beginning of a smile pulling at his lips. He could act any way she wished.

"And don the attire laid out on my bed," Daniel added.

Jake didn't offer any more arguments and hurried to make himself presentable.

A few minutes later, he and Daniel stood outside Amelia's cabin. Jake rapped harder than he intended, and the door flew open. He drew back.

A man dressed in robes stood in the doorway. Jake looked around the narrow passageway, certain he had knocked on the wrong door. He didn't recall seeing a clergyman on the initial voyage, but he hadn't checked under the bed either.

"Mr. Hillary, welcome. Lady Audley awaits."

Jake spotted Amelia beyond the man's shoulder. She wore an ivory gown with long matching gloves and stood beside a formally set table. Candlelight reflected off the gilded rims of the china plates and reflected in the crystal goblets while casting Amelia in a soft glow.

Jake's heart expanded, filling his chest fully. She truly was his angel on earth.

Amelia extended her hand with an inviting smile. "Please, come inside."

He passed the table set for two to reach her.

Daniel gestured toward the clergyman. "Allow me to introduce the Vicar of Trinity Church in Dunstable. Mr. Ramsey has agreed to perform the ceremony."

"Ceremony?"

Amelia squeezed Jake's hand and lifted her pretty face toward him. "There is nothing to impede our marriage on ship, so Captain Hillary tells me. As long as we have the vicar to officiate."

Jake grinned, probably somewhat foolishly. "You're far from home, Mr. Ramsey."

"As are you," the vicar answered. "Your brother provided me with passage many months back. Family commitments required my attention."

Daniel shrugged. "I'd hoped Mr. Ramsey would still be in New Orleans, and that I would be able to locate him. I couldn't be certain he'd agree to return to England, but as luck would have it, his commitments in New Orleans have ended."

Mr. Ramsey crossed his arms over his chest. "And what a generous donation Captain Hillary has made to the Church of England to provide for my needs on the journey." The vicar raised his eyebrows, apparently waiting for a response from Jake.

"Oh. Well, perhaps you would accept a sizable donation from me as well. We cannot allow a respected member of the clergy to go without the *basics* needed for survival."

Mr. Ramsey beamed. "Indeed, Mr. Hillary. You are a generous soul."

Jake glanced at Amelia. Hell. He would give half his fortune if it meant he could have her for his wife tonight.

"This is truly what you desire?" he asked her. "Our wedding onboard?"

"Very much."

"Then we have no reason to waste any more of Mr. Ramsey's time. Shall we?"

Facing one another, they waited to repeat their vows. Amelia's clear blue eyes held his gaze.

Mr. Ramsey cleared his throat. "Please repeat after me. I, Jacob James Hillary, take you Amelia Catherine Caine née Barton, to be my wife, to have and to hold from this day forward."

Jake echoed the vicar's words, offering his promise of protection and love to Amelia forever. A thick lump formed in his throat as she looked on him with love. "For better or for worse, for richer, for poorer, in sickness and in health, to love and to cherish; from this day forward until death do us part."

Nothing but death *could* ever separate them. Jake would fight off the hounds of hell before anything kept them apart again.

Amelia spoke her vows without wavering. "To love and to cherish from this day forward until death do us part," she finished, tears welling up in her eyes.

Mr. Ramsey grinned. "I now pronounce you man and wife."

Jake kissed his beautiful wife chastely before turning to accept Daniel's handshake.

His brother thwacked his back as he pumped

his hand before sweeping Amelia into his arms and placing a noisy smack on her cheek. She giggled like a young girl, setting Jake's teeth on edge. His brother should find his own damned wife.

"Yes, my days in New Orleans were a hardship," Mr. Ramsey interjected as if someone had posed a question to him about his experiences. "I didn't enjoy the luxuries of home. In fact, I—"

Daniel clamped a meaty hand on the vicar's shoulder and guided him toward the door. "Then you must join me in my quarters for dinner. I shall open one of the finer vintages I carried from England."

Jake smiled his gratitude as his brother removed the chattering man from their cabin.

Amelia glanced at Jake from beneath her wispy lashes. "I requested our meal be served here. Would you like to partake?"

Jake chuckled under his breath. He would definitely like to partake, but not of the dishes spread on the table. But a few more minutes wouldn't be the death of him. Besides, Amelia required more sustenance these days.

"I would love to sample the fine dishes you've chosen." He held her chair out, and she lowered onto the padded seat, her movements fluid and graceful.

He examined the plush scarlet counterpane covering their bed and the expensive dinnerware. "You've been shopping for our quarters."

Spots of pink brightened her cheeks. "I thought to make it more inviting since it will be our home for the next several weeks."

"Brilliant idea."

Amelia ladled lobster bisque from the soup tureen into

delicate porcelain bowls before setting one in front of each of them. The savory scent made his mouth water.

"Did the cook learn some new dishes?"

She wrinkled her nose. "Sadly, no. This will be our only gourmet meal."

"You have been secretive, Mrs. Hillary." Jake loved the way her new address rolled off his tongue, richer and more exquisite than the creamy soup.

"I'm sorry for teasing you last night and today. It was rather bad form, even though it was successful at keeping you away long enough to arrange everything."

"I'm certain you will find some way to make amends."

She offered an impish grin before touching her lovely lips to the edge of the spoon to sip the bisque. Those lips had been mesmerizing him for years.

After the soup, she served a spicy red fish and fresh asparagus salad with a delicate vinaigrette. Lastly, she lifted a domed silver cover.

"*Beignets,*" she announced, swirling her gloved hand over the powdered pastries. The way her sea blue eyes danced with excitement was enchanting. His wife had developed quite the sweet tooth over the last couple of weeks.

Jake snatched a puff pastry from the tray, and with his free hand, he gently tugged on her arm. "Come here, sweetheart."

Amelia replaced the domed lid and allowed him to pull her onto his lap. He touched the treat to her lips, but as she opened her mouth for a bite, he withdrew it to tease her.

She huffed. "Jake."

He chuckled before licking the powdered sugar

from her bottom lip. "I'm sorry, love. I know you have developed a liking for *beignets*."

Her eyes clouded. "I'm afraid I have liked them too much."

He adjusted her on his lap and wrapped his arms tighter around her expanded waist. "How does one like a delectable treat too much? If that's possible, I fear I will be guilty of overindulging on my wife."

Her gaze dropped to her belly. "You don't think I have grown too stout?"

"Good Lord, no. You've become a goddess. I can barely keep my hands off you."

Amelia laughed when he kneaded her fuller bottom and nuzzled her neck.

"If anything, you should worry I might keep a babe in your belly as often as possible."

"Even though being with child tends to make me unreasonable at times?"

"As long as you return to your senses eventually."

She twined her arms around his neck, pressing her voluptuous breasts against him. "I'll welcome any children you see fit to give me. I never thought I would become a mother or marry again, but now I cannot imagine my life any other way. I love you, Jake."

Threading his fingers into her silky hair, he drew her forward until their lips drifted as close as possible without touching.

"I worship you, Mia, and I always will," he murmured before sealing his promise with a kiss.

Read on for an excerpt from

Miss Lavigne's Little White Lie

BY SAMANTHA GRACE

Coming October 2012
From Sourcebooks Casablanca

New Orleans
June 20, 1818

GRANDMAMMA HAD ALWAYS SAID NOTHING GOOD happened under the cloak of darkness. The witching hour was ripe with men practicing their evil. Therefore, it was with much trepidation that Lisette Lavigne huddled together with her younger brother and cousin in the shadowy gardens of Passebon House, praying the night would conceal their escape from the wickedest of men, her betrothed.

The coarse language of Louis Reynaud's men carried on the sluggish air. They made no attempt to hide their presence outside the gate of her father's Vieux Carré home, and hadn't since their arrival two days earlier. The men had even followed her on a shopping excursion to Rue de Royale earlier in the day, confirming her suspicions. Her betrothed sensed she no longer wished to marry him, and he had no intentions of releasing her from their agreement.

Her brother shifted and whimpered softly. Hiding

in the gardens rather than tucked into bed at this hour would disturb any child, but to one with Rafe's temperament, a fit of temper could ensue at any moment.

Their cousin, Serafine Vistoire, placed a comforting arm around his shoulders. "There, there, sweet child," she murmured. "Look for your stars."

Rafe rocked side-to-side as he searched the starsplattered sky, soothing himself, at least for the time being.

The deafening trill of cicadas pierced the night, their ever-rising call tweaking Lisette's taut nerves. She forced herself to slow her breathing.

"Where are they?" she whispered. "Monsieur Baptiste said midnight."

Serafine nodded. The whites of her eyes stood out in the darkness.

What if they didn't come? The wedding was in two days. This would be their only chance to flee. Lisette's fingers tightened on her bombazine skirts until her knuckles ached.

"Good evening, *messieurs*." A throaty laugh floated on the heavy air, the call of a temptress. Relief flooded through Lisette. The distraction had arrived at last.

"*Sacré bleu!*" one of the men yelped. "Are you seeing what I see?"

"Whores. Whatta they doing here?"

"Perfect night to take exercise," one of the women purred. "Wouldn't you agree, gents?"

Her companion chuckled, her voice heavy with seductive promise. "*Oui*. Two virile *messieurs* like you must take exercise often."

Reynaud's man uttered a combination of unspeakable words that might have impressed Lisette under different circumstances, for he excelled at the art of vulgarity. She considered herself an expert, having developed an ear for inappropriate language while visiting Papa at the waterfront.

Rafe wiggled, his control nearing the limits.

Sweet Mary. This had best work, and quickly.

"Just for a bit? *S'il vous plaît.*"

"Damn," one of the guards muttered. "I'm gonna hate myself for this, but we can't leave our posts."

Really, the man's integrity was shocking. How did one go about locating such upstanding criminals?

"May I share a secret, mister?"

"I s'pose. What kind of secret?"

"As your friend implied, a pair of whores doesn't happen by on a lark. Perhaps you should think of us as a reward for a job well done."

"Reynaud sent you?"

Lisette held her breath as she waited for the woman's response.

"Shh. 'Tis a secret, remember?"

Both men chuckled as if they couldn't believe their good fortune. And anyone with sense would know better. Lisette was barely acquainted with her betrothed, and yet she understood he did nothing that benefitted anyone aside from himself.

"Ain't no harm in exercise, right?"

"Splendid. This way, sir, where we may enjoy some privacy."

"What about the garden?"

Lisette froze like a rabbit that had spotted the family pet. If the women led them through the gate, she and her family would be discovered. Frantic, she searched for a place to retreat among the potted flowers and garden statues.

"Flowers make me sneeze, monsieur. But I know a better spot for amorous sport."

Their voices faded as they moved away from the house.

Lisette crept from their hiding place and slung the bag of their belongings over her shoulder. "We must go quickly."

Seeing no one else outside on the walk, she pushed open the gate then captured her brother's hand. Dressed in all black to blend with the night, they headed toward the wharf.

No one spoke as they crossed Rue de Chartres. Moss draped like gauze from the gnarled limbs of the trees as they drew closer to the river.

Rafe dragged on her arm, forcing Lisette to stop. "I want to go home."

She reassuringly squeezed his hand and urged him forward. "But we have a surprise for you, remember?"

"I want to go home."

Serafine tugged his other arm. "Not now, *ma biche*. We must hurry."

Rafe had maintained excellent control up to this point, donning black clothing despite his abhorrence of the color and kneeling in the garden where dirt might soil his hands. Expecting anything more from him seemed unfair, but they required his cooperation now more than ever.

Lisette crouched at his level. "Shall I reveal the surprise now? We are sailing on a ship."

"A ship?" A twinge of interest colored his voice.

"Yes, a majestic ship called the *Cecily*. We must sleep close to the port for we cannot miss our ship."

"Cannot miss the *Cecily*." Rafe resumed his measured strides. "Baltimore flyer, clipper, frigate, Indiaman." He recited the types of ships he knew with a note of excitement.

She had handled her brother without much difficulty this time. Now if only they could enter The Abyss without drawing notice. Reynaud had nefarious connections all over New Orleans, and hiding among the derelict of the city was a risky endeavor. What manner of man must the captain of the *Cecily* be to commune with petty thieves and cut-throats?

Lisette forced her concerns to the edges of her consciousness. Captain Hillary's ship was the *only* ship departing for England and provided the sole means of protecting her brother. Nothing would deter her when it came to keeping Rafe safe.

❧

Captain Daniel Hillary loved two simple pleasures in life, a woman's supple curves beneath his body and his Indiaman with sails unfurled, forging through the ocean waves. But damn it to hell, women and the sea didn't mix, and based upon Paulina's determined eyes staring up at him, he was in for a row.

Why she chose to make her request *before* they had taken their pleasure was beyond him. They were still wearing their clothes, for the love of God.

He rolled off his handsome mistress and flopped to his back. "I don't allow women aboard the *Cecily*. End of discussion."

Paulina lifted to her elbow and frowned down at him. Her mussed chestnut hair made her appear as if she'd already been tumbled, increasing his discomfort. "That is untrue. What of the beautiful blonde woman?"

"She's my brother's intended. I can't leave her in New Orleans." He reached for Paulina, but she jerked back. "I'll leave more money this time. You will never know I'm gone."

She leaned over to nip his earlobe then trailed kisses down his neck. This was more like it. "It—is—not—the—money—I—want." She spoke between pecks, unwilling to abandon the topic after all.

Daniel sighed. Paulina resided in luxury. She wouldn't forfeit her comfort for weeks on a bloody ship, which meant she had another objective. He lifted her chin to look at him.

"Tell me what you want, and don't insult my intelligence by claiming you only want me."

He was aware of her other gentlemen benefactors, even if she believed herself discreet. His connections kept him abreast of the happenings in New Orleans, and the reports on Paulina's indiscretions could keep him occupied for the better part of a day. If he cared to listen.

She sat back on her haunches and pushed out her bottom lip. "Don't you want to be with me all the time?"

He linked his fingers behind his head. Paulina was a talented woman who knew how to please him, but he *didn't* want to be with her all the time. He didn't wish to be with any woman all the time, not after Cecily.

"I'm content with our arrangement." He didn't bother to tread lightly with her sensibilities.

As he expected, no hurt crossed Paulina's face, only

irritation. "Very well, but I *would* like some security. You spend more time in England than here now. I don't enjoy your protection as I once did. Nor do you bring me beautiful trinkets as in the beginning. I am not getting any younger, Daniel. My beauty will fade and my prospects will dwindle. I need to know I won't end up in the streets."

He cocked a brow. "This isn't your attempt at proposing marriage, I hope."

"You mock me." She crawled toward the edge of the bed.

"Wait." Grasping her around the waist, he pulled her back.

Paulina had been an accommodating mistress these last two years. He supposed he could fulfill one of her wishes, if they could get on with other matters.

"Tell me what you really want, my dear, and dispatch with the theatrics."

She turned in his embrace, victory shining in the depths of her brown eyes. "There is a house I fancy. I wish you to purchase it in my name."

"A house?"

He glanced around the exquisite boudoir with the Turkish carpet, gilded mirrors, and silk curtains, all gifts he had given her. Not to mention that horrendous ruby amulet draped around her neck, the fruits of her last sulk. It was a wonder she didn't walk hunched over from the weight.

When he had offered his protection, her home had required an extensive remodeling. He could ascertain no good reason to fund a different residence. "There's nothing wrong with this one."

She scooted to the far edge of the bed out of his reach and crossed her arms. "It is too small. In fact, the lack of space troubles me to the point where I fear I cannot perform my duties this evening." She tossed a sultry look over her shoulder. "A simple promise from you, however, would ease my mind."

Her petulant behavior was growing tiresome. Too tiresome. They had been through similar pouts when he'd last visited.

"Very well," he conceded, "then we shall consider our affair settled."

Paulina's eyes widened. "Pardon? Settled in what way?"

He climbed from the bed and fastened his trousers, no longer interested in satisfying his lust with her. "My man of business will complete the transaction." He shrugged on his waistcoat before grabbing his boots and jacket. "Consider the house your severance. Your services are no longer required."

Paulina gaped, frozen to the spot on the bed. "But Daniel. You cannot—Oh, Daniel, don't, please." She burst into tears, burying her face in her hands.

He stood there in awkward silence while she sobbed. *Devil take it.* What was he to do now? After all, she might genuinely hold a *tendre* for him.

Daniel took a step forward, prepared to offer a retraction, but Paulina chose that moment to peek at him.

Her dry eyes sent a flood of indignation rattling through his veins. Was there a bloody woman alive who didn't use tears to advance her agenda?

"Do give my best to Anderson and Molyneux." Plopping his hat on his head, he spun on his heel and stalked from the premises with no intentions of ever looking back.

About the Author

Samantha Grace is the author of *Miss Hillary Schools a Scoundrel*. It is her belief that everyone has a story worth remembering, and she cherishes her work with aging adults, immersing herself in their tales of eras gone by. She is happily writing her next book and loves blogging with fellow authors at Lady Scribes. Samantha is married to her best friend, strives to stay one step ahead of their two precocious offspring, and lives in Onalaska, Wisconsin.

Miss Hillary Schools a Scoundrel

by Samantha Grace

———— ❧ ————

He'll never settle for one woman…

Debonair bachelor Lord Andrew Forest lives for pleasure and offers no apologies. But he receives a dose of his own medicine when his family's entrancing houseguest beds him, then disappears without so much as a by-your-leave. He'd like to teach the little vixen a thing or two about how to love a man… if he can find her…

And she won't settle for heartbreak…

After the dashing man of her dreams is revealed as a lying scoundrel, heiress Lana Hillary is ready to seek a match with a respectable gentleman—if only they weren't so dreadfully boring. Unable to rein in her bold nature for long, Lana flirts with trouble and finds herself entangled with exactly the type of man she's vowed to avoid.

———— ❧ ————

"With heart and humor, Grace delivers a rich and winning Regency debut. Clever and charming, this tale brings in everything Regency fans love…"—Publishers Weekly *Starred Review*

For more Samantha Grace, visit:

www.sourcebooks.com

New York Times and USA Today Bestselling Author

Lady Maggie's Secret Scandal

by Grace Burrowes

❧

Lady Maggie Windham has secrets

And she's been perfectly capable of keeping them... until now. When she's threatened with exposure, she turns to investigator Benjamin Hazlit to keep catastrophe at bay. But the heat that explodes between them makes him a target too. In a dance between desire and disaster, it's not always clear who is leading whom...

❧

Praise for *The Soldier*:

"Captivating... Burrowes's straightforward, sensual love story is intelligent and tender, rising above the crowd with deft dialogue and delightful characters."—Publishers Weekly starred review

"There is a quiet, yet intense power to Burrowes's simple prose and such depth of feelings that it will be difficult to forget this marvelous story."
—RT Book Reviews Top Pick of the Month, 4½ stars

For more Grace Burrowes, visit:

www.sourcebooks.com

A Gentleman Says "I Do"

by Amelia Grey

Her writing talent is causing all kinds of trouble…

The daughter of a famous writer, Catalina Crisp has helped her father publish a parody that makes Iverson Brentwood's whole family the talk of the town, and not in a good way.

Because he's the reality behind the story…

Furious and threatening, Iverson storms into Catalina's home, demanding satisfaction, but the infamous rake has finally met his match. With her cool demeanor and intense intelligence, Catalina heats his blood like no other woman in his notorious history…

Praise for *A Gentleman Never Tells*:

"Grey combines wit and charm in another enchanting, delicious romance."—RT Book Reviews, 4 stars

"Well written and entertaining."
—*Night Owl Romance* Top Pick

For more Amelia Grey, visit:

www.sourcebooks.com

A Gentleman Never Tells

by Amelia Grey

— ❧ —

A stolen kiss from a stranger...

As if from a dream, Lady Gabrielle walked from the mist and into Viscount Brentwood's arms. Within moments, he's embroiled in more scandal than he ever thought possible...

Can sink even a perfect gentleman...

Beautiful, clever, and courageous, Lady Gabrielle needs Brent's help to get out of a seriously bad situation. But the more she gets to know him, the worse she feels about ruining his life...

Enter the unforgettable world of Amelia Grey's sparkling Regency London, where a single encounter may have devastating consequences for a gentleman and a lady...

— ❧ —

"A stubborn heroine clashes with an equally determined hero in the latest well-crafted, canine-enhanced addition to Grey's Regency-set Rogues' Dynasty series."—Booklist

"The book is delightful... charming and unforgettable."—Long and Short Review

For more Amelia Grey, visit:

www.sourcebooks.com

The Rogue Pirate's Bride

by Shana Galen

❧

Revenge should be sweet, but it may cost him everything...

Out to avenge the death of his mentor, Bastien discovers himself astonishingly out of his depth when confronted with a beautiful, daring young woman who is out for his blood...

Forgiveness is unthinkable, but it may be her only hope...

British Admiral's daughter Raeven Russell believes Bastien responsible for her fiancé's death. But once the fiery beauty crosses swords with Bastien, she's not so sure she really wants him to change his wicked ways...

❧

Praise for Shana Galen:

"Lively dialogue, breakneck pace, and great sense of fun."—Publishers Weekly

"Galen strikes the perfect balance between dangerous intrigue and sexy romance."—Booklist

For more Shana Galen, visit:

www.sourcebooks.com

Lord and Lady Spy

by Shana Galen

No man can outsmart him...

Lord Adrian Smythe may appear a perfectly boring gentleman, but he leads a thrilling life as one of England's most preeminent spies, an identity so clandestine even his wife is unaware of it. But he isn't the only one with secrets...

She's been outsmarting him for years...

Now that the Napoleonic wars have come to an end, daring secret agent Lady Sophia Smythe can hardly bear the thought of returning home to her tedious husband. Until she discovers in the dark of night that he's not who she thinks he is after all...

"An excellent book, full of great witty conversation, hot passionate scenes, and tons of action."—BookLoons

"The author's writing style, how this story is built and all of the delicious scenes, and the characters themselves are just so rich, so enjoyable I found myself smiling and absolutely enjoying every single page."—Smexy Books

For more Shana Galen, visit:

www.sourcebooks.com

New York Times Bestselling Author

Lessons in French

by Laura Kinsale

❧

He's always been trouble...

Trevelyan and Callie are childhood sweethearts with a taste for adventure. Until the fateful day her father discovers them embracing in the carriage house and in a furious frenzy drives Trevelyan away in disgrace...

Exactly the kind of trouble she's never been able to resist...

Nine long, lonely years later, Trevelyan returns. Callie is shocked to discover that he can still make her blood race and fill her life with mischief, excitement, and scandal. He would give her the world, but he can't give her the one thing she wants more than anything—himself...

For Trevelyan, Callie is a spark of light in a world of darkness and deceit. Before he can bear to say his last good-byes, he's determined to sweep her into one last, fateful adventure, just for the two of them...

❧

For more Laura Kinsale, visit:

www.sourcebooks.com

New York Times and USA Today Bestselling Author

The Virtuoso

by Grace Burrowes

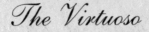

A genius with a terrible loss…

Gifted pianist Valentine Windham has little interest in his father's obsession to see his sons married, and instead pours passion into his music. But when Val loses his music, he flees to the country, tormented by what has been robbed from him.

A widow with a heartbreaking secret…

Grieving Ellen Markham's curious new neighbor offers a kindred lonely soul whose desperation is matched only by his desire, but Ellen's devastating secret could be the one thing that destroys them both.

Together they'll find there's no rescue from the past, but sometimes losing everything can help you find what you need most.

"Burrowes's exceptional writing and originality catch the reader and keep the story moving."—Publishers Weekly

For more Grace Burrowes, visit:

www.sourcebooks.com